THE
HIGHEST
STAKES

A N

EMERY LEE

Published by Sourcebooks Landmark, an imprint of Sourcebooks, Inc.
P.O. Box 4410, Naperville, Illinois 60567-4410
(630) 961-3900
FAX: (630) 961-2168
www.sourcebooks.com

Library of Congress Cataloging-in-Publication Data is on file with
the publisher.

Printed and bound in the United States of America.
VP 10 9 8 7 6 5 4 3 2 1

To my beloved Kasper,
upon whose back I dreamt my first chapters.

CONTENTS

PROLOGUE vii

PART I 1
  1. Of Victory and Defeat 3
  2. Of Sedition and Horseracing 17
  3. An Orphan's Tale 33
  4. Trial by Fire 57
  5. Corporal of the Horse 69
  6. A Bitter Rivalry 83
  7. Letters from War 93
  8. The Challenge 97
  9. Report from the Field 107
  10. Brothers-in-Arms 117
  11. A Hero's Welcome 133
  12. A Rogue's Heart 149
  13. A Wager for Love 161
  14. An Officer and a Gentleman 175
  15. The Rematch 197
  16. Broken Promises 213

PART II 223
  17. A Tale of Two Secrets 225
  18. The Business of Marriage 233
  19. Of Treachery and Extortion 239
  20. Return of the Prodigal 245
  21. The Devil Meets His Match 263
  22. Race to Gretna Green 275

23. The Betrayal 287
24. The Price of Integrity 309
25. King of the Turf 323
26. Salt in the Wound 339
27. The Reluctant Bride 351
28. An Unlikely Confidante 367
29. Love's Sacrifice 381
30. Military Justice 387
31. A Serendipitous Meeting 393

PART III 405
32. A Woman of Independence 407
33. The Turning Point 419
34. Heir to an Earldom 427
35. An Act of Vengeance 433
36. A Matter of Honor 441
37. An Old Flame Rekindled 453
38. Countess of the Turf 469
39. A Colonial Crown 473
40. A Revelation 489
41. An Irresistible Challenge 503
42. Retribution 511
43. Resurrection 521
44. Redemption 531

EPILOGUE 537

BIBLIOGRAPHY 539

ACKNOWLEDGMENTS 543

ABOUT THE AUTHOR 545

PROLOGUE

⸙

WILLIAMSBURG, VIRGINIA

*T*he blue roan colt had the finely shaped head and alert look of
his sire, with strong, straight legs, a chest deep and wide, a short
back with well-sprung ribs, and a highly muscled hind end inherited
from his dam.

Best of all, this colt lived to run! He was lightning off the line
and seemingly grew more energized with every stride. Christened
"Retribution," the colt represented all of his owner's hopes for the
future, a future in which that gentleman would finally be free to
move forward with his life without evermore looking back.

This race, a test of both raw speed and endurance, would be like
no other ever run in Colonial history, the victor gaining both the
fame and the spoils. The winning horse would be crowned the
indisputable king of Colonial racing, while the owner stood to gain
a purse of several thousand pounds.

The roan was slated to run among a field of over a dozen represen-
tatives of the Colonies' finest hot-blooded horseflesh—a surprising
number considering the exorbitant entry fee—but the high stakes
had acted as a dropped gauntlet to all who took pride in their racing
stock, and Virginians, in particular, were known for such pride.

Although sorely tempted to hire one of the many competent jockeys among his acquaintance and knowing that his actions might put his fine colt to some disadvantage, the man's compulsion to ride his own horse to victory was an overpowering and irresistible force. He needed this win more than anything he could recall, and a vicarious victory would never be as sweet. No. He must ride!

By entering his colt in the running, he had made the second most consequential wager of his life. The first, made nine years ago, had nearly destroyed him. Cheated, deceived, and betrayed, he had lost his love, his livelihood, even his country.

And now, on this momentous day, he would finally see if his patiently formulated plan, a plan that had preoccupied both his conscious and unconscious mind for eight long years, would come to fruition.

Only through this racing trial and, he prayed, a triumph to follow, could he be made to feel whole again. Only with this victory could he have retribution.

PART I

One

⁓

OF VICTORY AND
DEFEAT

LICHFIELD, STAFFORDSHIRE, SEPTEMBER 6, 1742

Robert Devington was growing more anxious by the moment. Once more he scanned the crowded and bustling paddocks. The call had already sounded for the first race in which Charles Wallace was to ride the gray mare, White Rose. The filly was entered in this particular race, a one-hundred-guinea challenge for maiden five-year-olds, young horses that had yet to win a race. It was a single four-and-a-half-mile heat, ten-stone weight, and about to start with her rider yet nowhere in sight.

With barely a quarter hour remaining to present the horse and weigh in, Robert was in an agitated quandary. Audibly cursing, he pulled the blankets from the mare's back, just to put them back on again. He considered the only alternatives before him: to deceive the racing judges by presenting the horse in Charles's stead and committing an act of fraud; or do nothing and risk both the forfeiture of Sir Garfield's entry fee—no paltry sum by any standard—as well as this fine young mare's best chance to win a race, a circumstance that would do nothing to improve his standing with his beloved's uncle.

His future with Charlotte was nearly a hopeless cause to begin with. He could scarce afford to fall afoul of her guardian's temper. Robert searched the milling crowd for the last time, desperately seeking a glimpse of Charles Wallace. Still none, blast it all! His last hope now dashed, he cursed with greater vehemence and led the horse out of her paddock to commit an act of fraud for the sake of love.

The Lichfield races, held annually in September, transformed the Whittington Heath, a three-hundred-acre sheep pasture, into the premiere event for all of Staffordshire. This hybrid of a horse race, garden party, and county fair attracted all classes of people from as far away as Derbyshire, the county's closest equine rival, but this year it drew an extraordinary number of persons of consequence. Lords and gentlemen had arrived from the North of England, Wales, and even the Scottish highlands, but as unusual as this was, never since its inception had this innocuous little village ever attracted a foreign dignitary.

By far, the most distinguished patron of the races this year was the elegant and illustrious Grand Ecuyer de France, comte d'Armagnac, Master of the Horse in the court of King Louis XV. Rumored to have travelled all the way from Versailles to procure a number of English running-bloods for the Royal stud, Monsieur Le Grand's visit to Baron John Leveson-Gower had propitiously coincided with the Lichfield races, over which Lord Gower would preside.

With the final preparations for the race in progress, Lord Gower and his eminent guest promenaded the grounds, surveying the field and assessing prospective stock to complement the Royal stud of France.

"I have heard for a number of years, Lord Gower, that the finest racing flesh resides across the Channel in England. I was of course loath to believe such a thing, but most curiously, after seeing so many specimens of excellence, I must confess that this might be so." He paused in his perambulations to admire a particularly sleek black stallion in one of the myriad paddocks.

"Do you know, what is the breeding of this horse, Lord Gower?"

"Hastings's Hawke? He is indeed a fine specimen! I believe he is by Francis Lord Godolphin's barb stallion, but I shall inquire further, if you so desire."

"The Godolphin again! He shall forever plague me, this horse!"

Lord Gower gave an inquisitive look, and the count bowed to him slightly.

"It is said that one of the finest producers of racing champions in England was first cast off by Versailles. A very foolish move by the Grand Ecuyer, was it not?"

"Am I to assume that you refer to Lord Godolphin's stallion?"

"Indeed! One and the same, but the name was not so. In France, the stallion was called by El Sham. You do not know the history of this horse, Lord Gower?

"Only these past years while he stands in Cambridgeshire, Monsieur Le Grand."

"Then I shall recount to you this story, *bien sur?*"

"Indeed, I am most intrigued."

"The stallion, El Sham, was presented to His Majesty as one of eight horses—*chevales pur sang arabes*—from the Sultan Muley Abdulah of Moroc. The grand riding master at Versailles, Monsieur de La Gueriniere, the man whom I appoint, finds this stallion wanting, you see. As he is small in stature and not of the form preferred for the dressage, he is cast out from the stud *Royale*. This same horse was then procured by your Englishman, Monsieur Coke, who brings him to England, where he soon becomes the sire of champions! So you see that I, *en effet*, am responsible indirectly for this horse leaving France, and now I come to England to find such a one to take back! *C'est l'ironie magnifique, n'est-ce pas?*" He recounted his tale with surprising good humor.

"Indeed, it is an amazing irony! But in all truth, this stallion's value was little realized at the first. When he left our poor departed Coke's hands for Lord Godolphin's stud, he was intended as a teasing stallion, used to prepare the mares for the services of his lordship's stallion, Hobgoblin. Apparently, he fought Hobgoblin for Roxana's honors, and the unintended byproduct, Lath, was a most formidable opponent on the turf. The fleetest since Flying Childers, some say, and now this former teasing stallion is making a greater name as a sire than Hobgoblin.

"Indeed, it may be of further interest that a son of his, called by Cade, is to run today. He is full brother to Lath and already proving as remarkable a runner. His first year at Newmarket, he won both heats of the King's Plate. His next year, he ran second only to Sedbury, a great-grandson of Colonel Byerley's Turk, another long-proven champion sire. I daresay we might yet see a match race betwixt the pair, but I should be in a veritable quandary where to lay my money on that one!"

"How I should like to see such a race!" remarked Monsieur Le Grand.

"If one offers a large enough purse, most anything might be arranged for the entertainment of *Le Grand Ecuyer de France*."

The trumpet called the first race, prompting the gentlemen to return to the viewing pavilion, the elegantly appointed structure erected in Monsieur Le Grand's honor. Built to Lord Gower's specifications, the covered and partially enclosed platform, which had employed a score of laborers for nearly two full for'nights, afforded a near bird's-eye view of the field, sheltered from sun, wind, and rain. Most importantly, however, the structure provided the requisite privacy for all of his particular guests, who now congregated in anticipation of the first race.

"As the races are set to commence," Lord Gower said, addressing his guests, "I suggest, Your Graces, lords, and gentlemen, that we take our places." He indicated the comte should be first to proceed. The French envoy was followed by nine of the most prominent and influential Tories in the British kingdom.

Though most were well known to one another through their positions in Parliament, there was little speech outside the mundane, until the liveried footmen, garbed also to honor the French dignitary, served platters of delicacies, poured the imported French wine, and were dismissed by Lord Gower. The host took no chances in protecting the security of this meeting.

Noting the white cockades adorning each guest's lapel or tricorn, said host raised his glass to the company. "As each of us today has both literally and figuratively committed a horse to the race"—his eyes scanned those of the group for reaction to this fitting analogy—"I solemnly propose a toast to the king across the water."

The day, which earlier promised to be sunny and brisk, had warmed with the noontime sun. The lumbering traveling coach, after battling miles of the wheel-sucking mire that barely functioned as a serviceable ingress in the best of times, finally drew near to Whittington Heath. This generously proportioned vehicle had conveyed a family of five ninety-some miles from South Yorkshire for the express purpose of the races.

Sir Garfield Wallace, master of the household, was a most avid turf follower, but with limited success to his credit. With his son riding in the first event of the day, he would have been one of the most fervent of spectators, but his damnable equipage was once again entrenched in the blasted muck!

The occupants of the coach fortunate to be nearest the windows espied the hundred acres punctuated with vendor booths hawking their wares of everything from mutton leg to bonnet ribbons. These were complemented by a half-dozen elegant pavilions serving as provisional banquet and concert halls.

Farther downfield, countless grooms and jockeys frantically hustled about to ready their mounts.

Growing edgier with each passing minute, Sir Garfield rapped impatiently on the roof, but his signal went unheeded by the coachman, who had already alighted—for the third time this day—to assess the extent of their plight.

With increasing agitation and with much greater power than intended, Sir Garfield forced open the coach door. Leaning out to bark his orders, he lurched forward, nearly toppling into the mire, saving himself only at the last by grasping onto the top of the coach door. Although he had narrowly escaped a disastrous tumble into the muck, this unfortunate gentleman found himself suspended, one leg in the carriage and the other dangling in midair outside, with his heft balanced precariously in between.

Charles Wallace, seated on the side opposite, moved with dispatch to aid his father, but his way was blocked by his sister, cousin, and mother, who wailed ineffectually and clutched at the elder gentleman's coat skirts.

Charles, now half-lying over the women, called out to his father as he reached, "If you will just let loose one hand…"

"Not another bloody word, Charles!" Sir Garfield blustered.

Rescue for the gent appeared from an unlikely quarter, as a young officer of the King's Horse stopped to observe the spectacle. "A true predicament, upon my word!" he exclaimed with a chuckle. He deftly dismounted in reckless disregard of the six inches of mud and then tethered his horse to the coach.

"Captain Philip Drake, at your service," he said, concealing his mirth with a flourishing bow. "Need I ask, sir, whether you desire to be inside or outside of the coach?"

"I bloody well shan't attend the races looking like a pig come from the sty!" the portly gent retorted.

Fighting to suppress an outright guffaw at the mental picture, the officer mastered himself enough to reply, "Then, sir, I shall do my humble best to lend my aid."

By this time, the bemired coachman had returned from beneath the rear of the vehicle, and betwixt them, he and the officer shouldered the gentleman's significant bulk, closing the door sufficiently for his son to pull him back into the coach.

"Such a chivalrous officer! Don't you think, Mama?" gushed a sweet and breathy voice, which immediately piqued the trooper's interest. He stepped closer to peer at the other occupants within the vehicle. To his pleasure, an angelic face did indeed complement the voice.

Red-faced and disconcerted in his struggle for composure, the portly gentleman offered gruffly: "My gratitude for your timely intervention, Captain Drake."

"If your desire is to attend the races, sir—"

"Wallace. Sir Garfield Wallace," the gentleman interjected.

"Might I suggest, Sir Garfield, that with your carriage thus entrenched, the labor of dislodging it from the mire might be greatly lessened by the removal of its occupants."

"Indeed, sir," piped up the coachman. "'Twould be a good deal easier empty if'n we must push it out again."

"And just how do you propose to proceed, Captain?" Sir Garfield glowered at the mud below.

"The coachman and I might, by crossing our arms, form a chair of sorts to convey you beyond the danger, from whence you might safely proceed to the nearest pavilion. Otherwise, I fear the races may be well underway before the coach is extracted."

"The races underway!" Sir Garfield exclaimed.

"Is the hour as far advanced as that?" Charles Wallace inquired anxiously. "I am to ride the first race, and on a filly sure to win, you know!"

As he glanced up at the noonday sun, the officer considered the question. "I fear they may have already commenced."

"Hell and damnation! We must proceed to the grounds at once!"

Charles had already alighted out of the door opposite, landing in ankle-deep mud. He remorsefully inspected his new riding boots before dashing off in the general direction of the paddocks in a desperate search of his groom and mount.

"Curse it all!" Sir Garfield swore again. "Four years and one-hundred-guineas entry fee to put my horse in this blasted race, only to miss it!"

"Then might I suggest we conduct your remaining party thither without further delay," said Captain Drake.

Forming the human chair, the two men strained to carry Sir Garfield the ten paces to the grassy heath. They followed with Lady Felicia, another sizeable burden, then returned for the two final and much lighter occupants.

Reaching the coach first, Drake hoisted the seraphic beauty into his arms. Well disposed to this notion, she wrapped her own arms tightly about his neck as he carried her.

"So very gallant, Captain Drake," she cooed while gazing dreamily into his eyes.

"Mayhap we shall become better acquainted these two days, my lady?" he suggested.

"One may always hope," she replied *à la coquette*. Their arrival on solid ground ended any further private discourse.

The coachman arrived, carrying the last occupant, Charlotte Wallace, and Sir Garfield offered another thanks but, having witnessed his daughter in the officer's arms, with less enthusiasm.

The party now safely assembled on the far side of the road, Drake bowed his departure, crossed the mucky path for the final time, and remounted. Without a backward glance, he waved down a fellow officer in the near distance and spurred his horse toward the racing paddocks.

His every motion was followed by Beatrix's intent gaze.

Robert Devington found he could barely squeeze into Charles's racing silks. He was now more than a bit worried about making the ten-stone weight for this class. Since attaining the age of twenty, his form had matured, and his added muscle had limited his rides to those assigning weight by inches or by the age of the horse. He didn't know if he would make the cutoff, reckoning now that he must outweigh the younger and slighter Charles Wallace by a good half stone.

His second worry, if he made the weight, was that this race was sanctioned only for gentlemen jockeys. Although Robert had jockeyed in races for nearly eight years, these events had allowed grooms and hired riders. This was not such a race. He approached the weighing station with pounding heart.

"Name?" inquired the clerk of the scales.

"Wall…," he began but hesitated. Charles might very well be known to these gents. Much better to take his chances with the truth.

"Name," the clerk repeated.

"Devington. Robert Devington. The horse is White Rose. Owner, Sir Garfield Wallace."

"I don't show a Devington on White Rose. Charles Wallace is to be up."

"Charles Wallace was unpredictably detained. I ride in his stead. Devington, Robert Devington," he repeated.

"This is a sanctioned race, Mr. Devington." The clerk spoke accusingly. "No grooms allowed. Gentleman jockeys only. Unless you are a kinsman, the race is forfeit."

"I am not in Sir Garfield's employ," Devington said, dissembling, and nonchalantly sat upon the scales. "I am betrothed to the gentleman's niece and therefore a kinsman."

The scales swung in the balance.

"Nine stone, twelve and one-half pounds," the attendant announced with raised brows.

Having made the weight by the skin of his teeth, Robert slowly exhaled. He was uncertain if he was relieved or not. Had he not made weight, he would have had a valid excuse not to go through with an act he would surely live to regret.

"Sign the register, then proceed with your mount." The clerk's voice was a no-nonsense monotone. "Next rider."

As he signed, Devington scanned the book for the other entries in his race. Nine had been slated to run, but strangely, six were now struck from the register: Merry Andrew, Traveler, Miss Romp, Cupid, Phantom, and Othello. All good horses. Curious why they should have withdrawn, Devington continued down the list.

The first name that had not forfeited was Lord Gower's own Slug, whom Devington knew to be a respectable runner but certainly not one to scare off the competition. Lastly appeared Hastings's Hawke, Lord Edmund Drake, Viscount Uxeter up.

The horse, Hawke, was said to be unbeatable in his class, and Viscount Uxeter was a man preceded by a foul reputation. He was a villainous rider with a passion for high-spirited but ill-tempered horses, and would bloody his mount's flanks before suffering defeat. He had proven as much last spring with Spanking Roger, son of the famed Flying Childers, and a superlative runner. The horse had lived up to expectations by running four seasons undefeated in all but one race—the one in which he had viciously tossed his rider. Spanking Roger's name thereafter became synonymous with malevolence, and Lord Uxeter had relished the challenge of owning and racing him. In the end, however, the fiery steed proved unequal to his rider, who pushed him to his very death in a match race.

The combination of names answered the riddle, and a chill of foreboding accompanied Robert to the starting post.

Robert's own mount, a mare affectionately called Rosie, was the first out of Sir Garfield's racing stud to show any real running potential. She was a scrawny foal and Charlotte's pet from the start. Truth be told, though none would ever confess it, Charlotte had trained the mare to run. Although Rosie came to this event green, Robert knew Charlotte had made her as fit as any horse on the Whittington Heath. But how game was she?

The young mare carried champion blood. She was by a Darley son, out of a Darley granddaughter, Amoret. With the noted stallion twice her grandsire, she had the blood of a runner, but did she have the heart to go with it? This was the remaining question to which he would soon have an answer.

Now less than five minutes to start, the bugler sounded the final call. Robert mounted the frisky mare and proceeded at a brisk trot to the starting post, where Slug's rider waited patiently astride the gelding, and Viscount Uxeter spurred his horse, Hawke, into a dancing frenzy.

The starter gave the command for the trio to line up and waited for all to settle before raising the flag, but Hawke, worked up to a nervous lather, broke forward in a false start. Lord Uxeter, realizing the error, jerked his horse to a hard halt and wrenched him back around to the starting post. Their horses now jigging in heightened anticipation, Devington and Gower had to circle for some minutes to resettle their excited mounts.

For the second time, the starter raised the flag. As it descended, the trio broke forth in a flurry of legs, lunging forward for a four-and-a-half-mile test of endurance, by a three-time circumnavigation of the track.

Devington knew his mare was up to the distance. Her daily routine for the past six months had included a spirited five-mile gallop on similar turf, but the day prior had been soggy, saturating the ground. The spongy turf pulled at her feet with every stride, but the going was as good as it was going to get.

Devington consoled himself that they at least had the advantage of the first race, before the track became completely pockmarked with hoofprints. The last riders would suffer the most disadvantage, as the now green surface became degraded by day's end to pure muck. With each lap of the track, the running would get slower and harder and try to suck the horses in.

It paid the rider to understand how turf conditions affect performance and how to manage even those things beyond a jockey's normal control. It was even more vital to understand how best to manage both the strengths and limitations of one's mount, even under adverse conditions.

The most superior jockeys were not always on the most superior horses, but were always the ones who knew how to ride smart rather than just hard. Devington was such a rider. He had acquired years of such equine wisdom under two of the best tutors: first his father and later Jeffries, the stable master at Heathstead Hall. In his relatively short career, Devington had ridden a hundred horses if he had ridden one, and he knew how to read them.

Keeping his mare well in hand, he studied the pair with whom he shared the field. Slug, he mused, was aptly named. He was the lazy sort. The type of horse with talent, but with a stubborn lethargy, having the inherent speed within him, but requiring the incessant driving of his rider to bring it out. This kind of horse required constant attention.

Devington knew this would serve him later. They would hang back just a notch and await the precise moment when Slug's rider would be too worried about driving acceleration to be aware of his competition. This is when they would grab the inside.

That Hawke was another case altogether from Slug was evident from the very outset, the moment he broke for a false start. He was a tightly strung stallion with a fine-tuned flight impulse, needing no encouragement from his rider to run. A horse of his kind ran with a frantic fear, as if his very life depended upon it, burning up excess energy that he could ill afford to lose on a field with worthy competition. Pushing a horse like Hawke with injudicious whip and spur would prove counterproductive, serving only to increase his stress and rarely inciting any willing or renewed effort to the fore.

The third type of runner, well represented by Rosie, the sprightly mare on whom Devington was mounted, was the willing partner. This kind was eager to please and attuned at every moment to its rider, anticipating and responding to the slightest cue of hand, voice, or leg. This was an honest runner, one rarely needing encouragement to perform, a horse to be trusted to run its own race to the best of its ability, simply guided by the intelligent rider.

Devington relaxed almost imperceptibly, trusting Rosie to pace herself for a while. As long as she didn't drop back or lag more than a length or two, he wouldn't drive her. Instead, he kept his eyes focused on the competition, reading every sign, developing his plan, seeking his advantage, riding this race to the peak of his horse's ability.

Either of the other two horses could be managed and run successfully, but success would depend completely on the skill and management of the rider, and Devington could clearly ascertain by the end of the second lap that Slug was decidedly undermanaged by his indolent jockey, and the high-strung Hawke was incontrovertibly terrorized by his.

By the start of the third lap, Devington was crouched low over the mare, well pleased and encouraged that Rosie was up in the bridle, holding her own, and keeping good pace with the two taller, longer-legged horses. Lord Uxeter was already plying the spur into the first bend, but Rosie, keenly aware of her rider, required little urging, voluntarily lengthening her stride to maintain her position.

By the end of the final lap of the arduous run, Lord Uxeter had completely used up his horse, and Slug had completely used up his rider!

Grinning with satisfaction, Devington seized the moment to claim the lead, murmuring low to Rosie, "It would appear, my lovely girl, the race is ours."

Two

❧

OF SEDITION AND
HORSERACING

Charles Wallace arrived breathless and perspiring just as Devington, with only a few furlongs to go, gave Rosie her keenly anticipated cue to seize the lead. The mare visibly coiled and sprung forward with renewed vigor. Her dainty legs sliced the air, barely grazing the turf with her flying hooves, and she overtook the harried Hawke to win a clean and undisputed finish.

Charles couldn't believe his eyes, but moreover, couldn't understand how Devington had managed to ride. The Lichfield races prohibited grooms. He feared there would be hell to pay once the breach was discovered, but for now he reveled with his friend who had just clearly beaten the unbeatable.

Sir Garfield arrived amid a plethora of congratulations on the fine performance of his mare, accepting the news with amazement, and made his befuddled way to the paddocks. How could Charles have possibly run Rosie in the last race? The second was already underway, and Charles had been only a few minutes ahead of him. There must be some misunderstanding, but he was loath to refute the glad tidings.

He arrived at Rosie's paddock just as Charles clapped Robert on the back. "Capital ride, Devington! I could scarce believe my eyes when I saw you overtake Uxeter. He's a veritable fiend in the saddle, you know."

"Rosie performed admirably," Robert replied.

"'Twas more'n just Rosie took *that* race."

"Devington!" Sir Garfield began just as Lord Gower appeared with his distinguished guest.

"Sir Garfield," Lord Gower said, "my most eminent guest wishes to be made known to the owner of the splendid mare who cleaned the field of her illustrious company.

"Monsieur Le Grand, may I introduce Sir Garfield Wallace of Wortley, South Yorkshire. Sir Garfield," he continued, "I present *Le Grand Ecuyer de France*, Charles de Lorraine, comte d'Armagnac."

Confounded as to how to greet a French dignitary, Sir Garfield's bow was so low and obsequious that his knees creaked, and stays threatened to burst. Failing to recall the elongated title, he tentatively began, "Munsoor..." and directed a pleading query to Lord Gower.

"Monsieur Le Grand," Lord Gower volunteered.

"Indeed. Indeed. *Munsoor Le Grun*."

The comte flinched at Sir Garfield's appalling French and responded, "*Mais oui*, I was most insistent to speak with the owner of this *cheval magnifique*, who claims such victory. And such rider superlative, he too must be congratulated, *non*?"

"Just so," Lord Gower agreed. "But I don't believe I am acquainted with your kinsman, Sir Garfield." He eyed Robert curiously. Sir Garfield flushed, but Devington interceded, saving them both from disgrace.

"Devington. Robert Devington," he offered with a deferential bow, thankful for having once aped Charles's lessons in etiquette and gentlemanly comportment. The gentlemen's reciprocal nods affirmed that his efforts had passed muster, but his bravado wavered when his lordship prodded further.

"What precisely *is* your kinship to the baronet, Devington? A nephew on the wife's side, mayhap?"

"N-no, your lordship." Devington vowed to stay as close as possible to the truth. "The relationship is by law rather than blood. I am betrothed to Sir Garfield's niece, Miss Charlotte Wallace."

"Indeed so? My felicitations to you. 'Tis peculiar I had heard none of this." He directed his inquiring gaze to Sir Garfield, who opened his mouth to refute.

Robert again interjected, "It has yet to be announced, your lordship, as Charlotte is but seventeen."

The reply satisfied Lord Gower. "'Twould appear congratulations are well in order, young Devington, on a superlative ride. Lord Hastings, the owner of the defeated champion, was near apoplectic when he saw you rout his prized stallion, ridden by his heir apparent, no less."

"More than worthy opponents," Devington said humbly.

"I privately confess to a belief that Uxeter is heavy-handed with his livestock, and 'twas past time for his set down. Now as to the point of this introduction, Monsieur Le Grand?" he prompted.

"Sir Garfield," the Frenchman began, "I had come to this country, you see, in search of a fine stallion for the stud *Royale*, but I tell myself, after seeing this performance of your mare, that one must never underestimate the value of the broodmare, *non*?"

"Just so," Sir Garfield replied.

"Then I should like to discuss with you the procurement of such a specimen as this mare. The King of France is a man *très genereux*, Sir Garfield."

"Indeed?" Sir Garfield's eyes lit with an avaricious gleam.

"What would you say to an offer of five hundred pounds?"

"'Tis exceedingly generous, Sir Garfield," Lord Gower encouraged.

Sir Garfield carefully posed his reply. "It is indeed, but the mare is yet young. This is only the first of what I suspect should be many successful racing seasons. I might gain as much in her race winnings alone, not to mention the sale of future offspring."

"'Tis a truth I should not doubt," the comte conceded. "As I perceive you are a shrewd man, we shall then forgo this *bourgeois* custom of bartering. I shall ask directly. Precisely what amount of *gold* should entice you to part with this mare?"

"No less than one thousand guineas."

"A thousand guineas! 'Tis not unheard of for a stallion, I think, but such is a price *très cher* for a mare, *n'est ce pas*?" He directed this last to Lord Gower.

Sir Garfield defended his stance. "She carries the Darley blood, top to bottom, proven blood of champions."

"I confess, Monsieur Le Grand, the blood alone will tell," Lord Gower espoused. "Darley's stallion has produced a prolific number of good runners."

"Très bien." He nodded. "If such is the case, I shall provide the purse you request on the morrow and will make arrangement to take the mare back to France after the races. *Enfin, Messieurs*. My business now complete, I am free to attend most heartily to *plaisir*. A good day to you, Sir Garfield." The party made their bows with great pomp, and the comte and Lord Gower departed.

"A thousand guineas!" Sir Garfield rubbed his hands gleefully. News of this sale would do more to establish his racing credibility than an entire season of wins.

"Sir Garfield," Robert began, "I feel compelled to explain my actions. With no sign of Charles, and the race beginning, I was induced to act."

In his delight of the moment, Sir Garfield had nearly forgotten Devington's act of deception. "'Tis of little consequence. 'Twas a clever and credible fabrication, by the by. Shows a quick wit," he added in grudging approval.

Perceiving in the baronet's good humor a golden opportunity to pursue his agenda, Robert pressed further. "Sir, as to the fabricated betrothal… I have made no secret of my feelings for Charlotte, and

I have reason to believe she reciprocates these sentiments. Though I have little to recommend me, I should do all in my power to care for her. I should desire nothing more in my life than to make this a betrothal in truth."

"Enough, Devington! We have had this discussion for the final time."

"But we have never discussed it at all. You have scarce given me the chance."

"Nor shall I! You are a penniless groom in my employ. My niece is a gentlewoman. There shall never be such a match. Promptly dismiss the notion from your head, lest I dismiss you altogether. You'd better serve yourself to rub down that mare. Come, Charles, I'm famished and in a mood to celebrate. There's food and wine in the pavilions."

Charles cast Robert an apologetic look but followed his father nonetheless.

Once more rebuffed and at a loss how else to achieve his goal, Devington directed his attention back to the mare. No sooner having done so, he was interrupted by an unfamiliar voice.

"Here, lad. I had a bit of luck on the last race, thanks to you." The trooper carelessly tossed Devington a coin purse. "There's ten guineas within," he volunteered. "Should hold you over for a spell, if you haven't a predilection for whores, gaming, or strong drink," he added the disclaimer. "'Tis but a fraction of my winnings, which before night's end will have completely vanished by all of the afore-mentioned vice," he said with a raffish smirk.

"By the by, lad, I caught that last from the overstuffed windbag. I deem you should better serve yourself to seek opportunity elsewhere. The King's Horse could use more crack riders." He threw the remark over his shoulder as he departed, leaving Devington stupefied.

Captain Drake left the dumbfounded youth to amble at a leisurely pace to the paddock reserved for the Hastings stud. He arrived to overhear a second dispute related to the prior race.

"But, your lordship," the groom pleaded, "'twas surely a fouled sinew led to his defeat. I seen he lost his action right at t'end, round that last bend, I seen it. Knewed he was off right then, I did. He wasn't hisself, on account o' it. But he'll be right as rain in a for'night. Wi' rest and me poultice, 'twill be no time at all. He'll be spankin' ready for Epsom."

"Shoot him," replied Lord Uxeter dispassionately.

"Surely ye canna mean it! He'll be right as rain in a for'night," the groom insisted.

"I've just lost a thousand guineas on him. I said shoot him."

"But, your lordship!" the groom begged as if for his own life. "Even should he ne'er run another race, surely he be good enough for the breedin' shed."

"This horse is not good for bloody dog meat," Lord Uxeter spat. "Upon the morrow, you shall present me this stallion's tail as proof you carried out my injunction. Otherwise, Willis, you shall find yourself seeking other employment."

"'Twas quite the showing today, Edmund," the captain interrupted. "I confess I may also have lost a great deal of money, had I bet it on *you*. Fortunately, I fancied the look of the little gray mare instead. 'Twas a magnificent payoff!"

"Piss off, Philip." Lord Uxeter spat in his direction and was gone.

"Ye be best not to goad 'im like that, Master Philip. He be of a murderous mind, he be," the groom warned.

"Edmund is a sadistic bastard. Now what's this rubbish about shooting the horse?"

"Ye overheered that, did ye?"

"Indeed. 'Twould appear a tremendous waste of a fine piece of horseflesh, wouldn't you say, Willis?"

"'Twould indeed, Master Philip. He be no screw, this one."

"So you say?"

"Byerley bred, twice over, he be."

"The Byerley Turk? I know of the horse. He was taken from a Turkish officer in the siege of Buda. He later served as Colonel Byerley's reconnaissance mount at the Battle of the Boyne. The horse was reputed to have remarkable courage."

"That 'e was, and later proved a fine runner to boot."

"Indeed? And this is his grandson, you say, Willis?"

"Aye."

"They say 'like begets like.' If it be so, he would be a worthy addition to the King's Horse. As an officer, I have forage allowance for a second mount. Hmm." He circled the horse and ran his hand down the stallion's right foreleg, feeling for heat. The horse shifted in discomfort as his hand touched the base of the cannon bone. He looked up at the groom. "What do you make of his injury?"

"'Tis naught that a bran poultice and se'nnight o' stall rest won't cure."

"Then I suggest you seek out some poor, decrepit cart horse with a black tail. Surely someone in Staffordshire can produce such a sad specimen for ten quid." Reaching into his pocket, he retrieved the sum in coin.

"Rest assured o' it, Master Philip," answered the relieved Willis with a toothless grin.

By day's end, eight races had been run with the surprising addition of a grand finale, a two-hundred-guineas match race between the two strongest contenders of the year. Mr. Martindale's Sedbury, another grandson of the Byerley Turk, and Cade, by Lord Godolphin's Barb. The contest would be a full three heats of four-mile distance, carrying twelve stone.

After having received this news with singular delight, Monsieur Le Grand turned to address his company. "My most distinguished *messieurs*, while having been received with the most pleasing hospitality within your midst, I am regrettably recalled to my purpose.

"I am come sadly, not for my gratification alone, nor solely for the acquisition of horses for the stud *Royale*. I am come, in truth, as envoy of His Most Christian Majesty, who has agreed after a much grave and extended consideration, to help restore Le Chevalier, the true and rightful king to the throne of England.

"When thirty years past, Louis XIV provided an army of several thousand French troops, the noble Scots rallied to their rightful king, but there was, I think, a decided lack of English zeal to restore Le Chevalier, *non*? But now you say the English people grow discontent and resentful of the Hanoverian Crown, who would make war with France for his insignificant German electorate."

Lord Gower replied, "It is our belief, Monsieur Le Grand, that in only a matter of months the English people will rally to the cause. The opportune moment of restoration is soon to present itself. We must be prepared to act."

"*D'accord*," replied the comte. "His Majesty is prepared to offer a fleet of thirty ships, and the troops numbering ten thousand. It is for this reason, I am come to England, to secure... shall we say... certain guarantees. Every favor of the Crown comes at some price, *non*? And these troops, they must be maintained."

"Precisely what manner of assurance does His Majesty have in mind?" Lord Gower asked warily.

"A pittance, as you English would say. Two hundred thousand pounds. An offer most *genereux, oui*?"

"His Majesty is infinitely benevolent," replied Lord Gower.

"Then I shall await your answer. All arrangements may be made through our usual friends," said Monsieur Le Grand. "And now I see the commencement of the race." He smiled and indicated the sinewy, sleek, and dancing forms of Cade and Sedbury proceeding to the starting post.

꧁

By six o'clock, the crowds had dispersed in preparation for the Grand Ball to be held on the far end of the race grounds. Though record numbers attended the races earlier in the day, the ball more than doubled that number, drawing those whose interest lay more in social events than in sport. Accommodations were made for all.

An open-air dance floor and hired fiddlers provided entertainment to the local folk, while luxuriously appointed and brightly lit pavilions served food and wine for the nobility and gentry. A half dozen such structures were erected in a circle surrounding an immense dance floor constructed within the center.

Having stayed to the last race at Sir Garfield's insistence, the Wallace party was among the last to arrive. Sir Garfield and Charles dragged behind the ladies Wallace, who meandered from one pavilion to the next inspecting, admiring, or criticizing those they passed by.

Beatrix moved about with an air of studied nonchalance, periodically shielding her eyes with her fan and scanning the crowds for a dark-eyed man in a scarlet coat with blue facings. Once or twice her pulse quickened, but the officer she sought failed to reveal himself.

Sir Garfield tolerated this circuitous perambulation by keeping his glass perpetually filled. Charles Wallace hung back from his clinging mother and sister to keep company with his cousin Charlotte. They had hardly seen one another since the carriage debacle, and Charles noted that Charlotte appeared even less enamored of the ball than he was.

"I trust your afternoon was diverting, cousin? I know how extraordinarily fond you are of the races," he said as the pair strolled along behind his twittering mother and sister.

"I hardly caught more than a glimpse of any of the races," she replied with dismay. "Aunt, in her belief that no decent lady shows her face near the track, scarce let me out of her sight. Did you arrive in time for Rosie's trial? I caught none of it and have been dying to know how she did. Though Uncle appears in exceeding good humor, he has not spoken of it, and I scarce dared to ask."

"'Twas a remarkable day indeed. I regret having missed the start of Rosie's race."

Charlotte's face fell.

"But the mare did run," he hastily added, "and she ran superbly, Charlotte. She routed Lord Hastings's Hawke."

"Splendid! Absolutely splendid, Charles. But how can it be? You can't mean to say that Robert rode?"

"Indeed he did, though I literally caught only the tail end of it. His riding in the last few furlongs was nothing short of brilliant. I'm convinced that none other should have accomplished it. M'father doesn't give the man enough credit."

"He never has. 'Tis so unfair of Uncle. Robert deserves the opportunity to prove himself. Uncle could have one of the finest racing studs in Yorkshire if he would only give Robert a chance."

"You bring up another point, Charlotte. After the race, Devington pressed his suit for you."

"Did he! Surely it was an opportune moment to do so! Uncle could not possibly have been in a better humor to listen. And?" She waited expectantly.

"And father threatened to dismiss him if he ever broached the subject again. I'm sorry, Charlotte."

Tears of frustration welled in her eyes. "I must speak with him, *now*, Charles. You must take me to him."

"But the ball," he protested. "The dancing will soon commence."

"What do I care? You know I despise these balls. Seas of faces I shall never encounter again. Scores of names I shan't ever recall, even if I cared to. Not to mention the dancing. I scarce can remember the simplest steps. Surely we can slip away for a short while."

"You can't claim to need air. We are already strolling out-of-doors."

"Then it must be infirmity."

"But that would require that I take you back to the inn," he moaned.

She regarded him with stubborn determination.

"Must you jut your chin so, Charlotte?"

The mulish look became a glare. "Will you take me or not, Charles? If you refuse, don't doubt that I shall slip away on my own, though with the grounds so ill-lit beyond the pavilions, I daresay I should need to carry something for protection."

He knew she would carry out her threat. Charles groaned in submission to the blackmail. Charlotte spoke briefly to her aunt, pleading a headache, but the lady was too preoccupied with her own diversion to pay much heed.

"Charles"—his mother turned to him—"I have noted a remarkable shortage of eligible gentlemen for dancing, particularly in light of the prodigious number who turned out for the races." She spoke deprecatingly. "You *will* return to lead your sister out to dance, should she lack partners. This is not a *request*, mind you."

The beleaguered Charles, wishing the world completely devoid of womankind, vowed to return as promptly as possible. Their excuses made, Charlotte and Charles then slipped away to the paddocks.

⁓

Mortified at the thought of dancing with her brother, Beatrix renewed her hunt for the officer she had selected to lead her out for the first dance, but he was nowhere in sight. Surely he was even now seeking her in the crowds. She had worn her very best silk gown in shades of yellow and gold to match her hair, but perhaps she hadn't made herself conspicuous enough.

"Mother, we have yet to inspect the last pavilion," Beatrix insisted.

"But we have already partaken of food and drink aplenty at all of the others," Lady Felicia replied.

"But Mama," she persisted, "there's a large crowd gathered hither. Should we not investigate? Mayhap there is something or someone of interest."

Sir Garfield interrupted his wife and daughter at this point. "Quite slipped my mind, m'dears, regretfully, as I know how these matters signify to ladies. There is indeed a person of great consequence at the races this year. Had the privilege to be introduced myself. 'Tis a *Monsoor Com d'Grun* something-er-other, come all the way from the court of *Louis Cans*."

"A French nobleman, Papa? A courtier of the king? How could you be so cruel not to say so earlier?"

"Indeed, Sir Garfield, 'twas unforgivably remiss of you," his wife scolded. "You must think of our son and daughter, who can only benefit from even the remotest connection to such a personage. You must perform introductions at once! But confound it, Charles is departed with Charlotte. You must contrive an introduction for him on the morrow," his wife insisted.

"Charles was present, m'dear, but 'twas a very brief encounter. He and Lord Gower came upon me for a matter of business."

His wife stopped in her tracks. "What possible business could you have with a French count?"

"'Twas a matter of a horse, m'dear. Seems the *monsoor* was quite taken with Rosie. Offered a thousand quid for the mare."

"A thousand, you say! 'Tis a king's ransom, Sir Garfield."

"Quite literally, madam," he said with a laugh.

"We shall be infamous for it!"

"'Twas quite what I thought, m'dear."

"Then surely we must be made known to this count, Sir Garfield." Taking her husband by the arm, Lady Felicia dragged him to the crowded pavilion.

By the time they were cognizant of the activities within, it was too late. The crowds pressed so tightly, there was scarce room to maneuver, let alone escape. The sixth pavilion, they discovered, was solely to entertain unencumbered gentlemen.

"Sir Garfield!" Lady Felicia exclaimed, attempting to shield her daughter's eyes from the open debauchery, but not succeeding before Beatrix had looked her fill, immediately spotting and fixating on her elusive quarry. Seated at a card table was her handsome officer. Resplendent in his crimson coat, his pristine breeches were further adorned by a voluptuous, painted doxy.

As if feeling the weight of Beatrix's gaze, Captain Drake glanced up from his cards, straight into her face, and without the least modicum of shame, winked!

With a gasp of outrage, Beatrix spun around to push and shove her way out of the tent. "How dare he amuse himself at my expense!"

For years she had been the one to mercilessly toy with the young men of her acquaintance. It had been her personal challenge to reduce them to pathetic little lap dogs who begged for her favors.

But not this man! Never had she been treated with such contempt. And to be cast aside for a painted whore was not to be borne! Oh, he would pay for this, Beatrix vowed. If ever he crossed her path again in this lifetime, he would surely pay.

Charles, preceding Charlotte by a pace or two, arrived as Robert, exhausted from the day, made ready to bed down for the night.

"Won't do at all, Robert," Charles declared. "If anyone sees you bedding down like a groom, 'twill be sure disaster. You must, at the least, retire to the inn. Surely there is a loft above the stables or some such to be had. Even failing that, you could make do in the coach, but let none see you now as our groom."

"Robert." Heedless of her cousin's presence, Charlotte stepped forward, extending her hands. Robert clasped them in his own, pulling her close. "I am so sorry I missed your ride. It must have been glorious! I wish with all my heart that I might have seen it. My uncle is in such rare good humor this evening."

"He has reason. Your filly has garnered him fame and fortune in one fell swoop."

"I doubt the fame should last long, and the hundred guineas was hardly a fortune by my uncle's account."

"Then have you not heard? Charles, you craven," he accused. "You've not told her yet!"

"Told me what, Robert?" Alarm reflected in her eyes.

"He has sold her, my love. Sir Garfield has sold Rosie to some pompous, painted, and befrilled French count, who is taking her to France after the races."

"Rosie? France? I don't understand! Rosie is mine!" Charlotte protested. "No one cared for her but me! I'm the one who believed in her, nurtured and loved her, taught her to run. You all would have cast her off as nothing! Even Jeffries had failed to see her potential. How could he do this to me?" Sobbing, she threw herself into Robert's comforting arms.

"Your uncle is a man completely devoid of sentiment, Charlotte. You know this. He cares naught for anyone lest they serve him a greater purpose, and today Rosie served him well. 'Twas at your expense and to his shame, and I'm deeply aggrieved by your loss." Robert spoke with earnest eloquence.

"But look at the bright side," Charles said cheerily, "her exceptional performance today earned her a place as one of King Louis's broodmares. She shall live out her life as a queen of equines in the stables at Versailles. Quite an honor, if you consider it, Charlotte. And I can't say I've ever seen m'father more ebullient."

"Even so, Charles, I fear his humor shall never be sufficiently charitable where I am concerned," Robert remarked.

"Surely m' father shall come around in time."

"Never, Charles. The day shall never arrive that he will perceive me as an equal."

Charlotte ardently protested. "Don't say so!"

"Today, so that your uncle might have his racing victory, I went so far as to announce myself your bridegroom. After thus perjuring myself for his gain, he was offered a thousand guineas for the mare. Knowing I should never see a more propitious moment, I pressed my advantage. I begged that he should grant our betrothal in truth, but he threatened to give me the boot. He means it, Charlotte. As long as I am in his employ, I shall never be more to him than some mindless lackey!"

"What *he thinks* signifies nothing! I know you for the man you are, and *you are* the man I love." She stroked his cheek with tenderness. "Only this is of consequence. If he will not be moved, then we will just run away together. I have my father's timepiece and my mother's pearls. Surely they could sustain us for a time."

"But only for a time, my love, and notwithstanding that I could never allow it. As it is, without your dowry, we could scarce feed ourselves. No, my love, I am resolved to make my own way and return to you only with respectability and means. Unless I can provide for you in at least a modest semblance of the manner to which you are accustomed, there should be a perpetual cloud dimming our happiness."

"How can you say so?" she pleaded. "*Our love* is what matters."

"Charlotte, a woman must respect the man she marries, and should I fail to support a wife and family by living hand-to-fist, I would never be worthy of your respect or your love. I *must* make my own way."

"But how? You aren't going away?"

"I must."

"B-but for how long?" Her voice broke; her heart wrenched.

"That I cannot answer, my love, but we are young. We have time." He drew her hands to his heart.

"When will you leave?" Her lip quivered.

"Soon."

"Oh, my love. My only love." Charlotte flung herself into his arms.

Three

AN ORPHAN'S TALE

*C*harlotte Wallace was thirteen when her uncle's carriage came to collect her three weeks after her parents' accidental deaths. Sir Garfield Wallace's instructions to his London man of business were brief and concise: close up the house, auction off the contents, and dismiss all the servants, save one to care for the child. His directives left Charlotte in an empty house, awaiting the arrival of a man she hardly knew, to take her to a home she had never seen.

Upon the appointed day at precisely the appointed time, the grand coach-and-four arrived at the modest house on Mount Pleasant near to Grey's Inn Road.

Perched upon the window seat of the second-floor salon, Charlotte peered apprehensively through the window, hoping her first glimpse of her uncle would provide a glimmer of hope for her future. The vision meeting her eyes did little to diminish her qualms. The footman opened the carriage door, and the portly gentleman wedged himself through the narrow opening and descended. Brushing off the footman's assistance with a frown, he straightened his waistcoat, righted his crooked periwig, and lumbered to the front door with the chastised footman following behind.

Catching her charge spying out the window, Letty pulled the girl briskly away. "Come, Charlotte. Ye don't want yer uncle to catch ye. 'Twould not be good manners, and ye daren't make a bad impression, seein' he's the only kin come to claim ye."

Charlotte valiantly battled the incipient tears, but her quivering lip gave her away.

"Oh, my poor lamb! It breaks me heart, it does, after what ye been through, but ye needs t'pick yer chin up. 'Twill be a'right in the end. Ye go to a grand house in the country wi' two cousins to keep ye comp'ny, and rest assured, Letty'll never leave ye."

"But I don't even remember them, Letty, not any of them!"

"I can't doubt it, lambkin. Ye were very young, mayhap three or four the last time that ye visited the Yorkshire kin, but 'tis no matter, luv. Yer cousins'll come to be like brother and sister to ye in no time."

"I pray you're right, Letty."

"Rest assured, my duck. 'Twill be all right in the end." She offered an encouraging wink, which Charlotte returned with a forced smile. A rap sounded briskly at the door, and with no other servants to answer it, Letty left her charge.

Wasting no time on formalities, Sir Garfield entered the foyer, nodding curtly to the maid, asking gruffly, "Where is the girl?"

"Above stairs, sir. Me name's Letty, sir," she offered with a deferential curtsy. "I've been with the household since Charlotte were a babe."

"I don't require your complete history," he answered irritably. "Take me to her."

A heated flush brightened Letty's cheeks. "Indeed, sir. I'll take ye directly."

"And the bags? Are her belongings packed? I have little time to waste."

"Yes, sir. We was told to expect ye and have been ready this past hour or more."

"Simmons, see to the baggage!" Sir Garfield commanded the footman.

Nervously fidgeting in the salon, Charlotte rose hastily at the sound of the heavy footsteps signaling her uncle's approach. Letty's curt nod from the doorway reminded Charlotte to curtsey, lest she forget decorum.

"Uncle," Charlotte said in tentative greeting.

He inspected her with a long, critical sweep. "How old are ye, gel?" he demanded.

"Just thirteen, Uncle."

"Small for your age. You don't look near so robust as your cousins. Not sickly, are ye?"

"N-n-o, Uncle."

Letty interjected hastily, "Nay, sir. The child's in the best of health."

"Good. Ye have quite the look of your mother about ye but not half the looks of my Trixie," he proudly asserted. "A rare beauty, that girl."

For want of a reply, Charlotte nodded.

"A timid thing, aren't you?" he remarked.

Always described as a spirited child, Charlotte drew breath to differ, but Letty directed a quelling look. Mindful to make a good impression, Charlotte maintained her silence.

The cursory introductions completed, Sir Garfield was wont to be on his way. "You know why I've come?" he asked rhetorically.

"Indeed, sir. I am most grateful for your exceeding kindness and generosity."

He nodded with a satisfied grunt, and the party set out for Yorkshire.

For Charlotte, the journey was scarce more than a blur, hours on end bouncing and jostling in the closed carriage, her uncle snoring and sputtering and otherwise ignoring her. At least he had allowed Letty to travel within the coach rather than outside on the driver's seat. The maid's presence fortified Charlotte.

After three interminable days, the coach halted at the gate of Heathstead Hall. Pulling back the curtain, Charlotte gained her first view of the long gravel drive that meandered up a lush green

landscaped hill to an imposing brick, Georgian manor house. The
carriage struggled up the steep drive until the door opened and the
steps lowered for their descent.

"Heathstead Hall. Your new home," her uncle stated proudly.

Wide-eyed and speechless, Charlotte was thankful for Letty's reassuring hand squeeze before she alighted the carriage. Mechanically
going through the motions, she would later have only vague first
impressions of her new family.

Her Aunt Felicia, a plump and powdered woman, near smothered
Charlotte with a cloyingly effusive welcome. "Why, Sir Garfield,
what a little darling our Charlotte is! Welcome, my dearest, into
the bosom of your new family. I am Lady Felicia, but we shan't
stand on ceremony. You must call me Aunt. Now come and meet
your cousins. They've been overcome with rapture in anticipation
of your arrival, my dear." She looked to her children and propelled
a fresh-faced lad, akin to Charlotte in age and stature, toward her.
"Here is Charles, but where is Beatrix?"

She frowned that her welcome party was incomplete. Beatrix was
nowhere in sight.

"She was here only a moment ago, Mama," Charles answered.

"'Tis no matter, my dear," Sir Garfield replied. "Charlotte will meet
Beatrix in due time. For now, let us just see the gel properly settled."

"Indeed, Sir Garfield. The rooms are all prepared."

"I leave all in your capable hands," he replied absently. "I am off
to inspect the broodmares." Having fulfilled his obligation to safely
deliver his niece, he departed without another thought.

"Always those confounded horses!" Lady Felicia cursed under her
breath. "I just don't understand what's become of Beatrix."

With her sudden arrival in her uncle's household, Charlotte's world
turned upside-down. She was regarded with disingenuous sympathy
from her aunt, indifference from her uncle, jealousy and resentment
from Beatrix, and seemingly no more than tolerance by Charles.

Charlotte had been adored by her parents, and by her father in particular, who treated her more as a son than a daughter. For this reason, she perceived Charles as her most likely ally and determined to cultivate a friend in her male cousin.

Her first opportunity presented early one morning, shortly after her arrival, when she espied Charles departing the house. Stealing surreptitiously through the back courtyard and gardens, she followed him down the narrow path to Sir Garfield's prized stables. Trailing in stealthy pursuit, she bypassed the carriage house and pressed on toward the broodmare paddocks, where arrested by a warm nicker and the approach of a sleek and glossy little chestnut mare, Charlotte completely forgot about Charles.

With her head held high, the little horse trotted merrily to the fence and nuzzled the girl. Her warm breath tickled Charlotte's cheek. Completely and unreservedly captivated, Charlotte reached out to stroke the velvety nose.

A voice spoke from behind. "That mare is Amoret. She's Darley blood, you know."

Startled, Charlotte flushed.

"I saw you following me," Charles said, his grin accusing.

"I wanted to explore the grounds but didn't know my way around."

"No matter to me. You don't seem half the trouble of my sister."

"I promise not to be any trouble at all. Though we lived in the city, I have a great fondness for the out-of-doors. My papa used to take me to the park to play every day when I was a child."

Charles considered her for a moment. "I've never been to a great city, leastwise not outside of Leeds. Can't rightly say if I should be keen on it or not."

"There is so much to do in London! There are people everywhere, strolling in their finery at St James or riding their horses in Hyde Park."

"I should hate to confine my riding to a mere park."

"But Hyde Park must be a hundred acres or more!" she protested.

"A hundred acres is nothing," he scoffed. "Heathstead Hall covers nearly a square mile."

"But Hyde Park has the Serpentine," she challenged.

"The what? Sounds like a bleedin' snake museum."

"Don't be such an addlepate, Charles! The Serpentine is a great man-made lake within the park. Papa once took me punting there. We had a lovely day." She blinked rapidly. Her mouth quivered.

Charles looked away visibly discomfited.

"You mentioned riding in that serpent park," he said. "Do you ride, Cousin?"

"No, but Papa always promised me…" Still fighting the incipient tears, her voice dropped to a whisper.

His question had failed to serve its purpose. Flustered by his second botched attempt to distract her, Charles tried again. "Well, would you like to? Ride, that is?"

The mare immediately nudged Charlotte's hand, as if encouraging her. Charlotte's eyes suddenly grew wide with delight. "Do you mean to teach me?"

"I could start you in the basics I suppose, though t'would be best to put you in Jeffries's hands. He's the stable master. Though he mostly works with the running bloods, he's also charged with our instruction, mine and Beatrix's, that is. 'Tis a waste of time on *that* girl," he added contemptuously. "Beatrix is afraid of anything with four legs."

"I should not be afraid at all," Charlotte answered intrepidly, determination replacing her tears.

"A bit of fear is a healthy thing," he advised. "Horses are powerful beasts, even the most docile ones, but if you truly wish to learn…"

"Oh, I should! Indeed I should!"

"Suit yourself, then," Charles replied gruffly, secretly pleased that his flash of brilliance had drawn his cousin out of her melancholia.

"You go to the Hall and change into your riding habit. I'll instruct the groom to saddle Beatrix's old gelding for your first lesson."

"But, Charles," she began timidly, "I should like to ride Amoret."

"You don't understand, Charlotte. This one is of pure racing blood. Even if you attempted to ride her, you'd *surely* risk your neck. Nay, you'll ride the swayback gelding, leastwise until you develop a seat."

Charlotte regarded him forlornly. "But I haven't a riding habit."

"Bother," Charles replied, and then surveyed her from head to toe. "Well, we're of a size, I daresay. Have your maid fetch some of my riding breeches. You'll be riding astride anyways, as I know naught of a lady's side saddle. Now run along, Charlotte!"

Beatrix, who had earlier spied on her brother and Charlotte, arrived unexpectedly in the stables garbed in her velvet habit and haughtily demanded her horse.

"Ye be riding then this morning, miss?" Jeffries inquired with surprise, knowing her distaste of horses.

"Indeed I shall. 'Tis a glorious day for it. Don't you agree little brother?"

"But Charlotte was to accompany me, Trixie," Charles protested, "and there is no other suitable horse for her, aside from Lancelot."

"He is *my* horse. Charlotte will just have to petition Papa for her own, as she shall not be riding *mine*."

Obediently, Jeffries led out Lancelot and lifted Beatrix up. Charles sent his young cousin an apologetic look but mounted his own horse to accompany his sister for what he knew would be an exceedingly dull ride.

Forlornly, Charlotte watched her cousins disappear from sight. Why did Beatrix hate her so much? Dejected and fighting tears of frustration, she wandered to the broodmare paddocks, alighted the top fence rail, and settled there, watching the horses peacefully graze. Noting her presence, Amoret left off cropping her patch of clover to float across the paddock in a daisy-cutter stride. Her enthusiastic greeting, although nearly knocking Charlotte from her perch with a playful toss of the head, served as some consolation to the girl's despair.

"'Twas naught but jealousy prompted that." Jeffries nodded in the direction Beatrix and Charles had ridden. He spoke absently, casting a lazy gaze over Charlotte. "I've no doubt wi' a few lessons ye'd soon be ridin' circles around that pair. 'Tis too bad there be no other suitable mount for ye."

Charlotte stroked and scratched the mare, who happily nuzzled her in kind. "Is there nary a one, Jeffries?"

"Nay, miss. The lady Felicia don't ride, and Sir Garfield, bless him, is grown so in bulk that he be nigh too big for the saddle. The rest be but carriage horses, broodmares, and yearlings."

"But what of Amoret, here? She is quite biddable, is she not?"

"That she is, but she's bred to the hilt for running, miss, and no mount for a young lass just finding her seat."

"But, Jeffries," she protested, "did you not just say I might soon be running circles around my cousins?"

"Indeed so, but 'tis a great distance 'atween a biddable hack and a courser, miss."

"But they both have four legs, don't they? I fail to discern the difference."

"Do you not, indeed?" He chuckled indulgently. "Then ye'd best study more closely. Come wi' me miss." He handed her down from the fence and led her across the stable yard to the carriage horses, a grazing group of big-boned bay geldings.

"Fine old English stock, they be, Yorkshire coach horses and unsurpassed for carriage work. If we compare this great gelding to Amoret over there, you see how he was bred to drive? You see it in long, well-muscled neck, the power of his forequarters, with his broad, deep chest. His shoulders are big, strong, and built to pull. His back is long, withers low. His legs be short in relation to his carcass but heavy in bone. This is a hardy breed, long-lived and docile in temperament, but not built for speed. Now cast yer gaze back to Amoret."

The contrast was unmistakable, even to Charlotte's uneducated eye.

"A horse bred for running has a well-chiseled head on a long neck, is high in the withers, has a deep, narrow chest, a short back, good depth in the hindquarters, a lean body, and long legs. A racehorse is a completely different creature, bred for dash, spirit, and bottom. Not for a lass to hack about the countryside."

"But Amoret is *the very picture* of docility," Charlotte protested.

"Aye, she may have the look of a lamb, but on the turf," he added with a scratch under Amoret's chin, "this one has the heart of a lioness. The difference lies not as much in the form of the horse but in its spirit."

"Amoret, a lioness? I can't conceive such a vision."

"She's right docile enough now, but don't mistake this one for no soft-hearted jade."

"How do you mean?" Charlotte sat forward with a rapt expression.

"This mare is from one of the great running families, ye see. It's deep in her blood. Her grandsire was the Darley Arabian hisself."

"Indeed?" she responded with wonderment. "But who is this Darley?"

"I was but a lad working at Aldby Park stud when Thomas Darley brought a horse all the way from the Syrian desert to Yorkshire. No more handsome beast have I ever seen. The Darleys knew he was a prime one. They stood him 'specially for their own mares, taking few outsiders. And they got some of the best whatever ran in these parts: Childers, Almanzor, Aleppo, Cupid, Brisk, Daedalus, Dart, Skipjack, Manica, and Lord Lonsdale's Mare."

"They were all winning racehorses?"

"They all could run like the wind, but the primest of the get was crack as any horse in his time or ever since. That was Flying

Childers, bred right over yon at Doncaster, out of a daughter of Old Careless, another what was the best o' his time."

"Did you ever see him run, Flying Childers?"

"Right enough, I did. I disremember the exact date, but 'twas the Beacon Course at Newmarket. Flying Childers bolted over it, well over four miles of hill and dale, in seven-and-a-half minutes. Bless me, miss, if I ever seen another horse run like that! His next races was all won for lack o' takers, so early on the Duke of Devonshire put him to stud. 'Twas his full brother what sired this 'un right here." He rubbed Amoret's ears.

"Is it truly so, Jeffries?"

"Aye, 'tis so."

"But Amoret doesn't race."

"Not any longer, she don't. But in her heyday, no mor'n half a dozen years back, she was right full o' piss 'n' vinegar, Amoret was. As game a little filly as they come. It was at the two hundred guineas for fillies in Hambleton that I first seen her. 'Twas on the Round Course, which was dedicated to runnin' only mares since the time of Queen Anne. I was up on Lord Portmore's Favorite, Isaac Cope from Middleham was up Amoret, and Johnny Singleton rode Lord Rockingham's Lucy. A gamer lot of fillies never was than that trio.

"And this little mare run that course up the hill, round the bend, and down the straight as if driven by the devil. She could flirt wi' the best of 'em for half a day and give 'em treble the distance in her time.

"'Twas a sad day I laid eyes on her at the blood sales, right dwindled to naught and lookin' like a rail. Sir Garfield wanted naught to do wi' her, but I knowed what she was, carrying the blood of the royal mares of King Charles on the one side and nicked wi' the full brother of one of the best runnin' horses e'er lived on the other."

"Indeed? What had happened to her that she went to auction?"

"Same's happens to many o' the best runnin' mares. Raced young and hard, pinched o' feed to keep their carcasses light 'til they be too weak and broken to run anymore. Then when the runnin' is completely wasted from 'em, they be turned out to the breeding shed completely sapped of juice and in no condition to propagate.

"Full in flesh and vigor is what a broodmare should be. Drained in body and spirit, a mare's in no condition to breed, leastwise not and produce a strong, healthy foal."

Charlotte looked at the mare pityingly.

"She had a yearling filly still suckling on her and further dragging her down, while she was breeding again. Bred back to her own sire, she was. Damned incestuous habit, goes against natural law, if'n ye ask me." He spat in disgust. "If'n the Almighty don't countenance such breedin' habits in man, why should man practice it in his lower creatures? But the high and mighty ones has some queer notions on blood. I'd as life nick a Darley granddaughter like her wi' a Byerley blood any day. Best of blood top and bottom, but there you be." He ended his tirade with a gesture of resignation.

"But what then became of her foal? You said she *was* bred, not *is* bred."

"Though we weaned her filly what was draggin' 'er down and give her the best of victuals to pick 'er back up, she slipped the foal right enough. 'Twas much to be expected, considering her miserable state."

"But how could anyone be so cruel and negligent to such a lovely animal?"

"Ignorance and neglect abound wi' running bloods who don't keep their owners flush in the pocket. The lot of the racer is to run and win or to breed winners. A blood horse that can do neither is nigh useless. Even with this one's high breeding, if she don't produce, she'll soon be back at the auction block."

"Does my uncle intend to breed her again?"

"Sir Garfield won't abide to keep her about if she don't earn her oats, but she be not ready to breed back again. She's had no time off to soften her condition. Like as a farmer need leave a hard-worked field fallow for a season, the racing mare must be roughed off for a time. Her owner didn't care to rough her off. 'Tis some wonder she even took on the first leap, but a mare that don't get a rest and time to recover throws a weak foal, matterin' not what blood she's bred to. Moreover, continuous breedin' will only make 'em go barren well afore their time."

"But what of the filly? You said you weaned her filly, didn't you? Did my uncle keep her, Jeffries?"

"Aye, and a right scrawny thing she be. That's her o'er in yon paddock. The gray. Daughter of Whitefoot she is, and her blood goes back to the White D'Arcy Turk. She be bred well enough, but as feeble as she looks, she's more'n likely to be useless as a runner. Mayhap her blood will tell as a broodmare, but I've a fair notion not to trouble training her to run. Sir Garfield has some colts what look to be far better racing prospects."

"But 'tis hardly a fair assessment to make so soon. You've not even given her an opportunity to prove herself," Charlotte protested indignantly.

"Mayhap so." He shrugged, adding philosophically, "Yet oft expectation fails where 'twould appear most promising, and nigh as oft it succeeds where hope is coldest. 'Twere never more true a sayin' than with blood horses."

"Well, I for one think she deserves an opportunity, especially having come into the world at such a disadvantage."

"You've a tender heart, lass."

"Maybe I just understand what it's like for her to be abandoned like that."

"Aye, lass, just mebbe ye do."

"Jeffries, since you have so little time and have already deemed her a poor prospect for racing, might I train her?"

Jeffries laughed. "You! Ye've ne'er even been in the saddle! What would you know of training a horse?"

"Well, nothing," she answered defensively. "But you could teach me couldn't you? You could give us both a chance." Her wide eyes spoke much louder than her voiced entreaty.

"Training a racehorse ain't hackin' about the heath, miss. 'Tis hard work, and not at all suitable for a young lady."

"But I shall prove my mettle to you if you give me the chance," she pleaded. "I'm made of much sterner stuff than you might think." She jutted her chin mulishly.

Suddenly moved by her eagerness and determination, Jeffries spoke without weighing the possible consequences of his actions. "If ye truly have a mind to learn the blood horse, I reckon there be no better teacher for ye than Amoret." The mare answered by rubbing her head against his shoulder.

"Do you mean to say you'll actually let me ride her?" Charlotte's face lit, and her pulse quickened.

"She grows heavy and idle out to pasture. Some light exercise can do her no harm. We'll start ye on the longe line with her tomorrow morn, if'n ye can be up and mounted betimes. The boys muck and feed well afore the cock even crows and are riding by first light. If ye can drag yerself from yer pallet afore light, none should be the wiser." He gave her a conspiratorial wink.

"You mean Beatrix. She never rises early."

"Then ye'd best be at the rubbin' house by daybreak."

"Indeed, I shall! I am a very early riser. I regularly watch the sun come up," she prevaricated with a broad grin and then turned to Amoret. "Until the morrow, my lovely."

She kissed the little mare on the nose and departed with a skip in her step.

༄

Charlotte spent the night in restive anticipation, springing from her bed at the first crow of the cock. Pulling on Charles's shirt and breeches over her shift, she yanked on a pair of his cast-off boots and pulled a cap over her plaited hair. Careful not to disturb Letty, she then slinked out of her chamber and down the back stairs, avoiding the kitchen where the cook was already about her work. Charlotte then exited a back door and surreptitiously edged her way through the gardens.

Her heart fairly skipping in anticipation, Charlotte strode eagerly down the gravel-laden pathway and along the waist-high yew hedge to the stable block. The gray slate roofs of the low red-brick buildings had only begun to reflect the rays of the rising sun. By midmorning they would cast their shadows upon the large, bedewed, grassy plot in the yard's center, but for now, the yard was a low hum of activity.

Charlotte wandered to the center of the bustling stable yard, watching as seven or eight boys methodically carried out their morning chores. One or two of them yawned and stretched, with stray pieces of straw and litter still clinging to their hair and clothing from the night spent in the lofts above the stables.

They set about their work, leading horses out of their boxes, fetching buckets of water, and mucking out the nightly refuse from the stalls. She had been to the stables on many prior occasions. Why had she never noticed any of this activity before?

Someone, presumably one of these same boys, always had her cousins' horses ready and waiting when they were appointed to ride. Upon their return, the boys collected and tended the horses and then faded back into the woodwork from whence they had emerged. She had never before given thought to all that was required to care for a stable of twenty-some horses.

Impatient to locate Jeffries and be about her own business, Charlotte dismissed further reflection. She scanned the yard, expecting to find her own saddled mare or, at the least, for someone to take notice of her. Ignoring her presence completely, the grooms continued about their morning routine, much like ants busy on their nest.

With Jeffries nowhere in sight, she looked about, huffing in disappointment mixed with annoyance. Suddenly she remembered. Jeffries had said to meet him in the rubbing house.

But which of these confounded buildings was the rubbing house? Turning about, she attempted to arrest the attention of a small boy straining to transport his manure-teemed wheelbarrow to the dung pit.

"Excuse me, lad?" Charlotte began. The boy glowered and continued on his way.

"Pardon me," she said louder now and grasped him by the sleeve. The slight pull was all it took to completely unbalance his precarious load and dump the manure—all atop her boots.

"Bloody hell! Look what ye done," the boy cried.

"Look what *I've* done? I'm sorry to have made you spill it, but I was simply looking for the rubbing house."

"'Tis over yon, ye muttonhead!"

"Muttonhead? There's no occasion for rudeness. If you hadn't overloaded your cart…"

"If ye hadn't come along and pulled me o'er, it ne'er would have happened. But now ye'd best clean it up afore Jeffries or Devington comes along."

"Me?" she replied incredulously. "I'm not the clumsy oaf who dumped it. It's not *my mess* to clean."

"Well, I ain't about to be last to finish me chores. Devington is back from Doncaster and will have me turning over the reeking dung pit instead of breaking me fast wi' t'other chaps."

"Well, I'm sorry for you, but that's nothing compared to what *you've* done to my only pair of boots, you ham-fisted lout!"

"'Tweren't me what pulled the wheelbarrow arse over teakettle, ye wantwit! Go bugger yer mother, and then lick yer boots clean!"

"Why, I'll box your ears, you brazen-faced little jackanapes!" Charlotte made a fist as if to try, but the boy flew at her first. They both tumbled onto the pile of manure in a wild, tangled flurry of thrashing limbs.

The commotion caused by the circle of cheering and jeering stable boys drew the attention of the head groom, who was leading his fresh mount out from the rubbing house. Hastily tying his horse, Robert Devington strode furiously across the stable yard to break up the mill. He tore apart the dung-covered combatants by the scruff of the neck. Turning first to the smaller of the pair, he cuffed his ear. "Jemmy! What the devil are you about? It's nigh past feeding time; you've still half your stalls to muck."

"But it ain't me what started it!" Jemmy whined. "'Twas the new chap what turned over me cart!"

"I don't give a groat who started it! Now get about your business before I tan your arse with a riding crop! And now for you, lad." He turned ominously to Charlotte and stopped mid-sentence, gaping at the spectacle she presented with her oversized clothes pulled awry and stained with ordure, her cap askew and nose oozing blood.

"Who the blazes are *you*? Or better said, *what are you!*"

Charlotte brushed a clump of dung from her flushed cheeks with the back of her hand and haughtily met his stare. "I was simply looking for the rubbing house where I am to meet Jeffries. Now if you would kindly direct me, I shall trouble you no further." Her voice was husky and quivered with righteous indignation.

"You say Jeffries sent for you? He told me nothing of a new boy." He regarded her closer, quizzically.

Charlotte refused to enlighten him. "The rubbing house, if you please?"

"The rubbing house"—he pointed over her left shoulder—"is the squat building hither."

"Thank you," she replied with as much dignity as she could muster. She turned on her heel and marched to the indicated building where, as promised, Jeffries awaited her with Amoret.

"Thought ye must be yet bedbound, miss." Puzzled by her appearance, he regarded her head to toe. "A right tussle wi' the lads is not what I expected when ye said ye'd prove yer mettle. Ye look nigh like ye been drug through the yew hedge backwards! By the looks of it, ye been well initiated into the world of the stable grooms." He chuckled.

"Indeed I have, but I'd rather not speak of it, if you don't mind," she said crossly. Desiring to divert the subject, Charlotte surveyed the low-roofed, poorly ventilated building where Amoret and another heavily blanketed horse stood tied. "What is this place, and why is it so stifling hot in here?"

"'Tis where the running horses are saddled to ride and rubbed down after their exercise."

"But why would you not saddle in the stable yard where it's cooler?"

"'Tis all well and good for the saddle hack, but the racehorse must be kept in condition. This requires sweating the beasts to remove spare flesh what weights 'em down. Though I've no great likin' for the practices of some what calls themselves training groom in Newmarket. I seen 'em destroy good horses by keepin' 'em always in a box wi' no air and covered in rugs three or four layers deep, turnin' the stables into a blessed Turkish bath.

"They send the horses out daily for 'strong exercise,' two or three times doubled wi' rugs, sometimes even addin' a woolen breast sweater and a hood. They put 'em through a four-mile gallop, and they returns heavin' in the flanks and lookin' like buckets of water was thrown over 'em. After this, the animals be scraped, rubbed down, wiped dry, and new clothes put on 'em afore goin' back in the hot box, where they breaks out in fresh sweats.

"This routine what some swears by, workin' 'em to exhaustion then clothin' and stovin' 'em, does naught more'n drain their juices such quantities as to destroy their strength and spirits."

"What a cruel and inhumane practice!" Charlotte exclaimed.

"Now I don't be sayin' a weekly sweat don't do a horse good," Jeffries said. "The cumbrous flesh a fat horse carries tears down his sinews when he runs. I lief run a horse lean than large. A horse don't never meet wi' his destruction by runnin' light in the carcass. But as to the sweats, all things be best in moderation. It be nigh easier to pull down than to put up flesh on a running blood."

As he spoke, he removed the three layers of rugs from the gelding. Scrutinizing the horse beneath the blankets, he gave a low whistle, murmuring curses to himself. "What's he thinking, the Bart, 'specting me to train a screw like this!"

"Whatever do you mean?" Charlotte asked.

"He be from the best sire, and 'he cost too much not to be good, Jeffries,' the Bart says." The stable master snorted in disgust. "Horses run in all shapes, lass, but always best when the shape is *good*."

"But I've never seen a coat with such a coppery sheen. He's akin to a new penny."

"Ye must look beyond the coat! Too many judge a horse's condition by the color or shine. This one be bad-kneed and built downhill. His croup's nigh taller than the withers. A horse that's ill-formed can't tolerate the training. He's thick-winded, too. He'll be roarin' like a lion afore the second mile."

"But how can you know which ones will be any good?"

"It begins in the breedin' shed, by selecting proven blood from a running family on *both sides*. Too many breeders care only for the sire and the damsire, givin' no heed atall to the dam herself. Begin wi' good blood then make sure the horse be well put together and full of vigor. The rest be in the training."

"But what will become of this one?" Her hand moved over his coat of satin.

"I says, by 'is looks, Sir Garfield would do better training that aged broodmare"—he indicated Amoret—"than this four-year-old."

"Amoret? Do you really think so?"

Jeffries chuckled. "Nay, miss. Her runnin' days be well past, but wi' exercise, she'll regain the vigor she lost in the last foaling. Some light rides on the heath will be good for the twain of ye, though I doubt yer Uncle would be too fond of the notion. Now then, time's a wastin'. We'd best be about your lesson."

Charlotte looked at him blankly. "But I don't know what to do."

"Then it be high time ye learn."

He conducted Charlotte into the harness room. The air was permeated with the rich smells of leather and neatsfoot oil. Several boys were at work cleaning the saddlery. Charlotte scanned the rows of gleaming leather as Jeffries moved to lift Beatrix's saddle from its rack.

"But isn't that a side-saddle, Jeffries?" She asked, regarding the saddle askance. "I don't want to amble along side-saddle like the fine ladies who parade on Rotten Row. I want to *really* ride, like the lads do. I want to hear the thunder of hooves and feel the wind in my hair."

"So you've a mind to ride the cracks, do you? 'Tis not the thing at all for a lady, ye know."

"What do I care for that? Please teach me to ride astride, won't you?"

"Ye truly think ye be up to the task?"

Charlotte lit up. "Yes indeed! If you'll only but show me."

"It'll be the devil to pay if'n the Bart should get wind of it," he warned.

"I promise he won't. I'll come to the stables before anyone is up at the house. Please, Jeffries."

The wide hazel eyes did him in. The stable master sighed in capitulation.

"Thank you, Jeffries!" Turning back to the saddlery, she asked, "Now which one shall I use? This one?" She indicated another saddle.

"Not unless ye be plannin' to leap the hedgerows chasin' foxes," he said with a twinkle in his eye.

"Mayhap not right away," she answered in all gravity. "But I fail to see the difference between any of those without the leg horn on them," she said with consternation.

"Then look more closely. Ye see the seat? This rise in the front is called the pommel, and the back is the cantle. On a hunting saddle, the pommel be low so that the rider can rise up in his seat to better take his fences."

"Oh, I see." Charlotte approached what looked like no more than an elongated leather pad. "And this one, Jeffries?" she asked.

"Ah, that be a racing saddle."

"But there's nothing to it! How does one even secure it to the horse?"

Jeffries pulled out a wide woven strap. "This is a surcingle. It goes over the saddle and around the horse's belly."

"It doesn't look like it would be very secure," she remarked skeptically.

"That be true, lass, but 'tis small and light, made that way to not interfere with the horse's running."

"We'll use this one." He pulled an exercise saddle from the rack, along with a blanket.

"Now, lass, bring me the snaffle. He indicated an entire wall covered with leather headstalls hanging from their hooks.

"What is a snaffle?"

Then commenced her lesson in bits and bridles.

After learning the basics of riding tackle, Charlotte was ready to commence her lessons upon Amoret. Waiting until the grooms and horses were going about the morning exercise and the stable block all but deserted, Jeffries instructed her in riding astride.

Her first few lessons were conducted with a long length of rope attached to the bridle, which Jeffries used to control the horse, while Charlotte learned equilibrium in the saddle. Greatly surprising the stablemaster, Charlotte proved to have a natural rider's seat and was confidently poised in only a matter of days. A fortnight later she and Amoret were leaving the exercise paddock and trotting freely out of the stable yard, with the mare tossing her head and snorting in delight.

With elation Charlotte and Amoret explored the open heath until unexpectedly encountering that horrid undergroom astride Sir Garfield's prime racing prospect. He had snuck up from behind, taking her unawares. Well, in all fairness, he hadn't *exactly* snuck up. He had spoken first, called out, but startled her nonetheless.

Charlotte was tongue-tied and paralyzed with fear that he would discover her identity and betray her to her uncle, and her only happiness would come to an abrupt end almost before it had begun. With a racing heart, she followed her first impulse, spurred her mare into action, and fled.

Needing little encouragement from her rider, the spirited mare sprung. Nostrils flaring, tail in the air, she surged forth, increasing her stride with each drawn breath. The young man, struggling to catch them, hung closely over his own horse's neck, spurring, encouraging, but still losing ground until the mist of the heath swallowed them. The sprightly Amoret was lightning on four legs!

Arriving back at the stable yard breathless, Charlotte dismounted, but Robert arrived hot on her heels. He swung agilely down from his saddle to land directly in her path.

"You bloody little reckless fool! Do you have no care for either yourself or your horse? She could have easily caught a hoof in a rabbit hole out there and broken a leg, or thrown you and broken your neck. Though by my first impression, the former would surely be the greater loss."

"How dare you lecture me, when you were in pursuit!"

"The difference is after ten years of riding that heath, I know every warren on it. You don't! Besides the fact that you ran that poor broodmare ragged. You can't ride a horse like that that's out of condition!"

"But Jeffries said I could take her out for an airing, and she loved every minute of it!" Charlotte replied.

"Because she was born to run, and you asked her to! A game little mare like that would run herself to death before quitting!" Charlotte cast a guilty look at Amoret's body, now coated in sweat and white lather.

"When the boys here exercise, they take their mounts for a light hack. That's a sedate trot and easy canter, not all out and hell-for-leather. A horse that's out of condition must be brought along easily, not worked too fast or for too long. You need to retrain the horse how to carry herself and strengthen her with light exercise, short gallops, short sweats, and regular rough offs, lest you destroy her legs."

"But that's not how *you* were riding!"

"It's *my job* to run the cracks, the ones who are already properly conditioned and ready to run. Did they teach you nothing where you came from, lad? And what *is* your name, anyway?"

"I'm *not a lad*," she retorted, pulling her cap from her head, "and my name is Charlotte. Pray excuse me; my horse requires cooling."

For days following the incident, Charlotte feared that Robert would betray her to her uncle, but after a se'nnight of agony, Robert had not spoken a word. His behavior was puzzling. With caution, Charlotte resumed her rides, but to her consternation, Robert began to appear every morning on the heath.

With her breath catching and her pulse racing, she had run. Run from any promise of friendship or love. But before long, she looked forward to their meetings with a fluttering heart and unexplained anticipation. Their morning rides became an exhilarating game of chase that Charlotte relished with sheer abandonment. For these few hours each day, Charlotte could take flight from her otherwise tightly controlled universe to share together this freedom and world without boundaries.

Over time, this unspoken, nameless attraction between them continued to blossom, refusing to dwindle or fade, though they had little opportunity to foster or nourish it. Slowly and patiently, Robert's sheer persistence in the chase had revealed his heart, and Charlotte came to realize the nameless thing between them was love.

Four

⌒∽⌒

TRIAL BY FIRE

*C*aptain Philip Drake swaggered down the line of crimson-coated new recruits, scrutinizing the would-be troopers with cynicism. Callow young men, barely off their mother's teat, with visions of grandeur in the King's Horse, he scoffed.

At barely three-and-twenty himself, the young captain was one of over sixteen thousand Englishmen who had joined the British Army as part of the Pragmatic alliance to defend the territories of the new Queen of Austria after a French and Prussian invasion of her territories.

George II, wearing dual crowns as King of Britain and Electorate of Hanover, headed the alliance, but acting more to secure his own German electorate than to honor the treaty with Austria.

The vast majority of British recruits desired nothing more than to fight Britain's age-old Gallic adversary. Although they had little concern for the threat to Hanover, French dominion across the face of Europe was another thing altogether.

Philip Drake was among this number and had purchased a commission with a small inheritance received on his twenty-first birthday. He had joined the King's Horse Guard with a desire to find purpose in his otherwise meaningless existence of drinking, gaming, and whoring, pursuits shared with his peers, other younger sons of nobility.

Already an able horseman, Drake was prepared for grueling hours in the saddle, but on the training field, he discovered he was a near prodigy in the art of swordplay. With his natural confidence and cool head, he had the true makings of a cavalry officer, although he had lacked the necessary funds to advance his career. Fate, however, intervened, and Philip Drake, the ne'er-do-well scapegrace of his family, became a captain of the King's Horse through a game of chance.

His first campaign, spent mostly garrisoned in Flanders, had failed miserably to live up to his expectations. Instead of riding gloriously into battle as he had envisioned, his entire regiment spent six months with thumbs up their arses whilst their generals dithered and the French amassed across the continent.

Disillusionment led to fond reminiscences of his "worthless" days of gaming, drinking, and whoring. His former life may have been meaningless, but damned if he hadn't enjoyed it more!

Increasingly restless and bored to distraction, newly commissioned Captain Drake began to drill and sharpen his men, lest in these months of inactivity they grow complacent, lazy, and dead... should the French and Prussians finally engage this muddle of a Pragmatic Army. In short order, the men under Drake's command were acknowledged as the best troop of the King's Horse.

With recognition of his success, the captain was recalled from Flanders to Horse Guard headquarters with orders to train the new Household Cavalry recruits for the coming spring campaign.

Now Captain Philip Drake faced his most daunting task: that of molding this pitiful assemblage into a troop worthy of the King's Horse.

As Drake strode the ranks of new recruits and their horses, his critical eye saw little raw material with which to work. A trooper was responsible for providing his own horse, and by the look of it, a full fourth of the nags wouldn't survive a march, let alone a battle!

Was this the best His Majesty could expect? He grimaced that any of this group might ride under his command. This was, after all, the unit bearing the Royal insignia, the best of the best, and their role was vital to the success of an army in the field. They were scouts, the eyes and ears of the generals, their watchfulness and intelligence-gathering crucial to strategic decisions. They were the protectors of essential supply wagons and escorts to dignitaries carrying urgent messages. They were expert horsemen and fearsome warriors trained for swift and unexpected attack at a moment's notice. They were a breed apart, but the captain saw little evidence of any of these traits before him.

"Mount your horses!" he boomed, watching each man pull himself into the saddle. His eye was caught by one particular trooper who vaulted with easy grace onto the back of a short-coupled, heavy-boned skewbald. The captain swaggered up to this young man, who saluted awkwardly, sitting tensely at attention.

"Name," the captain barked.

"Devington, sir. Robert Devington," the young man croaked.

"And what may I ask, Trooper Devington, is this sorry-looking beast? The King's Horse does not charge into battle on half-bred nags."

Trooper Devington's face flushed. "Permission to speak, Captain?"

He nodded curtly. "Permission granted, Trooper."

"Respectfully, Captain, although this horse was the product of an inadvertent coupling between a carriage-bred stallion and a racing mare, I believe him to be a superlative cavalry mount."

"You do indeed, Trooper Devington!" the captain roared and required more than a moment to compose his mirth before he could continue. "A superlative beast, you say? Pray tell me; upon what criteria?"

The crimson-faced trooper continued, "The qualities m'father taught me to look for in all horseflesh, Captain—soundness, sense, swiftness, stamina, and strength."

"Indeed desirable qualities..." The captain stepped back and circled around, scrutinizing the stocky gelding from every possible angle before snorting. "You actually believe *this* animal a paragon of the species?"

The captain's remark, traveling like wildfire through the ranks, was received with muffled chortles and coughs.

"Indeed I do. I'm no novice of horseflesh, Captain. On the contrary, I am well acquainted with this animal and confident in his abilities. He has demonstrated exceptional heart and stamina."

Now more irked than amused by the cockiness of this green whelp, the captain pressed. "And what of your skill, Devington? It would seem that only one of exceptional ability could mount such an exceptional steed."

"I hold my own, sir," he replied with quiet confidence.

"Hold your own with whom, Trooper? This is not the annual plowshare pull or the cart race of the county fair."

Trooper Devington's cheeks burned under the mockery. "Again, with due respect, sir, I can ride with the best of 'em."

"So you say, Devington, so you say... but are you willing to wager your career on it?"

Taken aback by the blatant challenge, Trooper Devington was at a loss to respond.

"Perhaps you didn't hear me, Devington," the captain repeated, his voice echoing through the ranks. "Are you willing to wager your career on that horse?"

"I'm not a gambling man, Captain."

"Not a gambler, you say, but indeed a braggart."

The captain addressed the full line of troopers in a booming voice. "There is no room in the Horse Guard for any whose words surpass their deeds." Addressing the trooper again, he commanded, "You may now prove your words, or dismount and return that wretched beast to your plowshare."

His future drifting completely out of reach, Devington blurted, "I accept any challenge of riding skill that you make, Captain."

"Do you now, Devington?" He paused. "I suppose you to be an expert swordsman, as well?"

"That would be quite an erroneous assumption, sir. I claim no experience or skill with either sword or pistol."

The trooper to Robert's right sniggered. The captain took mental note of him.

"No martial skill, you say? Yet you chose a military career?"

"These are skills I seek to acquire under your expert tutelage, Captain," he responded with sufficient humility to appease the officer, who now directed his attention to the sniggering trooper on Devington's right.

"Name, Trooper," he commanded.

"Prescott. George Prescott of the Derbyshire Prescotts," he replied smugly.

"Sir!" Drake barked. "I am your commanding officer, Prescott, and am to be addressed at all times as 'sir,' or better yet, as 'Captain.'"

Placing his arms behind his back, the captain paced down the ranks, speaking in an ominous voice. "You appeared prodigiously amused at Trooper Devington's inexperience with weaponry a moment ago, Prescott."

"He is ill-prepared for the Horse Guard, Captain."

"Indeed, it would appear so," the captain agreed. "And are you better prepared, Prescott?"

"I have studied, Captain, under the finest instructors of both horse and sword. My fencing master was a student of Sir William Hope."

"A student of Sir William Hope, you say? Then you are a virtual one-man army, to be certain. Perhaps we should send you to wage war single-handedly with the French, Prescott? The *Maison du Roi* will assuredly quake in their boots."

This was again met with muffled guffaws from the ranks.

"I, for one, have no fear of embarrassing myself," Prescott retorted, eyeing Devington with open disdain.

Raising his hands and looking about in mock wonderment, the captain stated to the assemblage, "I feel yet another challenge in the air."

He resumed his pacing but this time slowly, pensively, thumb and forefinger to his chin. The past months on campaign had been tedious, filled with nothing but vacillations of the various generals, endless marching, and repositioning of forces, followed by more dithering while the French moved decisively and conquered. He was damnably tired of it and frustrated by inaction. He relished this opportunity to hone his skills, if only on these pitiful recruits.

By the look of it, none deserved to wear the uniform, but the sorting of the wheat from the chaff would start today. Those few who made *his* cut would be worthy of the Horse Guard; the rest were free to join the expendable ranks of the infantry. It was time to test their mettle, and humbling this cocksure pair was the perfect start.

"It would appear, gentlemen," the captain said to the column of troopers, "that with this expert horseman and this master swordsman among our ranks, we should all benefit from an exhibition of their skills. The day's training is about to begin." *B'God, he hadn't enjoyed himself this much in a long time!*

Calling to his subaltern, the captain ordered his horse.

"Soundness… sense… swiftness… stamina… and strength," he repeated when the corporal returned leading a glossy ebony stallion. Leading the impressive charger to a position opposite the skewbald, the captain remarked, "What of Hawke here? By comparison, he would be near antithesis of your ideal."

Devington remembered this remarkable horse from his racing days. Although past his prime for the track, Hastings's Hawke was still a magnificent horse.

"A matchless beast to be sure, Captain, but I stand by my appraisal of Ol' Jack."

"Indeed, you say!" The captain laughed. "We shall soon test his mettle, as well as your own."

Stepping out of earshot, Captain Drake spoke again to his subaltern, who departed briskly to carry out the captain's orders.

"Well, gentlemen," the captain said to Devington and Prescott, "'twould appear the two of you just might make a whole. Furthermore, Devington, given the unparalleled claims you have made of the strength and speed of your *noble steed*, it shouldn't be out of the question to put him to the test against Hawke... while carrying you both." He paused while the company digested the outlandish challenge.

"You can't really expect this, Captain?" Devington was incredulous.

"Indeed, I do. This and more. 'Tis not an impossible feat to demand of a war horse, should one of your comrades be cut down or lose his own mount in the course of battle." The captain indicated the training field. "Do you see the effigies hanging in various positions around the field?"

The troopers strained to see the long column of straw-stuffed effigies of the French cavalry.

"Upon my signal to charge, you shall proceed against me and Hawke down the field. Your challenge is to be first to cut down each of the effigies. Thence you shall continue the circumference of the field at full gallop. Should you both remain horsed during this exercise, upon your return to this very spot, Trooper Prescott will engage my sword. You shall ride as one man and fight as one man. Do you comprehend?"

"All while mounted on this nag?" Prescott snorted with ripe contempt.

"Such dismay, Prescott? Trooper Devington has full faith in the beast," the captain replied with a smirk.

Prescott's eyes flashed with fury as he clumsily pulled himself up behind Devington while the captain agilely mounted his snorting black.

"This sorry nag had better sprout wings, Devington! *You'll* engage my sword if my career ends today because of you," Prescott hissed.

"Just concentrate on your swordplay, Prescott, and leave the horse to me."

"Are you ready, gentlemen?" The captain quirked a mocking brow. Both troopers nodded. In truth, the captain's plan was a simple exercise in humility, as the entire company would witness their unhorsing and humiliation upon the cannon fire he covertly ordered.

However, as the earth shook in repercussion from the booming thunderclap of the cannon, the captain had underestimated both the resolve of Trooper Devington and the sensibility of his sturdy gelding.

As ranks of troopers struggled to control their wide-eyed mounts, Devington's skewbald remained the least ruffled of the herd. Startling slightly, he recovered and responded readily to Devington's cue, and they galloped down the field toward their intended targets.

The captain was astonished. Even Hawke had reared unexpectedly, nearly unhorsing him. He had regained control only to see the trio well on their way down the field. Wheeling Hawke into eager pursuit, the lean hot-blood hastily gained lengths on the smaller, stockier horse. The pair drove hard down the field, and Ol' Jack approached the first target. Within slashing distance, Robert cued his mount, and Prescott struck in concert, skillfully cutting down the first of the straw-stuffed soldiers of the *Gen d'Armes*.

The thunder of hoof beats was closer upon them, and Captain Drake and Hawke came up alongside. Robert, leaning forward in his saddle, coaxed Ol' Jack, and the gelding, straining under the heavy burden, nonetheless surged with a grunt of renewed effort, fighting to keep pace with the leggy Hawke.

As the next target came into sight, Captain Drake pushed easily ahead, squeezed into position, and sliced through the rope. On release, the dummy swung back to strike the other pair of riders. Robert ducked, but Prescott was hit hard in the face, thrown off balance and onto the ground.

Devington cursed, recalling his own success and his very fate were entwined with Prescott's. Pulling his horse into a hard halt on its haunches, they executed a half-pirouette, and without missing a beat, Robert swept down from his saddle to hoist his companion back up. He spurred the horse again, and Ol' Jack gave his all in response, but they had lost valuable time. The captain had nearly finished the course by the time the trio were headed back down the field.

They had failed. He burned with the injustice yet vowed to endure to the bitter end.

"Ah, Troopers Devington and Prescott, you join me at last! Better late than never, I suppose," Drake chided. "Prepare your weapon, Prescott," the captain commanded, maneuvering his horse to face them and drawing his saber.

Facing the captain, Prescott blanched, now realizing the grave error in his boast. Although *somewhat* experienced with the art of parry, lunge, and thrust with a small sword, he had never actually "pinked" an opponent, but moreover, his practiced technique of lunge and thrust was not developed for mounted combat.

Bile rose in his throat, and his saber suddenly felt heavy, awkward, and unwieldy in his sweating hand. He shivered with apprehension. This weapon, the slightly curved cavalry saber, was designed for slashing one's enemy to pieces. And to manage from the back of a galloping beast was another matter altogether.

"We ride in hard and strike hard, Prescott, like a joust. We need to unhorse him, take him down rather than engage hand to hand. We can prevail only with speed and steadfastness. You'll never best him otherwise. He has the advantage," Devington counseled.

"You just keep this nag moving, Devington, and I'll devise my own strategy," Prescott retorted hotly.

"My patience has nigh worn thin, gentlemen." The captain spoke authoritatively and without his customary mocking humor. "Prepare to charge or be struck down where you stand."

The gelding jigged under the tension of his riders. "Are you ready?" Robert asked tersely.

"Control your bloody beast!" Prescott fumed.

Ignoring the remark, Devington saluted the captain to signify their readiness, then spun and trotted off some distance to prepare for the charge.

The subaltern signaled, and both men spurred their mounts into action, hurtling at a headlong gallop toward one another. The captain held his sword in tierce, blade horizontal, point to the fore as he charged forth. He immediately perceived by his opponent's position that Prescott would attempt a thrusting attack.

While effective on foot, the technique was awkward at best on horseback, due to a mounted man's need to lean the upper body in order to extend his reach sufficiently to execute. Even when well done, this attack threw off one's balance, making it child's play to become unhorsed by an opponent. Drake considered making short work of Prescott in such a manner, but decided against it. What a pity 'twould be to end the lesson before it had truly begun!

Trooper Devington struggled to maintain his equanimity as the captain fiercely and unblinkingly charged toward them. "Now, Prescott! Now!" Devington yelled when they came together in a flurry, but Prescott, disregarding Robert's counsel, maintained his blade for a thrust.

As his sword point approached the captain's torso, Drake effortlessly dodged, and at the last second, like a cat with a mouse, parried. The opponents' blades clashed in the first pass, and Prescott fought to maintain his precarious balance on the horse, knowing if it were the captain's intent to harm rather than humiliate, he would have been disarmed, unhorsed, and damnably lucky to escape the encounter unscathed.

Robert pulled hard and swift and spun Ol' Jack around in an attempt to disengage the combatants, but Drake pursued, and before Prescott could prepare his guard, the captain's blade sliced the air downward inches from Prescott's left ear. He followed swiftly with a backhand stroke, which Prescott successfully dodged, knowing that had the captain intended, he would be missing both ears.

Prescott attempted to parry, but a third and forth diagonal slice of the captain's blade had Prescott gaping at his torso as if expecting his entrails to be exposed.

Robert again valiantly attempted to extricate them from this merciless onslaught, pulling Ol' Jack into a second retreat then circling around for another pass.

The captain reengaged with a final swift and fierce horizontal cut on the forehand, striking Prescott's blade from his hand, effortlessly unbalancing and disarming him. He and his weapon dashed to the ground.

As Prescott lay stunned and violently retching, Devington unsheathed his own saber and sprung into action. Spurring his horse, he leaned from his saddle, and in one fluid motion, swept the ground and tossed his comrade's lost weapon to him, but before the stunned Prescott could even react, Captain Drake intercepted, catching it midair.

"Very neat work! Neat work, indeed! Lesson's over." He paused. "Though my intent was an exercise in humility for two insolent new recruits, ironically, you have prevailed with your tenacity and quick wits. Dismount and cool your steed, Trooper Devington," the captain commanded. "By the by, as the new Corporal of the Horse, you are entitled to house him in my stables."

Five

CORPORAL OF THE HORSE

*B*y early spring 1743, the newly created British regiments were dispatched to the Continent. Having spent months in idleness interrupted only by drills, Corporal of the Horse Robert Devington believed himself exceedingly ill-equipped when these orders finally came.

With half of Europe now drawn into the conflict over the Hapsburg lands and the King's growing anxiety over his beloved homeland, His Majesty had called the Earl of Stair, an old veteran of war under Marlborough, out of a twenty-year retirement and appointed him Field Marshal.

Although the allied forces were by treaty committed to Austria's defense, it was no secret to the British that they had been positioned only to prevent French aggrandizement into the King's own Hanover.

As part of an advanced guard, Corporal Devington was to assist with the transport of one hundred newly procured remounts, which the guard would march halfway across the European continent to Pragmatic headquarters.

The horses, handpicked by the Regiment's Riding Master, Major Lord Bainbridge, were from some of the country's finest stables, but as Devington walked the paddocks prior to transport, he marveled at the major's choice of so many young, untrained horses as cavalry chargers. His experience told him that Bainbridge's procurements, all sleek, snorting, prancing specimens, were not at all suitable for war. Had he not held such a subordinate position, he would have said as much. As it was, he held his tongue and attended to duties.

They were to transport an entire herd in an enclosed vessel in unpredictable seas. Spring squalls were notorious for rising from nowhere. Many ships and many souls over the centuries had perished in those deceitful Channel waters.

Although the crossing would take only a few days, the men would need to take every precaution to safely transport their live cargo. Preparation of the horses began with Major Winthrop's express instructions two days prior to departure: to provide each horse with half their normal ration of oats the first day, then only hay the second day, and nothing to eat or drink the morning of embarkation.

"A horse whose belly is distended with food and water only adds to the inherent peril of slinging them aboard the ship," he explained to Devington. "Moreover, a bit of hunger will encourage them to take to their food once on board and help them to become reconciled to their change of quarters."

"Are they all to be loaded by sling, then?"

"I should think the few old campaigners within this lot shall walk upon the gangway with little enough fuss, but 'tis the green ones we must have a care to. I daresay the majority of them won't take to the gangway by any amount of coercion. A properly slung horse cannot injure himself, as his kicks and struggles meet only with air. 'Twill be by far safer and more expedient to sling the young ones.

"For now, my orders are to leave off the oats and maintain them quiet as possible. It is also vital, Corporal Devington, to keep together pairs who are accustomed to standing side-by-side in the troop stables. If they are settled in the ship stables in their customary order of precedence, they will feed and stand quieter, taking comfort from a familiar presence in unfamiliar surroundings. They must load in proper order. 'Twill be a stressful day tomorrow, and nervous horses are prone to colic."

By first light, the transport vessels were lined up for a half mile along the south bank of the river Thames. The veteran cavalry horses, with Devington's Ol' Jack and Captain Drake's Hawke among them, boarded in the precise order agreed upon and with little to-do. Once they were settled below, Captain Drake then directed all efforts to loading the restive young herd remaining in the paddocks.

Devington led the first of the bunch to the landing, from which the sling was suspended. As the men approached with the contrivance that would be used to lift the horse, the wind caught the fabric and sent the canvas snapping and flapping akin to a sail. White-eyed, the colt shied in terror, snorting and bolting backward.

"Are you men daft?" Devington rebuked angrily. "You can't expect him to just walk up and let us catapult him into the air. The poor beast must be allowed to accustom himself to the apparatus. Now lay the bloody thing down on the ground so it will cease that confounded flapping!"

Obeying the harshly spoken command, the troopers lowered the canvas until it lay motionless and benignly blanketed the ground. Stroking and quietly murmuring, Devington led the quaking horse by degrees toward the object of its fear. Snorting loudly, the horse lowered its nose to the ground to sniff the fiendish fabric then jumped back in renewed alarm. With Devington coaxing, man and horse circumnavigated the sling, until, gaining courage, they walked warily across the monster.

"You there," he commanded a trooper, "take hold the head collar and stroke him while I accustom him to the feel of it." Taking up the length of canvas, Devington approached the horse's side.

"Easy now, my good fellow," he murmured and rubbed the fabric along the horse's body, causing its skin to ripple. Devington continued until the animal was desensitized to the sensation and relaxed his stance.

Captain Drake, passing by to oversee the progress of the loading, halted his inspection to inquire: "Precisely how many horses have you loaded, Corporal Devington?"

"Not counting the ones who walked themselves aboard, this is the first, Captain."

"Indeed? Your counterparts on the other transports have already slung a half dozen aboard."

"This horse was excessively afeared, sir."

"Are not they all? 'Tis not natural for a horse to fly." The attending troopers chuckled at the wry remark.

"Indeed you are right, sir," Devington answered, "but I would convince you that a bit of extra time and care now will greatly reduce the dangers to both man and beast later. If we proceed with gentle persistence, he will load undaunted the next time. If we make the experience traumatic to the animal, he will subsequently be over-wrought with fear, thus creating a danger to himself and others."

"Very well, Devington, have it your way. If, however, we are not loaded and ready to sail with the evening tide, it will be *your* neck. Understood, Corporal?"

"Perfectly, sir." He saluted and turned back to the horse. "Now then. He has all but tasted the thing and knows there is naught to fear. We may proceed to sling him."

The captain stood back to observe unobtrusively while Devington addressed the animal in caressing tones and two others passed the canvas under his belly. Reaching hastily for the breast girth, which would prevent the horse from sliding forward within the sling, Devington deftly secured it. A fourth man fumbled to fasten the breech band, which would in turn prevent backward slipping.

Once assured that the animal was secure, Devington stepped back with a cry: "Make haste, lads, lest he decide to panic. Take him up anon!"

With four strong men manning the pulley, the bewildered beast was hoisted ten feet above the ground and swung over the ship's hatch, where he was lowered with the greatest of care into a large opening to the stable deck deep in the belly of the vessel.

Two additional men stood between decks to protect the animal's head and legs from striking the sides of the hatchway as he descended below. Once his feet were on solid planking, three more troopers awaited to release him and lead him to the stall and straw bedding that lay prepared to receive him.

The sling was then returned and the next horse led up. And the next. And the next. The procedure was repeated thirty times, until the paddock stood empty and the stable deck was loaded to near its capacity of fifty horses.

Returning later that afternoon to find Devington exhausted and anxious to locate his own pallet after ten unbroken hours of loading horses, Captain Drake remarked, "You have scarce an hour to spare before the tide goes out, Corporal."

"We have loaded the lot of them, sir." As he spoke, he rolled his shoulders in an effort to loosen his tight and aching muscles.

"Not quite so hasty, Corporal Devington. One yet remains."

"I hesitate to naysay you, Captain, but the paddocks are empty."

"The last of the horses we transport was not held amongst those in the general paddocks. He has awaited his turn in the relative luxury of the Riding Master's personal stables," Captain Drake remarked with a quirk of his brow. "Major Lord Bainbridge has given express orders that his prized young stallion be loaded last and that he is comfortably housed in the large box reserved for use by the veterinary surgeon."

"Indeed? And what of the animals that might become injured or distressed on the voyage?"

"Major Winthrop will have to address the issue with Bainbridge. The matter is far above our lowly ranks to resolve."

"Very well. Where is this specimen of equine perfection that our Regimental Riding Master holds so very dear?"

"Ah," Drake exclaimed, "here is the precious cargo at last!" He indicated two slight figures being tossed and dragged across the grounds by a magnificent, thrashing, plunging beast.

The finely sculpted head, small hooked ears, and highly arched neck revealed the stallion's Eastern origins. Notwithstanding his behavior, the tautly muscled, raging beast was a true beauty to behold.

"Our eminent Riding Master, Major Lord Bainbridge, especially selected this one out of the procurements as his own personal mount, but the stallion has proven an irascible brute. He plies all the arts of snorting, pawing, biting, rearing, and striking at his handlers."

"Good God! A fractious fiend, if ever there was one. And we are to load him?" Devington asked rhetorically.

"You might consider this a golden opportunity to prove the effectiveness of your unique training methods." The captain chuckled.

"I shan't go this alone, Captain!" Devington replied as he observed the horse rear and strike again at one of the grooms. "If I had a day perhaps to work with him, such progress might be made with the rogue, but with barely an hour? 'Tis an impossible task you would ask of me."

"And if I should offer you a full for'night's relief from stable duty?"

Devington considered the bargain. "Two for'nights and five guineas, Captain. I shan't risk my neck for nothing."

"Done," he answered promptly and with obvious relief. "By the by, you sold yourself short, Devington. I should have gone ten guineas for the sheer entertainment. Indeed, I shall now undertake to find a restful spot where I might *safely* observe your magic." He grinned broadly.

"I shall require a long length of rope."

"Easily found on a ship. You there! Trooper Benton, is it? Cut ten yards from that line."

Taking up the cord tossed to him, Devington formed several loops, rolled his shoulders once more, breathed deeply, and turned toward the approaching horse.

Taking firm hold of the lead, Devington abruptly dismissed the men who had escorted the horse at near peril to their lives. Devington then released the shank with which they had held the stallion and quickly slipped his own makeshift halter over the horse's head and moved back, out of striking range.

"Now, my boy, give me your worst."

When the stallion realized the slack in his tether, he set himself to renewed and violent plunging. Holding the line in his right hand, Devington sidestepped to position himself parallel to the thrashing stallion's hip. Giving the horse several more yards of slack, he took up the remaining length with his left hand and purposely made a large arc in the air to startle the stallion into forward motion.

Anchoring his right arm closely to his hip to keep from being dragged, Devington again made the gesture, but rather than invoking the flight reflex he expected, the stallion spun around to face him. Rising again on his hind legs, he snorted and struck out with both forelegs. Devington narrowly dodged the thrashing hooves.

"Yes, my boy, you are indeed much faster, bigger, and stronger than me and an altogether superior specimen of God's creation, but I have seen your like before. Only one of us can be master, and it won't be you."

He swung the rope in another arc to the side of the horse's head. Dodging the rope, the horse landed and spun his hindquarters toward Devington. The captain then struck the horse on the rump with the rope. Surprised once more, flight instinct prevailed, and the horse launched himself forward to escape.

Perceiving his advantage, Devington continued to use the rope to drive the animal from behind, forcing the stallion to run circles around him. Around and around he encircled his handler, until exhausted and licking his lips in the first visible sign of submission, he halted. Flanks heaving, he turned to regard his handler warily.

"That's a good fellow. Nice and easy now." Devington advanced slowly toward the horse, taking up yards of slack rope and carefully approaching the stallion's head. Within four feet, he paused. The stallion snorted and shook his mane menacingly. He stood his ground, staring Devington down, but made no further move to strike.

"You're a restive brute, you are, but I don't believe you are truly vicious, though you do your best to convince me." Speaking calmly and quietly, he moved ever closer toward the horse's shoulder, until he reached out his hand to stroke the horse's neck.

The stallion snorted again but remained in place. Wary of the horse's every signal, Devington made his way around the animal, running his hands over every quarter. Coming last to the animal's head, Devington brushed the broad forehead. The horse lowered his head with a great sigh.

Taking the lead close to the halter, Devington walked the subdued beast toward the sling, which lay again on the ground. At first notice of the canvas, the horse abruptly stalled. Snorting, he took three quick steps backward. Ears pricked forward in curiosity, he regarded the canvas suspiciously. Observing the flickering ears, Devington released some slack. The young stallion moved guardedly forward. Halting inches from the canvas, he stomped his foot and jumped back, his gaze never leaving the object.

With sudden boldness, he strode forward, reached his head down, took the fabric up in his teeth, and tossed it about while trotting a small circle, his tail raised triumphantly in the air.

"A born cavalry mount, b'God, for the one who can master him!" Drake remarked with astonishment. "You've an undeniable gift, Devington."

"I won't rest on my laurels, Captain. Horses are a whimsical and capricious species. I'd rather load the beast before he changes his mind."

Foregoing dinner for his berth, Corporal Devington collapsed and fell instantly into deep slumber. His rest was short-lived, however, interrupted by a violent list of the ship and followed by the groan of his cabin mates as they tossed up their accounts into the chamber pots. Soon following suit, Devington was on his knees with seasickness and heartily thanking God Almighty that His hand of Providence had not guided him to join the Royal Navy!

By first light, the storm had passed. The trumpet sounded, calling all to duty. Though he was relieved of stable duty and barely recovered from his infirmity, Devington was compelled to the ship's stables to see how the horses had fared during the turbulent crossing.

Finding Ol' Jack next to Hawke and quietly munching his hay, the corporal moved on to the other end of the stable deck where he found one stall door kicked loose from its hinges. Though all the horses' heads had been tied tight and short to prevent movement, one of them had managed to break free of its head collar and was no doubt wreaking havoc among the rest of the herd. He didn't go far before he located the renegade, who stood bullying the men who had come to clean and feed.

"You again!" Devington said to the stallion. "I should have known you as the malefactor."

The gray acknowledged him with a snort and challenging toss of his head.

"I'll see to this one, lads," Devington said to the troopers and took down a canvas head collar and lead from a peg on the wall. He slowly and steadily walked forward. The stallion promptly pinned his ears back and turned his hinder end to face the corporal.

"Tut. Tut, my man. I shan't allow such disrespectful behavior; such insolence cannot be tolerated in His Majesty's Horse. Discipline must prevail, you know."

Standing clear of the horse's flying hooves, Devington rebuked the stallion's rump with a smart pop of the lead.

Kicking out in vexation, the horse snorted and then turned again to face his antagonist. Devington stood firm, unruffled, and unintimidated. Almost imperceptibly, the stallion licked his lips and dropped his head.

"There's oats and hay aplenty back in your box," Devington said softly, moved to the horse's head, and deftly slipped on the collar. "Play time is now over, my man."

He led the miscreant to the first empty stall. Gathering some oats as distraction, Devington entered the box with the intention of examining the horse's legs for injury; but still restive and distrustful, the stallion circled with widened eyes and pinned ears. Not wanting to distress the horse further and impair the progress he had made, Devington decided to leave him to settle and see to the others.

By this time, Major Winthrop had arrived to make his twice-daily inspection. Proceeding down the rows, he assessed the general condition of the horses. Spying Devington exiting the gray's box, he halted.

"Corporal! What have you done with Bainbridge's gray?" he demanded. "He was at the other end of the stable deck when I saw to him last evening."

"Major." Devington saluted. "Not so. He broke free during the night, apparently kicked down his door. I moved him to this box to assess his legs for injury."

"And what knowledge would you have of a horse's legs?" Winthrop posed the question condescendingly.

"Enough to know he shall require a bran poultice to his right hock. There is visible swelling, but he appears not to favor it over-much. I doubt 'tis more than a self-inflicted strain from kicking down the door. With rest and a poultice, I would guess him sound in a matter of days."

"I daresay Bainbridge shall put little stock in *your opinion* regarding his animal. Stand aside, and I shall give him a *proper* examination."

"Would you care for my assistance, sir?"

"I should doubt it."

Devington shrugged his resignation but stood closely by and grinned as Winthrop entered the box. Within moments, the gray commenced a fit of plunging, kicking, and thrashing that made any attempt of examination impossible. Finally called upon to assist, the corporal spent nearly an hour patiently soothing and pacifying the stallion's volatile temper, all while Winthrop watched in amazement.

"Very well, I shall leave it to you to apply the poultice, Corporal Devington. And what is your assessment of the others? Beyond this renegade, how are they holding up?"

Devington noted that rather than condescension, the major made this address with what might be described as a modicum of respect.

"Other than some minor abrasions, for which I have applied standing bandages, I detect no great injuries, but I fear stall number five begins to colic."

"So you say? Then what would you do for this *first case* of colic? I warn it is nigh impossible to cross the sea without losing at least one thusly."

"One would normally commence to hand-walking at the first sign, but 'tis impossible to do when he must remain confined below decks."

"Then he must have three pints of warm water injected into his rectum to stimulate his bowels to move."

"I have already done so, sir."

The major regarded him quizzically. "Then mayhap my services as chief veterinary surgeon are superfluous?"

His rancor led the corporal to humbly volunteer, "Major Winthrop, sir, having been raised my entire life with equines, I have seen most every ailment and have no small experience of veterinary medicine. I sought only to help in your absence."

"Is that so, Corporal? Then pray, what is your professional opinion regarding this particular patient?"

"To massage his gut and promptly administer a colic remedy."

"And of what is your *colic remedy* comprised?"

"Two drams of ginger and one-half ounce of black pepper instilled in half a bottle of gin diluted with one pint of warm water."

The major raised his brows. "Ginger, eh? 'Tis a well-known remedy in humans for all manner of belly pain, and I suppose the intoxicating effects of the gin might serve as a sedative. But while I find your recipe interesting, I prefer to adhere to cures based on sound medical science. I shall administer two ounces tincture of opium and two ounces spirits of turpentine in one pint of warm water. I shall return anon, and you may administer this physic, as well as applying the bran poultice to Bainbridge's gray."

"It will be done as you wish, sir." Devington saluted.

"Gin and ginger," the major mused and walked away.

❧

By the time they docked at Ostend, three horses from the other ships had been lost to colic. Several more had perished by struggling and fighting so violently during the unloading that they had broken legs, dashing them against the hatches, or had breached the canvas sling and dropped into the sea. To Devington's credit, his entire herd was slung to shore with little fuss and no incident.

With all of the horses now unloaded and picketed, the troopers of the Household Cavalry spent three more days in Ostend, awaiting the ships conveying the supply wagons that would carry the forage and the accoutrements necessary for their march.

On the morning of the fourth day, the reveille trumpet was muffled by the soggy gray dawn. The day of decampment had arrived in the midst of heavy April rains. Waking cold and damp from his bed of straw above the tavern stables, Devington pushed his bedmates aside to pull on his boots and supervise the morning routine of mucking, feeding, watering, and grooming.

Though temporarily exempt from stable duties, Devington still retained charge over the care and feeding of the horses, whose importance superseded even the needs of the men. The valiant men of the King's Horse would be permitted to take their morning rations only after caring for the animals upon whom they depended to carry them.

Devington shortly joined Captain Drake and Major Winthrop, and the trio proceeded through the stables and picket lines of their troop horses, inspecting each one, until meeting the troop's farrier.

"How goes it, Tom?" Winthop asked as the farrier pounded the final nail into the hoof of the last troop horse on the picket line.

"Spent the past two days reseating shoes and painting tar on the soles of all their hooves, Major. 'Tis all can be done to prevent the thrush, though I daresay 'twill be all for naught. Wi' such heavy rains, we'll be marching for at least a for'night in the mud. Inevitably, a number of 'em will be footsore and oozing black pus afore we see Ghent."

"The tar should make a difference, as long as it's applied regularly," Devington remarked.

"Should it be reapplied twice or thrice per se'nnight, Tom?" Major Winthrop asked.

"Thrice… if'n the supply holds that long," he remarked dubiously. "Elsewise, the troop horses be ready to march, sirs." He then amended hastily, "Leastwise, all save one. Unmanageable brute he be. Look at this." The farrier lifted his smock and lowered his breeches to expose the deep purple tooth marks that marred his broad, bared buttocks.

"I might well hazard a guess which one it was." The Captain regarded Devington knowingly.

Six

A BITTER RIVALRY

*A*fter having seen to the men and horses, Devington washed down the last bite of dry black bread with a gulp of bitter coffee. Throwing the tin muck in his haversack, he slung it over his shoulder.

He then secured his accoutrements to his saddle, placed his new pistols in their case in front of his pommel, taking special care to protect his pouch of gunpowder from the damp. After making a last adjustment to his saddle girth, Devington straightened his sword and took up his carbine, whose butt would rest in the bucket on the right side of his saddle with his picket pole strapped securely alongside. Once he made his final checks, the corporal mounted—a clumsy business at best—while balancing two weapons and a four-foot picket pole.

When the trump sounded for parade inspection, Devington was ready and responded eagerly. With an encouraging pat to Ol' Jack, he wheeled and trotted off briskly to join his squadron, easily identifiable by their blue facings and housings, made conspicuous by a sea of crimson.

Locating his own Sixth Troop of the King's Horse, Devington hastily fell into the second line center, directly behind Captain Drake, whose height alone would have placed him in the front line if his position had not. Although of medium height, Devington was consigned to the more diminutive middle ranks, sandwiched front and aft by the taller men.

To Captain Drake's credit, his entire rank and file marshaled with precision and alacrity. They set out, smart-stepping in rigid scarlet columns. Their rifles clanked as they swung against their sabers, and the ground quaked with the low, rumbling thunder of their iron-shod chargers' hooves in rhythm with the kettledrum.

They marched through days of whipping wind and pelting rain, making field camp every night, with rarely a dry stick to start a fire, sleeping in wet clothes, and eating the coarse bread and dried meat that comprised the daily ration. Striking up camp every dawn, they repeated the routine, day after day. The journey, although onerous enough for the callow recruits, proved debilitating to a number of the young, green horses, who had to be put down for foundering.

After three arduous weeks of heavy marching in such deplorable conditions, the troops finally gained the Flemish city of Maestricht, temporary field headquarters of Field Marshal Stair, commander in chief of the Pragmatic Army. Their respite, however, was dismally brief.

After having wasted months in his unsuccessful effort to press the Dutch to join the alliance against her neighbor, France, Lord Stair's patience had finally expired. Frustrated and eager to engage, Lord Stair ordered his forces to decamp from Flanders. Without Dutch support and against the counsel of the Austrian and Hanoverian general, the field marshal advanced his British forces into French-occupied Franconia and marched resolutely up the hills of Killersbach, drawing up lines of battle in full sight of the French generals, who completely ignored the taunt.

Failing to engage even the interest of the enemy, the British Army moved farther up the river to join the Austrian and Hanoverian regi-ments. Stair and his Pragmatic generals continued to vacillate and dither, failing still to agree on a single plan of action, forcing their respective troops into the mundane and restless routine of regimental life while the French set up camp on the opposite bank of the river, patiently waiting to make their move.

For Devington, the monotony of the routine gave him far too much time to ponder. He missed the rolling Yorkshire hills and the morning "breezes" on the heath, but most of all, his heart yearned for Charlotte.

ᔪᔭᔪ

June 1, 1743

My Dearest Love,

I write from our regiment's encampment outside the city of Aschaffenburg in Franconia.

To my great disillusionment, my soldiering days thus far have differed little from my days as the under groom at Heathstead Hall.

I rise each morning before dawn, awakened by the trump of reveille, and push aside my four tent mates, who cram each night into our seven-by-nine-foot canvas shelter. We report for roll at five of the clock and then stable call at five and a quarter, during which time all troopers feed and groom their horses. At half past six, we receive a sparse breakfast.

Watering call ensues breakfast, which while garrisoned requires carting hundreds of gallons of water to the picket lines, or if encamped, marching the horses a full mile or more to the nearest watering place.

Drills and arms' practice take place from nine until eleven, with a brief respite prior to our noon meal of beer, dark bread, and cheese. The afternoon continues with troop reviews and mounted drill, followed by dismounted drill to prepare for battle on foot. The four-thirty trump signals water and stable call once more, with all troopers repeating the morning care of our mounts.

Once the horses are settled for the evening, the men partake of the evening meal, usually a watery soup with more bread, unless those of us not assigned to patrol are free for a few hours of leisure. In this happy event, we sup at a public house where the bill of fare barely surpasses that of the encampment. The Germanic folk subsist in great part on potatoes, cabbage, and all manner of greasy sausage. The beer, however, is more than tolerable.

The evening tattoo at approximately eight of the clock signals the barkeeps to close the taps and sends us back to our respective quarters for bed checks.

As to our Germanic brothers-in-arms, with whom we are united in name as one Pragmatic Army, I can assure you of a vastly different reality. There is mounting tension and a decided lack of camaraderie between the British and German troops who are daily more convinced that we wage war with France solely to protect Hanover.

The only cement in the Pragmatic alliance appears to be our mutual and absolute detestation of the French, which far exceeds our animosity toward one another. Nonetheless, fear of French domination has not been sufficient to cohere our generals on a battle plan.

But while finding ourselves in this sad state of limbo, I contrive to busy myself with my duties as Corporal of the Horse. My responsibilities in this office, I confess, are ill-defined and varied. One day I am the right hand of Captain Drake as he inspects his troops, and the next I might be acting veterinary assistant to Major Winthrop, whose respect I have finally managed to win.

'Tis nonetheless a post, for which I am exceedingly grateful, as it has allowed me firsthand knowledge of all the regimental horses. The most extraordinary of these is by far the Riding Master's personal, a beauteous specimen, whose behavior has been so unruly and rancorous that Winthrop was induced to conduct a physical examination, lest there be some unknown injury that incites his passions.

Finding naught physically wrong, and having seen me manage the stallion better than any of his other handlers, Winthrop asked if I should care to try him under saddle in order to assess his back.

Relishing such a challenge after months of ceaseless marching, I saddled the horse. After completing the deed (with no small difficulty!), I was preparing to back him, when arrives Bainbridge demanding to know why the gray was out of his stables!

At this juncture, I discovered our Riding Master to be a man of great self-conceit and jealously possessive of his horses. With no allowance for explanation, he snatched up the bridle reins and mounted, whereby the animal commenced any number of capers.

Charlotte, although the man is highly regarded by the regiment as its most superlative horseman, I can by no means concur but for his propensity to violence. Without compunction or hesitation, the major applied whip and spur to the horse so zealously, I believed he was bent on flogging the wickedness out of him. His actions only incited the full and uninhibited passion of the irascible beast, who thrashed and tossed himself about, bucking, plunging, and rearing in furious rebellion. Nonetheless, he failed in all his attempts to unseat the major, who gave back in full measure.

At length, Bainbridge succeeded in beating the horse into an angry, resentful submission. Convinced that he alone had tamed the untamable and mastered the unmasterable, the major's vanity was satisfied, but I could see clearly in the gray's eyes that he had conceded only the battle but not the war.

I am gratified to know that the horse's spirit remains unbroken. Capricious and cunning as he is, he will undoubtedly invent many schemes to oppose what is demanded of him by brute force. The major does not comprehend that the key to governing such a one is to gain his trust and respect by degrees, until he willingly comes to submit to his master. No man has yet, or ever will, gain a point over a horse in any but this manner. I am thankful to Jeffries for this wisdom.

I must now close, my dearest love, but know you are ever in my thoughts.

Your Most Devoted,

R. D.

Finishing his letter with a sigh, Devington laid down the quill upon the crate-table, folded the foolscap, sealed it with wax, and stuffed it into his left breast pocket. Rising from the camp chair, Devington turned to his captain. "I thank you for the use of your tent," he said. "I first feared I'd never have the leisure to write, but then when I did, I lacked the implements to do so."

"I am happy to oblige, Devington, but if you are now finished with your correspondence, I say we locate Winthrop and quit this accursed compound. With His Majesty's arrival, there should be no dearth of entertainment in the town… or at least in the taverns."

The Pragmatic Army's flagging spirits were greatly elevated by the arrival of King George, who assumed Supreme Command of his army. Sporting the gold sash of Hanover over his military uniform, he and his second son, the Duke of Cumberland, and their escort of Hanoverian Guards on their Hanoverian-bred horses, rode through the encampments and reviewed the troops.

Revelry permeated the town and filled the taverns as men pressed shoulder to shoulder into the crowded taprooms where Austrians, British, and Hanoverians mixed company and cheered the arrival of His Britannic Majesty. As much beer spilled as flowed, and the bawdy ballads sung in indiscernible tongues were drowned out only by the raucous laughter.

Pushing up to the bar, the three British cavalrymen squeezed in amongst a group of Hanoverians, who eyed the trio head to toe disparagingly. The most senior of the group, a captain, greeted them with a smile of overt disdain. Turning back to his compatriots, he said, "*Die Englisch, Sie glauben Sie Soldaten sind. Bah! Sie sind nur die Schafe in Wolfe Kleidung!*"

In answer, the group broke into hearty guffaws, drained their tankards, and poured another round.

Standing closest to the Hanoverian captain, Major Winthrop spoke in a low voice to his two countrymen. "Though I am no linguist,

I have mastered the basics of High Dutch while in this accursed country. It is my belief that our Hanoverian comrades-in-arms have just referred to our English army as 'sheep in wolves' clothing.'"

"Sheep?" Devington's hand went impulsively to his sword, a gesture not missed by either his friends or their antagonists, who abruptly ceased their chuckles.

"We need not begin a war within this taproom, Devington. Pray rein in your temper and allow me to handle this," Drake answered coolly, breaking the mounting tension. Pasting on a smile of affability, he then turned to the offending officer.

"So, *meine guten Kapitän*, you would presume to affront the very *English sheep* who have come to protect your inconsequential little electorate? I might ask you where were the brave Hanoverians whilst the English *sheep* mounted the hills of Killersbach to confront the French wolves?"

"What do you English know of making land war?" the Hanoverian jeered, ignoring the question. "Your field marshal is an old man. Your troops want *disziplin*, and your *Kavallerie*, mounted on inferior nags, is a mockery."

"Now he even dares insults our horses!" Devington cried. Drake shot him a quelling look.

"Even your king acknowledges the inadequacy of the *Englisch Kavallerie* and their horses. He brings from the Royal Stud at Celle the finest of Hanoverian mounts for himself, the duc, and his *Hanoverian Guard*."

"Inadequate, you say? Then I suppose you would not hesitate to back your claim?" Drake replied with icy composure.

"*Die Englisch* would drop *die Gauntlet, ja?*"

"Just so, *meine freund*. Sadly, as dueling between officers is prohibited, I cannot defend the honor of my countrymen with my sword, but by horse is another matter. There is no man among you who can outride an English cavalryman."

"So you think, *ja*?" He translated the British officer's remarks, and his compatriots laughed at the ludicrous idea that an Englishman might better a Hanoverian in any endeavor.

Tamping down his rising temper, Drake responded with dead calm. "There is no doubt of it, *Herr Kapitän*, and I stand ready to back my claim. I challenge your best Hanoverian horse and rider to a contest of speed, strength, and stamina against our English finest."

"A contest, you say?"

"Indeed, a contest. I propose a bloody race."

⌘

"Mark my words, Captain, he won't like it."

"I wouldn't be so hasty to judge, Devington. There is no love lost between our Field Marshal Stair and his Hanoverian counterparts. They have opposed his every move and completely hamstrung him this entire campaign. Furthermore, he is well aware that his British troops are as low on morale as we are on bread. As an old campaigner, he knows the danger this creates."

"Assuming he does not forbid the scheme, what is your plan?"

"I'll send a message of appointment to *der Kapitän Ranzau*."

"So *you* propose to ride?"

"*I am the one* who issued the challenge. And there is no better suited mount than Hawke. In his racing career he suffered only one defeat, and *that* was due only to a strained tendon," he stated matter-of-factly.

"I beg to differ with you, Captain. If you recall, I was the rider who defeated him, and Rosie would have won regardless. She was still as fresh at the finish as when she began."

Drake quirked a brow.

"So you would pull rank on me, knowing I'm the best suited for the task? Though I know none who would criticize your manner with a horse, Captain, you know there is no better rider in this regiment than I, and no stouter horse than Ol' Jack. Besides, I carry a full stone and a half less than you. The weight will be very telling on the horse for the distance you propose."

Major Winthrop's arrival from Field Marshal Stair's headquarters interrupted their discourse. Drake and Devington regarded him expectantly. As Winthrop spoke, his face was grave.

"The field marshal asks if you both fully realize the repercussions of what you have proposed—that this trial could further ignite the animosities within our camp."

"The possibility had come to mind. 'Tis precisely why I thought you should go as emissary to Field Marshal Stair to beg his approbation."

"Damn-it-all, Winthrop, what was his response?" Devington demanded.

"That is not so easily answered. His reply: Firstly, he offered 'to hang the damned lot of Hanoverians,' then catching himself, he offered up *any horse* in the entire regiment for the deed... including his own."

"So! The field marshal himself has given us the wink and the nod. I daresay he is more than eager to finally see a Hanoverian set down," the captain said with deep satisfaction.

"That may be so, however, he also stated that if asked by His Majesty, he will profess to complete ignorance of the affair, and lastly, he threatened that the challenger of this race will most certainly face the courts-martial... if he loses. Now I ask, gentlemen, if you are still so hell-bent on your scheme?"

"Indeed a good question. Notwithstanding these caveats, are you still so eager to ride, Devington?"

Perceiving his opportunity to prove himself at last, Devington answered with bravado, "You wish to win, don't you?"

"To think I had amended my opinion that you are a cocky upstart," the captain declared wryly. "You are quite sure of yourself, then. What do you think, Winthrop?"

"I must side with Devington. He handles a horse better than any man I know. A veritable centaur is our young corporal."

"Then I suppose it's settled. We shall meet the Hanoverians three days hence at sunup. 'Twill be a race like no other, from Aschaffenburg to the village of Dettingen and back again. 'Tis nigh on six leagues across rough country and surely a distance to test the mettle of man and beast."

"But who shall judge?" Winthrop asked.

"I suppose we must have a man placed at Dettingen, but one who has no vested interest."

"The Austrians, mayhap?" Winthrop offered.

"Know you any trustworthy man within D'Ahremburg's camp? One who would have no stake in the outcome?"

"I am acquainted with my Austrian counterpart. He and I have had many a discussion between the colic and the gripe. He owes me a boon and 'twould be no bad thing to have a veterinarian on hand after nearly a ten-mile run. I daresay he would show no favoritism."

"Then, gentlemen… let the games begin."

Seven

❧

LETTERS FROM WAR

*A*s had become her habit, Charlotte rose before the sun, but rather than snatching on her riding clothes as was her custom, she lit a candle and drifted dreamily to the mahogany box on her dressing table, where she retrieved her letter.

It was from Robert and the first word she had received since his departure from Woolwich nearly three months ago. Sick with worry, she had spent that time sleepless and without appetite, but now she knew he was safe. Robert was alive and well and thinking of her always, just as his image never completely vanished from her own mind and heart.

With tears of joy, Charlotte tenderly opened the pages she had read and reread a dozen times since receiving them from Jeffries only the day before. As she committed his words to heart, her eyes caressed every pen stroke.

Corporal of the Horse! Robert had already been promoted to corporal. He was well on his way to achieving his ambitions and making his mark. Soon, she reassured herself, soon he would return for her. He would appear one day in his handsome uniform and throw her up behind him and together they would ride away, just as she had dreamed they would.

Holding the pages against her breast, she spoke her morning prayer for his continued safety and returned to her dressing table to replace his letter inside her treasure box, along with her father's silver watch and her mother's single strand of pearls.

Now changing her shift for Charles's castoffs, which Letty had freshly repatched for her, she drew on her boots and moved stealthily through the quiet house. She exited the back, passing silently by the kitchens, and followed her well-trod path to the stables with a renewed spring in her step and whistling tunelessly as she went.

"Good morning, Jemmy," she said cheerily to the gangly young man at work grooming a leggy gray gelding while the other boys still busied themselves shoveling and carting the muck.

"G'mornin', miss." He paused with the curry to pull his fore-lock diffidently.

"You've finished the mucking already?" Charlotte smiled teas-ingly, reminding him again of his impudence at their first meeting. In those early days, Jemmy had stood in awe of Robert, and as Charlotte had grown in Robert's esteem, so had she reluctantly grown in Jemmy's.

Now, in Robert's absence, he had somehow deemed himself her de facto protector. He tended her horse, accompanied her on her rides, and stood as sentinel to guard her secret from those who would not condone her regular presence in her uncle's stables.

"Indeed so, miss. I started early so's yer horse would be ready."

"My horse?" She regarded Jemmy askance. "Where is Amoret?"

"Jeffries has took her North. The Bart had a mind to breed her to Hobgoblin."

"Indeed? The get of that cross would be twice Darley bred. I would think breeding her with Godolphin's stallion would result in a superior cross."

"You mean the old teaser stallion what is makin' such a name for hisself?"

"Yes. He is the sire of Lath and Cade, both exceptional runners. Breeding Amoret with him would blend the blood of two exceptional families, the Darley and the Godolphin. But if she is gone, who now am I to ride?"

"Don't ye fret about that, miss. Jeffries told the lads you was as able to ride the cracks as any of their sorry arses. 'Scuse me, miss." He blushed. "Forgot meself."

Ignoring his slip, she flushed with pleasure. "Jeffries said that?"

"'Deed he did. Says since Robert left, you was the only one could ready the runners for the fall season. Says you was to have yer pick o' the lot of 'em... that is, any but Rascallion."

"Rascallion?"

"He be the Bart's newest crack, miss. Bought yesterday. He be bred to run and looks right enough, but his temper is rightly soured. A vicious bast... er... beast, that is. Jeffries has his hands full, if the Bart 'spects 'im to run come spring."

"Indeed? I should like to take him out then."

"Not *that one*, miss. Jeffries need get 'im in hand first."

"Then who *am I* to ride, Jemmy?"

"This one 'ere is a fine colt, miss."

"Tortoise?"

"Indeed. Jeffries thought you might take to the idea, given that he's full brother to Rosie and all. Robert done started 'is training afore he left. Said that if he can run like 'is sister done, the Bart might finally have a go for the King's Plate. Jeffries has high hopes for him, even if it is wi' Master Charles up. Yer cousin is a right enough chap, ain't 'e? If'n not, ye might teach this horse o' his a trick or two."

"Charles's horse? Indeed I should not!" She laughed. "Charles has been ever kind and is my only friend within the family, though he rarely dares stand up to my uncle or even to Beatrix's bullying. Poor boy, though competent enough, he is not a gifted horseman, and sadly, that is the only accomplishment my uncle cares about. I fear he shall never live up to his father's expectations, and I think Charles knows it, too. No, I will return his kindness by teaching his horse good manners. Charles needs every advantage in a race. I'll finish up and saddle this one myself, if you want to go ahead and get your own mount ready."

"'Tis a'ready done, miss." Jemmy broke into a gap-toothed grin. "There be no need for ye to dirty yerself anymore groomin'. 'Tis a job for the lads."

"You know I don't mind the dirt," she protested. "I enjoy caring for the horses, though I am nonetheless grateful for your help. But if you are ready, let us not dally! I need keep my rides short these days. I dare not risk discovery. Beatrix would relish any opportunity to sour my uncle's temper against me."

She lightly tossed the saddle pad upon the gelding's back, placed the saddle behind his withers, and buckled the girth around his belly. Jemmy, meanwhile, slid the bit into the horse's mouth and drew the headstall into position. Charlotte then took the reins from Jemmy's hand and led the gelding out into the misty stable yard, where Tortoise tossed his head with delight.

"You're a fresh one this morning," she declared and sprung up into the saddle. "Jemmy," she called over her shoulder, "catch us if you can!" And Charlotte cantered gleefully out of the yard.

Eight

❧

THE CHALLENGE

*D*evington awoke on the appointed day, his mind and emotions awhirl. His opportunity to distinguish himself had finally presented itself, and he had grasped it with both hands, but his burden was multiplied by the weight of his entire regiment upon his shoulders. This race was a matter of honor.

He dressed with deliberate care, not desiring to give the Hanoverians any fault to criticize in his appearance or bearing. He lastly strapped on his sword, and taking up his riding tack, he walked briskly to the officer's stables, where his horse had been housed for the night. The corporal was surprised to encounter Major Winthrop and Captain Drake arrived ahead of him, and moreover, devastated to see Captain Drake walking the limping gelding out of his stall, whereupon Major Winthrop pronounced him dead lame.

"The devil he is!" Devington cursed. "Just yesterday he was rock solid."

"'Tis far from the case today. Nigh on three-legged lame, he is. Here, take him out a few paces at the trot."

Taking the horse's lead, Devington forced the gimping animal forward with a smart swat on the rump. After ten paces, they circled back with Jack's head jerking spasmodically upward with every step of his right fore.

"I found naught amiss in the sinews," Winthrop remarked. "I suspect it might be his right forefoot."

"Have you hoof testers?" Devington asked.

"Aye. We'll test him," the vet concurred.

Captain Drake located the device while Winthrop lifted the horse's foreleg and braced it between his own knees. He then clamped the hoof between the calipers and gently compressed. The jolt of the horse's body instantly confirmed his suspicions.

"'Tis an abscess, right enough. The good news is that the ailment is completely curable. I'll drill into the sole a wee bit, and a few days of mud packed with Epsom salts and vinegar will draw out the purulence. He'll soon be sound enough to march, but the bad news is he shan't be running any race today. You must find yourself another mount, Devington."

"Confound it all! I've no time! I've no doubt the captain's Hawke would give it a go, but I daren't push him such a distance with his old injury. This trial needs a swift athlete, a horse with grit to his very bones. Where can I find such a one with so little time?"

"If it's high spirits and an iron will you desire, I can think of only one such animal in this camp," the captain replied slowly.

"Indeed. There is one." The corporal and the captain exchanged knowing looks.

"You *can't* mean that notorious gray," Winthrop responded, incredulous. "Besides, Bainbridge will never allow it."

"Bainbridge answers to Lord Stair," Captain Drake interjected. "You said the field marshal offered up *any horse* in his army. Why should this preclude Major Bainbridge's stallion? Needs must when the devil drives. Besides, all will be forgiven, providing Devington wins."

"One would hope you know what you are about with *that one*, Devington," Winthrop said.

"It can be no other," he answered. With everything to gain— and everything to lose—he took up his riding tack and marched purposefully to the gray's stables, where he found the stallion pacing restlessly in his stall. Recognizing Devington at once, he uttered a low nicker in greeting, but then, as if remembering himself, he followed with a more menacing snort.

"I'm glad to see you too, my man, though I would wish it were under other circumstances. I require a boon, you see."

Accompanied by their seconds, much as a pair of duelists, the riders were appointed to meet at the Aschaffenburg bridge at precisely eight o'clock in the morning. Each rider departed his respective camp, dressed in his parade uniform and carrying his sword, pistols, and regimental standard.

While every attempt had been made to keep the matter quiet, word had spread in excited whispers, growing and swelling in rippling waves throughout the Pragmatic camps. Hundreds upon hundreds of British, Hanoverians, and Austrians formed a miles-long line, beginning at the bridge, crowding the streets, and skirting along the river path, which the riders would eventually follow nearly eight miles to Dettingen and back.

As the contenders advanced to the bridge, a party of British troopers hoisted the Union Jack and broke into a jubilant if unharmonious chorus of *Hail Britannia*! Devington paused his excitedly prancing horse to salute his country's flag, and the exultant Englishmen cheered. The startled gray reared, but Devington maintained his seat and calmly circled his agitated mount a few times to resettle him.

Arriving at the bridge, Devington and his opponent, one Captain Ranzau, faced one another appraisingly. Ranzau sat atop his large-boned, heavily muscled black charger. Standing well over sixteen hands, the splendid stallion towered over Devington and his lighter, lither gray, who danced, pawed, and snorted challengingly at his Goliath of an adversary.

"He's a fine one," Devington remarked appreciatively of the captain's black.

"He is *Sohn* of His Majesty's own *Gyldenstein*, one of the twelve best stallions *von* all Europe."

"That may well be true, *Kapitän*, but England is *not* part of Europe."

The Hanoverian flushed. "You English have so conceit of your horses, but we shall soon prove otherwise."

A trumpet sounded unexpectedly, startling both men and their horses. The herald caused a great commotion among the amassed soldiers, and the two riders regarded one another speculatively. Following a second trump, a group of riders came into view, now easily recognizable as an assemblage of His Majesty's Life Guards. The guards approached, headed by a portly, florid-faced young man in a highly decorated uniform.

"'Tis the Duke of Cumberland," Captain Drake reported quietly to Devington.

Abashed by the royal arrival and anxious of the repercussions, Devington and Ranzau moved to dismount, but the duke arrested them.

"As you were, gentleman," His Grace said to the pair. "I have come to verify for myself the report I received this morning of a challenge between His Majesty's British and Hanoverian Cavalries. Now, I would judge the rumor to be true." He spoke sternly, raking them with cool blue eyes. "Here we sit on half rations, with our supply lines cut and French all about us, and our troops would run a horse race?"

Captain Drake stepped forward. "Your Grace, Corporal Devington is not to be faulted. 'Twas I who issued the challenge, to avoid what might otherwise have been a nasty confrontation between your British and Hanoverian troops."

"And in so doing, you have marshaled the men and boosted pitifully low morale in both camps. I commend you, Captain. And now, I request the honor of commencing this race."

At the sound of the trump, the riders spurred their horses into action, clamoring down the crowded cobbles in a fierce flurry of hooves, accompanied by waving hats and a deafening cacophony of English and German cheers. The race was unlike any other Devington had ridden. The rules were simple: to be the first to reach the village of Dettingen and return, with the course completely determined by the riders.

Side-by-side, they galloped northeastward through the streets of Aschaffenburg until breaking into the open fields where the masses of British infantry and artillery were going about their morning routines.

Devington and Ranzau blazed through the middle of the encampment, causing men to scatter their weaponry and scurry out of the way. Hurtling now through the artillery, Devington heard the rumble of iron wheels and cracking of whips before he actually perceived the line of limbers and caissons stuck in the mud and blocking their path all the way to the riverfront. Hesitating, he pulled up his horse, looking right and left for an opening, while with a triumphant cry, the Hanoverian spurred his charger ever faster, and with a great and powerful spring, they cleared the cannon with the grace of a stag.

Devington sat frozen, momentarily bedazzled by the magnificent performance; then snapping back to attention, he wheeled his own horse with a mind to follow suit. Cantering back about twenty paces, he urged the gray forward, directly toward the cannon. At the final second of the approach, the stallion realized what his rider demanded. Suddenly balking, the gray propped on the fore and pitched Devington headlong into an artillery wagon full of gun powder. With his once pristine uniform coated with the black residue that had cushioned his fall, Devington rose and wiped the soot from his eyes in angry swipes. The stallion looked on, snorting and tossing his head victoriously with the success of his caper.

"I concede you've bested me once, my man, but 'tis a long ride yet to Dettingen." Gathering up his standard, Devington vaulted back onto the horse and squeezed narrowly through a break between the limbers and caissons.

With a cloud of dust in his wake, the Hanoverian was now barely a speck in the distance. "Damn! Damn! Bloody damn! You see what you've done?" Devington swore and urged his horse once more into a furious gallop. The stallion at first hesitated, but as if deciding to enter into the spirit of the game, surged forward in zealous pursuit.

Though yet ruffled by his unexpected unhorsing, Devington realized the Hanoverian had set far too aggressive a pace. The *kapitän's* vanity had compelled him to make a show as they ripped through the British camp, but their overzealous exertions would eventually tell. The captain, although on a stronger horse, was a much heavier rider than the corporal. Devington knew he had to gain lost ground, but there was no need to catch them. Not yet. For now, they would stalk.

On they ran, following the deep, wheel-creviced path toward the Austrian and Hanoverian cantonments just north of the village of Klein Ostheim. Half a mile from the village, the narrow road forked right and left, with the left leading toward steeply wooded hills and the army camp, and the right sloping downward toward the village on the river. The going here was known to be low and level for nearly a league, but the bridge passing over a rivulet feeding into the river Main was completely blocked by a farmer driving a large herd of sheep across the narrow bridge. It was at this juncture that Devington caught his quarry.

Cursing, gesticulating, and flailing his whip, the Hanoverian railed at the farmer, who shrugged in incomprehension and turned his attention back to his bleating charges. Arriving at the site, Devington surveyed the river, estimating the distance across at approximately twenty yards. The captain was not going to leap *this* obstacle! Perceiving his chance, Devington glanced down hesitatingly at the near-vertical embankment. Even if they could navigate the drop, the swirling currents made calculating the depth of the water impossible.

Directing the gray's attention toward the river, he spoke reassuringly. "Though you may not yet have tried it, most horses are quite adequate swimmers, at least for a short distance."

The gray snorted at the moving water but advanced unprompted toward the bank, where he stopped and licked his lips.

"Thirsty are you, old chum? Let us have a drink, then." Leaning far back in his saddle to help the horse to balance himself down the sharp embankment, the corporal coaxed the horse forward, but as they stepped toward the edge of the churning water, the earth gave way beneath, sliding horse and rider into the icy river. Devington made a startled cry, wresting the captain's attention from the farmer.

The snorting stallion floundered and splashed in an attempt to climb back up, but the footing was too loose and the incline too steep. Frustrated, he tossed his head angrily. Finding themselves belly-deep in water, Devington exclaimed, "It's sink or swim now, my boy!"

Sliding from the horse's back, he took hold of the stallion's tail and urged him forward. Paddling dog-style, the pair made their way steadily across the tributary to a rocky place on the other side, where they scrambled onto dry land.

With biped and quadruped both back on solid ground, the gray cast his rider a look of outrage then shook the water from his sopping charcoal coat. Soaked to his own chin, Devington pulled himself heavily back into the saddle, then stole a look over his shoulder to see the captain spurring and thrashing his horse, who refused to advance to the embankment.

Glancing down at the water sloshing from the tops of his boots, the corporal remarked deprecatingly to himself, "No one said we must arrive dry. Let's go, boy!" and broke into an easy canter back to the road, holding his mount well in hand, nursing him along with the knowledge that they had gained at least ten minutes on their opponent in the crossing.

Galloping in rolling strides, they continued onward past neat whitewashed cottages and golden cornfields, Devington glancing periodically over his shoulder for the Hanoverian. As he drew closer to Dettingen, Robert had become acutely aware of enemy activity across the river Main, catching sight through the trees of the French camps on the distant south side. Now, however, breaks in the wood revealed a glimpse of blue uniform on the *north* side!

In growing alarm, the corporal pulled up his horse, taking cover behind a thick row of trees on a small hill skirting the north side of the road. His vantage point gave an unobstructed view of the surrounds—clumps of trees and detached farms that comprised the village, and the river beyond. Clearly visible now were countless blue uniforms crossing the river by bridges comprised of boats linked and anchored to each shore.

The infantry had crossed and had already begun constructing trenches. Clearly the French were preparing to make their long-awaited move.

Pulling one of his pistols from its case, he realized its utter uselessness after having taken a swim in the river. Devington then withdrew his saber smoothly from its sheath and contemplated his next move.

Sensing first the oncoming rider, his horse sidled excitedly beneath him. Devington moved to warn the Hanoverian of the danger, but the French infantryman leveled his musket and opened fire, crying, "*C'est un espion!*"

The shot, fired true, took Ranzau on the left shoulder, knocking him clean of his horse. Responding to the alarm, a half-dozen French infantrymen appeared within seconds to form an irregular semicircle around the hapless Hanoverian, who with unwavering valor, regained his feet and brandished his saber.

"You think alone to fight us, eh?" The Frenchmen laughed. "You are now prisoner of le duc de Grammont, just as your foolish king soon will be."

Outnumbered and without aid of a firearm, Devington had little hope of freeing Ranzau, but with a diversion, perhaps the captain might yet free himself.

Taking a great breath of courage, Devington raised his own saber, and with a savage war cry, he leaped out from his cover directly into the group of infantry, dispersing the startled men in all directions.

Swiftly, he grasped the reins of Ranzau's horse and tossed them to the captain, who threw himself clumsily over the saddle. Desperately clutching his horse's neck, they bolted away amidst a firestorm of French musketry.

Nine

~∽~

REPORT FROM THE FIELD

*I*t was far later than usual when Charlotte snuck back into the house following her morning ride. She had taken Tortoise for his daily gallop, visited with Amoret who had just returned from Lord Godolphin's stud farm, and had looked on as Jeffries began putting the obstreperous young Rascallion through his paces.

Though Rascallion was old enough to be well under saddle, Jeffries had determined that his prior owner had completely soured him for riding of any kind and that the only way to manage him was to go back to the beginning in his training. As Charlotte watched, Jeffries calmly snapped the whip in the air, which set the horse into a frenzied fit of wheeling and plunging.

"A rebellious one, 'e is. In particular, 'e don't care much for a whip," Jeffries remarked. "Been properly soured wi' mismanagement, I'd say, but he be not completely unmanageable if'n he be placed in the proper hands. If'n his energy can be rightly directed, he'll be nigh to lightning on the turf. Easy now, me lad." Jeffries lowered the whip to the ground. Having sufficiently demonstrated his displeasure, the young horse then raised his tail and trotted off in a circle, as if it had all been his idea from the start.

"When will he be ready to ride?" Charlotte asked.

"Sir Garfield wants him to run come spring, but I has me doubts. Now if young Devington were here…"

Charlotte averted her face at the mention of Robert's name. It had been nearly a month since his last letter. Word had spread that the army had finally encountered the French, but nothing was yet confirmed. No news is good news, she kept telling herself to no great comfort.

Turning back to Jeffries, she offered, "I could try him."

"Nay, miss. Though you be as good as any of the lads, this one needs a strong hand to master."

"But if Uncle wants him to run in spring, who is to jockey?"

"The Bart has a mind to put the master Charles up."

"Charles! You doubt that I can handle the horse, yet you propose Charles to ride him!"

"I didn't say that I had a mind to put Charles up; 'tis your uncle what so desperately wants his son on a winner."

"And get poor Charles killed! Jeffries, you must let me ride. Perhaps I can gentle him enough for my cousin to handle."

"I'll think on it, miss, but 'tis well nigh breakfast time up at the house. You'd best move yerself along."

"Is it really so late?" Charlotte frowned at the position of the sun and trotted off anxiously to change her clothes for breakfast, but to her utter dismay, she encountered Beatrix on the staircase.

"Charlotte! Just look at you!" she exclaimed in horror at the mud-stained boots and patched-up boy's clothes. "Just wait until Mother sees you!" Her cousin made no attempt to hide her glee. Charlotte made to brush by, but Beatrix blocked her way. "Mother!" Beatrix cried over her shoulder. "Mother! Come quickly!"

"What is this shrieking, Trixie! Ladies do not shriek," she scolded from the top of the stairs. Then she shrieked, "Good God! Is that Charlotte? Go and change yourself at once! Letty shall burn those clothes, or I'll give her the boot! Imagine any niece of mine looking like a filthy beggar child."

"And the smell, Mother," Beatrix added. "Did you bathe in the dung, Cousin?" Her words were honey-coated venom.

"Now go to your room, and do not let me see you until you have bathed and transformed yourself into a respectable young woman. And I shall talk to your uncle about your riding. You have been given *by far* too much license to the stables. You must begin to comport yourself as a lady, Charlotte. What kind of gentleman would have such a hoydenish creature as you present?" Her aunt continued the harangue without giving Charlotte time to answer. "Now go! Go, child, and make yourself presentable! Go!" She gestured in a shooing fashion, and then with the air of a martyr, Lady Felicia descended to the breakfast room.

Charlotte ran to her room and the comfort of Letty's maternal embrace.

༄

It was nearly an hour later that Charlotte made her appearance in the breakfast room. Her uncle had finished eating and now sat engulfed behind the pages of his *London Daily Gazette*.

Red-eyed, Charlotte took her place across from Beatrix, who smiled smugly at the evidence of Charlotte's misery. Refusing to gratify Beatrix further, Charlotte directed her gaze down at her teacup.

With a flip of the page, Sir Garfield interrupted the silence. "Well, b'God, 'tis finally begun at last!"

"What has begun, Sir Garfield?" Lady Felicia asked.

"The war has begun."

"But I thought we were already at war?" Charles replied.

"We have played at war for two confounded years, but now the French have made it official. There appears to have been a bloodbath at a German village just northeast of Ash... Ash... Bah! Someplace in Franconia."

"Aschaffenberg, Uncle?" Charlotte volunteered, hoping her intuition was wrong.

"Indeed. That is the place."

"Wh–what has occurred?" she asked barely above a whisper.

"Appears the French, who outnumbered our men by some twenty thousand, crossed the river to the north and south, cutting off supply lines and with the intent of capturing our king. Upon word of this, His Majesty commanded a march for Hanua to meet up with Hessian reinforcements, but as they gained this village of Dettingen, they met with a French ambuscade."

Charlotte blanched, unable to speak.

Charles prompted, "What happened?"

"It says here that our brave king himself charged to the fore where his English Horse bore the brunt of the cannonade. He is recorded as brandishing his sword and crying, 'Now my brave boys! Now for the honor of England! Advance boldly, fire, and the French will soon run!'

"The Foot rallied. The Horse on the left flank charged with the trumpeter playing 'Britons Strike Home.' They became virtually surrounded by the Frenchies and should have been cut to pieces but for the arrival of the Austrian artillery."

Her face now spectral, Charlotte gasped.

"How did it end, Father?" Charles pressed excitedly.

"The French were repulsed across the river, forced to swim like ducks!"

"So we won!" Charles exclaimed, nearly jumping from his seat.

"Suffice to say, we had a lower body count, my boy," Sir Garfield responded then proceeded to read the statistics of dead and wounded.

With a cry, Charlotte pushed from the table, dropping her teacup, which shattered on the floor, and fled the room.

"What's amiss with the girl?" Sir Garfield asked vaguely.

"She's no doubt overwrought for news of Robert," Charles remarked sympathetically. "You remember he joined the Horse Guard, Father."

"Left me high and dry for the Horse Guard, eh? Serves him right if he's blown to bits. Now where's my copy of *Cheny's Racing Calendar*?"

❧

Ten days later, another letter came to Charlotte, again via Jeffries. She received it with trembling hands and stared blindly at the handwriting. Was it truly Robert's hand? Was he alive?

She was afraid to break the seal for fear of what news it might contain. With her heart hammering erratically, she sought solace and privacy in a corner of Amoret's stall, where she collapsed on a pile of clean straw. Sensing Charlotte's disquiet, Amoret turned her attention from her hay and ambled over, nosing the letter.

"It's from Robert," Charlotte said and stroked the mare's muzzle. Amoret's warm, grass-scented breath gently fanned her cheek. "But what if he wrote it before the battle? What if these are his last words to me? But there's only one way to know, isn't there?"

Amoret snorted agreement and nudged Charlotte's hand. Offering up a prayer, Charlotte thumbed open the wax seal.

July 10, 1743

My Dearest Charlotte,

I write you from our cantonment in Bergen, where we await our orders following our routing of the French at the village of Dettingen. I further pray my news will reach you prior to the official account of our historic battle, as I would not worry your heart to save my very soul.

The enemy, in far superior numbers to ours, was encamped in close proximity, only a few miles downriver. By a sheer fluke (a story I will recount to you later) I discovered their preparations for a preemptive strike. Returning to our camp with the utmost dispatch, I made my report, and His Majesty commanded an immediate withdrawal to Flanders, where Hessian reinforcements and supplies awaited us.

We struck camp stealthily before light and began our march without drumbeat, but upon approaching the village of Dettingen, we were met with an ambuscade of French cannons, which we were unprepared to counter. Our own artillery was several miles to the rear, from whence His Majesty had most anticipated the attack.

We were drawn out between the wood and the river and utterly vulnerable. The Horse was completely ensnared on either flank. The French artillery was stationed across the river on our left, and their Horse and light infantry were hidden in the wooded hills upon our right. Both commenced a vast outpour of fire upon us. We were caught in the very thick of it.

Our horses screamed. Men panicked. Sheer mayhem arose amongst our green recruits. Major Bainbridge, riding the magnificent gray stallion of whom I previously wrote, was carried into the direct line of fire. The horse was wounded and the major struck down. Captain Drake assumed command but struggled in vain to gain a fraction of control and some manner of order from the chaos.

His Majesty rushed to the fore upon report of cannon, entering valiantly and unreservedly into the midst of the fray, but his steed, like as many others, responded frantically to the fire, unseating His Majesty and charging off to the wood. Captain Drake sprang into action to shield the King into the protection of a nearby oak grove. Taking stock of our predicament, the King ordered our artillery to advance from the rear and commanded our infantry to a counterfire.

Our green recruits, however, having done naught more than march and camp for months, fired aimlessly, randomly, and precipitately. With precious few hits to their ranks, the French advanced briskly and with a tenacious fire, further weakening us.

The young Duke of Cumberland was next to arrive, courageously charging up from our rear infantry lines and taking command of the right flank. Cool, composed, and with remarkable presence of mind, he ordered the Foot to advance and fire. His propinquity alone rallied the men to respond with feverish fury. Even after taking a musket shot through the leg, Cumberland continued stoically in command, while our Horse and remaining infantry steadily closed ranks.

We now rallied against the French, who had broken our first line and penetrated the Scottish Fusiliers, but by this time several of our cannons were in play and wreaking havoc on them. Bit by bit, we drove them back before they ever reached our second line.

We had barely begun to regain ground when the fierce besiege of French cavalry began in earnest with a second wave. The famed Mousquetaires Gris charged us full force with two hundred horse! With slashing saber and smoking carbine, we fought like devils. We were now confronted with the enemy on all sides.

Forgetting nearly all I had learned, I cut and slashed blindly until charged by a French officer. Our horses screamed and collided. Jack, brave and true to the last, took a musket ball to the chest. Struck from under me, he crashed to the ground, breaking my leg and pinning me beneath him. I struggled in vain to free myself. I was defenseless.

My antagonist, now recovered from his own fall, approached with his saber to strike the deathblow. I knew my end had come, Charlotte, but of a sudden, he lurched to the ground, cleanly struck by musket fire. The hand of Captain Drake had delivered me. Clearly, our fates were sealed from that moment.

The battle raged interminably until our valiant English infantry rallied again and advanced for the final attack, driving back the remnants of French Horse and forcing the now battered and all but broken enemy to a hasty retreat across the river. Notwithstanding the sudden and massive withdrawal, their makeshift bridges collapsed, drowning no small number. The remainder swam like ducks to the opposite shore!

Of the two hundred French cavalry, fewer than fifty survived. We took a great number of their officers and men prisoner and captured nine cannons, as well as several of their colors and standards. Their losses exceed five thousand and ours about two thousand men.

My own Sixth Troop, by the hand of Providence, sustained only minimal damage, with but three men and four horses, and six wounded, including myself. Pray do not be worried for me, Charlotte. 'Twas only a break of the thigh bone and already healing well under Dr. Pringle's care—a rather crotchety Scotsman and Lord Stair's personal physician. He judges I shall be mounted again in no time. Indeed, I hope to ride through the gates of Whitehall on the back of the gray stallion.

As for him, he had taken a ball to the flank and lost the tip of an ear. I can only believe 'twas Bainbridge's vanity that caused his fall, and no fault of the horse. Winthrop conceded to retrieve the ball, if only to reward my service, and I shall take the horse in hand for the duration of my recovery.

As for the man to whom I owe my life, Captain Drake has deservedly received a field promotion for his multifarious acts of valor, and I have also been conferred a captaincy. Though I parted England a boy in soldier's clothing, I return a man who will control his own destiny, and that destiny shall be with you, if you would still have me, my dearest. I pray that I shall soon return to you. Until then, I most earnestly pledge my honor and my heart.

Your Most Devoted,

R. D.

❧

George II, the last British monarch to lead his own army, marched proudly through the gates of London with much parade and fanfare. The King's Horse Guard arrived weary and worn after weeks of hard riding and another accursed Channel crossing. They had reached their destination only a week before the slated victory celebrations. The city of London rejoiced to receive her heroes.

The inauguration of the month-long fete was the King's grand birthday parade, held at Whitehall Parade Grounds. After reviewing his Household troops, he presented the King's regiment of Horse with their new insignia, a golden oak leaf to commemorate their valor. The festivities concluded at Vauxhall Pleasure Gardens with fireworks and a symphonic performance of Handel's "Te Deum" composed in honor of the victory.

It was mid-December before the troops were at leisure and settled into winter quarters and finally free to pursue their own pleasure. For the captain, the novelty of London and nightly carousing had quickly waned. He'd been away from home for too long.

His heart ached for his Charlotte.

Ten

✑

BROTHERS-IN-ARMS

DECEMBER 1743

*R*ising well before daybreak, Captain Devington prepared to
depart his rooms in the crowded inn serving as garrison
for his company. Quietly fumbling in the dark, he bundled his
scant belongings into his pack and endeavored not to disturb his
snoring comrades.

Nearby, Major Drake stirred, bleary-eyed and groggy after
another night's carousing. "We're on furlough, you bloody sod!
What are you doing up before the cock has even crowed?" he
growled at Devington.

"I'm departing for Yorkshire, Philip. I've some unfinished business to attend."

"What the bloody hell is so damned pressing in Yorkshire that
can't wait until a respectable hour?"

"I told you, it's business. *Personal* business."

Intrigued by the evasive reply, Philip raised up on one elbow.
"Oh? I surmise 'tis a woman, then. Must be a fine piece of arse if
you're dragging your own all the bloody way to Yorkshire."

"Keep a civil tongue in your head." The warning was made with
a telling glower.

Philip smirked. "Indeed? True love, then. Didn't know you were a romantic, Devington. Didn't know you were a Yorkshireman either, come to think of it. Small wonder you joined the Horse Guard," he drawled. "From whence do you hail in the land of frightened sheep?"

"The South, if it's anything to you. Raised near Doncaster, and for your elucidation, the horses in the region outnumber the sheep."

"Indeed? Doncaster, you say? I hear of tolerable good horseflesh in Doncaster. I have on occasion witnessed a respectable Doncaster runner at Newmarket."

"Occasionally, you say! We run some of the primest flesh in England on Cantley Common!"

"So you fancy? You've not witnessed a race 'til you seen them run the Rowley Mile. Newmarket's where the real action is. My family has kept a stable for decades at Cheveley, outside Newmarket, and all prime Derbyshire stock."

"I quite assure you of the quality of South Yorkshire horseflesh, Drake. I find you surprisingly ignorant for a turf-follower, my friend. Who can be unacquainted with the famed Flying Childers? The stallion has one of the greatest names in the country, with an undefeated running career. Indeed, he won over half his races by default, as none dared challenge him."

"I am well acquainted with the Duke of Devonshire's celebrated stallion. He's a top producer of champions, and he stands *in Derbyshire*."

"You are once again misinformed. Flying Childers, the pride of the Duke of Devonshire, who once refused the horse's weight in gold, was born and bred by Colonel Childers *in Doncaster*."

"I shan't dispute the quality of this *one stallion* from the region," Drake grudgingly conceded.

"I contest that he was one of a number of exceptional South Yorkshire blood horses. Indeed, Colonel Childers knew a good thing when he saw it. He bred his dam, Betty Leedes, a second time to the Darley Arabian and produced a full brother, Bartlett's Childers, who still stands at Masham *in Yorkshire*. This blood-cross has produced many good runners: Smale's Childers and Lord Portmore's Grey Childers both come to mind, but the finest of the Darley grandsons to date, is probably Squirt. His was a most lucrative career. He won the two hundred guineas in '37 and again in '39 at Newmarket, and then followed with wins at Epsom, Stamford, Winchester, and Salisbury."

"I know well the reputation of Squirt, but I argue this fine horse also stands *at Derbyshire*. And what of Francis Godolphin's famed stallion? He stands in *Derbyshire*, and none dare contest the quality of his get. Thus far, they are without match. His son Lath won the thousand guineas in '37, and defeated your Squirt the following year."

"It might surprise you to learn that Lath was also indisputably *bred in Yorkshire*," Robert contested with no small pride. "I stand by my claim that our Yorkshire studs produce the finest horses in the country."

"I am duly impressed with your knowledge, Devington," Drake confessed, "but how do you come by such an intimate knowledge of blood horses?"

"I was probably mounted before I was out of leading strings. I spent my formative years riding anything with four legs. Worked as stable groom, under groom, racing groom, and later apprenticed in the North as a stud groom. Living no great distance from Doncaster, I had ample opportunity to follow my passion. Addiction, it is, the racing, sheer addiction," Devington murmured wistfully.

"So you fancy the races, Devington? Surprising. You've never struck me as a gambling man."

"Me, *gamble* on the horses? God forbid, man! Learned my lessons early on at the expense of others who were so imprudent. 'Tis a dirty business, that. I've witnessed countless men fall into utter ruination following a four-mile heat. No. My addiction is riding, chasing the wind, you know. There's nothing like it. No future in it, though.

"After my father passed, I had hoped to fill his shoes at Heathstead Hall but… circumstances as they were…" He paused as if hesitant to continue on that track. "Suffice to say, it came upon me to make my own way, and with no name to recommend me and no connections, my options were few."

"So you packed your belongings and Ol' Jack and made your way to Woolwich," Philip finished for him.

"Something like that, though the initial seed was planted in my head by a cocky young officer of the Horse who threw me a coin purse at the Litchfield races!" Devington grinned.

"Litchfield is where I procured Hawke. Damme, was that you, Devington?"

"One and the same, though I hardly caught more than a glimpse of you at the time. Later, at Woolwich, I didn't make the connection until seeing Hawke. I remembered the horse well. It was the race that I defeated that fiend Uxeter. How exactly did you come by Hawke, anyway?"

"That fiend Uxeter, as you so aptly describe him, is my half brother."

"I didn't know. No offense intended."

Drake laughed outright. "Oh, don't fear any insult on my account. He's an irrefutably arrogant sod and a blight on my existence. There's no love lost between siblings in my family. But to answer your question and to recount the rest of the story, when the blackguard lost the race, he ordered the groom to shoot the horse. So, given your history, one might say my presence at the Lichfield races proved serendipitous to both man and beast."

"It certainly was for me. I daresay I never should have entertained any notion of the Horse Guard otherwise, but here I am now, a lowly servant of the Crown. I never should have believed I'd make the cut that day. You didn't make it easy, by any means."

The major grinned, remembering their first meeting at Horse Guard training grounds. "And now you are returned a captain and a hero, by all accounts. Better a captain in the Horse than a major in the infantry, I say."

"A hero? I question that. I believe 'twas more the hand of Providence, or more accurately, the hand of Major Drake that preserved me at Dettingen."

"You have no cause for shame. You kept your head about you under fire and displayed remarkable valor for one so green. We are in a like position, you know, to have chosen a military career. As a second son, I am merely *spare to the heir*, as the adage goes. Edmund holds the birthright and all that goes with it. Miserable, ungrateful wretch. He'll inherit all, though not much more than a London townhouse and a manor rebuilt from a crumbling Norman keep. All I have to recommend myself to the world is an old family name. Even that's worth precious nothing without the title. Sorry, ole chap, forgot whom I was addressing," Philip added sheepishly.

"No offense taken. I am not ashamed of common birth; at least it was on the right side of the blanket, more than a great many sons of noblemen can claim."

"You have a point there," Philip replied dryly. "But although legitimate, I am the family scapegrace, the proverbial black sheep who has spent the past eight years following an ignominious expulsion from Harrow, doing my wretched best to live *down* to my family's expectations."

"But why?"

"My father, the Earl of Hastings, is a very exacting man," he said bitterly. "After Harrow, he cut me off and effectively washed his hands of me. I lived by little more than my wits for five years until attaining my majority and the meager trust left by my mother. After paying my debts, I purchased a commission. My only remaining alternative was the clergy. Can you picture me a clergyman, Devington?"

"You would have been a veritable disgrace to the cloth."

"Quite so," Philip agreed without shame.

"But if you truly desired to play the part of scapegrace, you have failed miserably, *Major*."

"Oh, I wouldn't quite say that; my advancement has not been wholly honorable."

"What do you mean?"

"I entered the Horse as a cornet but gained my captaincy by the hand of Lady Luck."

"Gaming?"

"I had a good night at the Hazard table, whilst Captain Simpson did not," he remarked dismissively. "But I begin to tire of the soldier's life, Devington. The past two campaigns have hardly proven the adventure I envisaged. 'Tis a hard life and hardly profitable. Now on furlough, I am resolved to scour the London ballrooms to find an heiress and be done with it."

"*You*, scour the ballrooms?" Robert scoffed. "You will surely be in good company. London is crawling with half-pay officers seeking a rich wife. Why not accompany me to the country instead? With the coming holidays, the capital will likely be devoid of heiresses anyway."

"I fail to perceive any advantage in leaving London."

"Doncaster may actually hold a prospect or two for you. Colonel Childers has three daughters. No doubt a bevy of marriageable ladies of their acquaintance will congregate at Cantley Hall or the surrounding estates for the Christmas season. Though most of 'em can't tell mane from tail, there will no doubt be heiresses among them."

Robert gestured grandly to their cramped and dingy quarters. "Care to leave all this grandeur and rusticate until we're called back, ole chum? Can't say I couldn't bear the company."

"'Twill be devilish going with only a for'night's furlough. Pushing hard, it's what, three days? I assume you're riding?"

"My carriage is in repair," Robert said ruefully.

"It'll be damnably cold riding, too. You'd best elaborate much more on the heiresses, ole boy."

"At this very moment stands a well-dowered and virtuous heiress, bounteous of charm, pining away for a handsome rogue to sweep her off her feet."

"Virtuous? That might be laying it a bit thick."

Recognizing his exercise in futility, Robert snapped smartly to attention. "Right then, I shall see you in a for'night."

Philip hesitated. "Mayhap I've enough of wine, women, and song... well, mayhap just the song, but what possible diversion can there be in bloody Yorkshire?"

"Mayhap a bit of racing. Weather permitting, they'll surely have a few training runs in preparation for the spring season."

Philip considered this for a moment and groaned as he pulled himself heavily from bed. "Allow me an hour, and I'll be in the saddle."

Surprisingly true to his word, within the hour he was shaved, packed, and swaggering into the stable yard, calling for his mount as the hostler, a grizzled Scotsman of indeterminate age, led out Devington's snorting, jigging, battle-scarred stallion.

"Son of a beast tried to bite me when I turned me back to the billets! No warning. Just barred his ugly teeth fur the attack! Daemon steed, that 'un!" Nostrils flaring and ears pinned, the gray repeated the offense.

"He wants another go at it. Be a sport, ole man!" Robert chortled. The indignant Scotsman threw the reins in his face, tromping off to collect the major's horse.

"I wonder, was it reward or punishment Winthrop had in mind in allowing you to keep that brute?" Drake innocently inquired.

"He eats only Scotsmen," Robert quipped. "He's actually as fine a horse as I've ever known, truth be told. Were he taller and less battle-scarred, I've no doubt he would have been appropriated for one of the colonels, or perhaps for Cumberland himself. They say he has an eye for horseflesh."

"He does, indeed, but I daresay the beast's reputation would have put him off."

"This horse has more heart than any I've ever known. I'd back him against anyone."

"Thought you weren't a betting man, Devington. Be warned that I might take up your gauntlet when we have the opportunity. Speaking of which, have you at least thought of a decent name for the animal? 'Captain Devington on Nameless Nag' doesn't have much of a ring to it." Drake smirked.

"I begin to think Mars, the god of war, might suit," Robert replied with a devious grin.

"The hostler would hardly disagree."

The sun was cresting the eastern horizon when the two young officers mounted up and set out on the North Road. Travelling for some time in companionable silence, each was lost in his own thoughts. Philip contemplated racing and rich, voluptuous heiresses.

Robert, conversely, brooded on his next course of action. He *would* offer for Charlotte again. He was resolute, but Sir Garfield was a cunning and ruthless adversary. His mind wrestled with the conundrum of how to win the man over. His expression revealed more of his thoughts than he intended.

Philip interrupted his cogitations. "You appear as if laboring with a veritable poser."

Devington didn't answer.

"At the risk of intruding further into your private world, I surmise that your *unfinished business* concerns a lady and your former employer. Were I not so well acquainted with your noble character, I'd be lief to suspect a dismissal following your seduction of the squire's daughter."

His companion answered the off-hand remark with a glower. "You pry into matters that don't concern you."

"Aha!" Drake laughed, unabashed. "I strike dangerously near the mark! Since you are so reticent to share your history, you compel me to follow the leadings of my imagination... and I own a very lively imagination."

"Lively or lurid?"

"Guilty as charged! Now, would you care to share your story, or shall I continue my summation based wholly on my deductions?"

"I fail to understand your interest."

"Rest assured, my interest is merely a passing fancy, but as you talked me into this infernal ride and have been less than a stimulating conversationalist for the last three hours, I am compelled to entertain myself."

Robert colored but ignored the remark.

Philip, purely for diversion, continued his narrative. "Very well, Devington, I shall piece together the facts of this tale you are so loathe to disclose. Pray feel free to interject as you see fit.

"You have a passion and obvious talent with horses but were passed over for the very position you had been groomed for and were, in essence, given the boot. But rather than taking the easy route and moving on to the Doncaster racing studs, you elected to leave all behind to join the Horse Guard. To what end?

"Now returned from the campaign, you defy reason by leaving the comfort and pleasures of London to ride all the way to Yorkshire in the dead of winter. No rational man would do such a thing.

"Evidence plainly indicates you are painfully and wretchedly enamored with some young woman. I surmise, nay *fear*," he amended, "that you intend to sacrifice your blessed bachelorhood at the matrimonial altar."

"Am I so damnably transparent?"

"Pitifully so."

"Well, you haven't all of it right, not by a long shot!" Robert said.

"No? Would you care to enlighten me?"

Having bared his soul to no one, Robert was weary of keeping his own counsel. Drake had proven a loyal friend and had even saved his life. He was also a man with broader experience and greater worldliness.

"It's a long story, Drake."

His companion shrugged. "It's a long ride, Devington."

Overcoming his reticence, Robert began his extended history.

"I was raised on the property of Heathstead Hall in Wortley, an estate owned by Sir Garfield Wallace, the man to whom my father owed his living. His son, Charles, and I grew up together, nearly as brothers. We spent many years of our boyhood riding, hunting the wood, fishing, cavorting, and even shared, or more aptly *tortured*, a tutor, the pious and pinch-faced Mr. Smythe.

"Sir Garfield's disposition toward me markedly changed, however, after the arrival of his orphaned niece, Charlotte. With his fortune, vast country estate, and children of comparable age, her situation should have been ideal, but this proved far from the case. Although her cousin Charles is an amiable chap, Beatrix is of another mold altogether. Vain, jealous, selfish, and spiteful, she resented Charlotte's arrival from the very beginning, making it clear she regarded her orphaned cousin as an interloper and a charity case."

"I have known many such women as you describe," Drake said. "I would argue this Beatrix's manner is hardly unexceptional in the circumstance. Your vision may be somewhat clouded, Devington."

"That may be, but you must perceive what an abominable position this poor girl was placed in."

"Quite so, that of a completely dependent poor relation, regarded little better than a servant. 'Tis a common enough plight," Drake remarked callously.

"You have no idea what she suffered living as a mere shadow under her uncle's roof."

"A pusillanimous miss. I marvel at your taste in women. Between the two, I profess a predilection for the vain and selfish cousin. Assuredly more spirited, at any rate."

"Charlotte lacking spirit? Then you would be duped as the rest of them. Only by the necessity of her situation has she cultivated meekness, but I know the real girl. I peered into her soul the first day I espied this waif-of-a-thing riding hell-for-leather across the heath."

"Ah! So finally, the tale piques my interest. Pray continue, Devington."

"Nearly five years ago, I broke up a brawl between dung-encrusted stable lads, and later while out for a training gallop on a misty morning, I unexpectedly encountered one of the same lads virtually flying across the heath. My first thought was to discover the identity of the one who would surely become my adversary on the track, and I was astonished to discover that *he* was a *she*!"

Robert then explained how Charles had informed him of his orphaned cousin's arrival, and how he began to look for Charlotte on her morning rides. "Whenever the vixen sensed my presence, she would turn tail and run, spurring me all the more to pursue. Mayhap that's what drew me to the girl, but I was bloody well intrigued."

"Chasing a little hoyden about the countryside a-horseback sounds too exerting for my blood," Drake scoffed. "Were I in your shoes, I should have sought out a plump and sassy dairymaid, most of whom, by contrast, expend their energies in a much more gratifying manner."

Robert ignored the sardonic remark. "The reward for me was well worth the effort. Unfortunately, Beatrix discovered our assignations and told her father. When he learned of my interest, he sent me to apprentice as a stud groom with John Bartlett in North Yorkshire. I remained there two years; hence, my intimate knowledge of the Northern horseflesh," he added in an aside.

"What of you and Charlotte?" Drake prompted.

"We were only fifteen and eighteen when I left, but we made plans to one day marry. When my father passed, I had expectation as well as hope, but Sir Garfield never gave me the first consideration in either case.

"I sold my father's meager belongings, as well as our livestock, save Ol' Jack. I had less than fifty pounds to my name. Of course my resentment of Sir Garfield only grew with the knowledge that this paltry sum was all my father had to show for a business partnership that garnered another man a fortune and a veritable empire."

"An empire? What do you mean, Devington? I thought we spoke of a simple country squire."

"On the contrary. Although of humble beginnings—a tavern keep, to be precise—Sir Garfield Wallace is an extremely wealthy man."

"Indeed? From a tavern to a fortune? I should like to know how this came about."

"'Twas in truth my father's notion. He was a private coachman for a genteel family in Doncaster and remarked one day over a shared tankard at Wallace's Blue Boar Tavern that it might be a profitable enterprise to start a public coaching service between Doncaster, Sheffield, and Leeds."

"One must credit his foresight," Drake remarked.

"Quite so, but Conrad Devington was never overly hindered with ambition. Garfield Wallace, however, was. Believing his establishment ideal to stage such a commercial venture, he and my father became partners of a sort."

"So I presume that this Wallace fellow put up the capital?"

"Precisely so. They began with a single coach-and-four. My father, with his keen eye for horseflesh, kept the business well supplied with strong, sound horses. In the first year, they were profitable and able to purchase additional coaches. My father then suggested breeding their own carriage stock to produce superior horses that could endure longer trips under heavier loads. Wallace compounded their initial success by building more inns and expanding the routes to include London and Edinburgh."

"It sounds like an extremely lucrative venture."

"It was; but my father had a partiality for gin. My mother, whom he loved dearly, kept him in line, but I was still in leading strings when she contracted smallpox. He never recovered from the loss and took heavily to the bottle from that time. He was never the same man."

"But what of the partnership? Did it dissolve?"

"Not precisely, but Wallace took advantage of my father's weakness, buying him out for a pittance during one of Conrad's drunken binges. Wallace then kept him on as stable master."

"Grasping bastard, eh?"

"You have no idea, Drake. Having tasted of riches, Wallace hungered for more, for what was yet out of reach. He had wealth but no social status, so he sold out and invested the bulk of his worth with the Society of Merchant Venturers."

"Invested with the slavers, eh?" Drake commented with mild distaste. "Barbaric business that, but I durst not assume the moral high ground. My father might own shares in a dozen such enterprises, for all my knowledge. I gather the investment was fruitful?"

"Immensely so. His profits on the Bristol slaving ships provided a yield sufficient to buy an estate and enter the ranks of the landed gentry. He then wooed the daughter and only child of a baronet and somehow finagled to come by the title upon his father-in-law's passing."

"Patents of nobility are a rare commodity *these* days, unlike centuries hence, when the Crown sold peerages to fill their private coffers. My own family's title traces back to James I, who supplemented his personal fortune thus."

"In Sir Garfield's case, he may have gained a title but has yet to achieve the heights of grandeur to which he aspires. He's a man who will use any means at his disposal to get what he wants."

"I am intimately acquainted with the archetype. I confess my own father comes immediately to mind," Drake remarked deprecatingly. "Although an interesting rags-to-riches tale, I still fail to see how this all relates to you, Devington."

"I warned you 'twas a long story, and beg your forbearance. Now where was I?"

"The shrewd, ruthless baronet made his fortune but yet reaches higher," Drake prompted.

"Indeed. Desiring to mix with the aristocracy, Sir Garfield focused his attention on the turf. He converted the stables, which once bred the country's finest carriage horses, into a racing stud, but my father had no experience of running bloods, so Sir Garfield was obliged to seek a competent man for the purpose. He found such a one in John Jeffries."

"The man who eventually took your father's stead."

"I don't begrudge Jeffries. He has been friend and mentor to me and is the devil of a horseman. I resent only Sir Garfield's duplicity, which led my father to drink himself into an early grave."

"This was when you were in North Yorkshire?"

"Indeed, my story now comes full circle. Upon my return, Sir Garfield promoted Jeffries to stable master. Although I had little after my father's death, Charlotte's father had left her a small dowry. Our monies combined should have sufficed to make us a very modest start, but Sir Garfield refused to consider my suit, and as you aptly surmised, sent me packing."

"You were no doubt in a state of mind to commit some act of folly."

"We discussed elopement."

"Mayhap not the wisest course of action, when one has not even a pot to piss in."

"Spoken in the words of a true sage, Drake."

"So we come back to the beginning. In an impetuously quixotic notion, you took your destiny into your own hands and left the girl behind to seek your fortune in the Horse Guard. And now you intend to claim your bride. What is your strategy?"

"'Tis what plagues me, Drake, as I yet have none."

Eleven

❧

A HERO'S WELCOME

YORKSHIRE, DECEMBER 1743

*A*fter three days with nary a break from the saddle, the officers'
suffering bodies ached for respite. Their very bones jarred
with each plodding step of their utterly spent mounts, but Doncaster
remained another half-day's ride. Gaining Sheffield—damp, cold,
and ravenous—the travel-weary pair drew up at the first public
house they encountered: the Dark Horse Tavern.

They entered the ramshackle stable yard and slithered wearily
from their lathered and drooping mounts. After settling their horses,
the pair dragged themselves to the tavern. The taproom reeked of
stale ale, and the smoky tallow provided meager illumination in the
cluttered, low-ceilinged space. Hungry beyond discrimination, the
pair collapsed at a corner table, wincing at the hard bench that was
so unforgiving to their saddle-sore posteriors.

Pausing little for conversation, they greedily devoured a meal of
bread, cheese, and mutton stew, chasing it all down with several
tankards of stout.

Now sated, Captain Devington leaned back from the table,
suppressed a yawn, and sleepily took in his surroundings. Major Drake,
hands clasped behind his head, directed his calculating gaze toward an

even dingier back room, taking in a small band of foot soldiers playing at cards. Devington noted his comrade's less-than-latent interest.

"Infantry," Drake humphed, scrutinizing the company more closely. "Devington," he asked, "do my eyes deceive me, or might it be our old chum Prescott?"

"Prescott, you say?" Devington grimaced. "I had hoped never again to cross paths with that blighter."

"Are you so poor spirited as that?" The Major grinned wickedly.

Robert refused the bait. He replied with another yawn, "I don't guess to know what you're about, old man, but I'm nigh fagged to death."

"It's bad form to go to the races with empty pockets," Drake chided.

"My pockets, although lean, are not yet empty. However, I know of no surer way to hasten that inevitability than to gamble what I have following little sleep and much stout. You're on your own, old chap; I shan't join you in your sport this night." Somewhat unsteadily, he rose to his feet.

"I find to the contrary that the prospect of sport has given me a second wind." Philip cracked his knuckles.

"On the morrow, then." Robert sighed, staggering to the staircase and up to their room.

"Oh, I daresay I shan't be detained overlong." Philip laughed and swaggered toward the back room.

It was mid-morning and Christmas Eve Day before the deeply slumbering men finally roused.

The first to wake, Robert blinked in an effort to orient himself. "Sheffield," he mumbled, remembering where he was. His critical gaze took in their less-than-pristine accommodations. "We must have been completely fagged," he remarked disparagingly and rose stiffly from the hard bed.

"What are you muttering?" Philip muttered. "And don't I recall already having this conversation about rising before the cock? Damme if one of us remembered it."

"Philip, it must be near noon. We'd best be about our business."

"*Your* business awaits, Devington, not mine. I took care of *mine* last night. While you counted your Yorkshire sheep, I perchance fleeced mine." He chuckled. "Fleeced them but good, I might say. As I stated earlier, 'tis poor form to attend a race without a farthing. Makes a very bad impression."

"Glad Lady Luck was on your side, Philip. Just remember she's fickle. You can only hope she returns to you at the track."

"No fear, man. I've never wanted for a lady. She'll return. She may even bring her twin, Lady of Fortune. I've always fancied a threesome." He chuckled again.

"Reprobate."

"The boot fits just fine," he quipped, customarily getting the last word.

"I do have important business to attend this morning, a long overdue call, so to speak. Would you be offended should I not ask you to accompany me? When I return, we can continue on to Doncaster."

"Don't fear for me, ole chum. I shall contrive to entertain myself. Perhaps our friend Prescott remains?" The devilish grin reappeared.

"Are you determined to cross swords with him again? He has company this time," Devington warned.

"You need not fret for my safety. He's proven himself no better swordsman on foot than on horse."

"So you say? And a poor loser as well, by the sound of it," Robert replied with mixed exasperation and relief. Turning to his ablutions, he approached the cracked and tarnished mirror at the dressing table, noting his disheveled appearance with a decided grimace. Discovering no water with which to wash or shave, he rang for the chambermaid.

Several rings and nearly twenty minutes later, the call was answered by the same voluptuous bar-cum-chambermaid who had tended the taproom the prior evening. Sizing them both up and down, she inquired in seductive tones, "And 'ow may I serve you 'ansome gents?" Placing a special emphasis on *serve*, Maggie directed Philip a wicked look, leaving no question as to her meaning.

While Philip quirked a brow in her direction, Robert ignored the exchange, answering, "Hot water, miss. I should very much like some hot water in which to wash and shave." He would have preferred a bath but knew such a request would be ludicrous in their present abode.

"Oh, I'll gladly wash and shave ya, Cap'n." The girl winked knowingly at Philip.

"Cheeky wench," Philip returned with a wicked gleam.

Robert retorted in his growing impatience, "No need to put yourself out, miss."

"Oh, I wouldn't say that," Philip drawled. "Maggie here can *put herself out* as she well pleases."

"I've pressing business and should like to be on my way. I've no further time to waste," Robert retorted and tromped out.

Ignoring Devington's outburst and fitful departure, Maggie cast her siren's gaze on Philip. With her hips sashaying, she slowly approached until they stood breast to chest, thigh to thigh. Placing both hands on Philip's shoulders, she gently but firmly pushed him back into a nearby chair and shamelessly rucked her skirts to straddle his thighs. Pressing her half-exposed breasts into his face, she breathed wantonly into his ear, "Now 'ow did you want *your* shave, Cap'n?"

c✐୨

Robert arrived agitated at Heathstead Hall. The morning had not begun well, and he still had no plan. Uncertain of his reception in the best of circumstances, he was chagrinned to appear the worse for wear. Yet unshaven and unkempt, he was in no state to call on Charlotte, let alone petition Sir Garfield.

Thankfully it was two o'clock, the traditional teatime at Heathstead Hall. He was unlikely to be seen by anyone at this time of day, outside of a groom or possibly Charles, his friend from boyhood, whose discretion he could trust. With relative confidence he could escape detection, he cautiously circled the house, sneaking to the backside of the stables where he hoped to find a champion for his cause in his old friend, Jeffries. But as fortune—or he thought more aptly, *misfortune*—would have it, he was startled by a familiar voice crooning in hypnotic tones to her mare.

"And how goes it today, my lovely? I will have you know I risked a capital offense on your behalf by absconding with sugar cubes from the teacart. I fear Beatrix will be exceedingly vexed to have no sugar for her tea today." Charlotte giggled at her mischief while Amoret eagerly devoured the contraband.

Drawn to her voice, Robert slunk into the adjacent stall. Even awareness of his scruff appearance could not keep him from her. "Charlotte," he whispered.

Startled, she spun around, spying no one. "Who's there?" she cried.

"It's me, Robert," answered a low voice. "Is anyone else about?"

"Robert!" she exclaimed breathlessly, her eyes searching the stable. "Robert! Where are you?"

"I'm in the next box. Is anyone else about?" he asked cautiously.

"Why, no. B-but why are you hiding in the stables? You have not deserted!"

"No, Charlotte." He spoke in a louder whisper. "'Tis nothing like that; I simply need to speak privily with you."

"We are alone at present," she reassured him. "I have dismissed the groom. There is none here but me, but I haven't long before I am missed for tea. Pray show yourself. I *must* see you!"

He rose cautiously. "If we don't have much time, I must come directly to my purpose. I have need of your assistance, Char—"

Stupefied, he gained his first vision of Charlotte in nearly two years. He gaped at the young woman standing before him.

Gone were the girlish braids and boy's breeches to which he was accustomed. Instead, there stood a vision before him. Her golden brown hair was elegantly coiffed under a frilled bonnet, and her cousin's ill-fitting garb had been exchanged for the snugly fit gown that revealed the transformation of his reedy little waif into a curvaceous young woman.

As incredulous as Robert was at Charlotte's metamorphosis, she was equally thunderstruck at her first sight of this scruffily handsome captain. She stared back at him with luminous eyes.

"Robert." She breathed his name, breaking the silence that held them. He, however, still gaped, to her increasing discomfiture. "You needn't look so surprised." She blushed furiously. "It was bound to happen, sooner or later—becoming a lady, that is. I had no choice," she protested. "Aunt Felicia and Beatrix…," she rambled on breathily.

Robert took her face in his hands, and her babbling abruptly ceased.

His kiss, swift and fierce, was unexpected and unnerving. His lips, simultaneously hard and soft, moved over hers and created ineffable sensations. Initially shocked to her core, Charlotte's response had been unschooled, but ardent. With growing understanding, she parted her lips and entwined her arms tightly about his neck.

Robert responded by deepening their kiss, and with this first real taste of her, experienced a quickening of desire. Charlotte sighed and leaned intimately closer, her soft curves now hugging his aroused body. Robert's mind ran rampant; he was becoming more lost to rational thought with every stroke of their tongues. They were alone and perilously near a large pile of clean straw... He shook the fog rapidly filling his brain and abruptly broke the embrace.

Weak-kneed, breathless, and bewildered, Charlotte regarded him with wounded, wide-eyed disappointment.

He took her hands in response to her unspoken question and raised them tenderly to his lips. "My love, I am come with an *honorable* proposition."

Cautiously quitting the stables, Charlotte scurried to the house for tea, and afterwards, waylaid Charles. Robert had judged his boyhood friend correctly. Charles was eagerly conscripted to play his part.

Next, after escaping to her room, Charlotte called for Letty and breathlessly divulged their plot.

Once enlisted, Letty snuck off to Jeffries's cottage to prepare Robert a bath. Jemmy was only too keen to join the conspirators and served as sentry over the stable yard.

After undressing and handing off his boots and less-than-pristine uniform, Robert bathed and shaved while Letty and Charlotte sponged, pressed, and polished all back to its former glory.

By five of the clock, bedecked in scarlet regimentals, adorned with the blue cuffs and facings designating the King's Horse, and with the gleaming captain's gorget adorning his neck, Robert Devington was every bit the resplendent officer. Mounting his charger, he decamped the stable via a hidden path and circled around to the front drive. Thence he reentered the gate and cued the eager gray into a springing piaffe. Dancing up the drive with proudly arched neck, the stallion carried the captain to the great house.

Charles, as planned, espied his erstwhile friend and alerted the remaining household of the hero's arrival. "Mother, Father, Beatrix," he said, summoning them, "'tis Devington returned, and a Captain of the Horse, no less!"

Charlotte, her aunt, and Beatrix swiftly quit the parlor, with the ensuing commotion interrupting Sir Garfield's afternoon coze. The baronet grumbled a diatribe on why a man could never find peace in his own home, only to be startled to full wakefulness by feminine exclamations of admiration and wonderment.

Hefting his ponderous bulk from his favorite chair, Sir Garfield threw his wig on askew and grabbed his silver-handled cane before lumbering out to investigate the hullabaloo that had his household in a tumult. He was stunned to see Devington on his prancing charger.

"What? Devington a captain? How is this possible?" Sir Garfield exclaimed in disgruntled astonishment that was soon overcome by fascination with the captain's horse.

Robert swiftly dismounted as Jemmy appeared to take charge of the captain's horse.

"Just a moment, boy." Sir Garfield stayed the groom. "Let's have a better look at this horse."

Sir Garfield ran his appraising eye over every line and muscle with grudging admiration, and the co-conspirators exchanged knowing looks.

"A fine looking animal, Devington. Might I ask how you have come by such a specimen?"

Devington nodded to Jemmy to take the charger off to the stables. "Spoils of war, one might say," he replied glibly.

"Is he indeed? You've seen action, then?"

"My Sixth Troop was among those at Dettingen."

"Survived the battle, did you?" Sir Garfield asked rhetorically. "You intend to make a career of it, I presume."

"Indeed, I do, sir."

"Then what draws you back to Yorkshire?" He watched intently for any subtle exchange between the captain and his niece. "'Tis a long way from any garrison."

"Homesick, one might say. I've been away for too long, and with a for'night's leave, I couldn't bear to spend the holidays in cramped London barracks."

"Can't say I blame you, but I didn't expect to see you return.

Leastwise not hale and whole," Sir Garfield said callously and cast another glance at his niece. Charlotte, playing her part, appeared dispassionate, the very picture of decorum.

"Then I beg forgiveness for disappointing you, sir."

"Sir Garfield," interrupted Lady Felicia, endeavoring to vitiate the growing tension, "you may continue to grill the poor boy after dinner. I *insist* he join us. After all, 'tis Christmas Eve, and Devington was *nearly* one of us for a number of years."

"Indeed, madam, indeed," Sir Garfield grudgingly acceded. Lady Felicia called her housekeeper and cook to prepare another place.

Robert considered the condescending tone of the invitation, meant to remind him of his station. It rankled.

"Indeed, Mama!" Beatrix chimed with affected adulation. "How dashing our Robert is become! And a captain so quickly. Our own dearest Robert *must* recount all of the battle of Gettinden."

"I believe that was *Dettingen*, Beatrix," her brother corrected.

Unrebuffed, Beatrix cast a hand to her breast. "How stirring to have a war hero among us!"

Though seething at her cousin's conduct, for her uncle's benefit, Charlotte displayed only polite interest in their exchange.

Observing Charlotte's detachment, Sir Garfield heaved an inner sigh that the enforced time and distance between the would-be lovers had finally made the cure. He refocused, with growing alarm, on Beatrix's display of coquetry as she led Captain Devington by the arm to the drawing room.

Surprisingly, conversation was far from stilted. The ladies desired to hear all about the sights and events in London. The gentlemen, having read several newspaper reports of Dettingen, were keen for a firsthand account.

"I just don't countenance this war with the French," Sir Garfield remarked, "while we had every reason to make war with Spain, with those infernal Spanish boarding and seizing our ships and destroying our trade! Wars are necessary to protect our commerce, but what is the point in spilling English blood for Hanover?"

Robert answered, "We entered the war to honor our treaty with Austria and protect her sovereignty. Without our deterring presence, Frederick of Prussia would have long since taken Silesia and Bohemia. And if the French resent our actions enough to threaten our king's Hanover, are we not as obligated to protect it?"

"Hanover!" the baronet scoffed. "The King uses the French threat to strengthen his German Electorate with British resources. Englishmen are sick to death of Hanover!"

"I confess your sentiments have permeated our army, sir," Robert said. "Field Marshal Stair and the Duke of Marlborough took umbrage to the King's preference for his German generals over his English counsel, and have both resigned."

"If Stair and Marlborough have both resigned, who then is to command?" Charles asked.

"At the moment, Lieutenant-general Honeywood is acting commander in chief, Colonel Churchill has the infantry, and Colonel Ligonier of the Black Horse Dragoons has overall command of the cavalry."

"Ligonier, you say? Didn't he fight the last Spanish war under Marlborough?"

"Indeed. He is a most able man. His Black Horse Dragoons were virtually surrounded by French and fought their way through the enemy lines at Dettingen. The colonel narrowly escaped capture. His Majesty later conferred upon him the honor of knight banneret, but the most compelling tale is that of Cornet Henry Richardson, who suffered thirty-seven wounds defending the company's standard."

"Thirty-seven? Good God!" Charles exclaimed.

"Incredibly, the man survived. He was presented the same blood-stained standard in honor of his exceptional valor."

The captain then spoke of the ball the Austrian general D'Aremburg had taken in the shoulder, and the Duke of Cumberland's leg wound, received at the hands of his own Austrian infantryman who mistook him for a French officer. Lastly he spoke of those fallen in battle.

Growing bored and truculent at the lack of attention, Beatrix lowered her napkin to her lap and reached under the table to stroke Robert's thigh.

Robert choked on his wine.

"Dear Robert, how overwrought you are," she exclaimed, all innocence. "And you are far too reticent about yourself. Pray recount how you earned your captaincy," she prettily appealed.

Robert maintained a somewhat stilted flow of conversation while restoring Beatrix's roving hand to her own lap, and detailed the battle, but resisted the temptation to expound and boast of his heroics.

Sir Garfield was keen to hear more of Cumberland, who at the tender age of one-and-twenty had so proven himself under fire.

"He behaved as bravely as any man could have, and the men rallied just to have him so near. They even sing his praises." Grinning, Robert broke out in tuneless song:

"Then rode up Billy the bold
Who ne'er was tried before
And shewd he came out of the mould
That could fight as well as were
For he bravely faced the foe
And fought by his father's side
When his leg with a ball was pierced through
Smart money my boys he cry'd."

Entertained thus, an hour passed and then two, prompting the ladies to withdraw and leave the men to their drink.

All having played out as Robert hoped, he waited for the conversation to turn to Sir Garfield's passion: his horses.

"They'll be soon getting ready for the spring season in Doncaster," Charles prompted, as they had earlier rehearsed.

"Will they indeed? Who will you be running this year, Sir Garfield?"

The baronet lit up at the chance to boast of the new addition to his stables. "I've Rascallion in training. He's half brother to the mare Rosie, who won herself a life of leisure in King Louis's stables."

"I well recall the mare. You believe the colt is as promising?"

"Indeed. Shows great potential, though Jeffries is loath to run him yet. Says he's not ready. But at four years old, I say he should be tried."

"You intend to run him at Doncaster, then?"

"Got my eye on Newmarket wi' this one! He'll be a contender for the King's Plate, mark my words. Grisewood's Bolton Starling son, a four-year-old called by Teazer, is in training at Doncaster. He was first in the King's Plate at Ipswich, and I hear he's to run at Newmarket come the spring season. I've a mind to see my Rascallion put Grisewood in his place. The colt just needs a trial to prepare him."

"As it so happens," Robert segued, "I've a mind to have a go at it."

"You plan to race? But you have no horse!"

"No? I refer to the gray charger. I believe he has the fire in his veins."

Sir Garfield sputtered at the notion. "A daft notion if I ever heard one, a war charger on the track!"

"I beg to differ. Mars is a stallion in his prime, and there's not a beast with more heart. He'll run or he'll die in the doing. I'd bet my all on it."

"Betting now, are you?"

"Are they running Saturday on the moor?" Robert inquired with studied nonchalance.

"Aye, weather permitting."

"Then I shall take Mars out for an airing, and we'll match anyone who shows."

"Ye'd best pray that none show, then!" Sir Garfield chortled. "Ye'll surely lose your shirt, and seeing that it belongs to His Majesty…"

Robert ignored the cut and replied with deliberate *sang froid*, "Then perhaps you would care to make a gentleman's wager? I challenge you, Sir Garfield, to a match race. My Mars against *any* of your prized bloodstock."

"What? A wager against your charger? A ridiculous vagary!"

"Is it so? Only a moment ago you said Rascallion was in need of a trial, and here I present the perfect opportunity."

"You think to challenge me?" Sir Garfield retorted. "For years I've bred the finest, and you think to best my horse? Presumptuous pup!" He snorted in contempt.

"Indeed I do, sir. If you're so confident of your horses, you have nothing to lose."

"Lose? I should not lose! Just what would *you* propose to wager, Devington?" he asked snidely.

"I should like to propose a breeding to your Darley mare Amoret. I've a mind to try Mars in the breeding shed, if he proves himself a runner, and I've always favored that mare. If my horse wins, I should like a foal out of her."

"And when you receive your sound thrashing, instead?" Sir Garfield challenged.

"I should propose the same; however, the resulting offspring would, of course, be yours. 'Tis a free breeding for you. You confessed admiration for the stallion. 'Twould be a fair wager."

"Ah," Sir Garfield said, ruminating, "but delayed gratification, you see; and what would I care for a horse of unknown blood?" He paused. "You may not be aware that Parliament has now prohibited any racing wager of less than fifty pounds. If you are so hell-bent to race, Devington, I'll accept your breeding wager, supplemented by fifty guineas." He regarded Devington shrewdly, anticipating a refusal.

"Then I accept your wager, sir." Devington's words were confidently if rashly spoken.

Sir Garfield sat back in his chair, considering the proposition further. "Charles will run Rascallion." Though he knew Charles to be no match to Devington in the saddle, he believed his colt so vastly superior that he would win regardless of the rider.

"But Jeffries says he's not ready," Charles protested, prompting Robert to raise a curious brow.

"Jeffries be hung!" Sir Garfield retorted. "'Twill be a good trial for both of you, before you ride him in the King's Plate in spring. I'll not suffer humiliation again as we did last May in Malton when you insisted on riding Old Screw. He was no match for the company. Routh's Frolic took the first race, Witty's gelding, Raffler, the second, and the Duke of Perth's Chance stole the third. You will ride Rascallion, Charles."

"If we are agreed," Robert prompted, "we shall meet at Doncaster Heath, Saturday next at ten o'clock."

"You may look forward to a lesson in humility, Devington." Sir Garfield's eyes gleamed at the prospect. "Think I'll retire on that note." Sir Garfield hefted his ample girth from the chair. "Charles will see you out." He nodded to the captain.

While they lingered over their drinks, Charles voiced his qualms about opposing Jeffries and running Rascallion. Knowing Sir Garfield's actions would prove to his advantage, Robert refrained from comment and diverted Charles back to talk of the war.

"I so envy you, Robert. If only I could join up," Charles said wistfully. "I've been tempted many times to go against the old man, but then I remind myself of my duty as the only son to conform to his wishes."

"'Tis not the adventure and romance you imagine, Charles. I would gladly trade shoes with you."

"But you at least had the freedom to choose for yourself, while my entire life is plotted out for me. Sometimes I wonder if I can bear it."

"I fully understand your yen to choose your own destiny. Is it not every man's God-given right to do so?" With this parting thought, Robert called for his horse and bade his old friend good night.

Robert had been perfectly satisfied that his plan had played out to perfection, until Sir Garfield had raised the stakes. Fifty guineas was still a paltry bet by racing standards, but Sir Garfield had done it only to put him in his place. He would have known it was a hefty wager for a captain. The sum represented more than a quarter's wage, and that was *before* the army deducted his allowances for food, lodging, and forage for his horse.

Robert had barely two farthings to rub together, let alone fifty guineas in hand. The combined value of his possessions would barely cover the bet, and a loss would mean selling his horse to cover it.

But, finally having a plan, nothing would now deter Robert from his purpose. He was resolved to see it through to the bitter end.

"We'd best be victorious, old man," he said to Mars, "or our partnership shall be very short-lived."

Twelve

&

A ROGUE'S HEART

*T*he next morning, Robert and Philip rode twenty miles to Doncaster. While Robert hoped to secure less shabby accommodations whilst preparing Mars for his run, Philip hoped the change of venue might provide opportunity to survey the field for his prospective heiress.

Arriving at the Black Lion in Firbeck, they found a large, well-lit taproom with two roaring fireplaces filled with the aromas of hearty Christmas fare. They feasted on goose, roast beef, Yorkshire pudding, game pie, several bottles of Portuguese wine, and various puddings and sweetmeats.

Having satisfied his appetite for food, Philip surveyed the room in his quest to gratify his near-consuming craving for sport. Philip pushed back from the table and sprawled in his chair. His keen eyes perused their surroundings, much as a predator stalking prey, but discovered little potential in the occupants of the taproom: a pair of elderly spinsters, an ancient who appeared deaf, and a genteel middle-aged couple.

Philip eyed the last gentleman and speculatively rolled a pair of dice between his long fingers, considering if he might offer a game of cards or dice. He promptly discarded the notion when he witnessed the gent meekly receiving an earful from his shrewish wife.

"Sir Horace," the woman sharply addressed the man, who dumbly studied the fire, "Did you even attend to one word I said?"

"N–no, my dearest. Ah... I mean, yes, my love."

She glared at him. "Here we are stuck at a horrid little tavern in the middle of nowhere on Christmas all because of your negligence! And if that odious public coach hadn't come along, we might well have frozen to death! Here I am once again obliged to make the most out of pitiful circumstances."

Sir Horace mumbled agreement about making the best of it, and redirected his morose stare to the hearth.

"But I expect it will all be soon forgotten. It is Christmas, after all. The time of giving." Her formerly acid tone was suddenly cloying. She regarded her husband expectantly.

"Uhm... er... ah... as to that my dear," he said visibly flustered, "with such an untoward event, and the numerous baggage we transferred..."

"Do you mean to say you have nothing for me?"

"No, my dearest. Of course not, my sweet, but I might have left it in the carriage, you see. One small parcel was all too easy to lose track of."

"One tiny parcel? When I have given the best years of my life attending your every need? And you lost it!" she exclaimed in indignation.

Listening to this exchange, Philip could no longer contain himself. "Good God, woman! You carry on like a common fishwife! What more do you want? You're warm and housed, safe from harm. You are undeniably well fed," he added, sizing her up. "You will retire to a clean and comfortable bed, and your equipage will be repaired. What more can you expect of a man?" The harridan's jaw dropped, shocked to the core at such unspeakable effrontery.

"And you, sir!" He addressed the gentleman with even greater vehemence. "Where the bloody hell are your ballocks? What the devil kind of example are you, behaving like an accursed sheep and allowing this… harpy (being the mildest word that came to mind) to emasculate the lot of us! Damme, if 'tis not enough to strike terror into any soul contemplating matrimony!"

His point made, Philip threw down his napkin in disgust, grabbed a bottle of wine, and quit the taproom for the peace and solitude of his chamber.

Robert made a hasty apology for his friend's erratic behavior and quickly beat his own retreat before the woman recovered enough to shriek her indignation. He forthwith joined Philip and kicked off his boots to slump into the second chair by the hearth.

"Dare I ask what *that* was about?" he asked his brooding companion.

"Mayhap I overstepped a notch, but damme if I could witness that spectacle any longer! To think I was actually contemplating the connubial state. God only knows what I was thinking. A king's ransom in dowry could never compensate for *that*!"

"What you witnessed, dear fellow, was obviously a loveless union. And 'tis likely what you will have if you seek marriage solely to increase your wealth. In my lowly world, people mostly marry for love and live quite happily. Some in poverty, but happily, nonetheless. You might consider it, Drake."

"Lovely sentiments, but what point is there in leg-shackling if not for gain? There is verily no advantage for me to face the same woman, day after day, year after year. Like this wine," he mused, inspecting the bottle, "'tis adequate for this occasion, but would I chose to imbibe the same every meal? I think not when there are so many other vintages to sample."

"Can you not even imagine a woman to whom you could be devoted?" The question, earnestly posed, received a scoffing reply.

"I hold no such illusions. Monogamy? Monotony? Daresay I confuse the two. Aphrodite herself could not entice me to the altar without a large dowry."

"Then you have my pity. In all your experience of women, you have yet to know love."

Philip's lips suddenly formed a grim, hard line. "What do you know of my life? I have indeed known what *you call* love, but my experience is far removed from your chimera, Devington."

Scowling into the fire, Drake continued. "I was barely twenty when I met a young widow of my father's acquaintance. She was nearly ten years my senior and bent on making up for a decade of lost youth while married to a doddering old man.

"I was completely smitten, and she was more than willing to initiate me to manhood. In time, I became nothing more than her pining lackey, while she regarded me as little more than an indulged pet.

"I found no such bliss as you ascribe to *love*, only regret and self-disgust. I had no contentment, no peace, only an intense jealousy of her affection, a restless angst, and a gut- wrenching vulnerability greatly exceeding anything I have encountered on the battlefield."

He took another long swig from the mouth of the bottle, continuing bitterly, "In my blind passion, I offered her love, eternal devotion, and even… my name, but she was too contemptuous of my proposal even to reply. After the affair lost its novelty, the jade cast me off. The anguish of the entire affair, by far, outweighed its pleasures. I grow maudlin," he stated with distaste, "'tis undoubtedly the wine." He grimaced and examined the bottle. "Empty," he said and tossed it away, along with his dredged-up memories.

The morning mist was still rolling over the heath as Robert and Mars rode to the Doncaster Common that served as the official racetrack, but he was unprepared for the amassing crowd. Spotting Drake and anxious to discover what had incited such a mob, he hailed the conspicuous crimson-clad figure threading his way toward the field.

"Appears I'm in luck today, Devington." Philip grinned. "The fine weather has presented a much-anticipated match race between the local champion and a new contender. Mayhap we should put your extensive knowledge of Yorkshire horseflesh to some good use?"

"How so?" Devington asked warily.

"Apparently a certain Mr. Martindale of North Yorkshire has a score to settle with the honorable Mr. Grisewood. 'Tis reported that Grisewood's Teazer soundly trounced two of Martindale's best runners this season past, and Martindale, unable to resign himself to such sound defeat, has issued a new challenge. What do you know of this Teazer?"

"Teazer, you say? I recall the horse from when I apprenticed at John Croft's stud in Barforth. He's by Bolton Starling, but one would be easily deceived by the look of him. 'Tis perhaps the secret to Grisewood's success."

"How so?"

"Teazer is remarkable for being so *unremarkable*. He stands barely thirteen-two. Though he appears the antithesis of a running blood, what the tiny giant lacks in stature, he well compensates in speed. He established a formidable reputation on the track. His first year out he won at Carlisle, again at Durham, and Grantham, and finally the King's Plate at Ipswich. He trounced a number of good horses."

"So you say?" Drake listened attentively and remarked, "Yet our worthy Martindale, who assuredly knows his competition, challenges him. The man is either supremely confident or a fool." He directed another inquiry to his companion. "Which would you wager, Devington?"

"I would first know whom he plans to run."

"'Tis a Godolphin son, called by Regulus."

"Regulus, by Godolphin? Though I've not seen the colt, he's likely the half brother to Lancaster's Starling, Martindale's favorite.

If Martindale has the aphoristic axe to grind, 'twould be curious for him to run the lesser of the pair. Gives one pause for reflection, does it not?"

"My notion precisely, especially as Martindale appears too impatient to wait until spring for his payback and even meets Teazer on his home training grounds."

"Then I anticipate the devil of a run today." Devington gestured at the throng anxious to lay their odds. "Surely fortunes great and small will be wagered over a four-mile gallop."

"I swore I heard from your own lips that you never play the horses."

"Oh, I'm not here to place a bet. I told you earlier I had business in Doncaster."

"I thought your *business* involved a woman. You made no mention of racing."

"It's a complicated matter. My purpose is related to both, but it appears my own appointment will be delayed this morning."

"Indeed? And just what appointment is this?"

Although initially reluctant to reveal his true purpose, Robert unfurled the events of the previous day. Philip was at once intrigued and amused. "This is your mysterious *business*? A racing wager?"

"But there is much more to this than the horse race." Robert expounded on his plan, to return to Heathstead Hall in spring to breed the mare and pursue formal courtship of Charlotte.

"So it is actually a wager for love." Drake laughed. "Your purpose is only to ingratiate yourself to the lady's uncle in the belief that he will then accept your suit?"

"Something to that effect," Robert answered. "I sought to turn his racing obsession to my advantage."

"Must admit I've heard of stranger bets, but your reasoning may be somewhat flawed, my friend."

"What do you mean?" Robert asked.

"If you win, what makes you think the blighter will favor your suit? You take altogether the wrong approach. Marriage among the landed class is a business arrangement made to each family's mutual advantage. The purpose is to advance one's standing. You might ask yourself what you bring to the negotiating table, Devington. What do you have to offer Sir Garfield in exchange for this precious commodity, his niece?"

"In truth, Drake, I have nothing at present but a promise to love, protect, and care for Charlotte. I'll never be a rich man, but her dowry and the eventual sale of my commission should afford us a modest living. We might even endeavor to breed some horses of our own, Charlotte and I."

"Though I regret to burst your bubble, the man undoubtedly has plans to marry his niece off to someone of consequence, someone who can advance his agenda. An impoverished earl, perhaps? It happens every bloody day," he stated cynically. "Besides, if he is so averse to losing a race, the very sight of you will remind him of his disgrace. 'Tis hardly the way to ingratiate yourself."

Considering Drake's arguments against his plan, Robert realized the flaw in his thinking. In consternation, he asked," Now that you raze my only plan, I'm compelled to ask if you've any better strategy?"

Philip mused a moment. "Why not give the man what he wants, the victory he craves?"

"You propose I should lose the race?"

"Perhaps. It's only a thought, ludicrous though it may seem. If it's the man's goodwill you desire…" Philip shrugged. "Consider, if you should concede the race to him, he might respond altruistically, the magnanimous victor and all that rot. In such a moment, he might be more disposed to attend to your plea."

Robert hesitated. "I see your point, but this alternative creates a bit of a snag."

"Indeed?" he asked sardonically. "Just how much is this *snag* going to cost?"

"Just how lucky were you at the cards the other night?"

"Lady Luck bestowed her graces generously," Philip drawled.

"If I am to lose, I need fifty guineas."

"Fifty guineas!" Philip hooted. "A bloody gentlemen's wager! Hardly worth the trouble."

"Unless you're living on a captain's wages," Robert said dolefully.

Realization dawned on the major. "Are you mad, Devington? You challenged the man without the funds to back your bet?"

"I had no intention of losing, but now you suggest a significant deviation from my prior plan. Whether I win or lose, I shall return to breed Mars to the mare. The difference is who shall own the resulting foal. At least he agreed to that much before he upped the ante. So now 'tis just the matter of the money, should I lose."

"But I contest that you risk all you have in this infernal wager. There are much easier ways up a woman's petticoat. Have you learned *nothing* in my presence, man?"

"Be wary how you tread, Drake," Robert remarked with a deathly glower.

"What, are you now going to call me out?" He laughingly dismissed the notion. "I fail to understand why you have made this ludicrous wager."

"For Charlotte; I intend to have Charlotte!" Robert cried.

"Not if you end up in debtor's prison. I credited you with more sense."

"I'll cover it. If nothing else, I'll sell Mars."

"The devil you will!" Philip rebuked him. "Just how do you expect to return to the Horse Guards without a horse? You've lost all sense! In the interest of your sanity, if not for your professed devotion, I'll back your infernal bet... if I'm able."

"What do you mean, *if you're able*? You just said you were lucky at cards."

"Indeed I was, but I've wagered it all on the first race, ole chap. Just have to wait and see what this newcomer Regulus is made of."

Robert awaited the start of the race, knowing his fate was in the balance.

~~

As the starting time approached, spectators to the private match drew in to the track in keen anticipation, with the breeders, owners, and local gentry finding reserved places on a raised dais overlooking the field. The other spectators milled about, seeking the best vantage point, and the contenders were led in.

Mr. Grisewood and Mr. Martindale had agreed that the single heat of four miles, two furlongs, was sufficient to trial the newcomer, Regulus, against the more seasoned runner, Teazer. The gleaming, snorting fifteen-one-hand copper chestnut took his position first at the starting post, appearing to tower over the diminutive Teazer, who innocuously resembled a prancing gray pony being led up to the start. Once at the post, both horses eyed each other, snorting, dancing, and tossing their heads. Their nostrils flared, and every visible muscle tensed in acute anticipation. Their riders balanced precariously on the restless mounts and edged closer to the mark.

With the signal, the horses launched forward in unison, surging forth and grunting their exertions with every stride. As they thundered past the crowd, their iron-shod hooves hammered the ground. Down the track, they fought neck and neck along the rail. They pounded down the turf, and clods of earth became projectiles in all directions.

In the first pass, the panting animals flashed by the frantic spectators, shoulder to shoulder, in a blaze of gleaming sinew. They rounded the bend. Teazer was visibly slipping, but every bit the fighter, he brought all to bear and rallied valiantly to regain the fore. Eyes glazing and mouth foaming, he pressed on. His jockey urged him furiously, but Regulus gained by inches, soon by feet, then by yards. By the final

bend, Teazer's supreme efforts had waned. The game was up for
Teazer, and in the end, he proved no match for the leggy chestnut,
who easily breezed him by. Regulus gleaned a clean victory.

With the defeat of the local champion, moans of agony over-
came roars of triumph. Mr. Martindale, however, was not alone
in his ecstasy.

"Looks like I've more than enough blunt to go around." The
jubilant major clapped a hand on his companion's back. "I'll back
your bet, Devington. Just tell me which way the race is to be run."

Devington considered his answer. "I suppose I am about to run
a losing race."

"Then when I double my winnings on your race, your debt to
me shall be quite forgiven."

"How so?"

"How do you think?" He grinned. "I plan to bet against you."

"Opportunistic bounder," Robert mumbled, watching his
comrade swagger off to place his "sure bet."

At ten o'clock, the riders checked in, with the horses being
weighted by age and size. Rascallion, the younger, carried ten stone,
while Robert's mount, perforce, carried twelve. The single heat of
three miles was shorter than normal but also gauged to equalize the
age difference of the contenders.

This anticlimactic challenge of two unknowns, following Teazer-
Regulus, drew few but the most die-hard spectators. Among them,
Sir Garfield awaited the celebration of his assured victory, while
Charlotte watched expectantly, absorbing the final preparations and
the horses advancing to the start. With intense concentration, she
unconsciously angled forward, her hands clenched in her lap. In her
mind's eye, she was positioned to ride.

As the gentleman jockeys came forth, Jeffries made his way to
his young master's side. His instructions were tersely spoken. "If'n
ye hope to ride him to the finish, Master Charles, ye'd do well to

give me yer ridin' crop. This 'un be none too fond o' it." Without comment, Charles handed the object to the trainer. "And don't ye be too generous wi' the spur neither, or this horse will run the race wi'out ye," Jeffries warned him ominously.

Already nervous, Charles struggled to maintain control over the unruly chestnut, who jigged sideways and thrashed his way to the start.

Conversely, Robert cued Mars quietly, almost imperceptibly, and the horse pawed the ground, arched his powerful neck, and locked his gaze intently on the horizon. He sensed that Mars had coiled, akin to a spring. The horse was prepared to launch.

Awaiting the signal, Robert and Charles slanted over their horses' necks. Their fingers tightly threaded the reins. Their legs locked in position.

The starter signaled. Mars exploded like a lightning bolt, with greater power and speed than Robert could have imagined. Wholly engaging his hindquarters, he stretched forward. Running nearly nose to earth, in a peculiar style of his own, he drove forth with an astonishing intensity that left Rascallion in the dust.

Fearful after Jeffries's instruction to give any direction to his horse, Charles rode as little more than a passenger, not caring who crossed the line first, as long as he remained horsed.

With the finish in sight, Robert was at once euphoric and dismayed. Rascallion was truly a good runner, so he had counted on a challenge, had hoped for a good fight, but never in his wildest dreams had he envisaged such a blistering start. Mars, never trained or tried to race, had already such a strong lead that no attempt to pull him up would go unremarked.

Robert's only option: submit to the will of his steed and chase the wind to the finish.

He relaxed the loop of rein through his fingers, leaned forward, stomach to withers, with his face to the wind-whipped mane, and held on for the ride, resigned to face the music later.

The race called without question. Mars had completely distanced his challenger and was the clear champion. Sir Garfield watched agog, with his greatest hopes, pinned on his best prospect, torn asunder.

Philip was nearly purple with suppressed fury. "Incredible! Simply bloody incredible! What in the devil's name are you about, Devington?" He glowered once he was capable of forming coherent speech.

"It didn't play out as I intended. Honestly, Philip. I knew he would make a good show, but by the time I realized what a lead we had, the race was nigh run. What else could I do?"

"I lost a bloody fortune on that race!"

"Perhaps we might yet turn this around," Robert offered hopefully.

"Just let it rest!"

"But I haven't told you about the mare."

"What do I care about the bloody mare?"

"Half of the wager was that I should breed Mars to one of Sir Garfield's mares. She's a daughter of Bartlett's Childers, and a good one, I tell you."

"I recall your fondness for this lineage," Philip remarked with little interest.

"The mare's a producer, Drake. Her first filly, White Rose, ran only one race and was sold to the king of France."

"I recall *winning* on that one," Philip remarked acerbically.

Ignoring the remark, Robert continued, "With the right stud, the right blood, we could produce an unbeatable champion."

"Precisely what has this to do with me?" he snapped.

"In for a penny, in for a pound? You fronted me the fifty guineas, so I propose a partnership. I offer you one-half ownership in the offspring."

"You propose half ownership in an *unborn* horse as repayment?"

"Surely a good racehorse is worth what you lost?"

"The horse would need be bloody Pegasus to cover what I lost! But let's have a look at this mare."

Thirteen

✧

A WAGER FOR LOVE

*F*ree to travel cross-country, the two officers preceded Sir Garfield's lumbering coach to Heathstead Hall by a full half hour. They dismounted in the stable yard, handed their horses off to the younger groom, and then proceeded to the house, where its mistress, who hadn't the least interest in horseracing, awaited her husband's return.

A footman led the gentlemen to the morning room, and Devington made the introductions. Lady Felicia eyed the major speculatively. "Drake?" she said, repeating the name. "I've a peculiar notion we've met before, but can't seem to place you."

"Having never before visited Yorkshire, madam, I might ask whether your family have perhaps any political connections? My father and brother are both in Parliament."

"No, Major, we do not. But 'tis of no moment. Undoubtedly 'twill come to me soon enough. Now, gentlemen," she continued, "would you care to join me for a dish of Bohea while we await our racing party? I had expected their arrival in time for tea but am disappointed again. Sir Garfield's horses seem to always take precedence."

The clattering outside announced Sir Garfield's arrival, whereby the two men took leave of the lady to greet the coach. They arrived outside just as the footman lowered the steps.

Though Philip had accompanied his friend only to provide moral support, he soon realized the serendipity of his decision when Beatrix made to alight from the carriage. Robert had come to claim his prize, but Philip now espied his own trophy in the baronet's daughter.

Unaware of the company, Beatrix said with a giggle over her shoulder, "What a vastly entertaining ride, Charles! I thought dearest Papa was in danger of apoplexy! I fail to comprehend all this ado over a silly little horse race."

Intercepting the footman, the major reached up to hand the lady out of the carriage. Beatrix's giggle died on her lips.

"So we meet again." Philip's voice was low and smooth but his lips smoother as they brushed her fingertips. Frozen, Beatrix blinked three times before her brain could process the vision or compose a response. Here stood the same man, the raffish captain, who had ridiculed her.

"'Twas the Lichfield races, was it not?" His eyes mocked even as his lips spoke the reminder of her humiliation by his hand.

She flushed, taken unawares, but recalling her vow of vengeance, she reclaimed her equanimity with an artful reply. "Are we acquainted, Major? I'm afraid I have not the least recollection of you."

"But I remember it well," Charles said, exiting the carriage. "'Tis the same chap who came to our rescue when we were entrenched in that devilish mud. Trixie, you *must* recall it," Charles insisted, soon joined by Sir Garfield and Charlotte.

"Regretfully, Major, the event signifies with my brother, but alas, my poor memory fails." Her vindictive glint belied the mendacious response.

Realizing her game, Philip suppressed a wicked chuckle. *Hell hath no fury, eh? We'll just see about that.* Beatrix had dropped the gauntlet, and Philip was not one to refuse a challenge.

With an infuriatingly rakish grin, Philip replied, "I am chagrinned, my lady, in having made such a poor and forgettable impression. A grievous discredit to my rank and station, for which I am compelled to make amends."

Beatrix gave this man further study. Did he still mock her? She would surely exact vengeance for his scorn. She vowed to bring her charms to full measure. She would enslave him, make him beg as no man had ever begged. She would hold nothing back to achieve her aim: the complete degradation and utter humiliation of Philip Drake. Her decision made, she applied herself immediately and unreservedly to her purpose.

"Amends, you say?" She flashed her most beguiling smile and placed her hand on his sleeve, allowing him to lead her into the house.

Once inside, Charlotte and Beatrix excused themselves to change, and Sir Garfield withdrew to his study for a stiff drink, mumbling about settling the bet after tea.

Lady Felicia, abashed at her husband's inhospitality and less-than-convivial manner, and secretly eager to further Beatrix's acquaintance with the major, ordered tea served in the solarium and then instructed a footman to prepare a chamber for the two men to refresh themselves.

Once in the privacy of the bedchamber, Philip ventured languidly, "Beatrix was none too concerned with her father's losses today."

"Beatrix? She's a vain and frivolous chit. She hasn't the least care for money, leastwise not the spending of it," Robert added dryly.

"But one would expect her to have more care for her dowry," Philip artfully segued to his purpose.

"She needn't worry on that account, I assure you."

"Do you indeed?"

"Nigh on twenty thousand, I've heard."

Philip's interest was decidedly piqued. "You do say, Devington? How reliable is your source?"

"Her cousin, Charlotte. Why the interest?"

"You promised heiresses, as I recall." Philip's indolent tone did nothing to assuage Robert's growing unease. He instinctively balked at Drake's setting his mercenary sights on Beatrix.

"I meant in Doncaster, not here at Heathstead Hall," Robert said.

"I beg to see the difference, and I daresay you owe me after your *brilliant* performance this morning."

Mortified by the truth, Robert suppressed any further protest.

Once retired to her chamber, Beatrix set about formulating her battle plan. She took particular pains with her toilette and selected her most flattering day gown. The pink silk bespoke innocence, but she bade Letty lace her stays as tightly as achievable, to display her bosom to best advantage.

With her blond curls newly coiffed, she rehearsed a sultry moue in the looking glass, and then an enticing smile, and rubbed her teeth for shine. Her vanity now well satisfied, she went to Charlotte's dressing room to ply her with questions.

"Charlotte, what do you know of this Major Drake? What has Robert said of him?"

Charlotte was surprised by her cousin's keen interest in the major. Beatrix had never shown sincere interest in any other gentleman. She answered warily.

"As an officer, Robert is in admiration of him. He has described the major as capable, competent, and brave. He exhibited great valor in battle. Outside of that, I know little of the man."

"But what do you know of his family?"

"I believe he is the son of an earl, but 'tis the limit of my knowledge."

"From a noble family?" Beatrix furrowed her brow. "But he has no title, Charlotte. Do you suppose he is heir to one? But then surely he would have introduced himself with at least a courtesy title such as *Sir* Philip Drake or Major *Lord So-and-so*, if he was heir to one. Even Charles, as first son of a baronet, is eligible for knighthood at his coming-of-age." She frowned again, posing the question almost to herself. "Since *you* are no help, I suppose I must make it my objective to discover for myself." *And then make him grovel at my feet for forgiveness*.

Beatrix wafted gracefully into the solarium, gushing disingenuous apologies, just as Lady Felicia began pouring tea. Charlotte followed demurely in her wake.

Accepting the obvious bait, Major Drake complimented Beatrix on her charming appearance, but his appraising gaze spoke volumes more. Satisfied she had achieved her aim to fix his interest, Beatrix lowered her eyes coyly in a perfect imitation of a blush.

Observing the interaction, Charlotte and Robert exchanged skeptical looks.

Yet ill-humored from the race and completely oblivious to the exchange between his daughter and the major, Sir Garfield fixed his morose stare on Robert. "Well, now you've won your wager, what have you in mind regarding the mare?"

Considering for a moment, Robert replied, "I have a mind to breed her to Mars in the spring."

"'Twas pure happenstance, your taking the race," Sir Garfield grumbled crossly. "Rascallion's by far the superior horse. Must've been off today. Damned fluke it was, nothing more!"

"He's a fine colt, Sir Garfield. No doubt he was off," Robert amiably conceded.

"'Twasn't even a proper race, for that matter," Sir Garfield continued, gaining steam. "A proper race would have been four miles and three heats! That's the true test. The true runner has bottom; still runs with vigor at the end, don't you know. Four miles, three heats: that's the true test!"

"Indeed." Philip encouraged Sir Garfield, perceiving a golden opportunity, the proverbial gift horse about to raise its head, if he would take the bait. He winced at his mixed metaphors then prompted, "Perhaps, sir, a rematch is in order?"

"A rematch?" Robert eyed his comrade speculatively.

"Yes... yes, indubitably a rematch is in order," Sir Garfield parroted.

"What do you propose, sir?" Robert asked cautiously, veiling his enthusiasm for Philip's stroke of brilliance.

"Yes. Indeed. A real race, b'God. Four miles, three heats."

Robert eyed him squarely. "I accept, Sir Garfield."

"If it is a real match, it must be a real wager, Devington," Sir Garfield challenged, fully expecting Robert to back down.

"Then I propose substantially higher stakes, sir." He paused for courage then took the ultimate plunge. "I propose Charlotte and Amoret should I win, and the forfeiture of Mars, should I lose."

Sir Garfield choked on his tea. "What do you say?"

With his heart in his throat, Robert enunciated slowly, "Should we again triumph against your Rascallion, I shall win the mare, as well as your consent to Charlotte's hand, if she will have me." He directed his gaze straight into her astonished hazel eyes. "Conversely," he continued, "should I lose, you shall acquire one fine gray charger, and I shall foreswear my feelings for your niece forever."

Charlotte was stricken at these last words.

"You would have me wager my own niece? You impudent puppy!"

"'Twould appear your stakes are too high for the gentleman's liking, Devington," Philip drawled.

"Stakes too high? Indeed not, you insolent whelp!" Sir Garfield furiously sputtered.

"Whelp, sir? I think the remark needlessly disparaging to my poor mother." The major smirked.

"Your mother?" Sir Garfield scowled, befuddled by the major's satire.

Robert regarded Philip intently with a silent plea to hold his peace. Sir Garfield needed no further goading. The man had never refused a racing wager in his life.

"Must mull this overnight," the baronet replied sullenly. "You'll have my answer on the morrow, Devington."

"On the morrow, then, sir." Robert said and bowed his dismissal.

While Robert departed in relative haste, Philip tarried, making his adieus in an obsequious fashion. He thanked his hostess for her congenial hospitality and displayed his leg in the execution of a most courtly bow. Advancing to Beatrix, he lingered longer than necessary over her hand. "My lady," he said for her ears alone, "I fear I provoked your father and have jeopardized my opportunity to make atonement for our prior meeting."

Beatrix lowered her head demurely for her mother's benefit, but her brazen gaze belied her innocent tone. "I am yet unconvinced of your contrition, Major." She accompanied the words with a practiced moue. "You have yet to pay penance."

Philip was all too familiar with such coquetry but played along. "Indeed, my lady? And precisely what… penance… have you in mind?"

"The penalty should match the crime, should it not?" she challenged.

"Indeed, so." Philip chuckled. *So, the little minx wanted to play deep, did she?* She ventured into unchartered waters if she intended to play with him. "I then leave it to your imagination, my lady." He made his departure.

Charlotte confronted Robert, intercepting him as he was leaving. "Why, Robert? Why take such a gamble, such an impossible risk? What are you about? Please make me understand," she beseeched.

"My dearest, dearest, love." He clasped her shoulders. "When I left you, I had no wealth, property, or title attached to my name. I departed with only the desire to elevate myself in your uncle's esteem. I had the naïve belief that my new rank might deem me an acceptable suitor. I had hoped to part with a betrothal.

"I realize now 'twas a false hope. Your uncle will never perceive me as either an equal or as a suitable match. As matters rest, we will never be together. You will soon be given to another, and I would have nothing beyond a hard and lonely soldier's life, with greater likelihood of an early grave than a prosperous future.

"Although it is an undeniably rash act, this is my only way forward. I have pledged to you and before God to take charge of my destiny and of *our* future. If I cannot earn Sir Garfield's favor, then I would incur his debt of honor. If I lose, I am no worse off, but if I win, I gain my heart's desire. It truly is no gamble, Charlotte. Do you see it now?"

"But, Robert, I have as much at risk as you. My uncle already has plans to take us off to London in a few months to arrange marriages for Beatrix and me. I'll do anything to prevent this and secure our future together. You must let me help."

"There's nothing you can do, my love," he said tenderly.

"But there is," she insisted. "You need to ready Mars, don't you see? Though he made an impressive showing today, it was a short race. Rascallion doesn't start as strong, but he has impressive stamina. I've seen him run, and I'm not nearly as confident of victory as you are. It is by no means assured, especially if Mars is not prepared."

"What do you propose?"

"Let me ride. I can ready him for you. You know I can outride even you. I proved it years ago. I can help. You *must* let me," she pleaded, knowing their future balanced on the outcome.

Arriving to overhear her entreaty, Philip retorted with a snort, "What rot! A woman to ride? I credited you with more sense, man! Take the horse back to Doncaster and hire a professional."

"Don't be so quick to dismiss her, Philip. She speaks the truth. I've told you as much before. Her suggestion is not without merit."

Eyeing Philip disapprovingly, Charlotte continued, "It must be very early, at first light. Only the servants are about before dawn. We can trust Letty, and Jeffries will be in Doncaster with Rascallion, at least until the race is over. A few coins should bribe the stable hands."

"You've yet to convince *me*," Philip interjected with clenched teeth, "and it's once again *my blunt* at risk. I've played the fool once on your account, Devington, and it's not a role I relish."

"Reserve judgment until you've seen her ride. We won't have Sir Garfield's final word 'til the morrow anyway. If you're not swayed by then, we'll off to Doncaster if he accepts the terms, though I doubt not he will. The man doesn't suffer defeat easily."

Charlotte concurred. "My uncle is entirely predictable on that score."

"All right, I withhold judgment until the morrow," Philip conceded grudgingly.

"Until the morrow, my little hoyden." Robert pulled Charlotte into his embrace and sealed their pact with a long, lingering kiss.

✒

They met at daybreak and rode in silence to the heath. The rising sun shed barely enough light to limn the laid-out course.

Robert cast his nostalgic gaze over the same great oak where the young lovers had first raced, and then over Charlotte, garbed once again in her cousin's cast-off britches. Drawing off her cloak, she pulled a woolen cap from her pocket and tightly tucked up her long, honeyed locks until well contained in the cap.

Philip stood askance while Charlotte and Robert exchanged horses and joined their heads to confer on the distance and course. This decided, Charlotte led the restless stallion a short distance away but did not immediately mount, as Philip had expected. Instead, she laid her hands on the horse and began murmuring in a low, hypnotic voice.

With skepticism, Philip watched her move around the horse, from neck to shoulder and down his foreleg, speaking to him and tracing every muscle with her hands. She continued her journey over his withers, back, flank, stifle, and hock. She memorized his very form with her hands.

Moving back to his head, she whispered and murmured in his ear. Mars was mesmerized by Charlotte's witchcraft and responded in his own language of snorts and nickers. He appeared hers to command.

With a sharp nod to Robert, Charlotte signaled her readiness to mount. Philip and Hawke then joined them at the start, in the belief that competition would help stir the stallion's blood.

They ambled the short distance to the oak, and the contenders took position.

Breathing deeply, Charlotte poised over the stallion's withers, reins woven through tightened fingers, her small body lithely balancing in the frame of the stirrup irons. As the stallion arched and tensed in anticipation, she forced herself to relax.

Robert gave the signal, and Mars, fully engaged in the hind end, let fly. He lunged forward, stretching into his peculiar gait. Gaining impulsion and with it momentum, he instantly parted company with Philip and Hawke. Were it a real race, 'twould have been a cruel hoax. Horse and rider disappeared like a gray ghost into the horizon, their hoof beats echoing in the silent dawn.

Charlotte initially struggled for balance, but within a few strides found her rhythm with the horse. She rode with intensity previously unknown to her. Gauging the time, the distance, the exertions, the pace, she no longer harbored any doubt the horse could run. But did he have the staying power, the "bottom," to last four miles at this bruising rate? Moreover, could he sustain for the two additional heats that would be asked, nay, *demanded* of him? Only the toughest and most tenacious survived such a trial uninjured in body or spirit.

Charlotte pushed him harder on the second lap, and he responded without hesitation. Instinctively watching, waiting, feeling, she hovered, belly over withers, hands along the crest of his neck. Her toes balanced in the irons, legs flexing along his sides, he felt to her akin to a bellows, flexing and contracting with every stride. She was lost in the cadence, the tattoo of hooves striking earth. Her only thoughts were of lightness: lightness of limb, lightness of hand, as she by degrees gave and took of the slack, rating him, pacing him, willing him to maintain his momentum, to persevere. She became one with the horse, losing herself in the glorious, ineffable thrill of their gallop.

Rounding the final bend, she urged further acceleration. He answered readily, lunging forth again, exerting his power to lengthen his stride for home. At once Charlotte understood Robert's confidence and why one who never gambled had wagered his all on this horse. Her racing heart lightened when the great oak came into sight. With a smug little smile to Philip, she pulled up to the waiting men.

"You've made your point," he grudgingly confessed.

The trio set out at a sedate pace for Heathstead Hall, well satisfied with both their performances. Charlotte handed the horse off to the bleary-eyed Jemmy and then scurried back to the house to dress for breakfast, where they would soon hear Sir Garfield's decision.

After giving Mars a vigorous rubdown, Robert turned him out in the paddock next to an indignant Amoret. The stallion, eager to attract the mare's attention, first snorted then powerfully arched his neck, tossed his head, and trotted in a springing stride up to the fence, where he nickered softly to her.

The mare, who had been cropping grass, paused to regard the eager stallion with haughty disinterest and then turned away. With her hindquarters facing him, the stallion curled back his upper lip, trying to better catch her scent in order to decipher her receptiveness to his nickered invitation.

This time the mare exhibited mild curiosity and ambled up to the fence. Eagerly, the stallion stretched his neck and reached out his head to sniff her more closely. Amoret, rather than showing any encouragement, demonstrated her repugnance with a squeal of displeasure and a lightning-fast strike of her foreleg. Contrary to the male's amorous inclinations, the mare was more disposed to kicking his teeth in. The hapless stallion, demonstrating good sense and even better reflexes, retreated from the peevish mare.

"'Tis not yet her season, my good fellow," Robert replied. "She will surely show more interest as the days grow longer."

Philip chuckled to the stallion, considering his own pursuit of Beatrix. "She merely plays hard to get, old chum. With patience, and above all finesse on your part, she'll issue her own invitation in due time."

The officers left the paddocks for the house and joined the family, who were still seated at breakfast. Lady Felicia again played the gracious hostess, and Charles greeted the pair genially enough. Beatrix feigned disinterest but stole covert glances at Major Drake. Charlotte concealed her apprehension by diverting her eyes to her teacup. Sir Garfield, however, was all business. Without preamble and forgoing any social niceties, he staunchly announced, "I shall accept the rematch with the following provisions: Firstly, it shall be run at Doncaster Common, three days hence. Secondly, the horses will be ridden by a hired jockey." Far from crestfallen not to ride again, Charles received the news with a sigh of relief, return by Sir Garfield's darkling look.

Sir Garfield continued, undaunted by his son's sullen visage. "Thirdly, they will run four miles distance and perform three heats, if required, to clearly declare a victor." He paused, scrutinizing the captain, and added the final proviso. "As to the wager, it shall be augmented by five hundred pounds. I accept nothing less. A bona fide race requires a true wager."

Robert's heart skipped a beat at this final pronouncement. At his rate of twelve shillings per day, five hundred pounds represented over two years' salary! It would be impossible for him to cover such a loss.

By issuing such a challenge, Sir Garfield had saved his own face. He had intentionally proposed stakes so exorbitant that Devington would have no choice but decline, but doing so would also compromise his honor as a gentleman.

Philip's ire rose at the gall of this game played at Robert's expense. Such men as this baronet were the lowest of the low in his estimation. He refused to suffer his fellow officer's debasement by such a pusillanimous sod, but given his recent ill luck, five hundred pounds was a devilish stiff loss to cover. He had a rule never to overextend himself and lived by this basic canon to avoid the humiliation of appealing to his family to cover his debts. Nonetheless, he vowed to support his companion. *In for a penny, in for a pound...* Catching Robert's eye, Philip nodded almost imperceptibly to accept the wager.

Though taken aback by the magnanimous gesture, Robert managed to choke out the words, "I accept your conditions, Sir Garfield."

The wily baronet, in belief he had outmaneuvered the captain, now found himself backed into a corner.

The race was most definitely "on."

Fourteen

An Officer and a Gentleman

Returning to the house, Charlotte was greeted by a summons from her uncle. "He wishes to see you in the library, miss," the footman notified her.

With foreboding, she straightened her shoulders and proceeded to his sanctuary, where he beckoned her to a chair. Charlotte perched upon it rigidly, expectantly.

"I wish a word with you, Niece," Sir Garfield began in deceptively cordial tones belied by his visage. Rising, he sighed deeply and commenced pacing with his hands clasped behind his back.

"Charlotte, as your uncle, it befalls to me to see to your future, to ensure you properly settled and espoused to a gentleman. Do not deceive yourself that I am ignorant of this romantic fantasy you persist in entertaining. I had hoped you had done with your foolish fancy when he went off to war, but since he failed to get himself blown to bits, I find I must needs deal with this once and for all. This infatuation with young Devington must come to an immediate conclusion."

"But, Uncle—" His dark look cowed her.

"A marriage, not unlike a business partnership, is an amicable arrangement at best. It is not to be entered indiscriminately and upon one's personal whim. One must consider the betterment of one's family, as in horse breeding, with sagacious deliberation to improve the stock. With no name, no holdings, and no future, Devington is of a decidedly inferior breed. He is not, nor will he ever be, a suitable match."

"But I love him!"

"*That* is of absolutely no consequence! Love is for paupers, those who have nothing else. The boy is not for you, so get this maggot out of your head once and for all! Henceforth, you are expressly forbidden any contact with that upstart. Do you understand?"

"But the race! You agreed to his wager!"

"Whatever the outcome of this ludicrous wager, you are to refuse his suit. Attend to me closely, Charlotte," he said, his voice threatening, "regardless of the outcome, you *will* refuse him."

Charlotte, who had scarce spoken a word during his tirade, sat pensively silent. She had almost known what he was going to say before he said it, but the knowledge didn't lessen the sting. He claimed to have her best interests at heart, but the truth was self-evident. Her uncle viewed her as nothing more than a commodity to advance his own ambitions.

He had used her father in the same way. When young Edward Wallace approached his brother with a desire to enter the clergy, Sir Garfield had refused. He had no use for a clergyman in the family. Instead, he had insisted that his brother study law or lose his financial support. Edward acquiesced and entered the Honorable Society of Gray's Inn, where he spent the ensuing decade repaying his brother with legal favors.

Although he never developed a passion for the law, he had found contentment with his wife and daughter. Charlotte's parents had loved one another deeply and were truly happy. Having seen this, Charlotte would settle for nothing less. She would never agree to a loveless union, and only Robert held the key to her heart, that sacred organ she had warily guarded. Her future would be with the man she loved, or with no one.

Misreading her silence, Sir Garfield brought the interview to a closure, gratified by the ease and success of his subjugation. Charlotte excused herself, and with a heavy heart, escaped to her room. Upon entering her chamber, she went directly to her treasure chest, the ornately engraved mahogany box on her night table. Opening the lid, she solemnly fingered her only valuables, her most treasured possessions—Robert's letters, a short strand of milky pearls tied with a pink satin ribbon, and a silver watch.

She knew the value of these items was only a fraction of the five hundred pounds Robert needed, but he had gambled everything to win their future together. Her sacrifice could be no less. Tenderly wrapping her treasures in a linen handkerchief, she slid the small bundle through the slit in her petticoat and into her pocket.

Lest anyone spy her, she exited the house through the garden and crept thru a neglected opening in the hedgerow, taking the well-worn path to the stables. Failing at first to see her beloved, she wandered over to the paddocks. Amoret greeted her with a warm nicker and trotted prettily up to the fence.

"How goes it, my lovely, with your handsome gent?" Charlotte crooned, stroking the mare.

"Not as well as he had hoped," Robert replied, striding up behind her. "Though I confess I had no real expectations for either of us until spring."

Charlotte turned, and Robert pulled her to him, encircling her in his warm embrace. Charlotte was suddenly hypersensitive of the rising physical tension between them. "Spring?" she asked.

"Aye. If all goes as planned. Spring would be a good time to wed, would it not?"

Hope rekindled in her eyes. "B-but what if—"

He hushed her with a finger to her lips and slowly traced them before inclining his head and brushing them with his own. Charlotte quivered involuntarily. Alarmed by her sudden clamor of emotions,

Charlotte backed away, fumbling for her pocket and the small package within.

"But we needn't wait, Robert, and you needn't risk everything in this wager. We could run away together."

"But how would we get by?"

"With these," she answered, retrieving her bundle and offering it with open hands.

Distraught by her sudden anxiety, Robert had neither need nor desire to inspect her gift. Probing deeply into those hazel eyes, he cupped her hands in his and closed them back about her offering. "Have faith," he whispered.

His kiss expressed the greatest reverence for her selfless gesture, and Charlotte responded with all her being. Any further speech was superfluous.

༄

Keen to learn even the most tedious and mundane details of army life, Charles detained Philip after breakfast. Callow and idealistic, he would have enthusiastically enlisted in the army had not his father dismissed the notion and any further discussion of it. Sir Garfield's interdiction, however, did little to stifle his son's interest in all martial matters, and most particularly in the current campaign.

"Major Drake, I understand from Robert that you've served with His Grace, the Duke of Cumberland?"

"Not precisely, Charles. All cavalry units were under Ligonier's command, but during the fray at Dettingen, His Grace rode bravely to the fore and assumed command of the left flank when our major fell and Ligonier was cut off. The duke took charge of the remaining Horse whilst His Majesty and Lord Stair commanded the Foot on our right. We were sure to be annihilated, but the men rallied, and the tide was turned, ere I shouldn't be standing before you."

"By all newspaper accounts, our forces soundly routed the French," Charles remarked.

"Indeed so, and had the advice of Lord Stair prevailed, we should have pursued them back to France with their tails between their legs."

"I wish I had been there," Charles said wistfully. "When do you return?"

"Devington and I report back to Whitehall within the se'nnight, and I anticipate preparations for the spring campaign to hastily ensue, lest the French take obscene advantage of our absence. I expect our troop transports will embark by mid-April."

At this moment, Beatrix appeared, feigning a search for her fan. "War again! Have you ever encountered a more ponderous household, Major? Papa thinks of nothing but his blessed horses, and Charles of nothing but the war. I fear I shall die of sheer tedium!"

"My frivolous sister gives no thought to such weighty matters," Charles remarked disparagingly, "even when thousands of Englishmen shed their blood."

"Englishmen shed blood? Why should you imagine such a thing, Charles?" she replied indignantly. "We are fighting Frenchmen, after all; how difficult can that be?"

Philip suppressed a chuckle. "One should never underestimate one's adversaries, my dear, even those more disposed to food, frippery, and fashion than fighting."

"But why should they not be? All the best styles come from Paris."

"Is this a confession, my lady? Have a care, lest I detain you for purchasing contraband French goods."

"I confess nothing, for fear of the reprisal," she teased.

Master of this particular dance, Philip didn't miss a beat. "As a British cavalry officer, I well assure you of reprisals, my lady."

"Indeed? And precisely what should you do with me, Major?" she taunted.

"Do you truly wish me to elaborate?" He spoke *sotto voce*.

Regarding him coyly, she placed her hand intimately on his arm. "You must enlighten me, lest I be tempted to commit any shamefully illicit act."

An interesting choice of words. The chit was wading deep now, but the question remained whether she actually knew how to swim.

His interest was piqued, but a change of venue was in order. "Perhaps I could elaborate... with a stroll?"

Beatrix acquiesced with a knowing smile, and the pair quit the morning room through the French doors, wholly intent on exploring the delights of her garden.

$\backsim$

Robert hailed Charlotte as she completed Mars's second training run on the heath. "You are managing him too heavily from his mouth," he said.

"What do you mean?" she asked a bit defensively.

"You are holding him too fast, which puts his frame all wrong and makes him heavy. Though any Newmarket jockey would advocate holding a horse fast in his running, I say it encourages him to run with his mouth open and in a fretting, jumping attitude, like a stag, with his forelegs pointed and head in the air. A horse that runs in this fashion works to excess. He strains his sinews, and his wind becomes locked. He will be used up early."

"What would you have me do differently?" she asked.

"Run him light in the mouth, and he will be willing and at ease and respond readily to your cues. His legs will be more beneath him, and his sinews less extended. He will be relaxed, exert less, and have freer wind, enabling him to run faster when you call upon him. Hold him, Charlotte, as if your reins were a silken thread as fine as a hair that you are afraid of breaking. *This* is how you should ride."

Charlotte absorbed his words intently and thenceforth gave the stallion a free hand.

Robert was immensely pleased with their progress. Charlotte had quickly learned to rate the horse, and he had run superbly, but the horse still needed a capable jockey. Robert struggled with his dilemma: Who would ride the horse in tomorrow's race?

Philip was an able horseman in his own right and might have ridden for Robert, but his size and weight of over twelve stone, compared to the average jockey groom at nine stone, was prohibitive. Jeffries would have been Robert's first choice, but he could not go against his employer. He would no doubt ride for Sir Garfield. Jemmy was among the best exercise riders but hadn't the experience to ride a true race. Though Robert racked his brain, he could think of no other competent rider with whom he could entrust his future.

He needed someone like Charlotte. She was barely eight stone and a crack rider, but women were strictly excluded from racing. He watched her dismount and continued to turn this over in his mind. Technically speaking, it was not a sanctioned race. He and Sir Garfield had settled on the terms without any specifics as to the jockey.

Unlike most gentleman of the turf, Sir Garfield was encumbered by his sheer girth and never rode his own horses. Charles had failed him in the prior run, thus his mandate for a hired jockey.

Though Robert heartily doubted Philip would embrace the idea, he was utterly convinced that Charlotte should ride. It was their best hope to win, but also at their greatest peril.

The night before the race, Charlotte pleaded a headache to excuse herself from dinner, with her ever-faithful Letty promising without hesitation to cover her prevarication until Charlotte's return after the race. Charlotte met Robert in the stables, and the pair journeyed to Doncaster so that Mars would be settled and well rested for the next day's event.

They arrived at dusk and located the stable block farthest from the track, where they could avoid unnecessary contact with others and reduce Charlotte's exposure.

Once their horses were comfortably settled, Robert found a wooden crate to use as a table and unpacked their saddlebags. Letty, in her foresight, had provided them a small meal of bread and cheese, as well as a flask of wine for their supper. After their brief repast, Robert gathered up a large pile of clean straw into a makeshift pallet and covered it with the woolen blanket from his equipage.

Exhausted from the day, he carelessly stretched out upon it, and Charlotte joined him, snuggling up against his side with her head resting on his shoulder. They lay quietly together for some time before Charlotte's whisper broke the silence.

"Robert, what will happen after tomorrow? When we win the race, that is? What will we do?"

He answered while hypnotically stroking her hair. "We'll begin our life, my love," he said simply. "We'll take the mare and the winnings and buy a plot of land. Mars and Amoret will be the foundation of our own racing stud. And with the sale of my commission, we shall purchase the best lot of broodmares we can find."

"Do you know so much of breeding to make a go of it?"

"I have my own theories, though some run contrary to the practices of most breeders."

"In what way?"

"Most men believe the quality of the get is solely determined by the sire. Although a number of stallions have proven exceptionally prepotent, I tend to believe the mare has an equally important role."

"What do you mean by *prepotent*?"

"Ah, 'tis a term I learned while working as a stud groom in the North. Namely, it describes a sire's ability to breed consistently true to type, to stamp his offspring with a high degree of desirable characteristics. In running bloods, this premise of prepotency is impossible to dismiss; however, many foolishly breed a quality stallion with an indifferent mare in the erroneous belief that she is only the vessel. I, however, have a strong notion that coupling such a stallion with a superior mare would produce the best possible result.

"Just look at the top horses of our day. Virtually all of the best runners have sprung from a very limited number of families, begotten by an even more elite group of sires. The Byerley Turk strain is probably the oldest of these lines. When bred to mares of no great quality, there were a few good horses, but when his blood was crossed with that of a well-bred mare of pure Eastern blood, the result was a filly named Bonny Black, who at fours years old beat thirty others at Black Hambleton and repeated the performance the next year. This *mare* later challenged any horse in England four times round the King's Plate course at Newmarket, with no takers.

"The offspring of this cross was the best possible combination. It is then hard for me to believe that one should disregard the importance of the mare, but I digress."

"You were speaking of the most prepotent sire lines," Charlotte prompted.

"Ah, yes. The second great sire line comes by the Darley Arabian, a horse that was also nicked with mediocrity until the fair Betty Leedes."

"I know this story!" Charlotte declared. "Betty Leedes brought forth the famous Flying Childers, and then through her second breeding to the Darley, produced Bartlett's Childers, who was Amoret's sire."

"Indeed, Charlotte. Amoret has exceptional lineage, precisely why she must be our foundation broodmare. Now as to the others we need for our harem, I would have a mind to also seek out mares of Byerley blood, as well as daughters of this Godolphin."

"You mean El Sham," she corrected.

"El Sham, eh? I surmise that Jeffries has entertained you with *his version* of this soon-to-be legend's history."

"Indeed he did! 'Tis such a romantic story, don't you think?"

"Perhaps it is all in the telling, dearest." He chuckled and stroked her cheek.

"Then perhaps I shall recount *my version* to you."

"Pray do so, my sweet." He smiled indulgently.

Bright-eyed, Charlotte began. "The story starts ten years hence. It is a dark, dreary, and rainy morning. An emaciated brown horse strains through the streets of Paris, pulling a water cart. The carter plies the whip to the poor beast, who is too weak to take another step and stumbles to his knees. The man raises the lash again, but the poor horse is too feeble and his knees too ravaged by the cobbles to pull himself up. Observing the incident, a passerby, a foreigner, stays the whip hand of the brute."

"And instead shoots the horse to put him out of his misery," Robert interjected.

Charlotte glares in indignation. "I thought you wanted to hear my story?"

"A million apologies, my sweet." He brings her hand to his lips. Charlotte frowned but was mollified. The tale continued.

"The foreigner is an Englishman and a Quaker, with business in Paris. His heart goes out in sympathy for the poor animal. He offers the carter three gold louis to buy the horse. The carter agrees, in the belief it will cost him more to dispose of the body. He unhitches the cart, and the Englishman, Mr. Coke, leads the horse back to his filthy stable, where to his immense surprise, he finds a blackamoor groom and a large gray cat.

"'What is this?' asked Mr. Coke of the carter.

"'It is a madman, a groom who accompanied the stallion from his homeland and is avowed never to leave his side.'

"'Never?'

"'Never, Monsieur. Queer beliefs have these Moors.'

"'And the cat?'

"'A curiosity. It rarely leaves the horse's side. So for three gold louis, Monsieur, you are now the owner of the horse, the groom, and the cat!'

"Poor Mr. Coke was quite stunned at first, but he did acknowledge the need of a groom to help nurse the poor creature back to strength. After several days, as the animal begins to improve, the gentleman realizes this is no ordinary horse. As poor as he appears, he is possessed of a beautiful conformation. He is exquisitely proportioned, with a small head on a well-arched and heavily crested neck. He is short-coupled with large hocks, tremendous quarters, and a high-set tail. But although he is of incomparable beauty, the stallion is fiery and headstrong.

"Knowing the stallion is too distinctive in appearance to be anything but Eastern bred, Mr. Coke makes inquiries of his friends at Versailles. He is amazed to learn that this pathetic creature was once the pride of the desert, one of the great blood stallions of the Bey of Tunis, given as a gift to the King of France, but was deemed by the equerries as too difficult to manage. This was how he came to the carter.

"Excited by this knowledge, Mr. Coke arranges to transport the new members of his family back to England but finds the stallion gentle only toward his loyal groom and his pet cat, Grimalkin. He is far too volatile for Mr. Coke to ride, so the gentleman gives him to a friend. This friend, failing also to manage the stallion, passes him along to another, and another, until his ultimate fate: this magnificent son of the desert, who once had a harem of the choicest mares of the purest, most ancient blood, was destined to become a lowly and despised teazer stallion for the racing stud of Lord Godolphin."

"Do you even know what that is, my dearest?" Robert interrupted.

"What *what* is?"

"A teazer stallion."

Charlotte blushed. "Yes. Jeffries was kind enough to explain to me that valuable stallions are not wasted with the preliminaries of mating; that a lesser stallion is often utilized to… to… to…"

"Prepare the mare for mating?" Robert offered.

"Yes. Precisely so," Charlotte added hastily. Robert's laugh rumbled deep in his chest.

"Are you quite ready to attend now?" she asked peevishly. He nodded with a smirk, and Charlotte continued her tale. "The pride and joy of Lord Godolphin was Hobgoblin."

"Another fine stallion of the Darley line," Robert volunteered.

"Indeed. And one he intended to breed to his most prized racing mare, the lovely Roxana."

"Do you know of this mare?"

"Only that Jeffries described her as unparalleled."

"In more ways than one. A flightier mare never was. She was of such an excessively nervous temperament that she had to be led to the starting post with a blindfold that was only removed at the word 'go'!"

"I would just call her a female of great sensibility and discriminating taste, Robert," Charlotte defended. "After all, she would have none of Hobgoblin. Though the tale is told that he refused *her*, I am not the least inclined to believe it. She instinctively knew him as the inferior male and had eyes only for El Sham, with whom she demonstrated all willingness. When he was removed from her and Hobgoblin led out to leap her, she repelled him most violently, calling instead to her love, El Sham. That stallion responded to her entreaty by breaking loose from his handler and attacking his rival for her affections.

"The stallions reared and pawed and rained blows upon one another. It appeared, at the start, that Hobgoblin, the larger of the two, would prevail, but El Sham sunk his great teeth into the other stallion's crest and wrestled Hobgoblin to the ground, where he lay stunned. Conceding defeat, Hobgoblin turned tail and ran away."

"And to the winner went the spoils?" Robert added with a grin. "And one year later, Lath arrived, one of the greatest racers of our day. The next year came Cade, and now we see the excitement surrounding Regulus, the third son of Godolphin to make his name on the turf in as many years."

"What was the word you used, pre..."

"Prepotent. Yes, the Godolphin has most definitely made his mark as a champion sire."

"Now you see what a lovely story that was?"

"Not near as lovely as the lips that told it." Robert gently traced her lips with his forefinger. Unconsciously, Charlotte parted them. Robert did not need a second invitation. Their lips met. He moved over hers gently at first, touching, tasting, softly probing. Charlotte responded tentatively to his exploration. He then pulled her closer, molding her to him, and she replied with a sigh and moved instinctively against him.

Such ready compliance was more than Robert had expected. His pulse quickened; his heart pounded painfully against his chest. He desperately yearned to hold her warm, supple, naked body in his arms. To lie with her, kissing, caressing, and breathing in her very essence.

Suddenly with a groan, he put her away and was on his feet, pacing to tamp down his raging fever.

Charlotte regarded him once again in bewilderment. "Please, Robert." She patted the blanket beside her, entreating so softly, so innocently tempting. "There's room for us both, and it will surely grow cold before the night is out."

Was she luring him in this guileless way? Or was she completely unaware of his struggle?

He responded with a scowl, knowing too well the inherent danger of lying together, even if she did not. They were completely alone and had the whole night ahead of them.

"Perhaps you should not be so trusting," he snapped more sharply than intended. "I am not impervious to temptation. *I am but a man.*"

"But I trust you," she said earnestly.

"Perhaps you should not," he replied, resolving right then to protect her honor by upholding his own. Ignoring her wounded look, Robert then gestured for her to bed down while he made ready to sleep against the wall opposite.

"As you will, then, my noble captain," Charlotte whispered and then closed her eyes and fell swiftly into deep slumber. Robert remained as he sat, keeping his silent vigil.

෴

Lady Felicia intercepted Beatrix and Major Drake returning from their interlude in the garden, from whence Beatrix emerged with a telling flush. Determined to encourage what she perceived as a burgeoning attraction between the two, Lady Felicia placed a possessive hand on Philip's sleeve.

"My dear major, do you find our company so lackluster that you would take your leave of us?"

"Indeed not, madam! But I have already greatly imposed. I have no wish to overstay my welcome."

"Pshaw! You will do no such thing. We are country folk here and do not abide by such stringent rules of society. On the contrary, we should not wish to be so soon deprived of your company. I insist you sup with us."

"Indeed, Mama," Beatrix readily agreed.

Philip received the invitation with unabashed delight. He would take full advantage to ingratiate himself to this family. Although Beatrix had thought to have him eating out of her hand, she had played right into his. Now he had an entire evening to dedicate to single-minded pursuit of his heiress and her twenty thousand pounds.

Philip Ian Drake was a born charmer and *raconteur nonpareil*. Although his quick wit and glib tongue had led to more than one caning at Harrow, the same talents had made him exceedingly popular with his classmates, and later, with his fellow cavalry officers. Philip could transform the most mundane event into a comic farce. No one was untouched by his sardonic wit when he chose to yield it.

His repertoire of military tales, political anecdotes, and sordid court gossip entertained and scandalized the Wallace family throughout the evening. He amused Charles with his boyhood pranks and followed with accounts of the Horse Guard, including his hazing of Troopers Devington and Prescott, a tale particularly well received by the chortling baronet.

Philip provided Lady Felicia with several juicy morsels of court gossip.

"Is it true that on Queen Caroline's deathbed she begged our king to remarry?" she asked the major.

"Indeed so. His reply was, 'No, I shall have mistresses!'"

Lady Felicia was aghast. "Surely he said no such thing!"

"There were several witnesses to the exchange. I fail to understand why his response should have surprised anyone at Court."

"Has the King so very many mistresses?" she inquired eagerly.

"Several former ladies of the queen's bedchamber, and even the governess to the Royal princesses. His Majesty is a vain little man who believes that keeping several women confirms his virility."

"Disgraceful! Absolutely disgraceful! But what of that Wallmolden woman?"

"Ah! You refer of course to the Countess of Yarmouth. Seemingly, Hanoverian mistresses surpass English ones in the King's eyes," he remarked sardonically. "Barely a year beyond the queen's passing, His Majesty imported her from Hanover, along with the bastard son he reputedly fathered. Mistress and bastard are both now naturalized and patented with lifetime peerages. She's the King's favorite, the *maitress en titre*, if you will.

"Our poor Queen Caroline, what she endured. God rest her soul."

"Every man has his weakness," Sir Garfield remarked with indifference. "But what of our new foreign secretary, Lord Carteret? I hear he has an uncommon fondness for drink. Surely this is much exaggerated."

"I assure you not, sir. I have it from Ligonier's own lips that our secretary spent the entire German campaign half-soused, though I daresay one with Ligonier's turpitude durst not cast the first stone."

"Indeed, you say?" Sir Garfield's interest was piqued.

"Consummate dissipation might be credited by many as far less egregious than debauching young girls."

Lady Felicia gasped.

"I beg your pardon, madam, for having spoken of it," Philip hastily apologized.

"Debauchery?" she repeated with diminished outrage at the salacious tidbit. "Beatrix," she commanded her daughter, "you must cover your ears."

Beatrix gaped and then protested, "I am not a child, Mama!"

"You heard me, Trixie," she repeated. "Cover your ears!"

Beatrix complied with a petulant pout.

"Now, Major, what is this about debauchery?" Lady Felicia said in a loud whisper and leaned forward eagerly.

Amused by such blatant hypocrisy, Philip obliged. "Sir John Ligonier has only a slightly lesser penchant for drink than our esteemed secretary, but a far greater proclivity for young girls. Though past sixty years, he reputedly keeps four separate mistresses. Although this alone is remarkable for such an ancient, the *pièce de résistance* is that the *combined* ages of said mistresses do not exceed eight-and-fifty years."

Performing the mathematical computation, the lady gasped in coalesced shock and delight. "Surely you hoax, Major!"

"Indeed not, madam. The man states that a woman over fifteen is past her prime and not worth his trouble. All evidence corroborates his belief."

"The dirty lecher!" she exclaimed in outward outrage but was secretly titillated. Now remembering her daughter, she tapped Beatrix on the arm, giving her leave to uncover her ears.

"Drake," Sir Garfield mused Philip's surname aloud. "Your family name's vaguely familiar. From whence do you hail?"

"East Sussex, if you please. The family seat is within an hour of London, though the earl, until recent years, spent a great deal more time in the capital than rusticating in the country."

"East Sussex, eh?" Sir Garfield paused. "I'm surprised you didn't seek your commission in the Royal Navy."

"Truth be told, I'm much more at ease in the saddle than on the deck of a ship," Philip replied.

"Never cared for the sea myself," Sir Garfield agreed. "Much prefer my feet on solid ground."

"What of your mother, dear boy? Does the countess reside in Sussex?" Lady Felicia inquired.

"The dear lady passed away of consumption nearly a decade ago."

"So sorry, my dear," she offered sympathetically. "Have you siblings?"

"One brother, Edmund, Lord Uxeter. He was born to the earl's first wife, who died of fever following childbirth. He's eleven years my senior, hence we've never been close. Staid and humorless type, exceedingly sober and excruciatingly dull. He has aspirations in politics and holds a seat in the House of Commons, though he recently sits as proxy for Lord Hastings in the upper house."

"So, your family has seats in both houses, you say." Sir Garfield digested this tidbit for future rumination. "What is your family's political affiliation? Whig or Tory?"

"The Earl of Hastings descends from a long line of Tories. Although the family claims remote blood connection to William the Conqueror, the patent of earldom was a reward by James the First to my great-grandfather for some long-forgotten favor. The family supported all of the Stuarts until it was no longer politically expedient to do so," he added dryly.

"The Earls of Hastings, past and present, hold very *accommodating* political views, thus my heritage has proven nothing if not resilient. This *tractability*, shall we say, has allowed the family title to survive one regicide, two civil wars, an abdication, a restoration, and several Jacobite uprisings."

"Jacobites! The whole damnable lot do nothing more than blather on impotently about restoration!" Sir Garfield said.

"'Tis ironic, is it not, that the throne of England was endowed by Parliament to the one man who truly didn't want it! 'Tis said of George the First that he knew nothing, he desired to know nothing, and he did nothing. The only good spoke of him at all was that he would have loved nothing more than to hand the English Crown *back to its heredity successor.*"

"I can't say which is easier to swallow: to live under the tyrannical Stuarts or under the war-mongering Hanoverians. George the Second will have us a bloody province of his beloved Hanover before 'tis all over. Mark my words on it!"

"Regardless of kings, sir, we are obligated by treaty to act in our allies' defense. Though I don't deny the King has his own agenda," Philip replied.

"Englishmen have no business fighting on the Continent. It wasn't enough to fight Spain; now we would commence hostilities with France," Sir Garfield said. "If an Englishman must die, better in defending one's own country, I say."

"But surely, Father, you would not allow France to overrun all of Europe?" Charles protested.

"Again this tedious talk of politics and war!" Beatrix rolled her eyes.

"As you say, my lady, immensely tedious," Philip agreed with warm sympathy.

"My dear gentlemen," Lady Felicia interrupted, "if the conversation is to continue on this bellicose theme, Beatrix and I shall retire to the drawing room. We shall not wait for you, so pray enjoy your port. And, Major,"—she paused—"I shall have a chamber prepared for you. It is far too late for you to ride back to your lodgings. Don't you agree, Sir Garfield?"

"Just so, madam. Just so," he agreed affably enough.

"My sincerest gratitude, my lady." Drake rose in a bow as she and Beatrix departed. The footman, leaving in their wake, promptly returned with several bottles of Portugal's finest vintages, and then produced several chamber pots, placed convenient to each gentleman.

While the footman returned to refill their wine glasses, Sir Garfield stood to relieve himself. "Thought I'd bloody well burst before the women left." As he filled the vessel, he grunted and then sighed with satisfaction. "It's damnably inconvenient to drink in mixed company!"

"Quite so, sir," Philip agreed, gratified that the baronet had at least the courtesy to turn his back to the table.

Speaking over his shoulder, Sir Garfield revisited politics. "So the question remains, Drake, where do you and your family stand?"

"Following family tradition, I daresay Edmund is hedging his bets," he replied with a smirk. "He has joined the so-called Patriot Whigs who pay court to the Prince of Wales."

Sir Garfield remarked, "Forming an alliance with the future heir shows foresight as well as ambition, I'd say."

"Quite," he replied curtly, uninterested in discussing his brother.

Resuming his place at the table, Sir Garfield took up his glass. "But what of *your* ambitions?" he asked.

"For the moment, His Majesty has my future in his hands. While we've thousands of troops on the Continent, it is said King Louis would render assistance to restore the Pretender."

"Do you give any credence to such talk?" Charles asked.

"The threat may be credible. The Scots are either gullible enough or naively loyal enough to raise the Pretender's standard yet again. 'Tis yet hard to say how much support they might garner among the English, but we could expect some trouble from that quarter." Philip's reply was pragmatic.

"What of your leanings, Major? You wear the King's regimentals, but do you favor the King, his heir, or the Pretender?" Sir Garfield asked.

"In sum, I am first and foremost an Englishman, loyal to my country to my very death. As to the King, I defer to the poet John Byrom." The major raised his glass in a sardonic salute:

"God bless the King, I mean the faith's defender,
God bless, (no harm in blessing), the Pretender,
But who Pretender is, or who is King,
God bless us all, that's quite another thing."

Sir Garfield thumped the table heartily. "Here, here. Damn the Papists, the Jacobites, and the Hanover-lovers, too!" he bellowed, now well in his cups.

"I would that I could join you in the army," Charles replied in growing resentment of his father's injunction.

"Ever seen a battle, Charles?" Philip demanded of the callow youth. "The cannon charge is deafening, the smoke acrid and smothering as it hits one's lungs. Ever seen a man die? Once he realizes he's hit, the sheer panic is replaced by a vacuous disbelief glazing his eyes as his lifeblood drains slowly away. Furthermore, have you ever killed a man? Once one has regained enough composure to survey the aftermath of battle, the stench of blood and grotesque scene of miscellaneous disembodied parts scattering the field is sickening. It's ubiquitous and inescapable. War is not the romantic drivel conveyed to us by poets, Charles. War is emphatically unromantic. It is massive and overpowering death."

"The man's right, Charles. War's a vile business, vile business!" Sir Garfield said.

"But it is one's duty and honor to defend one's king and country. A soldier's life has purpose!" Charles rejoined.

"'Tis no purpose at all for an only son! I say, leave war to the ones who can be spared!" his father retorted.

"Indeed, 'tis precisely why the *spare* son is so highly recommended," Philip remarked laconically.

"'Twas not exactly what I intended, Drake," Sir Garfield blustered.

"I comprehend *precisely* your meaning, sir," he replied evenly. "'Tis true, Charles, that some must fight. I would that I needn't; however, soldiering is one of few honorable professions open to a younger son. Some achieve glory and others an early grave, and I confess I aspire to the former." Philip laughed, altering the conversation's morose tone.

Sir Garfield stifled a yawn. "I aspire to a comfortable bed and a fluffy pillow. So I bid you good night, Drake." He then emptied his last glass of port, and on the second attempt, hefted onto his feet.

The younger men followed suit and staggered up the stairs to their respective chambers.

Having brought no change of clothing, Philip undressed for bed and moved to snuff the candle. He was arrested by a light scratch at the door. Snatching on his breeches, he opened it with a mild curse. There stood Beatrix, garbed in her dressing gown, with her long, blond hair tumbling freely over her shoulders.

His gaze raked over her, and his instincts overruled his judgment.

Casting a cursory glance down the hallway, he hauled her brusquely into the privacy of his room.

"Now what the devil are you doing here?" he asked.

Beatrix suddenly grasped the weight of her actions. She was alone with a man in his bedchamber. She trembled at her own daring, but any trepidation was now overcome by something more powerful... rousing... exciting. She had never before experienced such a physical awareness, such a heightening of her senses as in this illicit moment.

"I-I desired a private word," she began.

"And the matter was so urgent it could not wait until morning?"

"Quite urgent, I assure you." she said and boldly entwined her arms about his neck. "But suddenly I've forgotten what it was." She pressed herself against him and reveled in the sensation of the thin silk against his bare torso.

Philip tried to ignore the sudden stirrings of arousal. No *gentleman* would seduce a young woman under her father's roof, though one could debate who was the seducer when a nubile young woman appears half dressed at said gentleman's room in the dead of night.

He considered the point moot and attempted only halfheartedly to extricate himself from her hold.

"One would hope you are well aware of the danger you court in coming to my room like this," he said softly.

"Danger?" she whispered back provocatively. "What kind of danger?"

Purposefully he angled her hips to him and gripped the globes of her buttocks.

She gasped but made no move to retreat.

His low and husky voice breached the silence. "I believe you have just made a most irrevocable decision, my lady."

The line now crossed, there was no turning back.

Fifteen

THE REMATCH

❧

The morning dawned foggy with a light, misting rain, unfavorable conditions for spectators but advantageous to the incognito rider. Having garbed herself again as a lad, Charlotte tightly bound her bosom and even added light padding to her clothes in order to better simulate the male form.

She wore an oversized jacket, a muffler up to her chin, and her long honeyed tresses were tightly confined in a snug-fitting jockey's cap. Thus prepared, she waited impatiently to present herself for Robert's inspection.

He returned from his brief meeting with Sir Garfield and the racing stewards and declared, "All is in readiness, and Philip has agreed to assist."

"Philip?" she asked dubiously. "What can he possibly do?"

"Never underestimate the talents and resourcefulness of the man, Charlotte. Major Drake will sit with the Wallaces and do what he does best, provide diversion at any sign of trouble. I am entirely confident in his abilities and am astonished at how warmly the master of Heathstead Hall embraces him. He will play this to our advantage."

"I know he's your friend, Robert, but there's something about him I just can't trust."

"He is given to caprice, I'll admit, but he's been as a brother to me. Besides, how could I not trust a man who saved my life?"

"How could you not," she replied.

"Drake shall attend to Sir Garfield. Now, as to your disguise." He circled once to inspect her and grinned appreciatively. "You are *nearly* the same young scamp I first mistook you for those years ago. But wait, there is something missing..." He cocked his head, studying her. "Indeed, I have it." He grinned broadly.

As he stooped to the rain-softened ground, scooping up half a handful of mud, she looked her question, and to her chagrin, he smeared it on her face.

"It's not horse dung, but I had to do something to counter such a suspiciously pretty face."

She laughed outright at the shared remembrance of their very first encounter after she and Jemmy had milled in the stable yard.

Robert nodded approval at his finishing touch, and he continued coaching her. "Now you are a lad who has taken his mount for an airing. I believe you shall pass muster to any but the veriest scrutiny. Now, what is your name?" he grilled.

"Charlie Devington, your cousin, recently apprenticed in Lichfield."

"Just so." He nodded. "But when you speak, Charlotte, and don't do so more than necessary, remember to lower your voice and evade eye contact as much as possible. Avoid Jeffries. He is the one I am wary of exposing you. He won't be fooled for a moment by your disguise."

"But he has been a loyal friend to both of us for years. Why should you doubt him now?"

"Suffice to say I question his loyalty only if his livelihood at Heathstead Hall should come into jeopardy. I shouldn't blame him, of course, but pray try to keep your distance from him."

"I understand. I shall not let you down. We shall prevail, Robert."

"Yes, my love. We shall."

❧

Charlotte, in assisting Robert with the final preparations, was completely puzzled by his instructions.

"Hold his tail up for me, Charlotte. I daresay he won't care much for what I am about to do." Charlotte's eyes widened, and Mars kicked out to demonstrate his immense displeasure as Robert inserted a large syringe into the horse's rectum.

"What in heaven's name are you doing?" she asked in bewilderment.

He answered matter-of-factly, "Using every weapon in the arsenal. A bit of alum and water will cause him to tighten his sphincter muscles, thus preventing him from taking in air thru the rectum that might later cause abdominal cramping."

Robert then removed his neck cloth and tore a narrow strip from the fine linen. Charlotte looked her question this time.

"I am going to tie his tongue down," he answered the silent query.

"Why would you do such a thing?"

A horse's wind is every bit as important as his legs. With insufficient air, he cannot last. By tying it down, the horse's tongue cannot obstruct his airway while running."

"But you did none of this before," she remarked.

"I did not feel it necessary when challenged by no better horseman than your cousin Charles. But in this contest, we have need of every advantage."

Suddenly feeling the weight on her shoulders, Charlotte swallowed hard in apprehension.

At precisely 9:45 a.m., the jockeys presented to the clerk of the scales where Charlotte mumbled her responses exactly as rehearsed. The preparations moved forward without incident, until shocked and dismayed, Charlotte discovered the identity of her adversary. Rather than mounting one of his own grooms on Rascallion, Sir Garfield had hired Jake Harrow to ride!

Harrow was a small, mean-spirited veteran of the turf, who had reputedly never lost a race. He knew how to bully it all out of his horses, pushing them to their limits, and some beyond. All his mounts won, though some never raced again.

Charlotte was astonished that Jeffries would allow this cruel and callous man anywhere near a horse he had trained, let alone ride one of his best. Noticing for the first time Jeffries's conspicuous absence, she could only surmise he had no say in the matter. If so, he likely wouldn't even watch the proceedings. Her uncle was very desperate, indeed, to hire such as Jake Harrow.

At precisely ten o'clock, and in fine form, the sleek, leggy colt Rascallion eagerly pranced alongside the leading groom as he proceeded to the start. Once his rider mounted, the horse practically cantered in place in his impatience to start. Raring to go, the young horse appeared the sure bet, but as Rascallion pulled alongside Mars—snorting, head tossing, and eyeing his competitor—the jockey took him forcibly in hand.

Holding hard at the starting post, horse and rider gave their competition an aggressive once-over, scornfully eyeing Charlotte and her battle-scarred mount. "Bloody snot-nosed apprentice! Should have demanded another ten quid from the ole gaffer for this!" Jake snorted derisively and intentionally loud enough for Charlotte's ears.

Avoiding Jake's eye, Charlotte struggled to compose her jangled nerves. *Focus. Focus. Can't think about him. Breathe. Just breathe!*

Mars tensed in anticipation, but except for the occasional flicker of his ears, he was as a statue compared to the tightly wound beast beside him. One unacquainted with Mars might misperceive his manner as lethargic, but that would be a grave error. Mars didn't expend his energy injudiciously. He amassed it, kindled it into a pent-up flame, and at the signal would ignite with the sheer force of it.

Coiled and poised for his signal, the stallion closely attended to his rider. In the months following Dettingen, Robert had spent countless hours training Mars for battle and honing one key trait, a trait even deviant to the equine nature… patience. Patience was for the predator in stalking his prey, but to the prey animal, it was unnatural and perilous. Patience meant certain death.

As a charger, Mars had been taught to entrust his very life unto the master, to conquer his innate fear and charge without hesitation into the full fury of battle. In so doing, the horse had transitioned in his mind from prey to predator. He had learned to anticipate his master's signal and succumb to his will. He awaited that signal now, and as the starter lowered the flag, Charlotte gave Mars what he most desired. They were off!

Mars surged forth from the start, head low, nose to the ground, hooves digging and clawing at the soft, moist earth, tearing a blazing trail down the turf. Rascallion, long forelegs stretching, reaching, slicing the air, also broke remarkably strong. Both horses fought valiantly from the start for the elusive prize, the yearned for, coveted, oh-so-precious early lead.

Though Rascallion was unquestionably improved in the past few days, Mars was still stronger. With little encouragement from Charlotte, he lengthened his stride, eating up yards of turf, gaining a clean lead with Rascallion chasing nose to tail behind them.

Although Mars claimed his lead effortlessly, Charlotte's dilemma was how hard to press him. If she asked, he would put such distance between them that Rascallion would be hard at it ever to catch up, but this risked using Mars up. Although he performed superlatively in their training, Mars was a warhorse. Did he truly have the heart and soul of a running blood?

How long could he sustain this blistering speed? Moreover, could he produce the same in a second heat? Did he have it in him to answer when the time was ripe? As she debated holding back, these were the unknowns. They *needed* to take the first heat, but if she used him up to claim it, he might have nothing left in the second and be obligated to fight to the death in the third. If they won now and she preserved just enough of him to take the next, he need not run the third. Her decision was critical. Her future with Robert rested on her judgment.

Though it would mean a hotter contest now, she determined to conserve him. Almost imperceptibly, Charlotte's fingers crept along the reins. Remembering Robert's words about the silken thread, she took up slack by minute degrees. Mars reluctantly conceded his will, snorting in protest and letting Rascallion creep back into his line of sight.

Coming out of the bend and into the stretch, Rascallion clamored for the lead and surged forth with renewed vigor. Gaining momentum with his refreshed confidence, he crept up alongside Mars, but this wasn't enough for Harrow, who commenced his particular brand of "encouragement." Rascallion, always a willing runner, continued in rare form but was clearly resentful of the crop.

Charlotte had known Rascallion from his first days under Jeffries. She had watched the trainer work with him and knew his mind. She had never quite taken a fancy to Rascallion, as he been unpredictable and refractory at times, but he had come along well enough under Jeffries's firm but gentle hand. The trainer understood how to work *with* the horse rather than fighting against him, using firm and persistent persuasion rather than brute force to manage the colt's irascible temper. Some horses didn't take well to bullying, and Rascallion was one of them.

His ire was unmistakable in the angry glare of his eye and in the flattening of his ears with the jockey's every downward stroke. Charlotte had witnessed Rascallion's temper firsthand and mused with a faint smile that it might soon prove Jake Harrow's undoing.

Holding Mars in check, shoulder at Rascallion's flank, they pounded along, waiting and watching. Charlotte would let them hold the lead, but just barely, just enough to keep the pressure cooking. Holding this position and preserving Mars, she would watch their opponents for any sign of weakness or fatigue, any window of opportunity as they drew nearer the finish. She would not push needlessly but would wait until the time was ripe.

Charlotte smiled with renewed confidence in her strategy. Her fingers slowly played, releasing first an inch and then two of slack. Mars, in tune with his rider, took his cue, once more gathering just enough speed to creep up along the outside, now shoulder to shoulder in synchronous stride with the increasingly agitated Rascallion.

Harrow, conscious of their advance, was either too callous to care or completely oblivious to the growing distress of his mount, even with the clear warning signs his colt exhibited as he plied the whip. The heedless jockey, intent only upon the finish line, prepared to thrash more speed out of a horse that was rapidly coming unglued. The colt was near boiling point, straining under the jockey's brutality, now more concerned about the crop than the track under his hooves.

His distress suddenly morphed into something much more dangerous. His ears pinned flat to his head, his nostrils flared blood red, his tail thrashed in open rebellion, and his eyes rolled menacingly back in a final unheeded warning. Charlotte *almost* felt pity for the jockey and yet again encouraged Mars. Leaning closer, chin to his mane, she loosened her fingers and released more slack. In instant response, he surged forth, and Harrow raised his crop for the very last time.

Rascallion had had enough!

The colt insidiously detonated by slamming all of his forward momentum onto the forehand. Harrow pitched ten feet straight into the air, arse over teakettle, before landing in a ghastly tangled, muddy mass.

Once free of his tormentor, Rascallion rejoiced! He spun, bucking and rearing gleefully, and ran to beat hell, finishing half a length ahead of Mars. The mutinous colt then celebrated his freedom with

a victory lap and was halfway again around the track before the
elusive Jeffries materialized to take him in hand.

The crowd went wild to get a firsthand glimpse of the broken
body, while the physician called to examine the mangled Mr. Harrow
promptly announced the end of the infamous jockey's riding days.
He had finally met his match in the murderous Rascallion.

The stewards, aghast at such goings-on, having never before
witnessed such a grisly incident, called a special race meeting.
Charlotte, during the deliberations, slipped warily away from the
crowds. Meeting Robert, Charlotte dismounted, handing Mars off to
a waiting groom for hot walking while they awaited the decision.

Although Rascallion had technically crossed the finish line ahead
of Mars, even an unsanctioned race could not concede the win to a
jockey-less horse. The stewards unanimously decided heat number
one in Mars's favor and called for a one-hour hiatus, during which
time Sir Garfield was required to hire a new jockey or forfeit.

Sir Garfield called for Jeffries to ride, but the trainer adamantly
declared himself unfit. Sir Garfield had completely dismissed his
advice regarding Rascallion's readiness to run. He had compounded
this transgression against his trainer in hiring such a known scoundrel as Jake Harrow. Thoroughly disgusted by the travesty, Jeffries
outright refused to ride.

Charles, however, perceived in this moment his opportunity to
finally prove his worth to his father and to make atonement for his
first defeat. Willing himself to overcome his apprehension, he spoke
up. "Let me ride in the next race."

"Absolutely not!"

"But why not? I've raced him before!"

"And a damned poor showing you made of it, Charles," his father
said. "Besides, after what befell Harrow I could never allow it. Let
some other poor sod risk his fool neck."

Sir Garfield was furious but refused to cry off. He dispatched

Jeffries to hire another jockey, but remarkably, in a town full of racing stables, there was none to be hired, leastwise not to mount the "homicidal" Rascallion. Eyes bulging and purpling with rage, Sir Garfield bellowed that he would find another jockey if he had to scrounge the bowels of hell for one.

With opportunity so blatantly presented, Philip hadn't the will to resist.

❦

"What news?" Robert anxiously inquired of Phillip.

"Seems we have a predicament, ol' chap. Curiously, Sir Garfield can't find a replacement jockey. Even at quadruple the going rate, he had no takers. Superstitious lot," he scoffed. "Seems they all believe the colt demon-possessed."

"One can hardly blame them after that performance!" Robert chuckled. "Will he forfeit, then?"

"Refuses to cry off, but he's requesting a renegotiation."

"A what?" Charlotte interjected.

"A renegotiation of the terms," Philip replied matter-of-factly. "The original agreement was for each horse to carry a hired jockey, but Jeffries claims to have injured his shoulder chasing down the obstreperous colt. With no other jockey for hire, Sir Garfield respectfully requests a reversion to Newmarket rules: gentlemen only to ride."

Robert brightened. "This is exceptional news! I had feared Charlotte's discovery every moment, and Charles is no match for me. Never has been. 'Twill be an effortless victory."

"This is decidedly to our advantage, Robert," Charlotte agreed. "Charles is barely more than a competent rider."

Philip interrupted. "I fear you both labor under some misapprehension. Charles Wallace is not to ride."

"If not Charles, then who?" Charlotte asked, bewildered.

"Simply stated, me."

"Surely you jest, Drake!" Robert exclaimed in disbelief.

"I assure you, 'tis no jest."

"Just whose side are you on?" Charlotte exclaimed.

"Why mine, of course. When have I implied otherwise?"

"But why would my uncle possibly trust you?" she asked incredulously.

"We came to a mutually advantageous agreement," Philip replied blandly. "After some manner of negotiations, Sir Garfield put forth such an attractive offer that I could find no reason to refuse. You came to Yorkshire in pursuit of your ambition, Devington, and I came with mine. The ends justify the means," Philip replied unabashedly.

"The devil you say, Philip! This changes everything!"

"Indeed. The weights are decidedly a problem. I daresay poor Rascallion must now carry near thirteen stone."

"That's hardly what I meant! I say Sir Garfield should forfeit."

"He is unlikely to do so with any measure of grace, Devington. I should think it much more to your advantage to finish this business in a sporting fashion. Indeed, I have a strong yen for sport. Are you not up to the challenge, old man?" He goaded Devington with an arrogant arch of his brow. "It's been some time since we two have pitted our skill against one another. The training field at Woolwich last comes to mind."

"Woolwich was decidedly to my disadvantage, and you know it. The scales were balanced in your favor; you designed it so."

"Decidedly, Devington. I could hardly allow a green recruit to show me up in front of the ranks, could I? But I'll promise you a fair run."

"Think again, Drake, if you imagine besting me on the racecourse!"

"I count you a worthy adversary, Devington, though Rascallion appears more than capable of the challenge. 'Twas exceedingly ill-judged of Sir Garfield to place him in that imbecile Harrow's hands.

The horse simply wants for a rider with more finesse. Now what do you say? I have thrown down the gauntlet. Do you accept?"

"Bloody hell, Drake, I accept!"

With public executions the most popular entertainment of the day, word spread like wildfire of the continuation of the race featuring the homicidal horse. With their nominally suppressed appetites for blood whetted by the earlier race, the Doncaster populace thronged to the rail in eager anticipation of Rascallion's next performance.

Robert recognized the raw talent, the fleetness of the younger horse, particularly once liberated from his brutal jockey. Rascallion under pressure was volatile and easily rattled, but Philip Drake, an expert rider with a level head and a light hand, was just the sort to manage such volatility.

The major, fully cognizant of his mount's weaknesses, would ride him accordingly, and if he could sufficiently focus Rascallion to bring all to bear, he would be a daunting, if not invincible, foe.

Robert still harbored some doubt that Mars possessed the sheer swiftness to outrun the younger colt, especially with the onerous thirteen stone he must carry to even the odds. The going under such weight would prove arduous, but Mars was intrepid to the last, and when asked, would give all without faltering.

Robert rested unwaveringly in his horse's courage and strength of will, but Philip would know how to get the most out of Rascallion. He hoped he needn't press Mars for supreme efforts. Robert would have to ride smart if they would prevail.

Once mounted and ready, the two officers proceeded to the starting post. Mars, well collected, proceeded as before, keenly aware of his rider's anticipation. Philip had the rambunctious Rascallion surprisingly well in hand, and the snorting colt sidled up to the start. Saluting one another, they nodded readiness to the steward, who lowered the flag.

The two horses burst forward in unison, but Rascallion, encouraged by his earlier success, initiated his new rider with a wild bucking spree. Demonstrating great prowess in the saddle, Philip was unmoved and smartly pulled the colt's head up to regain control. Philip knew from the prior run that this colt was, in Newmarket jargon, a "fizzy" runner. Such types never bore heavy management. Rascallion needed to be eased along in his running. Rather than holding fast to the horse, Drake mystified the spectators by crouching low over the testy colt's neck and murmuring words of encouragement.

Under Drake's cool and calm management, Rascallion remarkably forgot his act of rebellion. He once again pricked his ears to dash forward with great celerity, anxious to regain his lost ground. Having now won his first round with the colt, Philip channeled Rascallion's surplus of nervous energy to setting his mind back on the field.

Robert laid low over the gray, his reins laced loosely through his fingers, while Mars galloped in cadence with his rider's pounding heart. Briefly closing his eyes, Robert sensed well before he heard the thunderous approach of Philip and Rascallion coming up hard upon them.

Mars waited, as if baiting the other horse. Rascallion's nose appeared at his flank. Mars still waited. The colt crept up. They were shoulder to shoulder arcing around the bend. The tension rose in Mars. His body recoiling, he pushed onward but made no attempt to accelerate beyond the pace asked by his rider.

Stretching forward neck and neck, Rascallion glared at the gray, tossing his head while his forelegs reached, slicing the air as they proceeded down the track. Refusing to yield, Mars matched stride for stride, hanging alongside.

Rascallion fought to shake off Mars and gain the lead, but the gray refused to give an inch. With a deep and audible groan, the chestnut heaved and strained in another vain attempt, but dogged in his determination, Mars unremittingly clung to Rascallion.

Mars now displayed visible signs of fatigue. His light gray coat was coated with sweat. Foam spewed from his mouth. His sides heaved with every new stride, yet he relentlessly persevered, his cadence never faltering.

The battle heightened in intensity, and the wild-eyed Rascallion began to exhibit chinks in his armor. In his frustration to break free from Mars, the chestnut gnashed at the bit and shook his head in ire. While his mount was holding up well physically, Philip struggled to manage Rascallion's undisciplined mind and bilious temper. Another push could drive the fitful young stallion over the brink. The pair of riders entered the home stretch. The moment of decision had arrived.

Philip knew the potential of the colt under him. Although volatile, managed properly, the horse was a winner, and Philip himself was competitively driven. He had begun the race with a single purpose: to win. His heiress and her twenty thousand could be his, but in the final seconds, his conscience pricked like a needle.

"Bloody hell!" he swore and imperceptibly shifted his weight into his seat, just cue enough to give his horse pause. It was all the advantage Robert needed.

Mars, the warrior horse, was the undisputed victor.

As the final seconds unfurled, Sir Garfield leapt to his feet and nearly tumbled from the dais. His triumph had once again slipped elusively through his fingers, or in his mind, through Philip's fingers. Sir Garfield stormed onto the field in a blustering rage to confront the dismounting major. "What the devil was that performance? You could easily have overtaken them! The horse proved it in the last run!"

Philip handed the hot colt off to Jeffries's tender care, calmly responding, "You forget the colt was riderless and therefore at some advantage."

"What game do you think you're playing, Drake? You let the damned bounder win!"

"You suspect I am in league with Devington? I assure you not, sir. Our arrangement was as much to my benefit as yours."

Philip impassively waited for Sir Garfield to fully and unreservedly vent his spleen, allowing him to run out of breath before answering the accusations flung in his face.

"With all due respect, *good sir*, the horse was coming undone, nearly over the brink, as it were. He's a fine runner but has an exceedingly fizzy temperament. He would have no future at all should I have pushed him beyond his limits. Racing is as much a matter of disciplining the horse's mind as it is his body. Many four-year-olds aren't mature enough to handle this kind of pressure."

"How dare you lecture me on my stock! I've owned runners since you were suckling your mother's teat, you insolent cur!"

"I repeat, it was to my advantage to ride the colt to victory, but that would have been his undoing. 'Twould have been a very short-lived victory and an ultimate crime if one ill-conceived match race ruined a promising career. In truth," he drawled, "I did you a great service by saving this good horse for future races."

In full accord with the major, Jeffries jumped in, "Aye, he be right, sir. I've said as much, but ye wouldn't heed me. Yer got a prime piece of horseflesh in Rascallion, but like yer prized burgundies, 'e needs a bit of age on him. Knew from the beginning 'twas no good, this race. The major done right by 'im. Though I daresay naught will convince ye o' it." The trainer snorted his indignation and took his young charge off for cooling.

"Believe what you will, sir." Philip turned on his heel. With his aspirations temporarily thwarted, Philip would console himself with a bottle of smuggled French brandy and a warm woman. He had a good notion where to find both, but he first sought out Devington.

"My congratulations on a hellava ride, Devington! Devilish good sport!"

This said, he departed, leaving the astonished captain to wonder, *yet again*, just what Philip Drake was all about.

Sixteen

༄

BROKEN PROMISES

Soon to be five hundred pounds richer, and with Sir Garfield's consent guaranteed, Robert's long-sought goal was finally within grasp. With the sale of his commission, Charlotte's dowry, and Mars and Amoret as their foundation stock, he and Charlotte would be well set to start their own racing stud. Perhaps they could leave Yorkshire behind and settle in Newmarket. Lost in his musings, Robert proceeded to Heathstead Hall, intending to press for a spring wedding.

Letty intercepted Robert upon his arrival and handed him a hastily scribed note from Charlotte. "She can't see ye, Captain. He's locked her in her rooms," the maid said apologetically.

His face flushed upon reading her words:

Dearest Robert,

I am disconsolate that I shan't see you before you depart, my uncle having now resorted to the crudest measures. Still unmoved in accepting your suit, there is naught to change his mind.

I had falsely hoped that upon your return, he would finally see you as a man worthy of his respect, and moreover, as the man I love. But alas, my dearest, he cares for no one's happiness but his own. I despair for our future unless we act soon. We must find a way.

Pray send me word as soon as you are able, and know that only you have my heart.
Your Most Devoted,
Charlotte

Struggling to maintain his equanimity, Robert sought out Sir Garfield, striding with grim determination past the protesting footman to Sir Garfield's sanctum. Seated behind his great mahogany desk in the library, the baronet glowered. "What is the meaning of this intrusion? I gave strict orders that I should not be disturbed!" Sir Garfield reprimanded the harried footman who had followed in Devington's wake.

Robert posed his response with forced civility. "As you might expect, sir, I have come to see our wager settled and to speak with Charlotte."

"Charlotte is indisposed," the baronet replied contemptuously.

"I request only a brief word, sir."

"As I stated, she is indisposed!" he repeated sternly as he sharpened a quill.

"I respectfully remind you of our agreement, sir."

Sir Garfield paused with his penknife before meeting Devington's eyes. "Our agreement, you say? I have no obligation to you. Our wager is null and void."

"What did you say?"

"A wager is an agreement of *honor* between two gentlemen," he said condescendingly, "but it is revealed to me that our race was run under most *dishonorable* pretences, Captain."

"What do you mean?"

"You know bloody well what I mean. My wayward niece rode disguised as a boy in the first race. I never should have believed it but for Charles. He recognized something familiar in the rider, as did Jeffries, and the stable hands confirmed it. I know all about Charlotte's surreptitious rides."

Robert's face was ashen. "The race was run fairly under the rules we established at the outset. The rider's gender was never specified."

"As you well know, Newmarket rules prohibit females from riding."

"I don't dispute this; however, the same rules specify only gentlemen to ride. When you hired a jockey, Newmarket rules no longer applied." He knew it a lame argument and should have saved his breath.

"At my behest, the Doncaster officials conferred and agree that women are exclusively banned from *all* racing. Moreover, this act of fraud is not your first offense. Under the circumstances, I was compelled to reveal your prior duplicity at the Lichfield races, and they unanimously agreed the race is forfeit. I have no obligation to honor the wager of a cheat, and this embarrassment will never blight the racing record of a clearly superior running blood. Moreover, you are officially banned from the turf," he finished with a self-satisfied gleam.

Banned from the turf? The man was bent to destroy him. Robert was at a loss to understand the reason behind such loathing. "I ask you, Sir Garfield," he said, enunciating his words with care, "is it that you can't stomach losing or can't stomach losing *to me*?"

The truth was that Sir Garfield saw in Devington's triumph not only his defeat on the turf but the ruination of all his long-laid plans. He was infuriated by his loss but even more by the threat Devington represented to *all* his ambitions.

Sir Garfield's success in racing was his means of achieving upward social mobility. Rascallion had represented his best prospect since the mare he had sold to the king of France.

Sir Garfield's second means of attaining his ambitions was through a marital alliance with a peer of the realm. With numerous noble estates teetering on the brink of bankruptcy, many aristocrats would deign to marry below their class, given sufficient pecuniary persuasion. Such was Sir Garfield's design for both his daughter and his niece, who were now of marriageable age. He would be damned to hell before allowing this presumptuous upstart to lay waste to everything!

"I won our wager, Sir Garfield, and will claim what is *mine*," Robert declared. "I will have Charlotte."

"Hear me once more, Devington; I will not ever sanction the union of my niece with a stable hand."

"I am no longer your infernal stable hand! You may think to keep me in my place, as you did my father, but I am *not* my father, nor will I ever allow another man to dictate my future and my happiness."

"Then seek your damned future and happiness elsewhere. Get out of my house before I throw you out!" Sir Garfield directed an unspoken command to the footman to conduct the captain to the door.

Robert hesitated but recognized he had no choice. His appeal had failed; the same scene had replayed. Again. What right had the man to snub him so? Robert had left Yorkshire with virtually nothing and returned a captain. He had gained the respect of his men as well as his superiors, yet Sir Garfield regarded him with nothing less than seething contempt. "Damn the man!" Robert cursed.

Finding no one about to carry word to Charlotte, he conceded defeat and headed for the stables, where he reluctantly saddled Mars and departed for Sheffield. He arrived at the tavern well after dark. After settling his horse, he headed straight to the near-deserted taproom, fully intent on drowning his sorrows. His customary small beer wouldn't dull *this* pain. Glancing above the bar, he read the placard: *Drunk for a penny, dead drunk for tuppence, clean straw for nothing.*

He tossed down thruppence, and the barkeep assured him of achieving his inebriated stupor with contraband gin. Devington lifted the bottle in salute. "Like father, like son," he mumbled. Forgoing the dirty glass, he took a great choking draught of the rotgut disguised as drink. Having eaten nothing since breaking his fast, several more swigs had him well on his way to his yearned-for oblivion.

Perceiving a familiar low rumble from the back corner of the dim taproom, Robert spun around. His bleary-eyed squint revealed Philip Drake fondling a woman who sat on his lap, giggling in obviously feigned protest. With a grimace at the bawdy display, Robert advanced a bit unsteadily toward the preoccupied couple. He thumped his bottle loudly on the table to announce himself, and then slumped heavily and unceremoniously into the opposing chair.

"Devington, what an unanticipated surprise," Philip drawled in apparent displeasure. Devington failed to respond but knocked back draughts of gin at a rate that impressed even the jaded major.

Now that he perceived his miserable friend was come to seek his counsel, Philip heaved a reluctant sigh and gently settled Maggie back on her feet with a not-so-gentle pat on her shapely derriere.

Nodding her understanding, Maggie gathered up their empty glasses, and with sultry look of promise cast over her shoulder, she sashayed away. Philip's gaze riveted on her departing bottom for several seconds before transferring back to Robert. He helped himself to a drink from the rapidly diminishing supply and then addressed his companion. "I scarce thought to see you so soon, but I surmise from your untimely appearance that matters failed to transpire to your expectations."

"No, it bloody well didn't turn out."

"What now, then? How shall you go on?"

"B'damned if I know."

"Well, old chap, let's take stock of the situation. Charlotte still agrees to have you?"

"I've no doubt of her devotion. Charlotte's constant as the sun."

"Although poetic, I question your metaphor. The sun disappears every night. What would this imply of her nocturnal fidelity?" He smirked, and Robert glowered.

"My apologies, Devington. A man in his cups is scarce expected to reason clearly or appreciate irony. So I shall endeavor to aid you. Now, where were we? Oh yes, her devotion. There is still some hope, then. I suppose you're now contemplating elopement?"

"I can't do it! Though I know she'd have me, I can't go to her penniless. The five hundred from the race, combined with her dowry, would have been more'n enough to keep her in comfort, but the old rotter reneged on the wager, and without his blessing, there's no dowry. I've naught to my name but a captain's wages and fifty guineas from the first race. If we elope, she'd be condemned to a life following the drum in a soldier's camp. She deserves better, much better." His voice fell, and he downed another draught.

"Indeed. The truest love and devotion are known to diminish with privation and penury. But we're soldiers, Devington. 'Tis the life we've chosen, or perhaps it chose us. On either score, a soldier lives by his fortune, and fortune is exceedingly fickle. My point is that it can change on a whim. The corpulent old bugger could pop off tomorrow; then what?"

"Charles'd inherit and assume guardianship of Charlotte."

"And would Charles follow his father's lead? Seemed an amiable enough chap to me."

Robert raised the bottle, pausing midair to consider this thought. "Really can't say what Charles's disposition would be. S'pose he might be amenable."

"Then, it appears you have some choices: either abscond with the chit to Scotland for a clandestine marriage and live thenceforth in your blissful poverty, or wait until Charlotte comes of age or her uncle expires, whichever comes first.

"In either case, Hope, Devington, may displace your present courtship of Despair. She's a distant cousin to Lady Fortune, whom I personally hold dearest, but I believe Hope much more constant in her attachments; thus I trust she will serve you well."

Clapping his friend on the shoulder, Philip continued. "Speaking of ladies has put me in mind of some unfinished business." He grinned broadly, taking up the near-empty bottle. "Think I'll do you a favor, old chap, and save you some morning agony." Philip rose and swaggered, bottle in hand, in search of Maggie.

Robert sighed deeply and passed out flat on the table.

Robert awoke cotton-mouthed, bleary-eyed, and aching, sprawled in a chair by the hearth in an unfamiliar room. Attempting to focus and make sense of the night before, he rubbed his bloodshot eyes. He then unwisely shook his cobweb-filled head, which answered with the strike of a thousand anvils, awakening the most violent nausea he had ever known.

Moaning in abject agony, he stumbled to his feet, knocking over a side table as he frantically sought the chamber pot. Finding it, he wretched relentlessly.

"Oh my, luv!" Maggie spoke in sympathetically dulcet tones. "Ye'd best be still," she advised, rising quickly from Philip's bed. Holding the chamber pot, she guided Robert back to his chair. "Now Maggie'll jes' run and get ye a little sommat to help cure yer ills."

She threw her gown over her shift and sought the major's assistance to do up her laces. Then Maggie stuffed her hair under her cap and slipped from the room.

"She has a warm heart, that Maggie," Philip mused. "If it weren't for her, your arse would still be passed out in the taproom." Only her pity for the lovesick captain, coupled with concerns of thieves and cutthroats, had cajoled Philip into carrying his comatose companion to his chamber.

"You're a saint among men," Robert groaned. "Pray remind me *later* how much I'm indebted by your tender mercies."

Maggie returned armed with a tankard of weak ale and a pot of hot tea, just about the time the captain's retching ceased.

"Hair of the dog?" Philip inquired skeptically.

"Got ye sommat better?" she retorted saucily and deftly righted the table, placing her tray upon it. Then bringing a pitcher of water and a reasonably clean towel, she ministered to the wretched captain, endeavoring to put him back in passable order.

"Now how about a shave, Cap'n? Ye refused last time, if'n I recall, but jes' you ask Major Philip what a steady hand I've got."

Sensing Robert's refusal, Philip interjected, "She really does mean a shave this time, Devington. It's a sure bet Maggie's hand'll be steadier than yours. Let Maggie set you to rights. After last night's indulgence, you're sure to slit your own throat." Answering for Robert, Philip gave her a nod. She left to fetch hot water and a sharp blade.

"That's what you really need, a simple, uncomplicated wench like Maggie. I've half a mind to keep her myself," he mused.

"And what of your heiress?" Robert asked.

"Completely beside the point. Said I'd a mind to *keep* Maggie, not leg-shackle to her. I'm utterly bewildered by your fixation on matrimony, unless of course you've gotten the girl with child. Is that it, Devington?"

Robert glared his response.

"Nay, the most honorable Captain Devington wouldn't do such a thing, would he?"

"I would never dishonor Charlotte."

"Do you mean to say," Philip asked incredulously, "that you've pined nearly five years for her, stoically awaiting the day you may legally claim your conjugal rights and release your pent-up passions? I'm completely confounded by it."

"And what if I should be killed, leaving Charlotte unmarried and with child? Unable to collect even my military pension? She'd be destitute."

"There are ways to prevent conception, Devington."

"You still don't fathom it, do you? That I *desire* to marry her."

"You've yet to live, man. With women like Maggie so plentiful, why do you seek bondage?"

"I've no interest in whores, Philip. Not every man adheres to your voluptuary conviction that marriage is the fatal penance to be paid only after a lifetime of license. Doesn't love exist in your hedonistic Utopia?"

"Love? I seem to recall having this conversation with you once before. Pray let me ease your mind that I am no agnostic of *love*. Quite the contrary, I worship faithfully at the altar of Venus. I am religious in my practice of *love* and endeavor to share it in a most self-sacrificing and altruistic manner." He finished this last pronouncement with a smirk just as Maggie returned.

"I can vouch for 'im, Cap'n," Maggie said with a chortle.

Robert finally surrendered, flopping unceremoniously into the chair, and Maggie readied to shave him. Once dressed and sufficiently recovered to travel, Robert scrawled a missive with Maggie's promise to ensure its delivery to Miss Charlotte Wallace of Heathstead Hall.

With her reassurance, the two officers departed for London.

PART II

Seventeen

A TALE OF TWO SECRETS

*C*harlotte waited impatiently for word from Robert. She had read his frustrated missive repeatedly during her for'night of confinement. Surely he would write again soon. He wouldn't abandon her, yet she was increasingly apprehensive. Her position in her uncle's household had never been comfortable, but now she suffocated from the oppression.

Sympathetic to his cousin's plight, even Charles's normal exuberance dimmed. In an attempt to release Charlotte from her mental, if no longer physical, imprisonment, he casually remarked at breakfast, "Since it looks to be a fine day, I had thought to take a ride to the heath." He looked to Sir Garfield. "Father, might Charlotte be permitted to accompany me? And Trixie, too, of course, if she should care to go?"

Beatrix surprisingly agreed. "I daresay, I, for one, could use the fresh air. It's become so stifling here." She glared at Charlotte.

Charlotte, brightening suddenly at the suggestion, dimmed as acutely with her uncle's reply.

"I am afraid that won't be possible, Charles. Charlotte no longer has a horse in my stables."

"I b-beg your pardon, Uncle?" Charlotte stammered, spilling her tea.

"You have forfeited such privileges by your recent conduct. I depart this morning to London and have instructed Jeffries to accompany me with the mare. She will be sold at the blood sale."

Charlotte gaped at her uncle.

"Though I intended to have this conversation later, I suppose 'twould be best to be done with it now, to give you time to contemplate the consequences of your actions, my girl." He paused to lower his cup to the saucer.

"You have proven willful and headstrong, Charlotte, and many a man won't tolerate such a wife. It is thus my responsibility to take you to task, as it were, and I shall do it for your own good, b'God."

"Your uncle is right," Lady Felicia interjected. "I have never condoned your hoydenish behavior. You need now practice the manners and deportment of a young lady. How else shall you ever expect us to make you a desirable match?"

Sir Garfield smiled approvingly at his wife then said to Charlotte, "You and Beatrix are both come of marriageable age, and with so few eligible prospects in the county, I am bound for London for the arrangement of nuptials."

"Arrangement of nuptials?" Charlotte repeated blankly.

"Indeed. My solicitor, Wiggins, has already made inquiries at my behest. There are several eligible prospects, all members of the peerage, who would greatly benefit from the largess of a well-dowered bride."

"Well-dowered, Uncle? Five hundred pounds would hardly be considered a large dowry."

"'Tis precisely why I instructed Wiggins to increase your dowry to five thousand. That should see you married well enough, if not quite as auspiciously as Beatrix. My only niece will not be wed to a former stable boy, even one who parades about in crimson regimentals."

"My dear sir, should not we discuss this matter privately?" Lady Felicia inquired.

Sir Garfield replied condescendingly, "No need to worry yourself over matters of business, my dear. There is little left but to negotiate the settlements."

"The settlements?" Lady Felicia prompted.

"Indeed, madam. How should you like to see our Trixie settled a countess?"

"Our Beatrix... a countess!" Lady Felicia exclaimed, her eyes taking on an avaricious gleam. "Is it to be so, Sir Garfield?"

"There is a particular nobleman, heir to a considerable estate, though diminished in fortune, to whom an alliance would prove advantageous. Our Trixie's dowry will provide a considerable bolster to his estate. Her only obligation will be to produce an heir to secure the future succession of the earldom. Wiggins indicates the gentleman was well disposed to discussion. I anticipate expeditious settlements and formal announcement of the betrothal upon our family's arrival in London."

Charlotte was incredulous that her cousin's future should be determined in such a callous and calculating manner. By this time, even Beatrix realized the implications of her father's machinations.

"But, Papa," she protested, thinking of Major Drake, "a title is all well and good, but how could I marry a man I haven't even met? What if we don't suit?"

"My dear Beatrix, marriage is an agreeable arrangement. As I have made the arrangement, you will be agreeable." Sir Garfield smiled indulgently, and she, blank-faced, took this in.

"Indeed, Beatrix," her mother agreed, "the most advantageous marriages are made thusly."

With her marriage all but arranged, Beatrix pulled her lightly arched brows together in a deep frown, once more counting the days since her last menses. Surely it could not happen the very first time?

She never should have gone to his room that night, but after tossing restlessly in bed, she'd crept down the hall to his chamber with only vague ideas of tantalizing him. She had intended to bewitch him with

her charms but soon found the boot on the other leg. Beatrix herself
had become drunk with passion. She now wondered at the cost.

Beatrix snapped out of her reverie when her mother asked, "But
what shall become of Charlotte, Sir Garfield?"

"Once Beatrix is settled, I shall deal with the wayward chit.
Finding a suitable husband to manage *her* may present more of a
challenge than I first believed. I have a mind to consider a widower,
mayhap, someone older to take the girl firmly in hand."

Charlotte's eyes grew wide in disbelief, and Charles jumped to his
cousin's defense.

"Father, how can you contemplate such a scheme? You speak of
marital arrangements in the same vein as taking a horse to auction!"

"Charles, it is *your* future in the making here! Through your
sister's connection, you will have entrance into the most privileged
circles, and through this so-called *scheme*, I shall ensure comfort
and security for both my offspring. What father could do more for
his children?"

Perceiving a cloud upon his sunny idealism, Charles could vouch
no further argument.

"Well then, my girls," Lady Felicia began breathlessly, "there is
little to discuss but much to do. Beatrix, you shall require a trous-
seau. Your present wardrobe is not fit for a countess-to-be. We must
also address Charlotte's dowdy appearance. It will not do to arrive in
London looking like backward country gentry. Come now, Beatrix,
Charlotte. We have much to plan."

Beatrix truculently trailed her mother and whined, "But, Mama,
why have I no choice?"

Lady Felicia reassured her with a pat on the hand. "My dearest
daughter, though it is a sad injustice, a woman seldom weds to her
own volition. The Good Lord bestowed upon males the greater
reasoning and intellect, thus it is for us women to obey them."

"But what if the man is a besotted lech… or a fusty bore… or ill-visaged, bad tempered, and deformed... or stingy, cruel, and close-fisted... or all of it!" she wailed.

"Trixie, I clearly sympathize, but pray cease the histrionics. As to your apprehensions, a clever woman can learn to manage her husband, even one who is... shall we say... less than desirable."

"But, Mama, *I don't want such a husband!*"

"Hear me out, Beatrix," she admonished. "If your husband should be faithless, affect ignorance. If he has a predilection for strong drink, feign tolerance; if he is choleric or sullen, be long-suffering until his mood spends itself. If he be a close-fisted despot, adopt a demure address. But if he be a weak and incompetent man, count your blessings, for you need only give him the very orders you should later receive from him. Lastly and most importantly, if you have wealth and position, your marriage need not be the least incommodious, regardless of your husband's temperament."

Beatrix scarce attended. Her father had arranged her marriage! He would never allow her betrothal to a lowly major of the Horse Guard when he had an earldom at hand. Though the match would make her a countess, she could not be pleased about it.

Beatrix was distraught, nearly overcome in her anxiety. If her husband suspected her prior indiscretion, an annulment would surely ensue, and with it, disgrace upon her entire family. It would be bad enough for her husband to discover her deflowered, but to wed while carrying another's child? She dared not even think of those repercussions!

"What am I to do?" she fretted to herself. Six weeks. It was now six weeks. Inspecting her abdomen daily, she was increasingly convinced she was growing with child and ever fearful some outward sign would mark her—that the truth would show in her eyes.

Ironically, she didn't feel guilty for her actions. If she had the chance, she would unhesitatingly do it again. Fear of the consequences distressed her. She could see no way out of her predicament.

She needed to confide in someone, but to whom? Perhaps Charlotte? Surely she would understand, would have compassion. After all, she was in love, and she wouldn't tell Papa. Whom else could she possibly trust? She resolved to speak with Charlotte, and it had to be soon.

Opportunity came unexpectedly with a trip to Sheffield under the guise of purchasing embroidery silks. To insure privacy, Beatrix insisted that Letty ride outside with the coachman. Although Beatrix made her best attempts at normal prattle, they had scarce departed ten minutes before she spoke. "Charlotte," she began tentatively, "I have a confession, something of a most private nature. I must tell someone, or I shall expire. Can I trust you?"

"What is it, Beatrix? Are you ill?" she asked, alarmed at her cousin's demeanor.

"No… not ill exactly… but before I speak of it, I need your promise, your solemn vow, that you will not breathe a word to anyone."

Charlotte was taken aback by this sudden desire for confidence. They had never been close, had never shared intimacies. This must be grave indeed. "Yes, you can trust me. I promise, Beatrix," she reassured, handing the girl her handkerchief.

With Charlotte sworn to secrecy, Beatrix inhaled deeply and blurted out, "I think I'm breeding."

"Pardon me?" Charlotte gasped.

"You heard me." Beatrix lowered her voice to a whisper. "I believe I'm with child."

"B-but you have never even met your betrothed!" Charlotte stammered in disbelief.

"Of course it is not by my betrothed, you peahen! But that is precisely the problem. It was Philip Drake." Beatrix spoke his name with a guilty smile.

"But when? How did this happen, Beatrix?"

"It was the night before you raced. And how? Are you quite certain you want me to elaborate? It's quite shocking." Beatrix giggled.

"There is no need to particularize. I've spent enough time with the broodmares to have figured it out. I just can't fathom it." Charlotte broke off with her cousin's indignant flush.

"And I suppose you are the innocent! I hardly think so, the way you run off with Devington at every opportunity."

"It's not like that with us, Beatrix. Robert insists we wait for the marriage bed."

"Then you shall have a long and lonely wait, as my father shall never countenance it, just as he will never allow me to wed Major Drake."

"He has asked for your hand?"

Beatrix's flush deepened. "Not exactly, or not yet." She recovered. "He intended to speak to Papa, but then you and Robert spoiled everything! But I shan't regret the doing, just my *undoing* as the result," she said defiantly.

"Oh my," Charlotte murmured, the repercussions dawning. "Beatrix, you must tell him."

"Papa would disown me!" Beatrix wailed. "I can't possibly tell him."

"Not your father; you must tell Philip. He has a right to know and no less an obligation to put things to rights. He must marry you."

"Marry me? Papa has made other plans. He shall never allow it."

"But under the circumstances, he has little choice. If the major is a gentleman, he will offer. No doubt it shall be horridly awkward with other arrangements already made, but I can't believe even Uncle could contemplate marrying you off while carrying another man's child!"

"But if I marry the major, I shan't ever be a countess."

"But I thought you were in love with him?"

"Well, I was, before I thought to be a countess." Beatrix pouted.

"You can't have your cake and eat it, too. Besides, you shan't be a countess once your betrothed learns of this. 'Tis hardly something you can hide for very long. In either regard, you must tell the major. It is your only recourse."

"But how?"

With her heart hammering, Charlotte fingered the envelope in the pocket of her petticoat. Although she had proposed a shopping trip, her real intent was to take a letter to the tavern maid who had served as Robert's courier to her. Could she trust Beatrix with her secret? But her cousin was far too self-absorbed with her own predicament to attend to Charlotte's doings.

"As it happens, I know how to privately convey a message." She could only hope that Maggie would be of a mind to help.

Eighteen

⚬❧⚬

THE BUSINESS OF MARRIAGE

*T*he portly, periwigged, and unfashionably clad man felt conspicuously out of place upon entering the doors of White's, London's oldest and most elite gentlemen's club. He was further abashed at the need to proffer his invitation, sealed by a longtime member, in order to gain entry to the hallowed halls, and even further mortified at his need to request assistance in locating the member.

Indeed, he had never even laid eyes on Viscount Uxeter, who had unexpectedly called this meeting. Sir Garfield mopped the perspiration, evidence of his discomfort, hastily from his brow and followed the lackey to a private parlor. The sole occupant was an elegantly dressed gentleman who sat engrossed in studying his drink.

The portly man was even further discomposed at the gentleman's prolonged hesitation to break from his trance and acknowledge his invited guest. Sir Garfield cleared his throat, and his lordship, foregoing even the most rudimentary of social graces, grazed him with a haughty stare. "Wallace, I presume?"

"Just so, my lord, just so," he replied with due diffidence.

With a curt nod, Lord Uxeter indicated the vacant chair. Taking his cue, Sir Garfield seated himself without ceremony and glanced admiringly about the room. "So gracious of you to sponsor me, my lord—"

The viscount's brows snapped together. "Sponsor you?" he scoffed. "I have no recollection of offering a sponsorship. White's membership is by election only."

Sir Garfield felt the heat of his flush at such an imperious set-down. "I had assumed with our talk of betrothal and your invitation..."

"You grossly misapprehend my purpose, sir," Lord Uxeter said and produced a packet of papers from his inner pocket. "I am in receipt of a most audacious proposition from my solicitor. Am I to understand that you desire a betrothal of marriage between myself and your daughter?"

"Exactly so, my lord."

"Pray let us be frank, Sir Garfield. If you design to align yourself with one of the oldest families in England, you are presumptuous beyond measure." His icy gaze penetrated right through Sir Garfield, and he slowly tore the betrothal contract into halves.

Sir Garfield considered the man and indicated the torn documents. "I shouldn't act so hastily in dismissing the notion, my lord. I fear you give no consideration to the advantages of the match."

"I need consider nothing beyond your low birth. Such a misalliance could only corrupt, indeed bastardize, a noble family line."

"Pray hear me out, my lord. I don't yet despair of overcoming your objections."

"You waste my time and your breath," Uxeter said with a sneer.

"My birth may be inferior, my lord, but I am possessed of a vastly superior fortune."

"What would you know of my family's affairs?"

"I make it my business to know. I am well aware of Lord Hastings's ill-conceived investments and the sorry state of your holdings."

"You overstep yourself!"

Sir Garfield's tone was placatory. "I fail to comprehend you aristocrats and your repugnance of discussing such dirty matters as money, but I plead your forbearance. Should we come to an understanding, I am in a position to refortify your fortune."

Lord Uxeter paused. "Is that so?"

"My daughter is possessed of a very generous dowry."

"How generous?"

He cast the lure. "Twenty thousand pounds."

Edmund regarded the baronet scornfully. "Not enough to taint the blood of a noble family." His voice dripped with contempt.

"But is not everything in life negotiable?" Sir Garfield remarked with a conciliatory smile.

"You wish to barter?" He was stunned at the man's effrontery. "*Gentlemen* employ solicitors for such business."

Disregarding still another set-down, Sir Garfield forced another smile. "Then *your solicitor* should be in expectation of an offer more worthy of your consideration."

"I should very much doubt it, sir." Upon that remark, Lord Uxeter rose and departed, leaving Sir Garfield vowing to buy the arrogant bastard's very soul if necessary.

"We shall see, my lord. We shall just see." The baronet leaned back in the leather chair with a self-satisfied smile and a growing sense of ease in his new surroundings.

JANUARY 5, 1744

The unmarked carriage arrived at Hastings House at precisely ten o'clock. The quartet of darkly cloaked figures descended, but rapping at the door was unnecessary. They were expected, and the servant who answered had his instructions. He led the gentlemen into a large book room with a blazing fire, where the host of this conclave awaited.

"Good evening, gentlemen." Lord Uxeter advanced and greeted his guests as his servant collected their doffed hats and cloaks.

"So good of you to play host," Lord Gower replied. "We must take care from this day forward to avoid any public venue." Lord Gower eyed the servant warily.

"Port or brandy, gentlemen?" Uxeter inquired. Noting his lordship's concern, he dismissed his footman. Lord Gower waited until the servant departed before continuing.

"With word of our friend's arrival in France, we must be ever wary of the minister's spies."

Edmund had never truly believed this plan, nigh on three years in the making, would ever come to fruition. For three decades, the Jacobites had ineffectually looked to France to help deliver their rightful king, but could the French really be trusted to deliver on their promises?

"You mention preparations, but how can we be assured of France's resolve?" he asked.

"The interests of Versailles finally converge with our own. France has never been more disposed to restoring the Stuarts."

Lord Barrymore interjected. "Our French agent, Lord Semphil, confirms eight thousand Foot and two thousand Horse already amassed at Dunkirk under Marshal de Saxe. The Brest squadron is also made ready.

"The French have provided fifteen ships of the line, four frigates, and sixteen troop transports. An additional three thousand of their number are to join our three thousand Highlanders in a coordinated invasion from the North while the prince lands on the Southern Coast and advances to the capital."

"We have confirmation, and the invasion is imminent," said Colonel Cecil. "But the prince requires more than our vows of support; he must subsidize the campaign, and his troops and munitions must be maintained. The restoration of our rightful king comes at a price, but those who lend their support will be justly rewarded.

"Twenty-five thousand pounds should secure your place on the Regent's Council, Uxeter, though the prince shall appoint his ministers as he will. Rest assured that he shall not forget those with him in his hour of greatest need."

Edmund eyed the gentlemen. How many men before them had plotted and schemed against the Crown of England, only to fail? The revolt of thirty years ago had led to executions and attainder of old and noble estates. Was he willing to take such a risk?

But should the Young Chevalier, Prince Charles Edward Stuart, succeed where his father had previously failed, Edmund might finally attain a position worthy of his talents.

This begged the question of whether the reward would be worth the potential price he might pay. It was a calculated gamble. His next question was how to come by twenty-five thousand?

Deciding to defer further contemplation, he only smiled and raised his glass to the assemblage. "To the Young Chevalier, Charles Edward Stuart, Prince Regent of Great Britain."

"To Bonnie Prince Charlie," they echoed.

Nineteen

❧

OF TREACHERY AND
EXTORTION

While heated debate on the war continued, the King and his most favored minister advanced preparations and appointed the new command for the spring campaign.

With the augmented cavalry numbers came a need for more horses. Procurement duty befell Captain Devington, who had gained a reputation for the keenest eye in horseflesh. Majors Drake and Winthrop were eager to join him at the Hyde Park blood sales.

Passing through the myriad of paddocks, they scouted hundreds of horses, in quest of the cavalry archetype: steady-tempered, big-boned, sound geldings. The gelding sale began at ten of the clock, and of the eighty-some horses run through the auction, only a handful passed muster under Devington's scrutiny. Once thoroughly vetted by Major Winthrop, they arranged to deliver the dozen or so select geldings to Whitehall.

The officers were just completing this business at the start of the broodmare sale, when quite by happenstance, Devington's eye caught the coppery glint of a familiar little mare led by the equally familiar Jeffries.

"The bloody sod!" Robert swore. "That's Amoret. I'll swear it! I can't believe Sir Garfield would go so far as to sell the mare."

"Is it truly surprising, given the scoundrel's conduct?" Drake asked.

"The bidding's about to commence. I'll be deuced to abide by it!"

"You have my sympathy, but we've two dilemmas. First and foremost, I'm bloody well strapped for capital. London's not an inexpensive place to entertain oneself, especially on half pay. Unless you are faring better than me, I have barely sixpence left to rub together. Secondly, where would you stable a mare? Our procurement orders are for geldings only."

"It doesn't matter how or where! We can't let her go."

"Are you really so persuaded?"

Major Winthrop overheard this exchange. "What has you so bedeviled, Devington?"

"That mare, sir, the chestnut just passed by. I know her."

"What the devil would the Horse Guard do with a fancy-stepping little mare? We are soldiers, not bloody fops! The cavalry can't use mares. Far too much trouble, they are. Our orders are for sensible, sound geldings."

"You misunderstand, Winthrop. She isn't for the Horse Guard. That mare belonged to my affianced, and her uncle owes me a foal from the same mare from a lost wager. He has reneged on the bet and apparently sells her as further reprisal."

"I see, indeed. So you wish to buy her back?" Winthrop asked rhetorically.

"Just so. But where to stable her?"

"Well, Devington,"—Winthrop clapped his companion on the back with a conspiratorial wink—"'twould appear the Household Cavalry has a previously unanticipated need for a broodmare. You can put her in the veterinary stables for the time being, just until you make other provisions." Robert reciprocated with a grin, and the trio proceeded to the auction paddock.

House of Commons, February 1744

Mr. Pitt's voice cried out as he indicated a sheaf of papers by his side. "I have in hand, gentlemen, a document confiscated by Admiral Norris from a packet bound for Scotland. It is dated December 23, 1743, and is a Commission of Regency for Prince Charles Edward Stuart, signed by the Pretender himself.

"Only ten days ago, the Young Pretender was headed for Calais, where the French fleet awaited him, and two days later our navy espied the Brest squadron off Land's End. I speak of a threat that is very real, the French invasion of England to restore the Stuart Crown. I only pray that there are none among this house so desperate or mad to join such an ill-considered attempt against the throne and our country."

With Parliament in an uproar over the imminent invasion and the risk of his discovery in the plot increasing, Lord Uxeter was livid at having to quit London at his father's sudden summons. Except through the earl's secretary, he had not seen or spoken to his father in months, but the old man now demanded that he drop all his obligations to return to Sussex.

Nothing appeared to be going his way, and his future had never appeared more uncertain. He burned with bitterness and frustration for his lagging career, and seethed with scorn and contempt for his filial duty.

Edmund arrived at the family seat of Hastings Park in an unusual state of agitation. He leaped from the carriage and snapped instructions to the footman. His appearance was haggard, as if he had not slept in days, and his manner, in marked contrast to his normal haughty self-possession, was impatient and edgy.

Standing outside the earl's door, he battled to compose himself enough to play doting son and obedient heir. When he entered the earl's chamber, however, he was stunned to behold his father's frail, feeble, and ancient appearance. Beside the blazing hearth, he was covered in rugs, and as Edmund approached, he discerned an audible rattle resonating with every breath the old man took. Mayhap his sudden summons was not much ado about nothing.

Supposing the earl asleep, Edmund conducted himself with less than his usual diffidence. He slumped into the chair opposite his father and studied the old man with insouciance. For all appearances, the earl was nearing death's door.

The stinging blow by the earl's cane gave sharp notice of his error.

"You insolent whelp!" the earl croaked, his gimlet eyes burning like a firebrand.

Recovering from the shock of the blow, Lord Uxeter smoldered his odium to force an apology from his lips. "Pray forgive me, my lord. I had thought you asleep and only sought to wait by your side until you awakened. I intended no disrespect."

"Your judgment is sorely lacking, Edmund. I seem to find you wanting in many areas these days."

"Then I am sorely grieved. In what manner have I displeased you?" His tone was appropriately contrite.

"You presume to the earldom, Edmund, yet you fail to honor my single request. I have long ignored the whispers from certain unsavory circles, the rumors that you run among those who are less than troubled by a repugnance to the unnatural. I now wonder why you are so loath to stand up to your obligations, and ask if these filthy rumors are not founded?"

Edmund had always maintained utmost discretion in his private affairs and had paid dearly for it. Nevertheless, he had enemies whom he could look to for motive.

"Nasty rumors are ofttimes generated by those who would most benefit from another's fall from grace. We live in times of great political unrest, my lord."

"You would blame political enemies? Yet your career has been considerably less than I expected. You were born to one of the oldest aristocratic families in England, yet you have failed to achieve anything remarkable. I begin to question your worthiness of an earldom."

His throat constricted, and Edmund responded with more inso-lence than he would have previously dared. "Whether you deem me *worthy* or not, my lord, I *am* your legitimate firstborn, and your heir. None may question my birthright."

The earl regarded his eldest son with a piercing stare. "You presume much, Edmund. While there is breath in my body, I will not allow the estate and possessions of four generations to revert back to the Crown! And to a Hanoverian Crown at that! *I am still the Earl of Hastings*, and I will see my wishes carried out, regardless of your birthright!"

"What do you mean? You cannot dictate the laws of the land. Patrilineal primogeniture guarantees my right of inheritance."

"Patrilineal primogeniture, eh? You think to hold inheritance law over my head? Although English custom dictates the eldest male to inherit an entailed estate, the Statute of Wills of 1540 guarantees my right to designate an heir by testament. Thereby, I may confer the right of inheritance upon whomever I wish."

Edmund was stunned.

"And since you have been so disinclined to heed my wishes, I am compelled to enforce them. *I can and shall* ensure my will prevails, Edmund, whether in this life or in the next.

"I have already met with my solicitors and have made my last will and testament. Upon my death, you shall have one year to produce a male heir. One year. Should you fail, my estate shall go to *whichever of my two sons* is first to beget legitimate male issue. Should Philip succeed where you have failed, he shall inherit all, and you shall be cut off completely."

"Philip? That wastrel! How can you even think it?"

"I am inclined to believe that since he embarked upon his military career, your brother is mending his ways. One may at least hope as much. I am further confident that news of my wishes might well provide him further... inspiration. I also trust this change in circumstance shall provide you with proper motivation. Perhaps you now fully comprehend the weight of an earldom, Edmund."

His first reaction was blind rage, but amidst it all, Edmund was thunderstruck. Had not Providence recently delivered a bride to his very door? He had initially dismissed Sir Garfield's proposition. Now he realized the twofold advantage. The timing could not have been more opportune. He could assure his inheritance, and the immense dowry would help advance his lagging political career. Edmund smiled placatingly at the earl.

"As a matter of fact, my lord, I had wished to make known to you news of my imminent betrothal."

"Your what? Of a sudden you would have me believe you intend to wed?"

"Indeed, my lord, the marriage settlements are already in progress."

"Don't think this news alone shall mollify me, Edmund. The will is made, and I will ensure it is executed. If you have indeed chosen a bride, you damned well better get her with child, and not in this leisurely manner in which you chose to wed! My time is running short, and I will not go to my grave unassured."

"I fully intend to comply with your wishes and produce an heir, my lord."

"And what of your betrothed? Who is the family?"

"As to the family, she daughter of a Yorkshire baronet. I am told she has a strong constitution and will undoubtedly prove sound to the task of bearing progeny."

Lord Hastings directed him a frosty stare. "A baronet? I once erred by wedding a woman of inferior birth. I will never countenance begetting the future heir of Hastings from common stock."

"Yet you propose to offer my half-bred brother an earldom?" Edmund sneered.

Twenty

⌒

RETURN OF THE
PRODIGAL

With the threat of French invasion, the remaining British
fleet not already engaged with France in southern waters
patrolled the Channel in force, and extra garrisons were dispatched
to the southernmost coast, where the landing was most anticipated.

Major Drake was placed in command of two hundred Horse
and a thousand infantry to patrol his home coast of East Sussex.
Devington, under his command, was starkly reminded what a
grueling taskmaster his friend could be. The major was assiduous in
preparing his men to defend their beloved shores.

He garrisoned the troops of Horse at Hastings Castle, a ruined
Norman fortification that had succumbed to the elements over the
centuries. Great sections of the castle, along with chunks of the soft
sandstone cliff face, had long given way into the sea, but it provided
an ideal vantage point to spot any encroaching vessels. He positioned
his cavalry units to patrol the cliffs and garrisoned the remainder of
his forces five miles to the north at Battle Abbey.

By February 16th, the French naval squadrons, under Admiral
Roquefeuille, set sail up the Channel to clear the way for the troop
and armament transports. On the 23rd, Roquefeuille—mistakenly
believing all the British ships to be at Portsmouth—sent a vessel on
to Dunkirk to signal Marshal de Saxe.

He was unprepared to meet four-and-twenty British ships of the line with orders to burn the French transports. The total destruction of the French fleet was virtually inevitable, but Admiral Norris tarried and deferred his assault. In the morning, Roquefeuille and the French fleet had slipped away!

Although Norris failed to pursue, Providence worked on Britain's behalf, with a fierce gale. Three days of punishing winds and squalling waves scattered and dashed the French transports, sinking some of the largest and wrecking others along the coast, devastating the French navy without a single cannon having fired.

Their few remaining ships returned to port, and the surviving troops disembarked to march for Flanders. The Stuart prince, having barely escaped with his life, was all but abandoned.

Major Drake's troops patrolled the coast for a full for'night before receiving report of the devastation to the Brest fleet, but fear of a second invasion attempt persisted. After another month with no French flagships sighted and no appearance of the Young Pretender, the British concluded they had held the domestic threat at bay.

With the crisis now averted, Drake left a handful of troops behind to continue patrols, while the rest were recalled for another deployment to Flanders, following France's formal declaration of war. All officers were given three days to take care of personal business and report to Whitehall.

Given his current proximity to home, Philip decided to make a much-dreaded but long-overdue visit to the ancestral estate before returning to Headquarters. Inviting Devington to accompany him, the pair set off on the twelve-mile ride.

"Misery does prefer company," Philip remarked as they mounted up.

"Just how long have you been away?" Robert inquired.

"Nearly five years, but not long enough by my estimation."

"Indeed? Why so bitter?" Robert asked.

"I would that I had only one reason, my friend," Philip replied ruefully, pulling a newspaper clipping from his inside pocket and handing it to Robert.

"What's this? I should hardly think you followed the social scene."

"On the contrary, I was quite thunderstruck by this news. Indeed, you may also be overcome with the incongruity."

Robert's eyes grew wide. The clipping was the betrothal announcement of Edmund Giles Drake, Lord Uxeter, heir apparent to Anthony Philip Drake, Earl of Hastings, and Lady Beatrix Wallace, daughter of Sir Garfield Wallace of Heathstead Hall, Wortley, South Yorkshire.

"Beatrix engaged to your brother? B'God, looks like the old sod has buggered us both. But what does it mean, Drake?"

"The announcement has already run in the Times, so I can only assume the settlements are made. I cannot help but believe it is retaliation for the lost race."

"But I wasn't aware of any connection between Sir Garfield and Lord Uxeter. How could this have come about?"

"It came about from my own bloody stupidity, that's how! After a fine dinner and several bottles of port, Sir Garfield petitioned me for a letter of introduction to my family. I was more than happy to oblige, thinking it might advance my cause. I erroneously assumed Sir Garfield desired an introduction into one of my father's clubs. I had no clue of any such devious intent!

"One can't but laugh at the irony, that through my own doing, my sanctimonious brother not only inherits the entire estate but now shall gain my heiress, as well. Though Edmund, I assure you, will not appreciate Beatrix's particular charms."

"Why do you say so? Although not to my taste, her pulchritude is widely remarked in Yorkshire."

"My brother is arrogant, conceited, and pretentious. He takes singular delight in exercising his erudition and intellectual prowess at the disparagement of others less gifted. He values political connections over friendships, and I have never known him to look sideways at a woman, let alone harbor any tender feelings toward one."

"Never?"

"I have never known him to keep a mistress or pursue any serious romantic liaison, though I have heard whispers regarding his particular preferences."

"Are you saying he's a sodomite, Drake?"

"I have my suspicions. Regardless, he will doubtless hold Beatrix and her charming prattle in utter contempt. 'Tis a veritable match made in hell."

"Might I interject that the deed's not yet done. You might decide just how badly you want her."

"I confess I had an indifference to all but her fortune in the beginning, but later I discovered at least one area of compatibility. I am convinced that we would get on tolerably well in our daily intercourse." He grinned.

"Quite so." Robert ignored the double entendre. "So what are you to do?"

"That, Devington, I have yet to decide."

Within two hours, Philip and Robert caught their first view of the estate. The manor was an imposing gray stone edifice set back several hundred yards from the cliffs—as if looming over them—in a vista of desolate grandeur.

"Most resembles an ancient keep from this vantage point, don't you think?" Philip asked. "Centuries hence, this region was a Norman stronghold. You'll find that many like structures, dating back to William the Conqueror, dot the coastline. The house, built on the site of a castle ruin, used many of the original stones."

The long drive to the manor gate was well landscaped at one time.

The numerous trees and shrubs were designed to lend the entrance a more welcoming appeal, but evidence of neglect abounded. Now, in the dead of winter, bereft of their leaves, they somehow enhanced the loneliness, the eeriness of the landscape.

Philip dismounted to open the gates, and Robert could not help remarking, "To be sure, Drake, 'tis not the most welcoming sight."

Philip laughed cynically. "Not by half, and you have yet to see the inside, dear boy! Do you now understand my lack of enthusiasm as well as my yearning for company?"

"Quite." They entered the deserted courtyard, and Robert gazed up at the weathered stone walls. "Charming," he remarked dryly.

"'Twas much more welcoming in my mother's time, I assure you. She loved flowers. They were everywhere, giving the old place almost an air of enchantment. There were half a dozen full-time gardeners about the place at that time." Philip's voice dropped off, and he gazed at the overgrown, ivy-covered walls and empty flowerbeds.

With no groom appearing at their arrival, the two men dismounted. Philip approached the large iron knocker on the massive door. He had barely laid it to rest, when the door opened to a most formidable manservant.

Recognizing the major, the somber face made a complete metamorphosis. "Why, Master Philip! 'Tis so long, I scarce recognized you. Welcome home!" Only his dignity and awareness of his position prevented the old retainer from taking the major into a joyful embrace.

"Thank you, Grayson," Philip responded, truly taken aback by the enthusiasm of his greeting. "One would hope my family will receive me so warmly."

"Certainly after such extended an absence," the butler replied, but they both knew it a lie. "You have brought a guest?" He looked toward the officer holding the horses.

"Indeed, this is Captain Devington."

"Welcome, Captain. We shall do our utmost to ensure your comfort." He turned back to Philip. "My apologies there was no groom to meet you. I will summon one, posthaste." He rang a bell and stated, "The staff is much reduced these days, you see. Half attend Lord Uxeter in the London house, and the rest care for the earl, who since his illness, rarely leaves his apartments or receives visitors. Shall I prepare your old rooms, Master Philip?"

"Please, and a guest chamber in the same wing for Captain Devington, but don't trouble yourself overmuch. I daresay it will be a short stay."

"When we received news of the army patrolling the coast, we had hoped to see your return, but we hardly dared expect you. 'Tis prodigious pleased I am, Master Philip." He grinned again. The hunched old groom arrived to take the horses, and the butler ushered them inside to the Great Hall.

"I trust there's a fire and a bottle of brandy to be had in the library?"

"Aye, Master Philip. His lordship still enjoys an active commerce with the free traders." He winked knowingly.

Philip answered Robert's questioning look. "The Sussex coast is second only to Cornwall in smuggling activity." He turned back to Grayson. "You mentioned my father's recent illness. Am I to understand this is something beyond his gout?"

"Sadly so. His lordship suffered an apoplectic seizure several months ago. Although much recovered, he retains a lingering weakness of his right side. You will perceive him much changed."

"Dare I ask if his illness impaired his faculties in any manner?"

"His faculties are yet as sharp as his tongue."

Philip ignored the impertinence and responded with good humor. "I appreciate the word of warning."

"My lord is currently resting above stairs, but I will announce you as soon as he awakens."

"And my brother? Is he also in residence?"

"He has been much occupied in Parliament since France's declaration of war, but he is expected this evening."

They entered the library, where Grayson took their hats and cloaks and set about building a fire. Philip, meanwhile, went straight to the brandy decanter. Pulling two chairs close to the hearth, he poured two generous glasses for the captain and himself and set the bottle on a table between them.

"Is there aught else you require, sir?" Grayson asked.

"Not at the moment." Philip met the old servant's eye with a murmur of thanks. The retainer, slightly embarrassed, mumbled about it being his pleasure to serve, and departed to alert the cook and supervise room preparations.

Now comfortably ensconced by a blazing fire, the two men nursed their drinks and warmed their chilled bones.

"Drake, it may be altogether impertinent of me, but why is there such acrimony between you and Edmund? Knowing you as I do, I find it hard to believe it stems only from the birthright."

"You are entirely impertinent to pry into my family matters," Philip chided, threw back his drink, and generously refilled the glass.

Devington regarded him expectantly.

"All right," Philip said, deciding. "You surmise correctly; it goes much deeper than the birthright. If you are so dammed interested, I'll air our dirty laundry." He paused to take another long swallow of brandy.

"I suppose I should begin with the present Earl of Hastings. Shortly after inheriting the title and estates, he married his paternal cousin. He had awaited her coming of age by design to merge the fortunes of two related families, and to ensure the purity of the family line, a notion no longer held by many outside the royal families."

"Is your family so very old and noble, Drake?"

"Old, yes, but noble? Mayhap ignoble is more apposite," he added ruefully. "It is said we descend from the blood of the Conqueror, but on the dubious side of the blanket. My great-grandfather persuaded James the First, for a handsome fee of course, to recognize the connection and thus issue the patent of earldom. But I digress.

"The earl's first wife died of puerperal fever following childbirth, but the babe, Edmund, survived. Grieving his wife but satisfied in having produced an heir, Lord Hastings returned to London and left the infant in the care of nursemaids. The earl was at that time one of the high Tories at Queen Anne's Court, but his fortunes changed with her death. The Act of Settlement, which rang in the Hanoverians, rang the death toll for the Tories. Less than a decade later, he lost the vast majority of his fortune with the South Sea Company. He then did what most noblemen in such positions do: he sought a rich wife.

"At five-and-forty, he married twenty-year-old Eugenia Forsythe, the daughter of a London merchant and the lady who would be my mother." He took another long drink as he reflected on his boyhood memories.

"Although she was anxious to make a successful marriage, the earl's excessive pride and arrogance destroyed the remotest possibility of happiness. The bastard never gave her a chance, but buried her in the country while he supported himself in town, largely on her dowry. I was born scarcely ten months following their nuptials. To this day, I am dubious whether the old man ever touched her again after my birth."

"And your brother?"

"Edmund was eleven years old and at school when the earl remarried. My mother endeavored to nurture a relationship with him, but even then he was jealous and exceedingly aloof. He was cruel and actively sought to damn me in my father's eyes. From the earliest age, I perceived that ours was no ordinary sibling rivalry.

"He was successful in this aim, as I have lived under my father's consummate disapprobation. Knowing I could never amend his bad opinion, I thought it a great lark to confirm his belief in my utter worthlessness. I chose to confound and antagonize them both at every turn, even at the expense of my own hide. I survived numerous birchings for my miscellaneous high crimes and misdemeanors, and I daresay the headmaster at Harrow earned his wings in heaven for all his pains. To this very day, I bear the scars of his labors to save my soul. Fortunately, he finally realized the futility of flogging my sins out of me, and I was expelled."

"Expelled? On what grounds?"

"The *coup de grâce* was the discovery of the late-night gambling Hell carried on in my room." He laughed.

"You were running a gambling Hell?"

"I was a most enterprising lad, Devington." He flashed a rueful grin. "But my venture came to an ignominious end."

"This must not have gone well for you."

"Indeed it did not, my friend! And by this time my dear mother had succumbed to her illness. I dared not return home, and although she left me a small inheritance, I was but sixteen and had no access to it."

"So, how did you get on?"

"By little more than my wits, for nearly five years."

"And your father allowed this life?"

"He cared little. He'd long written me off as a ne'er-do-well, blaming my inferior breeding. The bad blood, you know."

Philip refilled his glass and offered the decanter to Robert. He refused but prompted, "So why did you decide on the military?"

"By the time I received my inheritance, I had gained maturity and discovered a desire to prove them all wrong. So I purchased my commission. Now you have it: the *raison d'être* for my cool familial affections."

"Under the circumstances, I quite understand," Robert replied.

"Have no doubt that now here I'll perform my filial duty, but with any luck, I'll be spared further obligation for another three years."

Grayson knocked lightly on the door. "Your rooms are ready whenever you wish to refresh yourselves, sir. I have placed Captain Devington's bag in the green room as you requested."

"Thank you. I will show Devington to his room. No need to trouble yourself further, Grayson."

"As you wish." The butler departed.

Having drunk their fill of brandy, the officers stumbled up the east-wing staircase leading to the former nursery and Philip's boyhood rooms. The green room, two doors down from Philip's, had once housed his tutor, and there was a small study betwixt the chambers. Grayson had ensured a comfortable arrangement, with blazing fires in all three rooms along with basins of hot water and towels. Philip showed Robert to his room before retiring to his own.

Once in his chamber, Philip removed his coat and took off his boots, placing the articles of clothing outside the door, knowing they would be cleaned, pressed, and shined in time for dinner. He pulled his shirt over his head and washed. He then promptly collapsed, sprawled full-length on the tester bed. He had just closed his eyes when a light scratch on the door interrupted his repose. Grayson entered with his cleaned and pressed uniform and gleaming boots.

"Master Philip," he said, "the earl will see you now."

"Indeed? Might I inquire after his humor in learning of my arrival?"

Grayson hesitated. "My lord appeared almost... pleased."

"Remarkable," Philip murmured.

"May I also inform you that Lord Uxeter has arrived. He bids you and your companion dine with him at six. Is there aught more that you require, sir?"

"Just more brandy, if I am to deal with both my father and brother on the same day," Philip remarked, only half in jest.

"I shall see to it," Grayson responded soberly.

Philip groaned at the prospect of facing his father. He rose from his bed, raked a hand through his hair, and donned his clean linen and boots. He buttoned his coat and inspected himself in the looking glass. After Grayson's fastidious attentions, he was ready for parade. Although his appearance would have satisfied any of his commanding officers, in his entire life, he had never passed muster with the Earl of Hastings. Philip squared his shoulders and proceeded to his lordship's apartments.

❧

A half hour later, Philip knocked lightly on the captain's door.

"You look none the worse for wear," Robert remarked.

"On the outside only, I confess. I'm in desperate need of another drink, a dose of liquid courage, if you will, for what is likely to be a second trying engagement."

"It would sound as if you prepare for battle."

Philip's look spoke volumes.

"That bad, eh?"

"Quite." He grimaced.

The pair descended the stair and proceeded to the great dining hall.

"My lord Uxeter is seated within, sir," Grayson informed him. "The earl dines alone in his rooms."

The footman opened the door to the formal dining hall to announce their arrival.

"I see 'tis to be a cozy, informal gathering," Philip commented under his breath.

Noting Edmund seated in the earl's place at the table's head, Philip executed a less than deferential bow and remarked, "A bit precipitate, don't you think, Edmund? The earl was quite alive above stairs only a quarter hour ago."

Edmund responded with a haughty stare. The tension between

the pair was already palpable to the captain, who stepped forward
with his own bow, curious to assess the viscount for himself.

In observing the two brothers, he noted both were tall and lean,
but other than being of a comparable build, the pair stood in stark
contrast to one another.

Philip was of dark complexion, with a ruggedly handsome visage
and a mobile, sensuous mouth. His black gaze could be hard as flint
one moment or warm with capricious mirth the next.

Edmund was fair and had sharp, distinctly aristocratic features, with
his slightly aquiline nose and thin mouth set in straight, harsh lines. His
icy blue, humorless gaze was eerily penetrating and contemptuous.

"So young Philip has come back to the nest from which he was
tossed, or mayhap more like a young vulture come to circle the
carrion," Edmund drawled, but his lips formed a sneer.

Philip's skin prickled at the early provocation, but he responded
with indolence. "I credit you with a vivid metaphor, Edmund. I
should rather have expected some boorish remark about the return
of the prodigal."

"No doubt you've come to beg a loan to cover your gaming debts."

"Alas, I am come merely to pay long-overdue respects to our father.
Much as I hate to disappoint you, my finances are in tolerable order.
I have no need of money." He was immeasurably grateful at the truth
of it. Although perpetually low in the pockets while in London, his
luck ran true. He had at least managed to keep his head above water.

Perceiving his disadvantage in the first parry, Edmund's eyes
narrowed. "Why, then, have you *really* come?"

"'Tis nigh on three years since I have visited the ancestral home.
Is this not reason enough?"

Silence reigned while the footmen poured wine and brought in
the first covers. The captain moved to break the oppressiveness. "Do
you still maintain a racing stable, Lord Uxeter? Philip has mentioned
you have horses at Cheveley, I believe?"

"You know blood horses, Devington?"

"Undeniably, my lord. Raised and raced 'em."

"I don't recall seeing you at Newmarket."

"Doncaster racing," Robert amended.

"Doncaster!" Edmund scoffed.

Robert eyed him ruefully, remembering his prior arguments with Phillip. Obviously, these misbegotten views ran in the family. "I beg to differ with you, my lord. Many prominent runners hail from Yorkshire. Indeed, Major Drake and I recently witnessed one of Martindale's new colts trounce a Bolton Starling son."

"Martindale, eh? The pompous ass goes on incessantly about his stud. He's got a four-year-old he claims is undefeated under twelve stone. I've a mind to match him with Perseus for a thousand guineas. We'll then see if he stands by his claim."

"Perseus?" Robert queried. "Of what blood is he?"

"Only the oldest and purest of English racing blood, the Byerley Turk and Old Careless. He's full brother to Hawke, you know; both carry pure Eastern blood, undiluted by any *common* stock." He ended his intimation by directing Philip a contemptuous stare.

"I know Hastings's Hawke very well, my lord. He is a fine stallion," Devington remarked.

"*Was* a fine stallion. 'Twas a sad day when he was euthanized after injuring a leg at the Lichfield races."

"I remember this race, my lord, but I was unaware of any incapacitating injury," Robert replied. He and Philip exchanged knowing looks.

"I'm sure you were devastated, Edmund," Philip remarked.

"Just so. I thought the horse irreplaceable at the time, but Perseus shows even more promise. The blood will always tell."

This second insinuation sent the bile rising to Philip's throat, but Robert intervened. "But even the purest stock, my lord, can on occasion produce imperfect get. Indeed, this manner of inbreeding you advocate has proven to bring out either the best or the very worst in the offspring."

"I am affronted by your ignorance, Captain! Superior blood will always prevail, just as bad blood will eventually out."

Robert countered, "While I beg not a quarrel, 'tis well known that a number of highly inbred crosses have produced imperfect get. Flying Childers of the Darley line, by example, was one of the most successful racers of his time, but his full brother, Bartlett's Childers, was unfit to race due to a blood-vessel disorder thought to descend from the dam, Betty Leedes. She was also inbred with the blood of Darcy's Yellow Turk. As there are a number of highly bred racers with similar bleeding disorders, I suspect some connection to this particular breeding method. This is, of course, just my personal theory," he added.

The footman cleared the covers and refilled glasses. Philip gestured to leave a bottle close at hand. Robert noted he had barely touched his food.

"While on the topic of breeding, what of your family, Devington?" Lord Uxeter inquired.

"Undoubtedly common stock, my lord." Robert's self-deprecating laugh was met with Lord Uxeter's narrowed stare. "My father was first a coachman and later stable master for a South Yorkshire baronet."

"I am recently acquainted with a South Yorkshire baronet by the name of Wallace, a Sir Garfield Wallace. Do you know of him, Captain?"

"Indeed, my lord! My father was in the same man's employ from the very start of his coaching service."

"Coaching service? The man to whom I refer is a significant Yorkshire landholder."

"Indeed, 'tis one and the same man. Sir Garfield is possessed of a considerable fortune made in trade but is assuredly a commoner by birth. Are you acquainted with him through your racing stud, my lord? He has a considerable interest in blood horses."

Lord Uxeter's displeasure shone in the hardness of his eye and the grim line of his mouth. It was bad enough he should be betrothed to the daughter of a country squire, but a tradesman?

"Are you acquainted with the gentleman through horses, my lord?" Robert repeated.

"I don't recall the circumstances," he remarked dismissively.

"Sir Garfield Wallace of Yorkshire?" Philip mused artlessly. "It seems I've encountered the name. There was recently something related to his family," Philip uttered pensively.

"It is of no consequence!" Lord Uxeter snapped, throwing down his napkin.

"Precisely what is your connection, Edmund?"

Edmund exploded in a venomous outburst. "I didn't say, you accursed half-breed whelp!"

"Another interesting choice of words," Philip drawled, "especially given your choice of bride and your stated views on selective reproduction. Mayhap you'll produce a whole litter of such half-bred whelps."

"Damn your insolence!"

"It appears the *noble* viscount forgets himself. My apologies for my brother's poor *breeding*, Devington." Philip rose stiffly, and with a mocking bow, strode out.

When he arrived in his room, Phillip was thankful for Grayson's foresight. Forgoing the glass, he took a long swig from the mouth of the bottle, cradled it in his arms, and collapsed on the bed. He drank for some minutes, bemused even more by Edmund's behavior than what his father had revealed.

His audience with the earl had been, thankfully, exceedingly brief. Philip had spoken little beyond answering his father's questions. Although he wasn't fool enough to believe he had entered the earl's good graces, mayhap his military success had at least removed him from utter perdition. At least it was progress, he mused. He shrugged resignedly, took another drink, and pulled a crumpled letter from his inner pocket. It was written in a childlike, sloping hand and dated over a for'night ago.

My Dearest Philip,

 I pray that you forgive the impropriety of this message, but I must needs speak with you on a matter of the utmost urgency. 'Tis a matter most confidential and delicate, that may be made only unto your own ears. Time is of the essence, as we depart the first week of April for London. I await your reply with greatest anxiety and "expectation."

 Your Beloved,

 B. W.

He digested the brief contents. *Confidential and delicate disclosure? Expectation?* What the devil did that mean? Did she wish to personally inform him of her betrothal to Edmund? Unlikely, he thought. There were no promises between them. Indeed, they had little conversation at all during their last encounter. He grinned. Besides, the betrothal was already public news.

Did she wish to reveal that she was under duress? That she did not wish to go through with the marriage? If so, she could have written thus.

The next thought that sprang to his mind was nearly unthinkable. Although he had exercised less than his normal degree of caution, Philip couldn't believe in any undesirable consequences. Were it that easy, he'd have fathered a pack of bastards by now.

Nevertheless, if Beatrix *was* with child, 'twould certainly foil all Sir Garfield's schemes, let alone humiliate Edmund. *What retribution that would be!* The notion amused him.

When his brother had provoked him at dinner, he had been

tempted to expose his liaison with Beatrix, but he had bit his tongue. As a gentleman, his code would not allow him to ever willingly cause shame or embarrassment to a woman. Beatrix's letter gave him cause to address her father, but his sense of honor required that he do so with utmost discretion. He also could take no action until he knew if Beatrix was a willing party to the betrothal, or not. He filed this thought away in his brain for further reflection.

In examining the other side of the coin, Edmund had obviously contracted the marriage for financial gain. This knowledge alone would not have got under Philip's skin, as his own motives were equally rapacious, but the difference lay in Beatrix's destiny of misery should she marry Edmund, Lord Uxeter.

Although Philip was by no means in love with the girl, if he had to marry someone, he could do much worse. She was an heiress, after all, and he thought they would rub along tolerably well together. Indeed, he decided, all would be much better served, whether or not she be with child, if she were to marry him.

Having now muddled through the tangled web to some semblance of a plan, he resolved that he must intervene. He would confront Sir Garfield with her letter.

Twenty-one

THE DEVIL MEETS HIS MATCH

$\mathcal{E}$ach having a score to settle with Sir Garfield, Philip and Robert departed at first light for London.

"Tomorrow morning, you and I shall go unannounced to the house," Philip said. "While I demand my audience with the baronet, you shall arrange a private word with Charlotte. He has forced our hand, so we shall now see who wins his wicked game." Philip grinned, *wickedly*.

The next morning, with his uniform concealed in a dark cloak topped with a shabby-looking tricorn, Robert stalked to the servants' entrance, while Philip, resplendent in his dress uniform, called at the front door of the house on Upper Brook Street. An unassuming manservant answered, and Philip boldly entered the domicile.

"Major Philip Drake to see Sir Garfield. You will be pleased to announce me," he commanded the servant upon whose heels he trailed. Philip announced in sardonic tones as he barged into the master's study, "My felicitations on the happy announcement."

Sir Garfield, startled by the intrusion, nonetheless retorted, "You have no business here, Drake."

"On the contrary, sir," he replied blandly, "it is precisely my business that directs me. Though I have offered my felicitations, as propriety requires, I come to make known a slight... impediment... shall we say, to the pending nuptials."

"Impediment? There is no impediment. We had no formal agreement."

"'Twas an understanding, a matter of honor between *gentlemen*."

"Without a betrothal contract, you haven't a leg to stand on."

"True, unless our agreement had already been... consummated."

His intonation and choice of words caused Sir Garfield to blanch, but he hastily dismissed it as a bluff. "I have no time for your conundrums. Be pleased to make your departure, Major."

"As you wish, sir," Philip answered with mock civility and made as if to go, but turned to play his trump card. "I will, as a matter of course, recommend to my fastidious brother that a physician examine his bride-to-be. 'Tis an unfortunate nuisance for your daughter but an innocuous enough precaution on Edmund's part." He uttered this last with such calculating confidence that Sir Garfield wavered.

"Do you mean to imply that you dishonored my daughter? And under mine own roof?"

"I, dishonor your daughter? Indeed not!" Philip replied with self-righteous indignation. "More accurately, your daughter compromised me by coming to my room and seducing me! Nonetheless, I stand ready to forgive this heinous act and absolve her with the atonement of marriage." He flashed a taunting grin.

"Impossible! 'Tis all an accursed lie, damn you!"

"But what if I speak the truth? What if your daughter even now carries my child? Should you proceed with your plans, matters might become extremely problematic.

"Lord Uxeter could legally and without repercussion break the betrothal should the bride's virtue be called into question," Philip stated flatly, having now driven his point home. He waited for Sir Garfield to digest it all.

With a bellow, Sir Garfield summoned his daughter.

Beatrix arrived breathless, disarrayed, and confused, and followed by her mother.

"Sir Garfield, what is the meaning of this?" Lady Felicia demanded.

"This is not a matter for your ears, wife. I have need to speak with *your* daughter."

Beatrix's eyes lit upon Philip. "Philip, my love! You have finally come to speak to Papa for me!" Remembering her parents, she broke off, blushing scarlet.

Philip strode gallantly to her side. "My dearest, of course I have come in response to your letter. I only regret that my obligations delayed me so long." He raised her hands to his lips, regarding Sir Garfield ironically. "Have I now your permission for your daughter's hand?"

"She is spoken for, you audacious blackguard!"

"On the contrary, I have it on word from the family solicitor that the final settlements are yet unsigned, my brother having been called suddenly to Sussex."

"But 'tis already announced in the papers. There would be a scandal!" Lady Felicia exclaimed.

"Scandals should be avoided at all cost, would you not agree, Lady Beatrix?" Philip said softly and smiled.

"Y-y-yes," she answered, her eyes growing wide in apprehension.

Sir Garfield understood the implicit threat and realized his entrapment. His countenance darkened. "So, it is to be blackmail, then?"

"I confess to such thoughts when I first learned of the betrothal; however, I am confident of a mutually beneficial solution should we call a truce."

"The major and I have business to discuss, m'dear," the baronet said, addressing his wife. "Pray escort your daughter back to her rooms."

Beatrix directed Philip a pleading look answered with a reassuring flash of white.

Disgracing a lady was not the hallmark of a gentleman. He

despised putting her in such a distressing position; but needs must, as the saying went.

"All right, Drake, if I should call truce, what then?" Sir Garfield asked.

"I have a proposition in mind, something that should suit all parties."

"What sort of proposition?"

"Mayhap a sacrificial lamb, for want of a better phrase. I propose that you offer your niece as Edmund's bride, in lieu of Beatrix. He will care little, providing the dowry remains the same."

Sir Garfield, having already considered Charlotte's marriage prospects, digested this. It made little difference which of the girls married first, as long as the connection was to his advantage. "And why should your brother countenance such a thing? What possible appeal should Charlotte have over Beatrix?"

"You don't know my family, Sir Garfield. Have you not yet met Lord Uxeter?"

Sir Garfield colored at the remembrance.

"I see you have," Philip remarked dryly. "Charlotte's father was a barrister, a member of Grey's Inn, was he not? Men of the law are deemed of a higher social caliber than merchants. Hence, the alliance with a barrister's daughter would be more appealing to my noble family than an alliance with a former tradesman."

"You propose that I substitute the bride?"

"Why not? If the contracts are unsigned, they need only be revised. I shall then offer Beatrix the protection of my name in return for her dowry of twenty thousand, of course."

Sir Garfield, bowled over by the sheer audacity, grudgingly responded, "Quite brilliant m'boy. However, you overlook that the dowry is already pledged to your brother."

"Surely this is another negotiable point, Sir Garfield. No dowry; no wedding. No wedding would assuredly lead to dishonor and scandal. Moreover, should anything befall Charles, your heir through Beatrix would be a bastard."

"You've outmaneuvered me on the score of my daughter, but I'll be damned to bless you with a fortune for it!" he expostulated. "Besides, you have no proof of a child."

"Do you think to call my bluff? I regret it has come to this. I had wished to spare Beatrix further indignity." Producing her letter from his breast pocket, Philip presented it to her father.

Sir Garfield conceded defeat.

"I believe my proposal the best way forward," Philip remarked.

"Ten thousand pounds, Drake. I'll offer a dowry of ten thousand."

"Twenty thousand."

"I will see her in a nunnery first! Fifteen thousand, and not a penny more!"

Pleased with the ease of the negotiations, Philip agreed amicably. "Dearest Papa, I shall await notice that Edmund has agreed to the new settlements. Pray convey my warmest sentiments to my affianced." He departed with a self-satisfied swagger.

With impatient hauteur mixed with repugnance, Lord Uxeter waited in his carriage while the footman presented his calling card at the door.

Following his interview with the earl, Edmund had sent word to Sir Garfield of his change of heart concerning the alliance, but now the baronet had inexplicably changed the agreement by putting forward his niece. He had described the girl as genteel, demure, and obedient, but Edmund cared only that she was sound for breeding and came with a fortune.

These ruminations were interrupted by the footman, who lowered the steps with word the baronet would receive him without delay. His lordship gracefully alighted and paused to brush an imaginary speck of lint from his sleeve. He adjusted the Mechlin lace at his neck and cuffs, and advanced to the house. Another servant led him into the salon, where he paced the room edgily while awaiting the arrival of the man he remembered only as a loutish boor.

In his library, Sir Garfield glanced in the mirror to straighten his lopsided peruque and wobbled more than walked to the salon to greet his potential in-law. He was surprised by the arrival, given Lord Uxeter's distaste for business matters. He had expected the reply through a solicitor rather than the prospective bridegroom.

Had he anticipated the call, he might have abstained from so much drink, but he was still excessively put out by his earlier encounter with the younger Drake. Damn, but he was growing to dislike the whole family! The youngest son was an unscrupulous upstart, and the elder a patronizing, pompous ass, but he believed the connection would serve him well. He pasted on his most jovial smile.

"'Tis is a most unanticipated pleasure, my lord." While Lord Uxeter made a punctilious bow, the baronet advanced and engulfed the viscount's pale, well-manicured hand in his own beefy one. The viscount forced a smile that failed to reach his eyes. The man was exactly the coarse buffoon he had remembered.

"Please you to be seated, dear man." Sir Garfield assumed an armchair by the hearth, indicating another to his guest.

Lord Uxeter ignored the gesture with a brush of his hand. He spoke tersely. "Pray forgive my dearth of pleasantries, sir. I am here only to clarify your proposal and wish to come directly to the point."

"Indeed, indeed. Straight to business, I always say."

"If I understand correctly, you have put forward your niece as a more suitable bride. While I do not dismiss the notion, my betrothal to your daughter, Beatrix, is already announced. How do you expect this to be accomplished without a scandal?"

"If 'tis only that apprehension that concerns you, my lord, have no fear. *The Times* named a Wallace chit from Yorkshire. As my family is unknown in London, who would remark if you wed one

Wallace chit or another? I should doubt the matter would be heeded at all." Sir Garfield smiled broadly.

Lord Uxeter confessed the truth of it. Though his marriage might astonish some among his acquaintance, there would be no need to make explanations.

"Have you any other objections, my lord?" Sir Garfield asked. "The dowry is acceptable?"

"The dowry is adequate, sir." At thirty thousand pounds, it was actually a fortune, but Lord Hastings's will had provided the final impetus for his acceptance.

"Then there's naught more than to plan the bridal, eh?"

The man was no buffoon, after all, Edmund decided. This bumbling rustic just might be the proverbial wolf in sheep's clothing.

"Just look at this, girls," Lady Felicia said to Charlotte and Beatrix as she read the social section of the Times. "There are six-and-thirty betrothal announcements today. I have counted six-and-thirty! One of them is even our foreign secretary, Lord Carteret! The man must be well over half a century, and here he's taking Lord Pomfret's daughter, Lady Sophia Fermor, to wife. She is reputedly younger than Lord Carteret's own daughter! I am shocked her father should allow the match with such a despicable lecher. Shocking! You remember what Major Drake said of the secretary and all his young girls!"

"Mama," Beatrix interrupted, "the foreign secretary wasn't the debaucher. That was General... oh... General-something-French. The secretary is only a sot."

"Beatrix, a lady does not speak so!" she admonished. "But look at the settlements, Beatrix!" her mother continued. "Upon my word, she is to have sixteen hundred pounds per year jointure, four hundred pounds pin money, and another two thousand in jewels.

We must show this to your papa. As a future viscountess, you should have at least as much."

A maid interrupted to notify Lady Felicia of a guest.

"Well, who is it, Betsy?"

"I don't know, mum, but 'tis an elegant gentleman arrived by private carriage and with a manservant to boot."

Lady Felicia's curiosity was more than she could bear. She excused herself from the girls and breezed into the large salon. "Sir Garfield," she said, feigning surprise, "I was unaware we had a guest."

"Allow me to introduce Viscount Uxeter, m'dear."

"Lady Wallace? 'Tis a delight, I assure you." With an indifferent smile and perfunctory air kiss, Edmund accepted the lady's proffered hand. "Your husband and I have just concluded our business."

Cluing his wife, Sir Garfield expounded, "Indeed, we were just now speaking of the upcoming bridal. Lord Uxeter has condescended to wed our Charlotte."

"Charlotte? But what of Beatrix? 'Twas Trixie's betrothal we announced. My head quite spins! Surely you aren't saying that both girls are to wed Lord Uxeter?"

"A ridiculous notion, m'dear."

"But why do you say Charlotte? Beatrix is the elder and should rightfully wed first," she remonstrated.

"'Tis inconsequential which of the girls weds first," he informed his bewildered wife. "His lordship has deemed Charlotte more suitable."

"Charlotte! But she has not half the beauty or accomplishments of our Trixie! And what of the title? Beatrix was set on being a viscountess," she lamented as much for herself as for her daughter. Sir Garfield quelled her with a darkling look.

"I suppose it makes little difference. They are both of marriageable age," she grudgingly ceded then addressed the prospective groom. "You will stay for tea, Lord Uxeter? I shall send for the girls."

"S'pose it's nigh time to meet your bride, eh?" Sir Garfield added with a leer.

When his hostess rang for both the teacart and the bride, Edmund perceived no escape.

Beatrix entered first, with Charlotte demurely proceeding behind.

"Lord Uxeter," Sir Garfield began, "I present my niece, Miss Charlotte Wallace, and my daughter, Lady Beatrix Wallace."

Beatrix, paying little heed to the order of precedence in the introduction, stepped forward and dipped in her most graceful obeisance. "Lord Uxeter," she gushed, "how delightful to make your acquaintance. You are the second most pleasant surprise we have had this day."

He lifted an inquiring brow.

"Oh! I don't mean to *place* you second!" She giggled. "I meant to say that we learned this morning of a planned excursion to Vauxhall Pleasure Gardens. This was the first surprise. My cousin, mother, and I were just discussing it. Have you been to Vauxhall, my lord? But how silly of me; of course, you have been. We are only newly arrived from Yorkshire, you see, and pleasure gardens are quite novel to us." She waved her fan and flashed a beguiling smile.

"Indeed, I pine to see all the spectacles of London, but Vauxhall is first on the list. I hear there are even illuminations planned for the opening. In Yorkshire, one hardly has occasion for such things as fireworks. I can scarce describe my excitement!" she finished breathily.

"Your enthusiasm is quite overwhelming," Edmund drawled, appalled by this babbling bovine who seemingly embodied all his aversions to the feminine gender. The idea of marriage to this vapid, chattering cow was completely repugnant, regardless of her fortune.

Charlotte, lost in her own ruminations, had paid little heed to their visitor until Lady Felicia interceded and pushed her to the fore. "Lord Uxeter, my niece, Charlotte."

Lord Uxeter's gaze raked her as if inspecting a horse at auction.

"Pray present yourself to your betrothed, my dear," her aunt urged in a fierce whisper.

As realization crawled up her spine, the color drained from Charlotte's face. "M–m–y betrothed? B–but Beatrix?"

"There was a simple misunderstanding, dear girl. Nothing to trouble yourself with. All is most amicably resolved," Sir Garfield interjected while studying Lord Uxeter's reaction.

Edmund smiled charmingly and bowed over Charlotte's limp hand, immensely relieved that this quiet and unassuming young woman was now his affianced. "Miss Wallace," he began after her compulsory curtsy, "no doubt this is come as a surprise." His words were sympathetic, but his smile was cold. "Your cousin speaks of Vauxhall. Since your family is unacquainted with the pleasure gardens and their nuances, it would be my greatest pleasure to accompany you."

"We should be honored with your escort, my lord," Lady Felicia tittered.

"How gracious," Beatrix replied. Charlotte sent her cousin an unheeded look of panic.

"The pleasure gardens open at nine," Lord Uxeter continued, oblivious to Charlotte's discomfiture. "As one must cross the river by barge, my carriage shall collect you at precisely eight of the clock."

Edmund bestowed Charlotte a last appraising look and turned to Sir Garfield. "The contract shall be executed, sir." He then took his leave.

Charlotte's life had unraveled before her very eyes. Only this morning she and Robert had arranged an assignation at Handel's statue, but now with Lord Uxeter accompanying them, it would be impossible to sneak away.

Why had she and Robert not run off together when they had had the chance?

She had warned him their time was running out.

And now it had.

Twenty-two

RACE TO GRETNA GREEN

*A*rriving back at his quarters that afternoon, Philip found Robert wretchedly pacing the floors.

"You look a mess, Devington. What has you so bedeviled?"

"Charlotte's uncle has arranged to marry her off, and I am about to be dispatched to Flanders. I shall return to find her wed!"

"If Sir Garfield brought his family to London expressly for that purpose, he will certainly see her wed. With no dearth of noble blood hemorrhaging their estates, he'll have no difficulty achieving what he seeks. A generous dowry covers a multitude of sins, you know, even common birth. I stand as living proof."

"Then the deed's nigh done, and I don't see a deuced thing I can do about it!"

"Short of absconding to Scotland, there's not a bloody thing to be done."

"Are you advocating elopement? 'Twas the last suggestion I expected to hear from *you*."

"As your commanding officer, I could hardly suggest such a thing," he answered sternly.

"I thought my ears must have deceived me."

"However… were I to speak as a friend who has long wearied of your perpetual pining, I might be pressed to encourage the notion."

"It's not that I haven't considered it a thousand times, Philip. I live in daily fear of losing her, but I still have nothing to offer her by way of security. I could scarce put a roof over our heads on my pay."

"How much longer do you think to dangle after her? If you wait 'til you make your fortune as a soldier, you will lose her. It may be time to play your cards or fold them, Devington."

"I depart for Gravesend in a for'night. How could we possibly post to Gretna Green and back in time? Hard riding, it's got to be five days at least."

"Then I suggest haste," Philip answered.

Robert considered further. "We would have to leave straight away, tonight even. But how to steal Charlotte from under her uncle's nose?"

"The King's Plate is to be run in Newmarket day after tomorrow. Surely Sir Garfield will attend, and the event will last several days. If he is unaware of your departure, the deed will be done before he's the wiser."

"You must go to Newmarket and keep Sir Garfield diverted long enough for us to get to Scotland," Robert said.

"Newmarket? I suppose I could manage the sacrifice." Philip grinned. It would be no great hardship to pass a few days in three of his four best-loved activities: uninhibited drinking, gaming, and racing. Now if there were women as well...

Robert continued to mull over his plan. "But what should we do after the wedding? What then?" he mused aloud.

Philip laughed in mocking exasperation. "My dear boy, if you don't know what to do with the woman once you have her, there's no help for you!"

"That's hardly what I meant, Drake! If we do succeed, what shall become of Charlotte once I depart for the Continent? Even if I could find suitable apartments for her, I can scarce leave my new bride alone in London for who knows how long. And I refuse to see her as a camp follower."

"Let's consider the potential outcome, shall we? If naught goes awry, you will shortly have your precious Charlotte. I will have my heiress and her substantial dowry. Edmund will be jilted and humiliated, which is a bonus unto itself. Devington, the entire scheme so pleases me, I'll make you a wedding gift of a thousand pounds if you carry it off! You may then set her up comfortably in Flanders with the other officers' wives."

"A thousand pounds, Philip? 'Tis a small fortune."

"With Beatrix's dowry, I can afford to be munificent. All things considered, a thousand pounds is a veritable bargain." Philip chuckled. "You see how fortunes can change on a whim?"

"Then I'm decided. I shall go tonight and fetch my bride."

"I had begun to doubt you had the ballocks to pull it off, my friend."

As he thought through his plan, Robert ignored the jab. "We need to move quickly. Inconspicuously. Horseback," he said suddenly. "We must ride out of London and later pick up a stage from a coaching inn. We shall need Amoret, Philip. Charlotte needs a fast horse."

"This may not be such a good idea. It may be overtaxing to the mare and the girl."

"No need to fret; she won't ride all the way to Scotland. We just need to get a good start. Besides, the mare is rightfully Charlotte's to begin with. It's just a loan. By the hand of Providence, we'll be in Gretna Green by week's end if you ensure us that head start."

"You need not fear on that account. Newmarket will be bustling. Upon my word, I'll contrive to keep Sir Garfield busy, but my involvement goes no further, Devington. If aught goes awry, I can know nothing of your elopement… nothing, you understand." His gaze was intent. "I shan't jeopardize my own plans and future, even for our friendship."

"I fully understand your faithful and consistent commitment to your self-interests, Drake," Robert said.

"Just so. It's vital we understand one another on this point. Furthermore," Drake added, "I caution, as your superior officer, that we could be called back at a moment's notice. Should this occur, you must abort the scheme at once."

"I am painfully aware of the need to conduct my business expeditiously. Don't worry about me; you just don't lose your shirt on the races. We'll need that thousand pounds when all is done."

"Don't fret for my shirt; instead, you take care not to lose your ballocks. You'll have need of *them* when all is done!"

❧

"Is there any word yet, Letty?" Charlotte asked anxiously.

"Aye, miss. I've a note delivered by the coachman. He's an easy enough bribe, that one."

Charlotte took the note from Letty, reading it with trembling hands.

"What is the news from yer cap'n that has ye so fretful?"

"He has proposed an elopement this very night." She spoke with mixed emotions of elation and despair. How on earth could they accomplish it with so little time to plan?

Letty's face lit with excitement but wilted at Charlotte's tearful expression. "Why are ye crying, miss? Ain't it what you've wanted?"

"Aye, Letty, it's what I most wish, but 'tis impossible!"

"Miss, sometimes love runs a crooked course, but it don't mean ye can't get there eventually. The cap'n don't see no other way, to be sure. Lest ye want to find yourself hitched to his high-and-mighty lordship, you'd best take off to Scotland with the young cap'n."

"But if we are caught, my uncle will pull Robert before the magistrate so fast our heads would spin. He would face kidnapping charges, and I would be forced to repeat wedding vows to that wretched viscount. I couldn't bear it!"

"There now." Letty handed Charlotte a handkerchief to dry her eyes and blow her nose. "Surely there is a way. We just need to think of sommat to keep ye confined to your room for a spell, sommat that would give ye time to get to Scotland afore you're noticed missing."

"But how, Letty? How can I possibly buy us enough time to get to Scotland undiscovered?" She racked her brain for what to do. "How can I disappear without anyone's notice? I pled a headache when we stole away to Doncaster for the race, but it was only one night. 'Tis not an ailment that would keep Beatrix and Aunt Felicia away for days."

"Nay, not the headache," Letty mused aloud. "We need sommat else to keep folks away from ye, another ill. What ills could ye fake that would keep ye confined for a time? Not consumption, nor the smallpox. There's no way to invent them telltale blisters. Now think... what ailment could we fake?"

"Fever?" Charlotte answered. "Fever could be feigned any manner of ways."

"I don't ken that fever alone would keep yer aunt away from ye."

"Letty, I have it!" Charlotte exclaimed.

"What, miss?"

"It was in the paper just today. Lady Sophia Fermor had to postpone her wedding with Lord Carteret because she has contracted scarlet fever."

"Scarlet fever? To be true, 'tis very catching and 'twould keep ye confined for a for'night or more. I had it m'self as a lass. Shouldn't be too hard to invent, neither. A pot of rouge to pink yer cheeks, a touch of white face paint around the mouth. A bit of onion juice to shine yer eyes, and a hot brick under the blankets to make ye feel feverish. None will come near ye for fear of catchin' it. Jest trust Letty. We'll have ye married off sure enough." Letty grinned mischievously.

"Then we shall be off to Scotland this night. Letty." She paused.

"I shall need your aid to help cover my tracks, but when my Uncle discovers me gone..." She regarded her former nurse with a worried frown.

"Now don't ye worrit yerself about me, my lambkin. Let's just think how to get a message to yer captain in time."

"I'll write a note, Letty, and give you money for a hackney to Horse Guards. We don't have much time."

"Aye, miss. Now get yourself undressed and into the bed. I'll fetch the brick and slip into her ladyship's room for the face paint."

Hearing of Charlotte's malaise, Lady Felicia went immediately to her niece's room, but she stopped just short of the door when she perceived Charlotte's fever-glazed eyes, rubicund cheeks, and blanched mouth, all signs characteristic of scarlet fever. There must be an epidemic, she thought with a flutter of alarm. Just this morning, she had read of Lady Sophia Fermor's suffering the same fate.

"How is she, Letty?"

"She's feverish, ma'am, and needin' rest, but 'tis not so severe a case. A se'nnight in bed should see her right as rain, and I can nurse her for you. I've had the illness afore."

"But we were to attend the grand opening of Vauxhall. How am I to explain to Lord Uxeter?"

"She's in no condition to go out, ma'am, aside from it's very catching, you ken."

"You will keep me apprised should her condition worsen?" Lady Felicia asked.

"Indeed, ma'am."

Once Lady Felicia departed, Letty slipped out and hailed a hackney to deliver her to Horse Guard headquarters, where she located Captain Devington.

Recognizing the woman immediately, Robert flushed with panic. "What is it, Letty? Is something come of Charlotte?"

"Just the scarlet fever." Letty chuckled.

His concern heightened. "Charlotte's ill!"

"Nay, Cap'n Robert," she explained. "I come to tell ye we devised a plan, Charlotte and me. She's faking the illness."

"Is she?" he repeated, relieved and impressed with their resourcefulness.

"His lordship arrives at eight with his carriage. The miss will remain abed with hope they all depart without her. Once the house is empty, she'll meet ye by the garden gate."

"None could have devised a better plan, Letty. Pity you are a woman. His Majesty's army could use more talented strategists," he said with a grin.

"Sure enough we made a plan, but ye'll have to execute it wi'out mishap," Letty cautioned.

"The hour is growing late. You had best go before you are missed. Tell her I shall meet her as planned."

Letty paused. "Godspeed to ye both, Cap'n."

The elegant black town carriage with the gold emblazoned crest arrived at precisely eight o'clock. Lord Uxeter, elegantly attired in black velvet evening dress, alighted from his carriage only to learn from a flustered Lady Felicia that his affianced had suddenly taken ill.

"The *Times* wrote of a city-wide epidemic," she artfully dissembled. "I should have sent a note, but we have just learned of it, you see." She offered the anxious apology, correctly surmising that his lordship was not possessed of a compassionate nature.

"How very unfortunate for her, but if we are soon to be wed, we must be seen about in polite society." He spoke coldly.

"But surely you would not wish her taken from her sick bed?"

Gaining some mastery of his temper, Lord Uxeter replied, "A

ridiculous notion. Pray pardon my fit of pique, Lady Wallace. My deep disappointment prods my ill humor." His words were solicitous, but his manner barely concealed his displeasure. *Damned inconsiderate chit!*

"We shall say nothing more of it, my lord."

"But 'tis such a lovely evening to waste, is it not, Mama?" Beatrix interjected. "And Lord Uxeter has gone to so much trouble on our account, Charlotte would not wish for *us all* to miss the opening night. She would never be so selfish. Would she, Mama?" The question was posed rhetorically.

Lord Uxeter felt the trap closing about him. Would he be forced to bear alone the company of these two most fatuous and vulgar specimens of womanhood? His distress was alleviated only by the timely arrival of Sir Garfield and Charles Wallace.

"What ho, Uxeter!" Sir Garfield clumsily stepped out from the sedan chair and eagerly approached.

Edmund visibly flinched, anticipating another assault, but Sir Garfield, anxious to bring his son to the viscount's notice, offered only a perfunctory bow in greeting. He then put forward the honorable Charles Wallace, only son and heir to the Yorkshire baronetcy. Introductions accomplished, he amiably remarked, "Off to Vauxhall, eh?" He suddenly took notice of his niece's absence. "Where the devil's Charlotte?" he demanded.

"She's taken ill, Sir Garfield."

"The devil you say! Blast the girl!" he cursed.

Lord Uxeter, whose attention was drawn to the fresh-faced Charles Wallace, responded with greater compassion than he had previously expressed. "I doubt there is cause for alarm. The illness will soon pass with my betrothed in such capable hands."

"Indeed so, my lord," Lady Felicia agreed. "She is looked after by her childhood nurse. Rest assured, Charlotte will be right as rain within the for'night."

"She shall be advised to do so," Sir Garfield remarked. "She is a most dutiful and compliant girl, my niece." Suspicious of her sudden infirmity, he reassured the viscount with less confidence than he actually felt. "There is surely no reason to blight everyone's pleasure."

Edmund masked his displeasure. In reality, he would have liked nothing better than to forgo Vauxhall. He held far different notions of amusement. Suddenly, he smiled. "Why shouldn't young Charles join the party now we are reduced to an odd number?"

Sir Garfield lit up at the notion, eager to encourage his son's acquaintance with the peer. "A capital idea! Charles?" He looked to his son.

Charles flushed with pleasure to be included in the company of one who could help him navigate the sophisticated city. "I should be much pleased to attend, my lord."

He would have been surprised to know Lord Uxeter was equally keen.

❧

Robert arrived at nine o'clock and waited patiently at the garden gate. By ten, Charlotte had yet to appear. He paced anxiously. His mind raced in fear their plans were already foiled, until he detected the small, cloaked figure hugging the shadows.

Enveloped in darkness, he advanced toward her. Charlotte fell deeply into Robert's embrace. "I'm so sorry to be late, but my uncle was about, and then the servants…"

He hushed her swiftly with his kiss while cocooning her tightly against him.

"I had begun to think all was lost," he whispered warmly into her hair, but aware of the urgency of time, he wrapped his cloak about them and bustled her down the narrow lane to the waiting hackney. He spoke brief instructions to the driver and then helped her inside.

"Why Whitehall?" she asked.

"I'm afraid this bodes to be a long and uncomfortable journey," he apologized in advance. "We had little time to plan, and with no stage coaches scheduled for another day, we must set out by horseback. I shan't doubt it will be a hard ride. Do you think you are up to it, my little love? It's not too late to go back…" He searched her eyes for reassurance.

She returned his earnest gaze with one of steadfast determination. "I'm made of sterner stuff than you think, Captain Devington. Don't you know by now I would go to the ends of the earth with you?"

"Then all is indeed well, my love." He murmured his reply against her lips, but the carriage jolted and broke their embrace. Robert put breathing room between them and continued. "I've news to make the journey more tolerable, or at least less unpleasant, my dearest. I have requisitioned your mare."

"Amoret? You have found Amoret!" she exclaimed with joy and wrapped her arms tightly about him.

"Drake and I found her at the Hyde Park sale. I daresay she has missed you in equal measure, but I promise you shall be reunited forthwith. As to our journey, we'll ride only as far as Sheffield and then take the mail to Gretna Green. My plan is unformed after that, but we have several days before we need fret about it."

"Robert, it matters not as long as we get there. Once we are wed, the powers of Hades can't separate us."

The hackney pulled up outside Horse Guard stables, where the saddled horses awaited. The captain alighted first and then assisted her down. Inspecting her attire, he made a final suggestion.

"I have some clothes for you. 'Twould be neither safe nor wise for you to travel dressed as you are. Better if you're again disguised as a lad." Handing her a bundle, he led her to the stall housing her beloved mare. "You may change inside. You need not fear intrusion.

I'll keep watch, but pray make haste. We must put some long miles between us and your uncle this night," he said urgently.

"I won't keep you waiting."

Charlotte quickly changed and stuffed her gown and a few belongings into the pack that Robert secured to her saddle. He gave her a leg up, and then he mounted Mars.

Blessed with a full moon and a clear sky, they set out on London's Great North Road.

Twenty-three

THE BETRAYAL

*L*ondon's pleasure gardens had never been Lord Uxeter's milieu for entertainment. He despised the intermingling of the classes, milling about for no better reason than to gawk at one another. Nevertheless, he pasted on a smile and strolled the grounds with his party, pausing frequently along lamp-lit pathways for his guests to admire the statues, painted murals, imitation Chinese pagodas, triumphal arches, Turkish tents, and Italian ruins; all of which created the fantasy called Vauxhall.

After parading about interminably, they finally arrived at the box he had reserved in the grand arcade. An orchestra played above the teeming dance floor, and Edmund found the music unexceptional at the best moments and offensive to his ears at the worst. He was thankful to be obligated for only one dance set before the midnight illuminations, which he bore with little more than edgy tolerance.

After suffering nearly five hours of Vauxhall in his insipid company, he was nearing the limits of his endurance. Seeking any excuse to retire, he feigned concern for his fiancée, so the party returned home. Lord Uxeter took his leave of the ladies at their door but then turned to address Charles.

"I had in mind to go to one of my clubs for a drink. Would you care to bear me company?"

Eager for acceptance into Lord Uxeter's circle, Charles accepted the invitation, and they proceeded to a private house in St James. Lord Uxeter introduced Charles to a dozen or so men who passed the early morning hours between political discussions, rubbers of whist and piquet, and numerous bottles of wine.

A novice at cards, Charles sat out the play and did his best to feign interest in the political intercourse, but hard as he tried, he could not summon the slightest genuine interest. His boredom led him to imbibe more heavily than he realized. He soon passed out in his chair.

He awoke after a few hours, disoriented and alone in his lordship's company.

"Back to the land of the living, are you, young Charles?" Lord Uxeter gibed with his intense gaze.

Surveying the room through bleary eyes, Charles asked, "Is the comp'ny all departed?"

"Long since retired home or carried to a room above stairs, but I hadn't the heart to wake you. I daresay you are unaccustomed to heavy drink, but you will soon adapt to town life." He laughed indulgently.

"What pray is the hour, m'lord?" Charles asked while groggily rubbing his eyes.

"Just past daybreak."

"Daybreak? Hell and the devil!" Charles started suddenly to his feet.

Lord Uxeter raised a brow.

"M'father, m' lord! We're off to Newmarket today."

"Indeed? I go there myself. Has your father a horse in the race?"

"Indeed. He's pinned his hopes on Tortoise, and I am to ride."

"Then I perceive your predicament. I beg your forgiveness if I have put you out of favor with your father. 'Tis unwise to displease the one who holds the purse strings. I shall have my carriage put to anon and deliver you home. Perhaps we shall meet again on the field? I shall be running Perseus against the four-year-olds. 'Tis time and a half since I've enjoyed a race." He had not run at all since his humiliation at Lichfield.

Charles arrived home within the hour; still half foxed, he staggered into the breakfast room.

"Is that you, Charles? What do you think you are about, making me wait half the morning?" Sir Garfield demanded. "You knew we were to depart early for Newmarket. Most important races of the season! You'd best explain yourself, m'boy." He glowered.

"M'sincere aplolo... apologies, sir," Charles slurred.

"You're bloody well in your cups, boy!" his father retorted.

"Not m'flault, sir." He hiccupped. "Lord Ux'ter invited me to his club. I didn't s'pose you'd have me refuse."

"Uxeter, eh?" His glower morphed into a grin. "Well done, Charles! For God's sake, pour the lad some coffee!" Sir Garfield demanded of the footman. "You'll just have to sleep it off in the carriage. Now go and get yourself presentable. I will allow you half an hour before we depart.

"Escort the lad upstairs, lest he break his fool neck on the way," he told the servant, "and by all means, avoid Lady Felicia. She'll be up in arms if she spies him thus." Sir Garfield chuckled.

As Charles clumsily ascended the stairs on the footman's arm, misfortune met him in the form of his mother. Her gaze raked his rumpled hair and disheveled attire. "Charles! Are you just coming in at this hour? And in this... this... deplorable condition?"

His blank look failed to convey his innocence.

"I shall speak immediately to your father!" Lady Felicia stormed into the breakfast room. "Have you beheld your son, Sir Garfield?"

"Indeed. Foxed to the gills, ain't he?" He chuckled.

"This is no laughing matter," she insisted. "I question the wisdom of encouraging such a connection with Lord Uxeter. What kind of gentleman would keep a young man out all night and send him home in such a state?"

"Lord Uxeter is a gentleman of the town, and our boy is a man grown. You should be pleased he has been so initiated. Indeed, this may be a step in the right direction for our Charles. The boy has been in the country far too long. A binge or two will do him no harm. I assure you he will sleep it off in the carriage. 'Tis sixty miles to Newmarket."

"I'll warrant half a day's ride in a jostling carriage will make him positively ill. He'll rue last night's reveling then," she prophesied.

"You may well be right on that account, m'dear."

"Speaking of illness, Sir Garfield, should I send for a physician? Charlotte has not stirred since yesterday forenoon. Mayhap the girl should be bled."

"M'dear, you know I take little stock in such practices. Why don't you go to her room and see if she's in her right mind. If she's lost her wits with fever, by all means send for the physician."

"Very well, but pray wait your departure until I have seen her. I care not to be alone in London with a sick girl, you know."

"Charles has already put us behind schedule, madam. I shall not tolerate any further delay. The girl will be fine."

"Always the races!" Lady Felicia exclaimed with dismay and went to check on her niece.

Her rap on the door took Letty by surprise. "Who is it?" the maid inquired apprehensively.

"'Tis Lady Felicia, come to check on Charlotte."

"But she's yet sleeping."

"Then mayhap the physician should be dispatched. Open the door, Letty."

"But, ma'am, 'tis a very catching fever. You durst not enter," Letty answered nervously.

Growing suspicious, Lady Felicia insisted, "I'll just stand from the doorway. Sir Garfield departs for Newmarket forthwith, and I will not have his niece die in his absence. I demand you open this door. I'm not beyond calling the footmen to remove its hinges!"

Letty said a brief prayer for Charlotte and her captain, and trudged to the door. She turned the key in the lock and cracked it open. Lady Felicia pushed it farther ajar, spying the form under the bedclothes.

"Well, Letty, go rouse her," she demanded.

Letty dragged her feet toward the bed. "I dare not uncover her, ma'am, on account of the fever."

"Letty!" Lady Felicia shouted.

The forlorn maid pulled back the covers to reveal pillows in place of the supposed invalid.

"Where is Charlotte, you impertinent sneak? You will surely be beaten!" she threatened the maid.

"She has eloped, ma'am." Letty burst into tears.

"Eloped! Charlotte has eloped! Sir Garfield!" the lady shrieked, stirring the entire household. Clutching the quaking maid, she dragged her frantically down the stairs.

"What is all the infernal commotion?" Sir Garfield demanded.

"Charlotte has absconded in the night!"

"What! The devil she has! That disobedient, ungrateful little wretch! When?"

Letty now sobbed violently.

"Ye'd better answer well or be horsewhipped, gel!" His threat brought forth only more hysterics. Lady Felicia shook the woman out of her fit.

"After ye all went out t-to Vauxhall." Red eyed, Letty sniffed out her confession. "M-must've been about ten of the clock."

"Devington! Did she run off with Devington?" He interrogated the quivering maid but knew the answer.

"It w-was Captain Robert." Letty recommenced her wailing.

"Charles!" Sir Garfield spun to face his son. "I shall demand satisfaction of that scoundrel! We must find them before Uxeter gets wind of this. I shall not have everything ruined by that upstart!"

"But, Father," the befuddled Charles responded, clutching his throbbing head, "if we don't know where they went, how the devil are we to catch them?"

"Think, boy! Where could they go but to Scotland? They can't bloody well marry anywhere else."

"But they have a whole night's start on us. Impossible to catch them."

"Leave that to me, m'boy. Are the horses put to?" Sir Garfield demanded of the footman.

"Indeed, sir. The coachman's been waiting this hour or more."

"Come, Charles, I know just the man to assist in this hour of need." He spoke grimly, and the pair made haste to the waiting carriage.

Early morning traffic was sparse. They arrived at Whitehall within twenty minutes. Sir Garfield unceremoniously disembarked from his carriage and waylaid the first trooper he encountered.

"Major Philip Drake," he demanded. "I must see him at once!"

"Know you which unit he commands, sir?" the soldier asked.

"Horse Guards, of course! Why the devil would I come here otherwise? I have no time to waste on such impertinence!"

The soldier considered having some fun with the pretentious sod, but the man's purpling demeanor was so agitated, he thought wiser of it. "You might try the stables. A party of officers was departing for Newmarket this morning. He may have been amongst them."

Sir Garfield ungraciously spun around and barked to the coachman to carry them to the stables, hoping to catch his quarry. As luck would have it, the four officers had already departed, but Sir Garfield was resolute. He directed his coachman to the Newmarket Road, sparing not the whip.

Charles, now acutely experiencing the effects of his excesses, fell violently ill with the rocking and swaying of the pitching vehicle. Only fear of transferring his father's wrath onto his own head kept him from halting the coach. He suffered in miserable agony until he was finally lost to sleep.

They covered fifty miles in record time, pulling into the stable yard of the Crown at Great Chesterford just as the officers were mounting to depart the inn. Spotting Major Drake within the group, Sir Garfield abruptly halted and leaped from the coach, with Charles staggering behind.

"Drake! I demand a word with you instantly!"

Winthrop looked at the baronet and then cast Philip a quizzing look. Philip said with measured insouciance, "'Twould appear I am to be detained, gentlemen. Pray go on without me. I'll catch up anon."

Unperturbed, Philip dismounted, and the three remaining officers spurred their horses out of the stable yard.

"Might I inquire what has you in such a state, Sir Garfield?"

"You know damned well what this is about!" the baronet roared.

Philip blinked innocently and said with an ingenuous protest, "I am quite benighted, sir."

"I don't hold for a minute that you are ignorant or innocent of this… conspiracy! I speak of Charlotte and Devington. Do you deny knowledge of their elopement?"

"I am uninvolved in any such adventure," Philip replied impassively.

"Uninvolved, are you? Well, you are about to become very much *involved*, Drake. The brigand absconded with my niece last night, and I have every reason to believe they are for Scotland."

"As I am not the one who eloped with your niece, I fail to see how this concerns me."

"You, Drake, are this moment charged with retrieving my niece before she is ruined, or you shall not see a penny of my money. Beatrix will go forth to a nunnery before I let you get away with this trickery! I will not be made the fool twice!"

"'Tis a near impossible task you thrust upon me," Philip contended. "By your account, they have half a day's start, and I know not by which route."

"They can't have taken any public coach. I am well acquainted with the schedules. The Edinburgh stage departs on Tuesdays and Thursdays. The mail does not run on Sundays, and a private convey-ance would be far too dear for the likes of the captain. I surmise that they rode out on horseback."

Philip could not help appreciate the man's deductive reasoning. "You are likely correct in your assertion, sir."

"And as Devington travels with a woman, they cannot hope to outrun the pace you will set to overtake them."

"You may not realize what a neck-or-nothing rider Charlotte is, Father," Charles interjected. Excited by the prospect of a chase, he eagerly volunteered, "I'll accompany Major Drake. No doubt he will need assistance once he finds them."

"You'll do no such thing, impudent puppy! You couldn't even sit a horse in your present condition. Ridiculous notion! Besides, you are to ride in the King's Plate. We shall proceed as planned."

"But as your son and Charlotte's close male relative," Charles argued, "is it not my duty to defend our family's honor?"

"Under the circumstances, I think not, m'boy. You have no knowledge of swordplay, and Devington, although a scoundrel, is an experienced soldier. The major is much better qualified to take care of this ugly business."

Notwithstanding his longtime friendship with Robert, Charles was angered and humiliated to be brushed aside by his father as unworthy to the task. However, with no horse or weapon at his disposal, he had to swallow his pride and continue with his father to Newmarket.

"You have five days, Drake. Five days to return my niece. I shall have satisfaction! I hope I am completely understood in the matter." He issued a challenging look.

"Indubitably," Philip replied with a subtle clench of his jaw.

"Five days!" Sir Garfield repeated and strode back to his carriage, followed by his sulking son.

"Bloody hell!" Philip cursed, remounting Hawke and spurring him northward.

Robert and Charlotte rode through the night at a punishing pace, stopping only to rest and water their horses. By noon, with over sixty miles behind them, they arrived on the outskirts of Northampton. Famished and near spent, they needed a decent meal and a couple of hours rest if they were to continue any farther. Wary to avoid traffic at any of the larger coaching inns, they located a small tavern where the captain and his young *cousin* greedily partook of a hearty but rustic meal of meat pasties, bread, cheese, and small beer.

"Nothing ever tasted so good," Charlotte uttered between mouthfuls, heedless of good manners. "I feared I would drop from the saddle if we had to ride another mile."

"My fears exactly, young *Charles*," he tenderly reminded her of caution. "While I am accustomed to hard riding and sparse comfort, we have yet many miles ahead of us. If I bespeak a room for you for a few hours rest, do you think you might be able to carry on?"

"I appreciate your solicitude, but pray don't fear for me. I don't profess to being equal to a hardened soldier, but I am made of sterner stuff than you think. Allow me but a couple of hours repose, and I shall prove my fortitude." Her wan smile didn't fool him for a moment.

"I estimate another forty miles or so to Leicester. If we push, we can take rooms tonight at the Old Greyhound. 'Tis a clean and decent establishment with tolerable food. They frequently billet troops, so our presence should go unremarked."

Robert paid the reckoning for their meal and escorted Charlotte to the single shabby room over the tavern. Observing her ragged condition and their dingy quarters, he was overcome with guilt. He grasped both her hands in his. "You deserve so much better than this, my little love. I just pray you never grow to hate me for taking you away."

She had run away from a betrothal to a nobleman, who would have assured her a title and comfort, just to settle for an uncertain future with a penniless captain.

"Don't you understand, Robert? This signifies nothing to me." She gestured at their surroundings. "It matters only that we are together and free at last to make our lives."

A wave washed over him, a swell of love so powerful he thought he would drown in it. He never loved her more than in this moment. He wanted to pull her to him and bathe her in the depths of his love, but this was neither the time, nor, he thought more grimly, the place. Instead, he lay beside her on the narrow bed, holding her close, stroking her hair, sheltering her in the protection of his arms.

Basking in this moment, Charlotte pressed her head to his drumming heart. She closed her eyes, and instantly, exhaustion overtook her while Robert dozed in a soldier's hazy state of semiconscious vigilance.

"My little love, you deserve better, and God willing, I shall provide it," he whispered.

Philip Drake rode as if chased by the devil. Damn, damn, and bloody damn! His blood coursed hotly at his ridiculous errand: chasing a pair of runaway lovers across the country. This was one complication he didn't want, didn't need, especially since he had encouraged the elopement.

Devington had dangled helplessly after the girl, and Philip's machinations had finally compelled him to act, but in suggesting the notion, Philip never once considered that *he* would be coerced to pursue them. But what choice had he?

He had suggested Charlotte's betrothal to Edmund to solve his own dilemma regarding Beatrix. After all Philip had been through to ensure his future, he couldn't let it simply slip away, especially not if Beatrix was carrying his child. Even putting aside the dowry, he was not such a rogue as to allow her to wed someone else, especially his brother, under the circumstances.

He openly acknowledged his past rakish behavior, but at heart he was still a gentleman. Now forced to choose, he found he desired to act the part. His intentions were, for once, honorable; he wished to marry Beatrix. But only by retrieving Charlotte and destroying the other couple's happiness could he guarantee his own. His conscience pricked.

Though part of him hoped Devington would make this an impossible task, Philip was resolved to overtake them and return Charlotte to her uncle. He saw no other way. May the best man win, he thought grimly.

He knew they already had a twelve to fourteen hour start on him, but just how many miles they'd put behind them before stopping to rest was anyone's guess. Philip would ride hard to gain Leicester, eighty miles from Great Chesterford but over a hundred from London. He calculated his route would afford him a twenty-mile advantage, making up about four hours of their lead.

Even pushing hard, they couldn't be much more than halfway there by this time. An average soldier, traveling light on a good horse, could cover seven to eight miles per hour and up to seventy miles a day if he rested his horse sufficiently.

Philip doubted that Robert could maintain such a pace while riding with Charlotte, and he questioned whether they would have the resources to hire fresh horses. Unlikely. They would be more liable to keep their own mounts rather than entrust Mars and Amoret to some unknown hostler's care. Perforce, they would rest more frequently, thus losing several more hours of their lead. If

Philip changed horses, he could ride straight through to Leicester by midnight.

He estimated Robert and Charlotte would break their journey somewhere between London and Northampton. The girl couldn't possibly complete three hundred miles by horseback. It would be a cruel and arduous ride for a man, let alone a slip of a girl. They would continue on to either Sheffield or Doncaster, where they might safely stable their horses and pick up either the stage or the mail to Scotland.

Philip had little doubt he would catch up with them. He had already ridden the better part of fifty miles in six hours, a bruising pace. Hawke had been fresh and enthusiastic at the outset, but the distance had nearly spent him. Philip feared pushing any further, lest he seize up or grow lame.

"Sorry, m'boy." He patted the steaming horse's neck. "I fear we soon part company. The next coaching house or livery must be your home until I can collect you, but I've no doubt you'll appreciate the break." The horse nickered as if in agreement.

Drake lessened the pace, but by the time they reached the next village, Hawke had lost a shoe. The horse could go no farther. Finding no livery, Philip dismounted and led his drooping horse to the village smithy.

"Excuse me, good man," Philip said, addressing the burly smith, "might there be in this village a sound horse for hire?"

Busy at his forge, the man did not immediately respond.

Philip tied his horse and addressed him more adamantly. "I seek a horse for hire, man. The matter is quite urgent."

The burly man stood and surveyed the major. "Next coaching house and livery be twenty miles, in Leicester. Best ye try there."

"Twenty miles! This horse is past spent and going lame. I must acquire a replacement. How much to hire Goliath?" He indicated a big draught tied nearby.

"'Ow'd ye know 'is name?" asked the bewildered man.

Losing patience with this simpleton, Philip demanded, "How much to hire your horse? I shall require him only as far as Leicester, where I can procure something more suitable. Rest assured, I shall leave him at the nearest livery."

Perceiving opportunity in the major's urgency, the man greedily replied, "Two guineas."

"The devil, you say! That's highway robbery! I can hire a coach-and-four a full day for half as much!"

"Seems to me there be no coach-'n'-four at yer disposal, and seein' yer horse is nigh lame, 'twould seem ye got little choice. 'Tis no matter to me." The man shrugged, turning back to his forge.

Philip's ire rose at the outright usury, but he wasted valuable time. "I'll pay you one deuced guinea," he countered, "and not an infernal ha'penny more. Furthermore, you'll bloody well see to my horse! Should you unwisely refuse my offer, I shall requisition said horse in His Majesty's service."

Realizing the veracity of the threat, the smith grunted assent and left his forge to fetch the draught, while Philip pulled his saddle and pack from Hawke.

"I will be back in a few days to collect this one, and if, by happenstance, he is gone when I return, I will see you hung for horse thievery. Do we understand each other now, my good man?"

Philip tossed the man a guinea, but to his vexation, his saddle girth was several inches shy of accommodating the bigger horse. Rather than wasting more time and indignity haggling for the cart, Philip swung bareback onto the giant and spurred the sluggish beast into the bone-setting trot he was to suffer for the next twenty miles.

Finally reaching the livery at Leicester, the major dismounted, his fine breeches now covered in dirt and horse sweat. He handed the carthorse off to a sniggling groom.

Famished and fatigued, he arranged for a fresh horse and trod on to the Old Greyhound Inn, where he bespoke a room and inquired of the innkeeper if he had seen an officer traveling with a young woman. With the negative reply, Philip procured a bottle of wine and a stale loaf and made his way to his chamber. Little did he know, climbing into bed for the few remaining hours until sunrise, that Robert and "Charles," arriving only three hours earlier, occupied the next room.

❧

Startled by a log popping in the hearth, Charlotte abruptly awoke. "Robert?" she whispered to no answer.

Rising from the bed, she glanced around the chamber still steeped in shadow. Peering out the window at the lowered moon, she estimated an hour until sunrise but found herself alone. They had again shared a chamber, but this accommodation had two beds, and his was empty and bereft of his gear. Where was he?

A wave of panic threatened to choke her. Had he changed his mind and left her here? Alone?

Her fear rose to a fever pitch. She searched for her boots and then groped for her coat and cap. Pulling them on, she headed for the door, crashing into Robert as he opened it to enter.

"Robert!" Her voice quivered. "I feared you'd left me!"

"No! God no, Charlotte! How could you even think such a thing? I started the fire for you and left to make provision for our journey. You were so drained I did not wish to disturb your rest until the last possible moment. The horses are now ready, and I have stowed food in our packs to break our fast as we ride. We dare not tarry any longer."

"I'm so sorry. I didn't mean to doubt you, but waking alone…"

"You must never doubt me, my love. Never doubt me." He gripped her shoulders almost painfully and then checked his emotions. "We must be off now. We arrived late enough last night to avoid notice. 'Twould be wise to depart in like manner. We have over sixty miles to Sheffield, but I hope to make it this very night."

"We have come this far; I swear to persevere. Assuredly, I shall."

"Yes, Charlotte, you shall," he said, encouraging her with a tender brush of his lips.

❧

Philip rose with the sun, shaking the cobwebs from his head, his lids still heavy with the wine he had partaken of only a few hours earlier. His jolt to full consciousness arrived with the bracingly frigid water he splashed on his face before hastily donning his clothes. Taking up his pack, he broke his fast in the taproom and was off to the livery.

The young groom who brought out the horse, saddled and ready, inquired, "Be there more tidings of the Young Pretender?"

"None at the moment, lad. We feared invasion on the southern coast a few weeks back, but our proud navy prevailed."

"But what of the Scots? Is the army heading to the border?"

"There is yet no news of moment from the north. Why do you ask?"

"Just wi' two officers heading nor'ward, I thought ye might be carrying news," the boy offered.

"Two officers? Have you seen another heading north?"

"Aye, sir."

"Indeed? When did this other arrive? Was he a Captain of the Horse?" Philip demanded. "Was he alone or accompanied?"

"Can't rightly say when they arrived, but his uniform was like your'n. A stripling accompanied him. Left early, though; must ha' tended their own horses, as I was barely sprung from me bed when they rode out."

"Damme!" Philip swore. "How abominably obtuse! Why didn't I think to inspect the stables last night?"

"A friend of your'n?"

Philip didn't answer but sprang onto the startled horse almost before the groom released the bridle. Wheeling furiously, he departed the stable yard with a clatter of hooves.

With fresh horses after a full night's rest and extra forage, Robert and Charlotte set a more moderate pace than their frantic ride the day before. Easing their pace and breaking every fifteen to twenty miles, Robert was still confident to achieve Sheffield by suppertime, where they would take lodgings at the Dark Horse.

Although the accommodation was shabby, at least Charlotte would have the care of a woman after her long journey. He would order her a private room and a bath so that she might travel the rest of the way clean, refreshed, and returned to feminine attire.

From Sheffield, surely there would be service to Scotland. His hope was for the mail; pulled by six strong horses, it sped along at nearly ten miles per hour. Though not the most comfortable conveyance, it was assuredly the fastest. By mail coach, they could gain Scotch Corner by tomorrow nightfall, and then it was only a day's ride to the border town of Gretna Green.

He would finally have Charlotte. For now, it was enough.

He gazed tenderly at the girl by his side. In her present disguise, she was both the reckless little waif he first admired and the young woman he had come to love so deeply.

Feeling his gaze upon her, Charlotte smiled and blushed, as if reading his thoughts, but their moment was broken by the thunder of hoof beats. With one hand upon his sword hilt, Robert spun his horse around and spied a lone rider coming up hard behind them.

Though the rider was still a good distance away, he could make out the scarlet coat with its blue facings, the colors of the King's

Horse. It could only be a fellow trooper, but something all too familiar in the rider's posture set him on alert.

"Why the devil would Drake be coming north? He's supposed to be in Newmarket!"

"Drake? Are you sure it's Drake? Could he be recalling you to duty? Could he have changed his mind about helping us?" Charlotte's tone registered her growing alarm.

"I can think of no other reason for this pursuit," Robert said, "unless he thinks to retrieve you to his brother. I never would have thought it of him, but if blood is thicker than water…" He paused; then with slow deliberation, he drew his sword. "Ride ahead, Charlotte. I shall settle this. I shall meet you in Sheffield when it is finished."

"Finished!" she cried aghast. "Surely you don't mean to fight him!"

"I shall first determine his purpose, my love, but if he seeks to take you from me, he gives me no choice."

"You can't mean this!"

"I assure you, I do," he said vehemently. "I thought Philip my friend, but if my suspicion is justified, I swear I will draw his blood."

"Robert, I won't have it! We can still outrun him. That's our choice. We will push all the way to Gretna Green if need be!"

"'Tis now a matter of honor, Charlotte. Don't you understand?"

"No. I do not understand! You could be killed." Drawing breath, she challenged him. "If you truly love me, Robert, you will come now, and to hell with honor!" Without looking back, she cued Amoret into a gallop.

Robert squinted at the fast-approaching rider and then at the departing form of his intended bride. His choice now made for him, he cursed, resheathed his sword, and set his horse after Charlotte, with Philip in close pursuit.

Mars soon overtook Amoret, who was no match for the stallion. Pulling alongside, Robert spoke tersely. "For now, we ride. As I know this country better than he, mayhap we can lose him, but if he should catch up…"

"There is no need for violence when we can outrun him. But if he catches up, I pray you will see sense. What if you were wounded, or worse yet, killed? What should I do then?"

Robert was at a loss for reply.

The pair rode on, eating up the miles toward the Scottish border. Looking back over his shoulder for the third time in an hour, with no sign of their pursuer, Robert pulled up and gestured for Charlotte to do the same. Their horses, lathered and blowing, were in dire need of respite. They took shelter in a grove of trees. Charlotte looked anxiously southward. "Do we really dare stop?" she asked, breathless.

"I haven't sighted him," he said, meaning to reassure her. "At the pace you have set, my love, he is surely miles behind, and I fear the consequences if we don't," he said, his concern for the horses evident in his expression. "I daresay it will do us as much good as the horses to use our own legs for a stretch."

He helped her to dismount. With a grimace, Charlotte began walking out the cramps that had threatened her for the past five miles. "He knows our plans. What will happen if he catches up with us?" she asked, compulsively looking over her shoulder again.

"I have been trying to avoid the same thought. I still cannot make sense of it. Although he's unpredictable at times, Philip has been a good friend to me. I can only believe he is pressed into this chase against his own inclination. However, if he has decided it somehow suits his purpose to do so, he will be tenacious. I know him this well; he will invariably do whatever is in his best interest. He confessed as much before we left."

Charlotte noticed his unconscious fingering of his sword hilt as he spoke. Fearful of a confrontation, she urged, "We mustn't give him the opportunity. We must go on! How much longer can the horses last?"

"They must endure until Leeds."

"How much farther is it?"

"About forty miles, I'd say."

"You can't be in earnest! With the distance we've ridden, that will make near a hundred miles in one day!"

"I am dreadfully in earnest, my love. We might have caught a stage or mail coach in Sheffield, but he would anticipate this move and assuredly overtake us. I would lay coin he plans to rest there himself tonight. We *must* press on to Leeds."

"But we should kill the horses in the doing! Can they last a hundred miles?" She eyed their valiant steeds tearfully.

Robert's educated eye scanned the pair critically. "We've covered over half the distance already, and thus far, neither shows sign of lameness, though I worry much more for the mare than for the stallion. Hold up a moment, Charlotte."

Charlotte paused walking her horse. Now breathing easier, Amoret commenced to eagerly cropping grass. Robert ran his hands over the mare and paused to check her pulse. He commented after a while, "She's recovering well, and eating is *always* a good sign." He stooped to examine her legs and feet. "There is no sign of heat or swelling, and her shoes are yet tight," he remarked. "But there's no question they both need a rest." He fondly petted his own horse's neck. "We will tarry here a bit and let them forage, but I think the horses are fit to go on. We shall moderate our pace a bit and should still gain Leeds tonight."

Now reassured about the horses, he turned his attention to Charlotte. "My next concern is how you are holding up, my love. I almost regret this ill-fated escapade."

"Never say that, Robert! We are so close now. Two days ago, our future together was bleak, and had we done nothing, our fates would have been decided for us. I could not have lived with that. We have come so far. Surely we shall persevere!"

"Without mishap, we should arrive shortly after nightfall. Then I promise you a night of rest. Do you really think you can bear it, Charlotte?"

"It appears I still have not proven my mettle to you," she challenged. "I swear to you I will walk to Leeds before I give up!"

"My love, I believe you would try." He laughed wearily. "But don't doubt for a moment that I would carry you before I would ever let you walk."

⁂

Philip had spotted the pair miles earlier but maintained a discreet distance. He knew he could never match their speed once they discovered his pursuit. The horses carrying Charlotte and Robert were bred for stamina and speed, their blood a coveted mix of Eastern and highly cultivated native stock. Philip's livery nag was no match.

He wouldn't catch them before nightfall; however, catch them he would. They had to rest some time, and he had a strong suspicion where it would be. He pushed his horse doggedly northward to Sheffield.

Terminating at the livery, he stabled his hired mount and procured another for what he hoped would be his return to London. Not to repeat his prior error, he inquired of the stablemen whether they had seen a captain accompanied by either a lad or a young woman. None confessed to have seen the pair, but he wasn't surprised. Raised in this county, Robert easily could have found someone to harbor them.

His business in the stables completed, Philip proceeded to the tavern, as confident of Maggie's welcome as of her willingness to provide him with intelligence.

Upon his entrance, Maggie transfixed her eyes on the apparition. She had never thought to see *him* again. She cursed herself for all the false hopes she had once harbored where Philip Drake was concerned. She fought to compose her conflicting emotions and schooled herself to nonchalance. "If it isn't Major Philip. Can't say I expected to see you back in Sheffield."

"Nor did I, but urgent business carries me north."

Her heart wrenched. "Business you say?"

"Indeed, some most unfortunate business, that precludes any time for pleasure..." He regarded her regretfully, and when Maggie refused to meet his dark gaze, he continued back to his purpose. "For the moment my most pressing needs are for a meal, a bed, and any news you might have of Captain Devington and Charlotte Wallace. All at your pleasure, of course."

Beckoning young Jim to fetch a tankard, Maggie sauntered around the bar, wiping her hands on her apron. She led Philip to a corner table where they could speak privately. "Ye seek Cap'n Devington and Miss Charlotte, ye say?"

"They eloped and are this moment heading for the border. They've been riding for two days and are undoubtedly in need of rest. I thought it likely they would come here. Have you seen or heard anything of them?"

"Nay, ne'er a word. 'Tis about time, I say! Any fool could see they was pinin' for each other fierce-like."

"Precisely the problem, Maggie. Her uncle saw it and forbade the match. He has contracted her hand to another, and I have the unlikely fortune of retrieving her."

"Fetch her back! Ye cannot mean it! What right have ye to meddle? I thought him yer friend."

"The matter is more complicated than you could possibly imagine," he replied irritably. "Though I am pressed to act contrary to my inclination, I must return her."

"If that be so, ye can bet yer traitorous arse I know nothing of them!" Maggie's eyes flashed, and she slammed down the tankard, sloshing ale on him.

Philip's eyes danced in amusement. "Have you sufficiently vented your spleen?" He caught Maggie about the waist and pulled her onto his lap, kissing her hard on the mouth.

Maggie first averted her head but suddenly found herself responding, felt the stirrings of her body. It would be so easy to take him upstairs to her bed. She despised him in this moment... but she despised herself even more.

Philip had not at first perceived Maggie's condition, but now he noticed her fuller breasts and the slightly protruding abdomen that her apron concealed. Maggie was carrying some man's bastard. "A damnable waste," he cursed under his breath.

Maggie recognized his look of pity and regret. Her very soul screamed out to tell him, but her pride suppressed the scream. Abruptly, she pushed his hands away and stood, smoothing her apron.

"I know naught to help you, and I must be about me business now."

"Do you indeed?" he asked, the humor now completely vanished from his eyes. "If that is the case, I shall take my leave of you. I have pressing matters of my own."

As he rose to leave, Maggie's sob caught in her throat, but she said nothing until he departed, when she tearfully whispered, "It's your babe. For God's sake, it's yours."

Twenty-four

THE PRICE OF INTEGRITY

*C*ompletely depleted, Robert and Charlotte arrived at the outskirts of Leeds. After Mars and Amoret had faithfully carried them one hundred and eight miles in seventeen hours, the horses were ready to drop and their riders barely balanced in their saddles.

At the very first public house, Robert called the hostler to tend their mounts and then sought the landlord to bespeak rooms. He returned to find Charlotte sprawled asleep over her dozing mare's neck, with her head resting peacefully against the silken mane.

His heart tripped with love and pride at the girl's sheer grit, all for the love of him. He pulled Charlotte's limp form gently from the mare and handed her horse off to the groom. Robert then carried her to the inn and up the stairs to her chamber. He had procured two rooms this time, reminding himself that in just another day she would be his.

Charlotte never stirred while he removed her boots and settled her in bed. He then stumbled blindly to his own chamber, where he collapsed into a comatose slumber. It would be past noon before either of them arose.

Charlotte was first to stir, awakened by the chambermaid tapping upon her door. She pulled herself groggily from bed and approached the dressing table, where she caught a horrified look at the dirty, tangled mess she had become. Aghast at the first reflection she had seen of herself in days, Charlotte bespoke hot water and labored to put herself back in some form of order.

Resolving she had worn boy's clothes for the last time, she cast the filthy garments into the fire, but she was dismayed by the crushed and crumpled gown she pulled from her saddle pack. As it was her only one, she donned the pitiful garment with the consolation that she at least resembled a female once more.

Robert, meanwhile, awoke to the agitations of his stomach. They had ridden for seventeen hours straight and had slept another thirteen with little more than a crust of bread to sustain them. Rising abruptly, he washed with bracingly frigid water and then threw on his clothes in impatience to rectify the neglect imposed on their weary and abused bodies.

Tapping then on Charlotte's door, he found her awake, dressed, and greeting him with a pitiful moan. "Robert, I'm about to expire of hunger!"

"A matter soon rectified, my love." He grinned and offered his arm, and they proceeded down to the breakfast room. He escorted her to a table and left her to order food, while he sought schedules for the northbound coaches. By the time he returned, their meal of bread, cheese, cold chicken, and meat pies had arrived. Overwhelmed with hunger, they eagerly pounced on the repast.

It was several minutes before either spoke, and then only between mouthfuls.

"What have you learned of the coaching schedules?" Charlotte inquired between greedy bites of bread and cheese.

"To our misfortune, we've missed the morning departure to Carlisle, which would have carried us within ten miles of the border," he replied, pausing briefly to swallow some ale. "The Edinburgh mail, however, should be passing through at approximately four this afternoon. We could take it as far as Scotch Corner." He proceeded to devour half a chicken.

"How much farther from there?" she asked, washing down her meat pie with a most unladylike gulp of tea.

Robert held his answer, lest he choke on the drumstick he'd zealously torn from the nearly naked chicken carcass. Pausing only to swallow, he continued matter-of-factly, "'Tis seventy miles after that."

"Seventy miles! Still so far?" she asked in dismay as she tore a large hunk from their second loaf of bread.

"I'm afraid we lost a great deal of time sleeping, but I fear we would ne'er have survived otherwise. As it stands, we must break our journey at Scotch Corner, and from thence, take the next coach to Gretna Green."

She considered this, restraining herself to impatient nibbling on the remaining meat pie. "So we have two hours yet to wait on the mail?"

He nodded, taking another long draught from his tankard.

"Robert," she began, "would it trouble you greatly if I made some purchases while in Leeds?" She cast a dismayed look at her crumpled gown, adding, "I should so like to appear a proper bride."

"I would with my entire being, that I was a man of means who could have provided your heart's desire instead of absconding with you in this pusillanimous and clandestine manner." He ended with a helpless gesture knowing he barely had sufficient funds remaining to cover the rest of the trip.

Charlotte understood their financial difficulties and actually sought to pawn her father's watch and her mother's pearls, the items Robert previously refused to take from her. If her intentions were known, his pride would never allow the sacrifice.

"I have need of only a few small items. If you would but escort me to a shop."

"I suppose we have time," he said. "I'll take you directly, and then I must run by the livery to arrange for the horses. I can attend to them while you shop."

Robert escorted Charlotte to the haberdashery, but as soon as he was out of sight, she made her way to find a pawn broker. The first proprietor of such an establishment eyed her keenly when she withdrew her treasures: the silver watch and milky pearls. With a trembling hand, she offered them up for appraisal.

"One guinea," the man stated with a patronizing smile.

"One guinea? Only one guinea? The watch alone must be worth twice the sum, and the pearls are of the highest quality. Surely the pearls are worth more?"

"One guinea," he repeated with an avaricious gleam.

The price he offered was only a fraction of the items' worth. She was infuriated to be taken advantage of but feared to seek elsewhere, lest she receive no better offer and be forced to return and accept even less. Her stomach churned in indecision.

"I had presumed brigands haunted only the highways." The familiar voice came from behind her. "The lady no longer has need of your money."

Charlotte whirled to face Philip Drake.

"Be pleased to put away your baubles, my dear. I shall provide your fare to London." He put a strong arm about her waist and propelled her from the shop.

Overcoming her initial shock, Charlotte struggled vainly against his grip. "Philip! Just what do you think you're doing?"

He held her fast to his side. "Come along quietly. There is no need to draw attention. I am here to recall Devington, and at Sir Garfield's behest, to retrieve you back to your lawfully betrothed."

"My lawfully betrothed!" she hissed. "It was my understanding you barely stomach *my betrothed*."

"True enough, but there is more to this than you realize."

"Pray don't insult my intelligence, Philip. You covet only my cousin's fortune. I suspected as much from the start, but as Robert's friend, I gave you benefit of doubt."

"My reasons are my own," he snapped.

"But you professed to be his friend!"

"Friendship aside, Robert has no choice but to release you. He has a categorical obligation to obey his superior."

"How dare you interfere like this?"

"I didn't wish it but am now in a most invidious position. I am obligated by my honor to return you."

"But I will not go!"

Philip spoke quietly but compellingly into her ear. "Your refusal could put Devington in great danger. I can place him under arrest, you know. He could face charges."

"What charges?"

"Insubordination and absence without leave. If I am pressed, these are grounds for the courts-martial." Gripping her shoulders, he spun her to face him squarely. "Do you fully understand what I am telling you?"

"Y-you can't possibly mean it," she said, appealing to pitiless, dark eyes.

"I regretfully assure you I do. Don't challenge me," he threatened. "I suggest you come quietly, before Devington has wind of it. Regardless of what you might believe, I harbor a strong repugnance to stain my sword with my best friend's blood." His voice was rueful.

"Your friend? You defile the word!" Grating steel accompanied the retort as Robert drew his saber from its scabbard.

"Sheath your sword, Devington! That is an order. You have led me a merry chase, but I regret to say, my friend, you are run to earth. The hunt is over."

Devington was no match for him. Philip hoped the captain realized as much. Although Philip was prepared to cross swords, he hoped to avoid disgracing him in front of Charlotte.

"It is far from over. It is now become a point of honor, *Major*."
Robert weighed and balanced his saber with a fierce glower.

"Devington, this is senseless. On horseback, you have no match,
but you shall never best me with a blade. I order you for the last
time, Captain," he said with deadly calm, "Sheath. Your. Blade."

"It's been a long time since we have sparred, Drake. Are you still
so assured of your superiority?"

"I never intended this, Devington, but you edge to insubordination. Dangerously close. Pray consider your actions carefully." His
voice was low and ominous.

"I should advise you to remove your coat, lest the bulk hamper
you." Robert shrugged out of his own.

"No, Robert! Don't!" Charlotte threw herself at him. "You
could face the courts-martial over this! Please!" she begged.
"Please let this be over now. I will go back to my uncle. I could
not bear to see your life ruined for love of me. I could not live
with it!"

"No, Charlotte. It shall end today, but on our terms, not theirs.
We have been held apart by every deplorable means. I won't suffer
it any longer."

"But if you should lose."

"I shall not sacrifice my honor to these selfish, avaricious bastards.
I could no more stand as a man before you if I allowed it. If you love
me, Charlotte, stand aside."

Preparing for the inevitable, Philip shrugged out of his coat, tossed
it carelessly to the ground, and drew his saber.

Powerless to hinder this madness, Charlotte ran off to seek help
from anyone who might intervene.

Both men now faced one another, blades raised in silent salute. In
an act meant to both mock and intimidate, Philip boldly kissed his
sword hilt, preparing for what he reckoned would be a clumsy and
impassioned assault.

Unleashing his fury more nimbly than Philip had anticipated, Robert lunged into a swift thrust. Philip effortlessly parried and countered with a riposte, met by his opponent in a clash of blades.

Disengaging, Robert fiercely advanced again with a vertical slash. Philip agilely sprung back and dodged.

Perceiving his opponent's retreat, Robert dove in with a low thrust to the midsection. Philip narrowly evaded with a swift side-step. The blade tip caught his shirt and shallowly grazed his flesh.

Seeking only to disarm, Philip made a lightning-fast counterstrike, slamming his blade downward near Robert's sword hilt, but rather than disarming, the tactic drove the point of Robert's sword into the soft, trodden dirt.

By this time, the smell of blood permeating the air had drawn a small crowd around the dueling officers. Included in the spectators were several infantrymen, and their commanding officer, whom Charlotte had drawn from the tavern, begging them to stop the fight.

The infantry commander who had followed the near-hysterical girl stopped in his tracks at sight of the combatants. Lieutenant Prescott was unable to believe his eyes, or his good fortune. Fighting this illegal duel was the same pair who had humiliated him two years ago. He smiled.

The Articles of War gave him authority to quell all quarrels, frays, and disorders, even with those of superior rank, but Prescott saw no need to intervene so soon. If they did not kill one another, as he hoped, the same articles conferred upon him the authority to end the duel and place them both under arrest. Heedless of the girl's plea, he would act in his own good time.

The duelists fought, oblivious of the gathering crowd. In the course of yanking his buried sword from the ground, Robert spewed dirt straight into his opponent's face. Blinded, Philip staggered back in retreat, fighting to clear his vision, and Devington, perceiving opportunity, advanced.

Quickly wiping his eyes on his sleeve, Philip defended with a spin and slashed downward, connecting with the captain's thigh. The slice was long, clean, and deep.

Charlotte shrieked when Robert buckled in searing pain, fighting to maintain his feet.

"First blood, Devington," Philip remarked impassively.

"This isn't a game," Robert growled.

"Your injury hampers you. You have no hope of besting me. Certainly not now," Philip said.

Robert grunted and shifted his weight onto his left leg. "We fight to the last man standing."

"You really wish to continue?" Philip forced his impassive reply. "While I applaud your tenacity, *you* won't be standing much longer."

"I'm not finished with you by half, Major."

"As you wish, Captain." Philip bowed mockingly, rigidly determined to end this briskly.

Robert, unable to trust his right leg enough to advance, stepped back with a slight stagger. Philip slowly circled like a wolf around his wounded prey, looking for the most vulnerable moment to strike.

Attempting again to disarm, Philip aimed another powerful stroke just below Devington's sword hilt, but in attempting to parry, the captain brought his arm into the path of Philip's blade. Rather than locking swords as intended, the saber scored his arm, cleanly severing muscle and sinew.

Robert's blade clattered to the ground. He clutched his maimed arm, now spurting copious amounts of bright crimson blood, against his chest. Ashen-faced and drenched in his own blood, Robert swayed and then crumpled to his knees, cradling his mangled arm.

Philip froze for a moment, incredulous. He recovered with a curse.

"Damn you to hell, Devington! There's only one man standing

now!" Throwing his bloodstained saber to the ground, he strode off to find a surgeon.

With a horrified shriek, Charlotte threw herself upon Robert, but he was as unresponsive as a fallen statue. She frantically tried to staunch the blood still coursing in pulsating spurts. Charlotte prayed to God the surgeon would come quickly. There was so much blood, too much blood!

Whether in answer to her prayer or in response to Philip's dire threat to his life, the barber surgeon arrived to take charge of the wounded man. Now incapacitated by blood loss, Devington was carried to his lodgings while Charlotte followed helplessly.

Setting immediately to work, the surgeon managed to staunch the bleeding and plastered the leg wound. Tearfully sitting by his bedside, Charlotte strained to listen through the door as the surgeon gave his prognosis to Major Drake.

The leg could be saved if infection was averted, but the arm was another matter. The blade, slashing near the elbow joint, had sliced through muscle and tendon, nigh clean to the bone. There would be no saving the member. He advised taking it off with all dispatch.

"'Tis too damaged to repair, I fear. There is no surgeon so skilled that can reattach what your sword has severed, Major."

"That's not acceptable, damn you! The captain will be seen by a military surgeon, one accustomed to treating such injuries, before such drastic measures are taken. Do I make myself bloody well clear?"

"Major, 'twould be a se'nnight before such a surgeon could be dispatched. By that time…" He shrugged grimly.

"Then you'll bloody well stabilize him for transport and see him to the surgeon general at Westminster. Moreover, he shall arrive with two arms."

"And whom should I expect to bear the expense of this?" the harried surgeon inquired.

"All of this patient's expenses will be borne by Sir Garfield Wallace of Wortley. I've no doubt the man is well known in these parts, but you have my sword on it!" Philip swore angrily.

"Speaking of that sword, Major, I believe you left it behind," Lieutenant George Prescott interrupted.

"Prescott, is it? Quite the unexpected pleasure to find you in Leeds," Philip remarked, silently cursing his luck. He did not need these complications. Prescott had an axe to grind, and opportunity had presented itself.

"That's Second Lieutenant Prescott, of the First Foot," he replied smugly. "And I confess, the pleasure is entirely mine, Major."

"Quite." Philip noted the vindictive glint in the other man's eye as Prescott displayed the bloodstained weapon. "My gratitude for retrieving my saber, Prescott." Philip extended his hand to take his sword.

"Let's not be precipitate." He pulled it out of reach. "I believe this weapon shall be required as evidence."

"Evidence? Your interference is both unwarranted and unwelcome."

The Lieutenant reddened but pressed. "I think not, Major. I shall retain the weapon, as I intend to exercise my right, indeed my absolute obligation, to place both you and Devington under arrest."

"Bloody hell! The matter is between me and my subordinate and none of your damned business!"

"I gainsay you on that account, Major. The Articles of War expressly make this my business." He was immensely satisfied at having gained the upper hand over his nemesis and took no pains to hide it.

Philip's position was precarious. Although he had threatened charges against Devington, his had been a bluff to intimidate Charlotte into submission. The ensuing events, however, destined them both to face the courts-martial. Dueling, particularly between officers, was expressly prohibited.

He cursed under his breath. The damned hothead had brought it upon himself, indeed upon them both. Under normal circumstances, the commander in chief would turn a blind eye to a discreet settling of a point of honor, but their conduct had been anything but discreet. Two decorated officers had fought in broad daylight, with half the town of Leeds and a dozen infantrymen as witnesses.

Philip was backed into a corner. Knowing defense impossible, he chose the offensive. "I regret to pull rank, *Lieutenant*, but the prerogative is mine. My purpose in Leeds was to recall Captain Devington to duty. He disobeyed my direct order, and I intend to charge him with insubordination as soon as he is recovered from his injuries."

"Insubordination? Drawing a sword on one's superior far surpasses the bounds of insubordination, Major. Assaulting an officer is a capital offense."

"Mayhap so, Prescott, but once again, 'tis none of your concern. For now, the captain is unfit to travel, let alone face charges. Feel free to pursue your case most zealously once we return to Whitehall, but for now, you must defer your pleasure."

Prescott stared at his nemesis, feeling robbed but vowing to press forward and follow this through to the end. "To whom will you be making your report, Major?"

"To Ligonier, I would presume, as he is currently in command of all cavalry."

"Then I expect to see you when I report to General Ligonier. Until then, I shall retain the evidence."

"If you insist, Prescott," Drake said dismissively. "Now, if you will excuse me, I have other matters to attend. Good day, Lieutenant."

Philip knew the incident would be impossible to explain off. There were too many witnesses, and Devington was severely wounded. Charges were inevitable unless he could appeal to someone with influence, someone who wielded power over the very arbitrary military courts.

For now, he could ensure only that Devington saw Pringle. The rest remained to fate.

Charlotte sat endlessly through the night in silent, prayerful vigil. She dared not leave Robert's side, for fear he'd awaken and not find her near, or worse yet, that he might slip away from her.

She prayed for a miracle, that he could be whole again, that they might still escape together, but with the rising sun, she prayed most fervently for his life, so pale and still he lay against the pillows.

The barber surgeon, Dr. Wilkins, came early to reassess his patient, and Drake reminded him again of the peril to his own members should he fail to deliver the captain intact to Dr. Pringle.

His duty done, Philip proceeded without vacillation to bodily drag Charlotte away from Robert's bedside.

"But you can't expect me to leave him like this!" she wailed.

"He is under a physician's care, Charlotte. There is nothing you can do for him. I have vowed to return you to London, and return you I shall."

Arriving in the coach yard, she jerked her arm from Philip's grip, spurning his assistance with a hateful glare, and climbed in. As she awaited their departure, she sat in the carriage, silently seething, her heartbreak mixed with loathing, hot tears burning her eyes. Her hatred burned white, and had she Robert's sword, she would have carved out Philip's treacherous heart of stone without compunction. The thought brought a fleeting smile to her otherwise wan countenance.

Charlotte was thankful Philip followed on horseback, riding with the groom he had hired to help convey Mars and Amoret. She couldn't stomach his loathsome face, let alone suffer confinement in a carriage with him for days on end. Believing Robert's fate lay largely in his hands, she endured the journey, alternating between impassive silence and heart-wrenching fits of weeping.

She and Philip exchanged precious few words in their three days of travel together, until parting company at Leicester. The carriage driver was instructed to deliver Charlotte to her uncle's residence, while Philip rode back to the village where he had left Hawke. He collected the grateful horse, who though none the worse for wear, had no doubt suffered the indignities of pulling a cart while in the smith's care.

Paying the promised coin, Philip handed Mars off to his hired groom and vaulted back into his own saddle, on his own horse at last. It was a small comfort, for which he was thankful.

He had carried out Sir Garfield's wishes in order to secure his own future, but ironically, this future no longer held the same appeal. The course he had chosen now threatened to choke the life out of him. Philip closed his eyes, wishing the entire episode would fade away as a bad dream.

He needed a drink. Perhaps large enough quantities of cheap whiskey would drown his newfound conscience and dull his raw sensibilities.

Twenty-five

~

KING OF THE TURF

*N*ewmarket was first established as a premier racing center nearly a century hence by King Charles II, who was such an avid turf follower that he removed his entire court every spring and autumn to his favorite venue. Indeed, the Merrie Monarch was so enamored of Newmarket that he hired gentleman-architect William Samwell to build a two-story brick viewing pavilion overlooking the heath, and even the Rowley mile racecourse was named in honor of the King's favorite horse, Old Rowley.

Charles II, an expert horseman in his own right, even raced his own horses against the gentlemen of his court on these famed Cambridgeshire chalk downs. A true patron of the sport in every way, he established the first official rules, as well as the series of races called the Royal Plates, thirteen official races run in various locations throughout England.

Newmarket held the distinction of commencing the racing season each year with its six days of slated match races, culminating with the prestigious and highly competitive King's Plate. More than any other, this race lured hundreds of horses from scores of racing studs throughout England.

Now, with the advent of spring, this sleepy town once again sprung to life, transforming into a racing mecca. Turf-ites of all classes descended. Farmers delivering their cartloads of oats and hay jammed the byways into the teeming village square, competing with the owners and breeders who arrived in their carriages.

High Street echoed with the clip-clop of iron striking the cobbles, suddenly swarming with sleek, sinewy, snorting quadrupeds and their wiry young grooms. Jockeys and grooms eagerly employed themselves with their charges, proudly parading their coursers, conspicuously adorned in the brightly hued sheets of their masters' racing colors, and touting to one another the superiority of their masters' stock.

Meanwhile, said gentleman of the turf congregated in the public houses and crowded the cockpits. Lords and cock-keepers, grooms, and blacklegs rubbed elbows with talk consisting only of horses and cockfighting, heedless for the time being, at least, of the invisible boundaries that normally divided their classes.

The atmosphere was permeated with the sights, smells, and sounds of horses. The racing season had officially revived from its winter dormancy.

This was the scene greeting Sir Garfield and Charles Wallace upon their arrival at the Rutledge Arms on High Street.

Gazing about him in appreciation, Sir Garfield remarked to Charles, "A man's paradise is Newmarket, m'boy." He added with a lascivious wink, "We have before us a full se'nnight of gaming, drinking, cockfighting, and horse racing, with virtually no women, save the kind that enhance the entertainments."

As father and son were about to leave the inn yard, Charles noticed the late arrival of a familiar black coach-and-four with a gold emblazoned crest.

"I believe 'tis Lord Uxeter arrived," he remarked to his father. "Should we await him?"

"By all means, m'boy. We are soon to be kinsmen, you know." The men went to meet the carriage.

༃

Jeffries had arrived a week prior to ready Sir Garfield's runner, Tortoise, a son of Whitefoot out of Amoret, and full brother to White Rose, who had won her very first race at Lichfield two years past. Given the horse's mix of old proven racing blood from the likes of Darcy's White Turk and the Byerley and Darley Arabians, Jeffries had high expectations of Tortoise, particularly after his sister Rosie's early success.

Although the gelding had begun his training with Devington as his rough rider, Jeffries had entrusted the gelding to Charlotte, following her success with Rosie. Unbeknownst to Sir Garfield, it was actually his niece, Charlotte, who had prepared Tortoise to run.

"How does he go, Jeffries?" Sir Garfield asked as Jemmy brought the gray gelding into the rubbing house after his afternoon gallop. The rubbing grooms removed his three layers of rugs and began to massage him briskly with wads of clean straw.

"He be runnin' in high form, sir." Jeffries grinned conspiratorially. "He ain't like some o' these morning glories I seen the past se'nnight, what come out and breeze fresh as you please and wilt away in the afternoon race."

"That's promising, indeed," Sir Garfield said.

"Aye. I been watchin' 'em on the Gallops and waited for just the right ones before sending Jemmy out wi' Tortoise. He paced hisself well against Badger two days back and blazed a trail past Mr. Routh's Frolic, what won the Malton Plate. He had the Duke of Perth's Chance blowin' to keep up and stalked Lord Portmore's Othello with ease. Our boy will hold his own wi' the primest of the cracks, even if ye was to put a monkey on his back."

Charles, who was to ride, regarded Jeffries with a scowl.

"I didn't mean no offense, Master Charles," Jeffries hastily amended.

Sir Garfield, who had his own reservations about his son's ability to ride the horse to a victory, asked, "Who then is the greatest threat in this race?"

"There be several good ones, sir. Badger, by Partner, be one to watch, old Byerley blood, ye ken. Won three plates last season and is brother to Sedbury, who is now put to stud after winnin' nigh every race he ever run. Another is Phantom, what won both at York and Lincoln last autumn. Lord Godolphin's Hobgoblin was his sire, though I misremember who run him in the plates."

"What of the Bolton Starling sons? I hear this stallion produced three who will be running."

"Aye. 'Tis right enough, and nigh all of 'em's bred up at the Barforth stud."

"John Crofts," Sir Garfield grunted.

Jeffries nodded. "He's bred some of the best cracks, old John. None can deny it. His stallion sired Martindale's Torismond, the Duke of Ancaster's Starling, and Grisewood's Teazer, though I don't think to see that last one do much after he was routed at Doncaster by that young Godolphin colt."

Sir Garfield remembered the day only too well. It was the same in which Devington had routed Rascallion. The colt was never any good after that ill-fated match. "What do you know of Martindale's Torismond?"

"Torismond what won at Morpeth?"

"The same. That rotter always has a horse to beat."

"Then 'twould please ye to know that he scratched the King's Plate. Says why should he trouble for a mere fifty guineas when he's already won a thousand in a match race with Lord Uxeter."

"What do you say?" Sir Garfield asked in amazement.

"'Deed, 'tis true. They done run a match race on the last four miles of the Beacon Course right along the Devil's Ditch. 'Twas quite the sight, by all accounts. Lord Uxeter begun worrying his mount almost from the go, and by the time they hit the third mile, his Perseus was running wild-eyed and roaring like a lion. Lord Uxeter was still driving the horse like the devil himself and rousting him mercilessly to claim the race. Within yards of the finish, with blood streaming crimson from his nostrils, Perseus done collapsed.

"By the Hastings's groom, Willis's telling, Perseus was broken in wind and spirit. Willis done give his notice straight after that match, saying that was the last good horse he'll see destroyed by that son of a… son of…"— Jeffries caught himself—"*an earl.*"

"Indeed? That's capital," Sir Garfield remarked, unaffected by the tale. "There are now two fewer contenders in tomorrow's race."

Sir Garfield left the rubbing house with the happy thought that his time may have come at last.

Sir Garfield had done all in his power to encourage Charles's association with Lord Uxeter, in the belief that under the viscount's sponsorship, Charles would make his way with ease into the elite political circles, much as commoners William Pitt and George Lyttelton had done under Lord Cobham's patronage. He was eager for Charles to mix company with those men who wielded the most power, the same who attended these very races.

Charles Wallace, however, was as little inclined to politics as he was to racing. He yearned for nothing more than a meaningful pursuit. He still burned with resentment and stung pride from his father's thoughtless dismissal of him when he desired to go after Charlotte. His own father did not consider him capable of redeeming his family's honor.

He had long wearied of his father's control and of always deferring his own wishes. He had desired a commission in the army, as Robert Devington had done, but his father wouldn't hear of it. Instead, he pushed Charles to seek a political career or a government sinecure, for which he cared nothing!

Having no one else in whom to confide, and with his tongue loosened under the influence of strong drink—for which he had little tolerance—Charles spilled all to Lord Uxeter. In a single evening, Edmund learned not only of Charles's frustrated desires but of all the family secrets, including his runaway fiancée and Beatrix's delicate condition.

Edmund was livid! He had not only been cuckolded by Beatrix with his own brother, but Charlotte had eloped with a lowly captain. It was beyond humiliation!

For fourteen years, since first taking his seat in the Commons, he had managed his personal affairs with perfect discretion. Though it cost him dearly, he had never yet embroiled himself in the kind of scandals that brought others down. This tale, once out, would make him a fool as none other before him.

Controlling his gut reaction to lash out, he carefully examined the facts in his mind, evaluating the situation from every possible angle.

He vouched no denial that he had contracted the marriage for pecuniary gain and had already used the dowry to back his political ambitions, but this was only half the bargain. He still needed an heir to satisfy Lord Hastings and ensure his full inheritance, but marriage alone guaranteed no heir.

The very presence of the Hanoverians on the throne was evidence of this. Had the house of Stuart begotten any legitimate Protestant heirs, they would still hold the throne of England. But just as the English throne had ceded to a rustic German princeling, his own failure could see the earldom of Hastings fall into his half-brother's detestable hands.

No, he must produce an heir. Edmund carefully considered now how he might yet turn the circumstances to his advantage.

Beatrix was already with child, and a child of his brother's seed, no less! What better reprisal than to ensure his own succession through his brother's child. It was brilliant! Philip had saved him so much trouble by seducing the bovine slut. He could simply take the vapid, breeding cow to wife and pass the child off as his own. Edmund basked in the exquisite irony.

With this last thought, he escorted the inebriated Charles back to his father's lodgings, where he confronted Sir Garfield.

"But we should be ruined!" the baronet protested fiercely. "Drake knows about this child, Uxeter. He could expose us all. Indeed, he has already threatened to do so. We would never live down the scandal, and moreover, Charles's future would be destroyed!"

"Sir Garfield, we are intelligent men," Edmund said in his most patronizing tone. "Let us speak frankly. I have need of the dowry and an heir. You desire a place in government for your son. Should we forge ahead with this alliance, I shall soon be in a position to provide what you desire in exchange for my needs.

"Once I assume my father's place in the Lords, I can easily arrange for Charles to take my seat in the Commons, but my own assurances rest solely upon my father's good graces, which have proven fickle at the best of times.

"I must produce an heir before his death. Your daughter already carries a child of the Drake blood, which could assure me of my full inheritance, and what greater delight should I have than to deny Philip his own son and raise him as my own. Lastly, sir, by our allegiance, your grandson shall be heir to an earldom."

He paused to let Garfield reflect on the full weight of this.

"Indeed you are astute, Uxeter," Sir Garfield said with open admiration. "But what now of the major? He might still cause mischief. Should he succeed in retrieving my runaway niece, I have an obligation to him."

"Then should Philip succeed, I humbly propose another means of meeting your obligation."

Sir Garfield found Lord Uxeter's proposal eminently to his liking.

〜

Bewhiskered, haggard, and bearing all the physical evidence of his own grueling trial, Philip had ridden into Newmarket the night before the King's Plate. Had he arrived only a se'nnight ago, he would have enthusiastically joined the roistering, cheering the victories and commiserating the losses with the brotherhood of the turf, but his mood was far removed from revelry. Instead, he was single-minded and grimly determined to see this unexpected travesty out to its conclusion.

Knowing the scarcity of accommodations in town, Philip had procured a small room on the outskirts of Cheveley, where he ate, bathed, and drank himself into an exhausted coma. Rising betimes and brutally hungover, he made himself as presentable as his circumstances allowed and set out on his horse for the exercise heath in hope of locating Sir Garfield, whose horse he knew would be running in the final race.

The morning was crisp and foggy, but along the grassy knoll leading to the training Gallops stretched a long procession of vibrant figures, fading in and out of the rolling fog. As Philip drew closer, he could clearly delineate the colorful shapes of blanketed horses out for their morning gallops. Bedecked in custom-tailored and monogrammed clothes costing more than what the average man would spend on his own in a year, most of the horses were now wrapping up their morning constitutionals and returning to their respective rubbing houses.

Philip scanned the grassy plain for the man he sought, determined he would find him among the clumps of gentlemen and their trainers mounted on their riding hacks all along the hill. These early risers had come out to review their horse's form, spy out the competition, and strategize for their final run.

He had almost given up when he spotted Sir Garfield and Charles, accompanied by Lord Uxeter, within the groups inspecting those on parade. He rode up to the trio and dismounted from his horse.

"Well, if it isn't my dear brother, the major!" Edmund greeted him with a disdainful salute.

Sir Garfield regarded the major in surprise. "Drake? I'd all but given up on you."

Reciprocating the tepid salutation with a mocking bow, Philip answered, "Yet here I stand."

"But you are late. And empty-handed," Sir Garfield remarked pointedly.

Eyeing his brother warily, Philip replied, "An erroneous assumption. I have delivered your... baggage... as promised."

"Baggage, brother? Are you now demoted to delivery boy?" Edmund remarked snidely.

"I've ridden nearly six hundred miles in a se'nnight, Edmund," Philip growled. "Don't try my very fragile patience with matters that don't concern you." Philip turned to Sir Garfield. "I suggest we discuss our business in private."

"But this *baggage* of yours happens to concern me most intimately," Edmund interjected.

Philip glowered at Sir Garfield. "What does he know of this?"

Edmund replied blandly, "What do I know? I know that a decorated officer was dispatched to apprehend a wayward chit from the impudent cur who abducted her. If your so dangerous mission is accomplished, I commend you for your valor, *Major*," he mocked.

"But what has become of Devington?" Charles interrupted.

"Indeed, what of the errant captain?" Sir Garfield echoed.

"The young fool chose to fight a duel, knowing me the superior swordsman," Philip replied grimly.

"So glad you spared me the trouble, Philip. I find duels of honor highly overrated. But one question remains: whether or not the goods were... damaged." Edmund carelessly flicked an imaginary speck of dust from his sleeve. "He had the girl alone for three nights."

"They were yet a day's ride from the border. Since he had not yet wed the girl, the captain did not touch her. Devington has proven himself a man of honor, unlike the rest involved in this ongoing farce." His look challenged any to gainsay him further.

Edmund rose to the challenge. "Only a fool would believe her undefiled, but I suppose a simple physician's examination can confirm or refute the state of her virtue. But 'tis of little account now."

"Indeed?" Philip queried.

Sir Garfield directed Lord Uxeter a warning, which he ignored, saying, "Since all has been resolved, Sir Garfield, we shall speak again after the race." He directed a smirk at his brother, and Lord Uxeter took his leave.

What had just transpired between them? Philip asked himself and turned back to Sir Garfield with growing unease.

"Now as to *our* business, sir. I have done your bidding, though it was clearly contrary to my conscience and cost me dearly. In truth, no dowry could compensate for what I have lost."

Sir Garfield pulled a fat coin purse from his pocket. "And what would you expect as recompense for your *losses*?"

"There is no restitution for integrity," he said bitterly.

"On the contrary, Major. Integrity always has a price. To lose or to keep; there is invariably a cost. Some just pay more dearly than others." He tossed the coin purse to Philip, who made no move to catch it. Shrugging, Sir Garfield continued. "All will be settled in good time, Major, but I have first a race to attend. We will talk again when I return to London. You may call Wednesday at Upper Brook Street. Wednesday next," he repeated, dismissing the major.

With no interest at all in the races, Philip left the heath for his lodgings. Edmund and the baronet were playing some deep game at his expense. He could feel it in his very marrow. What had happened in the few days of his absence?

He was deeply unsettled, and the knowledge that he had soon to make his formal report at Whitehall only compounded his discomfiture. He still hadn't composed a plausible story to excuse the duel. It appeared increasingly inevitable that Devington would face courts-martial.

Though it was still morning, Philip bought another bottle of whiskey, taking it back to his quarters where he could brood undisturbed and drink himself again into mind-numbing oblivion.

ᥬᆑᦓ

According to long-standing tradition, the King's Plate was a race for horses, mares, and geldings no more than six years old the grass before. The race was run in three heats of nearly four miles, all riders carrying twelve stone, and no serving man or groom to ride.

Post time, mandated by the Articles Relating to Royal Plates, was at one of the clock. Privileged gentleman by the hundreds, preferring a bird's-eye view of the proceedings, crowded into the brick viewing pavilion. Those less fortunate elbowed their way through the horde to find their best place along the course. The King's Plate was about to begin.

Sir Garfield, pushing and prodding his way toward one of the pavilion windows overlooking the starting post, took his position. The vibrantly clothed runners in the King's Plate, twenty-three horses in sum, had begun to appear on the heath, each led by his outrider to the start.

The herd now visible on the field was the very prime representatives of English racing horses, in whose veins still coursed the blood of the desert kings from such far and exotic lands as Syria and Tangier, the stallions who were imported by the dozens to improve the native English breed. For the past half century, this imported blood had been selectively intermingled with that of the original royal mares received as part of the dowry of King Charles's wife, Catherine of Braganza, to create the matchless "thorough-bred" horse.

Though all the runners varied in size and shape, the unique form of the racer was unmistakable in each—the lightly sculptured head with large and aware eyes and attentively pricked ears. Their deep-chested bodies were long, sleek, and sinewy; their long, strong legs and powerful haunches stretching elastically in a fluid stride as they floated across the turf. Their every motion defined an ultimate state of fitness to run.

With six gray horses amongst the throng, only the yellow blanket and jockey silks identified Sir Garfield's Tortoise to his owner.

The horses approached the starting post, dancing in line, circling, pacing, jigging, jostling, edging ever closer to the mark as all eyes fixed on the starter's flag in anguished anticipation. With a squeal, a horse suddenly reared and broke the line, setting all into chaos.

Half a dozen others followed suit. Badger leaped forward, jolting Tortoise off balance and knocking him to his knees. Charles vaulted forward with the fall, found himself lying on his horse's neck, hugging for dear life, as Othello, a charging half-ton of horseflesh, came bearing down on them. Charles closed his eyes in terrorized expectation of impact, but at the last second, with a loud *tally-ho* from Lord Portmore, the leggy black leaped clean over them!

Unfazed by the episode, Tortoise calmly hoisted himself back onto his feet, and the much-shaken Charles unsteadily slithered back into his saddle. Minutes followed while the false starters circled back and reclaimed their positions at the post.

Charles Wallace had ridden a score of races in his reluctant turf career, primarily mounted on mediocre horses chosen more for their tractability than their fleetness. Tortoise, however, like his full sister White Rose, was one of those exceptionally rare equines who embodied the very best in temperament with superb athletic ability. Charles knew that in this mount, he was doubly blessed.

As the flag was raised, he awaited the signal with bated breath, forcibly loosening the iron grip he held on the reins. Instinctively, Tortoise poised himself to launch. The red flag dropped.

The pack exploded! Charles had no need to ply the spur. Tortoise lurched into motion, dashing off with the pack pounding down the heath. By the quarter-mile marker, the Duke of Somerset's Achilles had broken from the band to steal the lead, sending clumps of spongy turf heavenward in his wake. Phantom surged forth right on his heels, with Badger giving chase and Chance trailing the trio in fourth.

By the half mile, Charles and Tortoise were packed in the middle and compressed on all sides, with now nigh as many horses in front as behind. Surrounded as they were, Charles was unable to break loose. He balanced tensely in his stirrups, uncertain of his strategy, and floundered in this limbo.

Remembering the trainer's instructions to let Tortoise run his race, he gave the horse his head, and slowly, steadily, incrementally they began to thread their way through the crowded field pounding down the turf for a long and grueling four-mile run.

Charles leaned over Tortoise's withers, and they drove steadily on, the horse's hindquarters rising and falling in his own perfectly rhythmic pace. For now, they needed only to stay in play, just hold on and ride out the miles until the last few furlongs, when the pressure would be on and the leaders running out of steam.

Charles had no need to press Tortoise for raw speed in this race. It was a test of endurance, and Jeffries had assured him that Tortoise was no jade. The horse had endless bottom and would give all when the time came to break loose, but it was up to Charles to judge the moment.

As Charles and Tortoise drove relentlessly on, neither gaining nor lagging, the field began to thin out before their eyes. The horses began to shift, some moving up and others dropping back, losing their positions to the stalkers, the horses that would shirk the lead but incessantly drive and push the leader to ride himself out too soon.

As the final bend of the Round Course approached, the thundering herd folded in upon itself for the last time and geared into sudden acceleration. One by one, the runners fought to claim their positions. Early leader Achilles had now fallen into sixth, and Badger struggled to push back into fourth, but suddenly Starling appeared from nowhere to pull ahead into third.

With only a quarter mile to go, the time had come. Bellying onto Tortoise's neck, Charles lightly plied his whip, and the gelding responded like a fresh starter. With a grunt, he stretched out and pounced. Claiming his prey with every stride, he blazed past the flagging Othello, coming eye-to-eye with Phantom. He drove on, lunging past Miss Vixen to creep up on the startled Starling, and breezed past effortlessly.

To his amazement, Charles found himself in the lead and flying past the finish. By the wave of his flag, the steward signaled the distance post. Tortoise had won, distancing half the field.

Full of brandy and in fine spirits, Sir Garfield rejoiced at his success. Charles and Tortoise had taken both the first and second heats and won the King's Plate. The baronet was determined to commission an equine portraitist to render his champion's likeness for all posterity. He and Charles were discussing the artistic merits of John Wootton versus newcomer James Seymour when Lord Uxeter arrived.

"My congratulations to you, Charles, for having proven yourself on a field of your betters. 'Tis the talk of Newmarket." Lord Uxeter's sardonic greeting drew Sir Garfield's immediate attention.

"But he proved *himself* the better man, my lord," Sir Garfield challenged.

"I should only say I proved I had a better horse, Father," Charles interjected wryly, remembering Jeffries's earlier remark about the monkey.

"Your modesty becomes you, young Charles." Lord Uxeter smiled.

"A drink, my lord?" Sir Garfield offered a glass, which Edmund waved impatiently away.

"No. I shall not tarry now the racing is done. Personal matters demand that I depart for London forthwith." He spoke tersely, still bitter from the loss he could ill afford. "If it pleases you, I should like to send for my bride immediately."

"Indeed, my lord. The sooner all is settled, the better, I say," Sir Garfield agreed.

"Then I take my leave of you. Charles," he said, addressing the younger man, "will you accompany me back to London? So tedious, these journeys, when one travels alone."

Charles looked to his father, who nodded his acquiescence. With a bow to Sir Garfield, Edmund left with his new protégé in tow.

Twenty-six

SALT IN THE WOUND

*R*obert awoke to pain, sharp and searing in his right arm, and a dull, throbbing ache in his head. His body was stiff and weak, weaker than he could ever recall. He tried to raise himself in the bed, but his arm refused to cooperate. He collapsed with a groan back onto the pillows.

A stern voice spoke in the dim light. "So, back to the land of the living, are ye, Captain?"

The voice was familiar. He'd heard it before, but his mind was still muzzy. "Where am I? And who the devil are you?" His throat was so dry he could barely croak the words.

"Easy there, lad. Ye'll be wanting a drink afore any lengthy conversation. Ye've been nigh insensible since delivered from Leeds."

Leeds? Why had he been in Leeds? With a jolt, Robert's memory came flooding back, filling his vision with the nightmares that he now realized were his reality. His life was torn to pieces. As he remembered it all, hatred and despair burned through him.

"Just how ye survived the ordeal 'tis beyond my ken." The rough Scottish brogue sprung from the soberly dressed man who stepped into the dim light and drew a flask from his satchel. "But here ye are to be patched up at my hands."

He proffered the flask to the captain, who closed his eyes to refuse, as if in doing so, he could shut it all out. But his visions would not be vanquished. He wanted to die. He wished that death had already taken him, that Philip had finished the job rather than leaving him broken and emasculated before the woman he loved. He averted his head, scorning the proffered drink.

"'Tis not the way of it, lad," the physician reproached. "'Twill ease yer pain. Ye can drink it yourself, or I will funnel it down yer gullet, but you will drink, nonetheless. The arm needs to be examined and the wound cleansed. Ye'll appreciate the draught once I commence."

Now placing the voice with the face, Robert realized he was again under John Pringle's care, the surgeon general who had set his broken leg at Dettingen. "Dr. Pringle," he murmured.

"Aye," the doctor answered, pleased with his patient's new alertness.

Robert scanned his surroundings, a sparsely furnished room with a hard cot and close stone walls. "Where am I? How did I get here?"

"One thing at a time, lad. Ye'll drink a wee dram first, and then we'll talk."

Robert glowered but knew he would gain little by further refusal. He reluctantly accepted the drink, sputtering on the unexpected contents of the flask. Pure whiskey.

"'Tis from the high country, lad." The physician laughed. "In my twenty years of physick, I've ne'er found a surer cure for all manner of ills than Highland whiskey. 'Tis this same potion I used to bathe yer wounds in hopes of staving off the infectious fever."

As Robert watched Pringle cut away the bloodstained bandages to expose his mutilated appendage, he was dubious of the treatment's efficacy. Waves of nausea suddenly rocked his mutinous body at the sight.

"You've lost much blood, lad. The artery was nigh severed, ye see, and the arm should ha'e come off. 'Tis like now to putrefy, but Major Drake—"

"Don't speak that name!" Robert cried and then groaned from the exertion.

The physician raised a brow but methodically continued his examination. "Ha'e it yer way, then. *The nameless major*, he wouldn't hear of amputation. There was no talkin' sense to the mon. So, at the risk of yer life, he put ye on that infernal conveyance and brought ye to me. Your leg wound was clean enough and pieced back together, but God knows what I can do to save the arm. I need appeal to your sense of self-preservation, Captain Devington, and advise it better to lose the arm than lose yer life."

"My life, you say? What is left of my life?"

"You are much changed from young mon I knew at Dettingen. What reason ha'e ye to be so bitter?"

"There is naught worth saving, Pringle."

"Och, surely I know this ailment," he said sagely. "'Tis a disease that admits of only one treatment."

"What would you know of it?"

"Ailments of the heart? More than you think, mon. Medical science has proven the only cure is the possession of its object."

Robert laughed bitterly. "'Twas seeking such a cure that put me in your hands, Doctor."

"I had suspected. The lass would'na ha'e ye?"

"'Twas not the lass, but the family."

"Aye," he replied sympathetically. "Come, mon, ha'e another dram of whiskey."

Robert reluctantly took another draught and gasped when Pringle poured a splash over the wound and began to probe. The deep gash extended cleanly through the biceps muscle and the tendon. Pringle determined the main artery, also near-severed, would diminish blood flow to the appendage, but this was the least of his worries.

The captain's elevated pulse, weakness, and pallor, combined with the inflamed tissues, confirmed Pringle's fear of sepsis. Although bloodletting close to the injury site was the traditional treatment, the doctor was no fool. His patient had lost too much blood already and was far too weak to sustain further bleeding. Surveying the maimed appendage, Pringle advised Robert that if he survived at all, he would likely never have use of the arm again. He once more advised amputation.

Sunk in despair and heedless of the admonitions, Robert resolved to leave his fate to Providence. If he succumbed to infectious fever and death, so be it.

"Ye tie my hands to save ye, Captain," Pringle responded, shaking his head in dismay. He had treated many such young men in his time; strong, able-bodied men who succumbed to infection, slipping into fever, delirium, and eventual death, death caused by infection secondary to their wounds!

Pringle was one of few physicians who yet grasped the concept of infection by unseen organisms. Since his promotion to surgeon general, he had worked tirelessly to contain and cure disease in the army, already making headway in containing dysentery in the garrisons by isolating its victims from the general population.

Although he understood the process, after innumerable experiments applying different agents to treat wounds, he had yet limited success in discovering an effective anti-septic agent. The whiskey with which he had cleansed Devington's wounds was one of his more promising experiments.

With a helpless shrug, Pringle administered his patient a dose of laudanum to ease his pain and then helped himself to the flask of whiskey. He could do little to save the captain's life once the wound putrefied, but without his patient's will to fight, the surgeon's work was futile. Pringle resolved in the name of Hippocrates to discover the identity of the girl who held Captain Devington's life in her hands.

A week following her arrival in London, Charlotte was confounded to learn that Beatrix had been given in marriage to Lord Uxeter. Why had her uncle taken her from Robert if he had intended to give Beatrix instead? It made no sense! Nothing in her world made any sense at all!

She failed to comprehend what atrocious crime she had committed by falling in love. The past two years of her life had been punishing. Her heart had been broken when her uncle first sent Robert away, but his return had given her reason to hope. They had dreamed and planned, just to have their dreams dashed to pieces.

Elopement had been such a romantic notion, but the reality was harder than she could have conceived. Only their love and their desperation had given them strength to press on. They had almost succeeded, were only a day's ride from the border when Philip caught up with them.

Why had he done it? He held no love for either Sir Garfield or his brother. Why had Philip turned his back on his best friend? Indeed, it went much further than that. He had nearly killed Robert! All for what? Beatrix was now wed to Philip's brother.

Charlotte had not seen or spoken to her uncle since his arrival from Newmarket days ago, but this morning he had sent for her. At precisely ten o'clock, she was to appear before him in his library. At the appointed time, the grate of the key turning in the lock admitted her aunt.

"Charlotte, I am come to take you to your uncle."

"I don't understand what he wants of me," Charlotte said with tears in her eyes and despair in her heart. "What is my duty when Beatrix is married in my stead? Of what possible benefit was my return?"

"Your uncle does not suffer duplicity kindly. He regards you as a willful child and will chastise you as such. This is all I am free to say."

"I meant no disloyalty to him, but why should I not have any say regarding my own life?"

"You were overindulged and spoiled by your parents, Charlotte. Their marriage was not the way of it. I have told you that a woman rarely has charge of her destiny, especially in her marriage. The best she can hope for is a comfortable match with a man she might learn to manage."

"But why can't marriage be for love? Why should love be forsaken for expediency?"

"Charlotte," her aunt said more sternly, "I begin to think you no more sensible than Beatrix. Your obligation is to your family. You owed your uncle obedience for all we have done for you. You have forgotten your duty while in your romantic bubble, but the bubble is finally burst. It is not, nor ever was meant to be, you and Devington. You must accept it. I just thank God you are back in the bosom of your family with no one the wiser. Your escapade could have ruined us, you know! Now, Sir Garfield expects you in the library. Hasten along; his good temper shan't last if you keep him waiting."

Charlotte followed her aunt to her uncle's sanctum, reminded of her prior audience in his library at Heathstead Hall when he first lectured her on marriage and duty.

"Take a seat, m'dear." He gestured to the straight-backed chair facing his desk and pulled his timepiece from his pocket.

"Uncle…" she began.

He raised a quelling hand in her direction. "Any moment now, Charlotte, and all will be made clear." Now disregarding her altogether, he leaned back in his chair, arms crossed and eyes closed in repose, as if waiting for something… or someone.

His strange and atypical behavior magnified her apprehension tenfold. Her uncle was prone to blustering whirlwinds of temper passing like brief but violent storms. The man sitting before her, however, was calm and stonily resolved.

Charlotte tried to emulate his nonchalance, but her fingernails raking her skirts and her toes curling and uncurling in her slippers betrayed her, if only to herself. An eternity passed before she heard the ring of rapid and heavy footsteps advancing toward the library; two sets of footsteps, she thought.

Literally shoving the footman out of his path, an enraged Major Drake barged into the room, shaking a fistful of papers in Sir Garfield's impassive face.

"Just what the bloody hell is this?" Philip bellowed.

"Ah, Major, I see you have been attended by my solicitor. All should be in order, as we agreed—"

"As we agreed? The devil, you say!"

"Major! Curb your tongue or be removed from the premises."

"This is bloody well not what we agreed, you execrable, conniving sod!"

"Major, aside from a few minor revisions, you are in receipt of the marriage contracts, and by your acceptance, you shall obtain a bride and considerable dowry. This is more than generous on my part, though you, of course, retain the right to refuse."

"My bride was Beatrix! Your daughter Beatrix, whom you well know is carrying my child! Moreover, the agreed dowry was fifteen thousand pounds, Sir Garfield. We had settled upon fifteen thousand!"

"Major Drake, consider your position carefully. Firstly, you duped me into receiving you into my home with open arms then set out in the most debase manner to seduce my daughter! You then forced a betrothal by means of extortion. Although immensely vexed, I, in good faith, provided you opportunity to earn your way back into my good graces and charged you with the timely retrieval of my runaway niece.

"My instructions were clear, Major: return Charlotte within five days. You failed. Thus other arrangements were made. In all magnanimity, however, I have offered my niece's hand and five thousand pounds as compensation for your efforts. You may take it or leave it."

Charlotte, yet unnoticed by the distracted major, gasped. "You couldn't possibly mean this, Uncle! You couldn't possibly give me to this selfish, heartless brute who left his best friend lying in blood!"

"My dear, you are headstrong, disobedient, and rebellious. Overall, I consider you and the major well matched. One might even say you deserve one another; however, I am not heartless. You desire a choice, so I shall give you one.

"You may marry Major Drake, or when I toss you out of my house, you may make your way in this world as you came into it. If 'tis freedom from my tyranny you desire, Niece, your wish is granted. It is absolutely your choice."

Charlotte disbelieved her ears. How could he threaten such a thing? "I would have nothing. No home. No money. Nothing! Is this some cruel joke, Uncle?"

"Am I laughing?" His voice was soft and expression stony.

Philip blanched, incredulous at the position in which he found himself. His actions had already done irreparable damage to Robert and Charlotte. This he regretted deeply. It was bad enough he had prevented their marriage, but now matters were gone from bad to worse. He needed time to think this through and figure a way out of the trap.

Desperate to stall the proceedings, he addressed the baronet. "Sir Garfield, please permit Charlotte and me a moment to speak privately."

"Very well. You may have a moment, but don't try my patience. Either of you," he said to Charlotte pointedly before stepping from the room and closing the door behind him.

"Charlotte," Philip began.

"Don't even speak to me, you... selfish... treacherous... pig!" she snapped with all the venom she could muster.

"This was not my idea. You must know this."

"I would sooner hang myself than have you!"

"I might say the same; however, our verbal combat does nothing to resolve the dilemma and, moreover, will do nothing to help Devington."

"Robert? What do you care of Robert?" she spat. "You left him for dead in Leeds!" Tears stung her eyes.

"On that score, you're grievously misinformed. Devington is currently at Whitehall under the care of the surgeon general, the most respected physician in London."

"He's in London? I must go to him! You will take me to him, Philip!"

"'Tis not so easily done. Although wounded, he is still under arrest until sufficiently recovered to face charges. It is highly unlikely that you would be permitted to see him."

"First you tell me he's in London, and then you tell me I can't see him? Do you take pleasure in tormenting me? You black-hearted... bastard!"

"Charlotte, you need to rein in your overwrought emotions if we're to figure a way out of this."

"I would sooner be on the streets than have you!"

"As it stands, 'tis precisely what your uncle has in mind."

"But he wouldn't. He couldn't possibly do such a thing!"

"Do you honestly believe that? I, on the contrary, believe your uncle capable of just about anything."

"You would coerce me, then? I said I would hang myself before having you, but on reconsideration, I quite fancy myself as a widow."

"I have no plans to depart this earth anytime soon," he replied aridly.

"Then you'd best sleep with one eye open if you think to wed me, Philip. I'll cut your treacherous heart out without a second thought." Her murderous glare nearly convinced Philip she meant it.

"Listen to me. I desire this sham no more than you do, but we find ourselves betwixt a rock and a hard place. I implore you to go along with the ruse until we can contrive a better solution."

"I won't have it!"

"I'll take you to him."

Her attention arrested, she remarked, "I thought you said I couldn't see him? That he is under guard."

"Go along, just for the time being, and I'll take you to Robert. I swear. As for the marriage, it shall be in name only. Of my attentions, you need have no fear whatsoever."

Charlotte curiously couldn't decide if she was relieved or insulted by the remark, but she considered the rest. Even if her uncle was bluffing and did not turn her out, she was no more than chattel to him. Philip offered a way out from under his tyranny. She could see Robert, and perhaps he could somehow escape? Perhaps they could still run away together. At least she had hope. "How do I know I can trust your word?" she asked skeptically.

"I've never lied to you… to either of you."

"You turned your back on your best friend! How can you expect me to trust you after that?"

"I'm no hypocrite. I have never denied putting my own interests first, but whether you believe it or not, it grieves me deeply how events transpired. Whilst I know not if he will recover, I brought Robert back to London to save him. I am resolved to do all in my power to make restitution.

"By this marriage, I shall receive five thousand pounds dowry and vow to look after you on Devington's behalf. You will be at your uncle's mercy no longer. Furthermore, as I am in His Majesty's service, I will spend most of my time abroad, troubling you little with my so contemptible presence.

"This will be simply a marriage of expediency, for both of us, and should Devington be acquitted, the pair of you may yet be together."

"But I should not be free. How do you suppose we could be together when I bear your name?"

"As this union is in name only, our failure to consummate would provide grounds for annulment."

She considered this. It seemed plausible. "If I do agree, this must be kept secret, Philip. Robert must never learn of it. Promise me he will never know. He would see it only as further betrayal. 'Twould more surely kill him than his wounds."

"As much as it is within my power, I shall keep it from him. I can promise no more than that. Please believe I wish neither of you further heartache." It was the solemn truth.

With this last, Sir Garfield impatiently returned, not so secretly hoping they had refused one another. Five thousand pounds was no pittance, after all.

"So, Major, do you take the girl as your wife or forfeit the five thousand?"

"You leave us little choice, sir. I would not see the girl thrown onto the street."

"Nor would you forfeit five thousand pounds, Major. You need not feign the chivalrous knight." He then addressed Charlotte. "If this is your decision, the arrangements are made to carry us to Fleet Street. I see no need for delay." Nodding her silent acquiescence, she proceeded numbly, by all outward signs, resigned to her fate.

With contempt in her eyes and revenge in her heart, Charlotte Wallace would wed Major Philip Drake.

Twenty-seven

THE RELUCTANT BRIDE

*C*harlotte stood trancelike with her uncle's hateful form invading the periphery of her vision. The vicar's lips moved, and she responded, but the words failed to penetrate the cloud around her brain.

Philip stood equally stony, expressionless as the long-dreaded shackles closed about him, threatening to strangle him, and he choked out his vows to the gin-reeking vicar who joined them in this unholy state of misery.

The nuptials concluded, Sir Garfield renounced his guardianship of Charlotte with a few brisk strokes of the quill. Philip followed his entry in the register, grimly and briskly scrawling his name, made barely legible by the tremor of his hand.

As the ink dried upon the register, the gazes of the panic-stricken bride and groom met with the simultaneous thought, *"Dear God in heaven, what have we done?"*

Only Sir Garfield exuded delight, having now proven he was not a man to cross. His scoffing remark broke the silence. "Well, ain't you going to kiss your bride?"

Charlotte's eyes shot daggers at the mere suggestion, triggering a hoot of laughter. "My felicitations to the happy couple." Tears of mirth rolled down his fleshy cheeks. "Now the deed's done, I s'pose I must be off." Still laughing, he made to depart the shabby dwelling, asking, "By the by, where shall I send the girl's things?"

Philip regarded him blankly. "I'll send word," he replied, lacking any immediate recourse.

Sir Garfield looked inquiringly but was unmotivated to probe further. What did he care? He was thankful to be free of the ungrateful wretch. Served her right, marriage to the rogue. He would surely burn through the five thousand in a year. With that last thought, he departed Fleet Street with a smug glow.

What in bloody hell am I to do with her now? Philip was unaware of his audible sigh.

"You promised to take me to Robert," Charlotte said matter-of-factly, as if she had read his mind.

"What?"

"You *promised* to take me to Robert if I went through with this," she insisted.

"I didn't mean today! I gave you my word and shall keep it, but 'tis not so simple a matter as you imagine. I can't just whisk you in past armed guards."

"I can't bear to imagine him locked in some dank and dingy cell."

"He's hardly locked in a cell. He's under the surgeon general's care, and as an officer, he will be treated with the utmost courtesy, at least until charged."

"Charged with what? Why should Robert face a trial? You provoked him, and then you nearly killed him, while you stand with barely a scratch! As his accuser, you could surely put an end to these senseless proceedings!"

"On that score, you are dead wrong. The very fabric of the military is based on discipline in the ranks. Officers, in particular, are expected to set the example, adhering to a strict code of conduct, a code of honor, one might say."

"Honor? *You* dare speak of honor?"

Ignoring her retort, Philip patiently continued. "Striking a supe-rior officer under any circumstance is one of the gravest offenses. Such transgressions do not go unpunished; moreover, the penalty could be most severe."

Charlotte blanched as white as her lace cap. "You can't mean the gallows, Philip! He couldn't possibly be hung!"

"I have done all in my power to see him charged with the lesser offense of insubordination and have petitioned the court and many fellow officers on his behalf. There is little more I can do."

"And what does your noble institution deem suitable for insub-ordination, Major? A thousand lashes with a cat-o-nine-tails?" she retorted, full of rancor.

"Five hundred lashes would be closer the mark; discipline in the ranks must be retained at all costs."

"Good God, Philip, you don't jest?"

"I wish to God I did."

ᐸᔈ

Philip hailed a passing hackney, speaking little as he bundled Charlotte's desolate form into the coach. He glanced irritably at the girl who wept silently against the carriage squabs. God knew why she suddenly and inexplicably had become *his* responsibility. Only for Devington's sake had he vowed to look after her. He just needed time for his mind to untangle the mess. The jarvey inter-rupted his cogitations.

"Where to, Cap'n? I gots to make a livin', ye know. Wi' eight brats to feed, I ain't got all day, ye ken?"

"Just drive," Philip barked.

"And the direction?"

Where to take her? He needed to find a suitable abode and someone he could trust to look after her. Without thinking, he blurted, "Bedford Street, Number Ten."

The jarvey looked at him blankly.

"Between Covent Garden and Westminster," Philip snapped. "Proceed down the Strand."

"Aye, Cap'n." The hackney lurched, jerking Philip back against the squabs.

The devil take it! Why the deuce had he spoken that address? He thought it long forgotten; at least that's what he tried to tell himself. Nevertheless, he needed her. No, he corrected himself with a mental shake, she was simply the first who came to mind. Nonetheless, he racked his brain to think of anyone else as the hackney made its way to the house located just far enough from Covent Garden to be respectable.

The hackney halted in front of the neat brick dwelling, and Charlotte roused herself enough to look out of the window and down the quiet street. "Where are we, Philip, and why have we stopped here?"

"I am paying a call on an old friend, one who might be disposed to assist. Pray wait here until I summon you," he replied more tersely and alighted from the hackney. Philip then instructed the jarvey to wait and tossed the man treble his normal fare.

Although intimately familiar with this address, he hesitated, still questioning why he had come to this house he had not set foot in for five years. Pushing his qualms aside, he marshaled his will and strode purposefully to the door, knocking briskly.

"My lady is not receiving at this time, sir," the answering maid responded to his request.

"Pray inform your mistress that Philip Drake wishes to speak with her. I am a longtime acquaintance come on a matter of personal import. I believe your mistress will forgive my breach of etiquette in appearing unannounced. I request only a brief moment of her time."

She eyed his uniform and manner appraisingly and then conceded. "Be pleased to follow me, Major, and I will inquire if my lady will see you."

The maid led him into a small but cozy drawing room and left him to cool his heels while awaiting the favor of his erstwhile lover, Lady Susannah Messingham.

Susannah was a common-born woman blessed with both rare wit and uncommon beauty. At a tender age, she had escaped life as a vicar's daughter by marriage to a wealthy knight of the shire, but her marriage had barely lasted a decade before the worthy squire expired of a heart seizure. He left her childless and widowed at the age of eight-and-twenty.

In her widowhood, however, Lady Susannah suddenly discovered a newfound freedom, a life of license and gaiety she could never have previously imagined. She threw herself headlong into the pursuit of pleasure, determined to make up for her lost youth, and quickly burned through both her fortune and her reputation.

As her financial state neared a crisis, she determined to mend her ways with another respectable marriage but realized her folly too late. Now past the first innocent bloom of youth, the only proposals she received were less than honorable in nature. Against her better judgment, she accepted a *carte blanche* from a marquess, but said lover's declaration of undying devotion lasted only until a French opera dancer stole his fancy.

Her reputation tarnished beyond redemption, she sold her London townhouse and settled for a small abode near Covent Garden. She endeavored to live an independent life, avoiding the downward spiral of other women who fall on hard times, women handed off from one man to another until their beauty finally wasted, they are discarded on the street.

Instead, Lady Susannah chose to supplement her modest income by hosting private card parties and entertaining select gentlemen friends, men of her *own* choosing, who were mainly of her late husband's acquaintance. She was akin to many semirespectable women subsidizing themselves in like manner, but Lady Susannah was among the most circumspect.

To his surprise, Philip had experienced distress rather than satisfaction in learning of his former *inamorata's* fall from grace, but was far from understanding this damnably pervasive feeling of protectiveness for the woman who had so spurned his professions of love.

With sweating palms, Philip waited in her drawing room. Had she changed? A knot formed in his stomach, and he cursed himself for acting the bloody schoolboy, but she always had that effect on him. Perceiving the light approach of a lady's slipper, he moved to the window and struck a casual pose.

Lady Susannah entered the room as breezily as if she had just met him at yesterday's garden party. He turned from the window, arrested by her emerald eyes. She was as beautiful as ever. The past five years had been kind indeed.

"My dear, dear Philip! Such an indescribable delight to see you!" She offered her hand with a dazzling smile.

"Sukey,"—he accepted her proffered hand—"a long delayed pleasure." His gaze never left her face as his lips grazed her knuckles with leisurely deliberation. "You are every bit as lovely as when I first met you surrounded by all your lovelorn swains."

The role of gallant was far easier to resume than he could have imagined, he thought sardonically.

"*All* my swains? You tease me, Philip!" She chuckled throatily.

"They were innumerable, but I think none admired you more than I." *Now where the hell did that come from?* The confession rolled effortlessly off his tongue. He abused himself for falling back into his position as her lapdog.

He watched her, mesmerized, as she moved toward the loveseat and silently indicated the place by her side. Ignoring the gesture, Philip disciplined himself to remain standing. He braced one arm casually on the mantle, as if to anchor himself in place. "No doubt you wonder what has brought me to your door after so long an absence." His query was casually posed.

"One should never question a gift, my love." She smiled and again gestured invitingly. "Pray sit with me, Philip. We have much to catch up on."

He glanced at the empty space and redirected his gaze out the window, pretending something had caught his attention. He still found her bewitching. It would be so easy to let the past just slip away, all too bloody easy. Just a few hours in her bed, and it would all be a long lost memory. God, he was so weak!

He shook himself for still entertaining such thoughts of her and reminded himself she was nothing more than a heartless, self-serving coquette willing to sacrifice love for comfort. The thought brought him starkly back to his purpose.

"I regret this is not a purely social call, Sukey. I have come in need of a favor."

"A favor?" She raised a brow inquiringly. "What manner of *favor*?"

"'Tis a simple matter of lodgings for a well-bred young woman, temporarily consigned to my care. I have always known you to be discreet, and I require discretion."

"Discretion? Is the young woman your ward... or your mistress, Philip?" Her expression hardened.

"Rest assured she is *not* my mistress. You might call her my *provisional ward*," he replied ambiguously.

"And this is but a temporary arrangement?" Her voice was guarded.

"Quite," Philip answered. "But I am not at liberty for further disclosure." His quelling look stemmed her questions.

"Very well, then, I suppose I could accommodate such a simple request. Now, who and where is the girl?"

"Her name is Charlotte Wallace, and she waits in a hackney outside."

"In a hackney? Quite sure of me, were you, Philip?"

"I had hope that you would not deny an old... *friend*."

They had been much more than that. "No, Philip, I shall not

deny you," she replied. "Pray invite the girl in, and I'll call for tea."
She turned to ring the bell, hiding her hurt at his aloof manner.

Philip returned to the waiting coach to conduct Charlotte to her
new abode, knowing she would be safe in Sukey's care. At least the
girl had someone to watch over her until he could think of more
suitable arrangements. For now, it would have to do.

"You're just going to leave me here?" Charlotte asked, wide-eyed.

"What more do you expect of me?" he snapped. "Lady Susannah
is a trusted friend. You could not be in better hands."

"What do I expect? I expect you to take me to Robert! I fulfilled
my promise to carry out this farce. Now it's time for you to honor
your word."

Ruffled at her repeated affront to his honor, Philip snapped. "I
told you it may take some time to arrange. A military hospital is no
place for a gently bred woman. I gave my word that you shall see
him. You have no choice but to trust me."

They entered the house, and Philip made the initial introductions.
Having fulfilled his most pressing obligation, he departed, much
relieved to have the girl off his hands.

Charlotte had other ideas. She didn't fully trust Philip's word or
his supposed efforts to help Robert. Now left to her own devices,
she resolved to locate him on her own. On this point she was single-
minded, determined to her very marrow but in possession of only
two facts. He was under a surgeon's care and was soon to face the
courts-martial. Given these particulars, her search would logically
commence at Whitehall. Surely there would be a military hospital
nearby. With her plan vaguely formed, she vowed to find Robert.

Robert's body, weakened by blood loss, waged a losing battle against
sepsis. His raging fever pulled him into restless delirium, causing him
to murmur one moment and rant the next, mostly unintelligibly.

Pringle struggled to learn anything from his patient's ravings that might help to turn the tide in his favor, but thus far discerned only the name Robert agonizingly repeated: "Charlotte."

Fearing the battle near lost, the conscientious doctor stepped up his efforts to learn the identity of the girl. Although he hoped finding her might bring an entirely new set of healing arts into play, at the worst, the young captain might at least spend his last hours in the arms of his beloved.

Pringle had seen this scenario play out repeatedly, wounded patients lost to infection. It seemed a battle he might never win, yet he vowed to persist in his work. Frustrated with his ineptitude, Pringle retired to his office, cramped and overflowing with his medical texts and research notes, to find some clue, anything he might have previously overlooked in his quest to discover an effective "anti-septic."

A sudden disturbance outside tore his attention from his notes. Perturbed at the disruption, the surgeon general left his desk to investigate, desirous to confront and punish the offender. He was taken aback to discover the instigator of the fracas was a mere chit of a girl demanding entry at the hospital gate.

"Now look 'ere, missy, ye'd best be off," the distressed trooper said. "Ye have no business 'ere."

"If you refuse to let me see the patient, I demand an audience with the chief physician!" She jutted her chin obdurately, refusing to be moved.

"Ye'll see nobody, missy. Light skirts ain't allowed in the 'ospital. Now be off." The young trooper who attempted to remove her received a smart kick to the shin for his trouble.

"Light skirt! How dare you make such a presumption!" Eyes flashing and cheeks aflush, Charlotte jerked her arm from his grasp.

Dr. Pringle fought to restrain his chuckle upon beholding this diminutive young woman thoroughly harassing the trooper. "The surgeon general is a very busy mon, *miss*. Might I know which patient you inquire after?"

Fearing that someone in higher authority was about to turn her away, she took a completely different tack. "There is a patient within, sir, whose family is exceedingly anxious about him. I have come seeking word of his condition." Her voice was tearful.

"Are ye family, then?" Dr. Pringle asked.

"I suppose ye'll now claim to be his sister." The trooper leered.

"I am no doxy," she retorted.

The physician inspected her skeptically and replied apologetically, "Indeed not, miss, but you can understand the trooper's error in finding you arrived alone and requesting to see a patient."

"Indeed I do not understand, sir!" Her reply was indignant. "I am come only to inquire after Captain Devington."

"Your name, miss? And what kinship do you claim with the patient?" Dr. Pringle asked, hoping the captain's mystery lady had delivered herself to his door.

She hesitated to answer. While she could claim no entrance by kinship, she was by law, anyway, the wife of a senior officer. She was desperate enough to use any means at her disposal to gain entry, even if it meant *this once* acknowledging her status as a major's wife.

"Mrs. Philip Drake." She nearly choked on the words as she forced them distastefully from her lips. "That is, I am the wife of *Major* Philip Drake."

He had prayed Devington's love had come as an angel of mercy, but these hopes were dashed.

"Only immediate family is allowed visitation privileges, Mrs. Drake. As you are no kin, I am afraid your request is denied."

Charlotte tried another tack still, immediately softening both voice and demeanor. "But the captain has no living kin, aside from an elderly and infirm aunt in Chelsea. As a close family friend with

connections to the Horse Guard, I am come on her behalf, you see."
She smiled tentatively at Dr. Pringle. "I understand he's in a grave
condition. I desire only a moment and just a word with his physician. Just a very short moment, if you please?" Her imploring hazel
eyes ultimately softened the Scotsman, winning her case.

Dr. Pringle acknowledged surrender. "If 'tis the surgeon general
ye seek, lassie, I be he. Dr. John Pringle." He bowed curtly in introduction. "I suppose I'll grant ye entry afore ye lay a veritable siege
to my hospital." He offered his arm obligingly to Charlotte and
escorted her to the captain's room.

Charlotte gasped upon her first glimpse of Robert, aghast at the
pale, gaunt form. His hair plastered to his brow, he lay in a nightshirt
soaked in sweat from the raging fever that racked his body.

"Aye, lass." Pringle looked at her reprovingly. "Ye see why the
sickbed is no' a place for a delicate young lady."

"It's just that he's so… changed. I was not prepared to see him
thus." Her voice broke in anguish.

"Aye. 'Tis very grave, I fear, this fever. Should ha'e broken by
now."

"His prognosis?" she prompted with trepidation.

"Tenuous at best, lass."

"Please let me sit with him, Dr. Pringle," she pleaded.

He considered the request. "'Twill not hurt his cause, though I
dared hope ye were another."

Charlotte looked her question.

"Are ye acquainted wi' a lady named Charlotte, lass?"

Taken by surprise, she was unsure how to respond. "Y-yes. I am
acquainted with such a young woman. Why do you inquire, sir?"

"'Tis a name he mumbles, and I fear only her touch will stir him
to fight for his life."

"Let me try, Dr. Pringle. Please, I beg of you, please just let me sit
with him and hold his hand. He will know my voice."

He surveyed his patient gravely and then softened again under
the imploring eyes. "It canna hurt for an hour, but not a moment
longer." With this concession, Dr. Pringle departed to do his rounds
in the other wards.

Charlotte moved to pour a basin of cool water. Dipping a cloth,
she lovingly bathed Robert's face, gently following the planes of
his features. She achingly studied the hollow cheeks and bluish
circles beneath his eyes and traced the line of his brow, brushing
the damp hair from his forehead. "Dearest Robert," she whispered,
"please come back to me." Gripping his limp hand, she brought
it to her lips.

Too preoccupied with her sorrow, she didn't immediately perceive
the subtle change in his ragged breathing and the blink of his eyes
in response to her whisper as he fought to distinguish whether the
voice were reality or another dream.

"How did this ever happen to us? I believed in my heart of hearts
we were meant to be. I ask God every day why our love was so cursed
while others so undeserving flourish. I can't comprehend, though I try."
As she continued her prayerful weeping, her tears fell freely in rivulets
down her cheeks, dropping unheeded onto their clasped hands.

Dr. Pringle spied her thus when he returned to escort her from
the hospital. Walking her back to the gate, he bowed politely.
"Good-bye, miss..." Pringle looked embarrassed, addressing her
apologetically. "So bad with names, lass."

"Charlotte. Charlotte Wallace," she blurted, covering her mouth
when she realized what she had let slip, as if she could pull back and
trap the reply years of habit let spring so freely from her lips.

"Indeed you say, lass." He grinned slyly. "If 'tis a secret ye guard,
ha'e no fear. Upon my word as a Scotsman, 'twill stay betwixt us."

"It's so very complicated, you see."

"I'll not prod ye further."

"Thank you, Dr. Pringle. May I come again on the morrow?"

"Aye, I'll leave word with the guard."

Charlotte hurried back to Bedford Street, assuming Lady Susannah would follow the habits of a lady of fashion, not rising before noon. She was thankful to have judged correctly. Her absence had gone unremarked.

Rising shortly after sunrise the next day, Charlotte padded the bed with pillows in the event a maid should enter to start a fire and report her room empty. Making her way quietly downstairs and slipping out of doors, she had little success in hailing a hackney so proceeded to walk most of the way to Whitehall. Just as well, she considered, having little coin to spare.

Arriving at the gate, her hackles rose upon encountering the same trooper who had hindered her the day before. Arming herself with a deep breath, she marched forth, prepared to do battle.

The trooper's deferential greeting stole the wind from her sails. Clearly, Dr. Pringle had paved her way. "My apologies to ye, miss… er… missus, fer yesterday. I'd no idea, ye see…"

Charlotte, in a much more charitable mood, responded with as much dignity as she could muster. "I shall endeavor to accept your apology for your abominable conduct of yesterday, Trooper…"

"Wiggins, ma'am. Trooper Joshua Wiggins."

"I will forgive your conduct yesterday, Trooper Wiggins, provided I can count on your discretion."

"'Scuse me, ma'am?"

"Your discretion, sir. As you pointed out so vividly yesterday, it is highly irregular for a *lady* to visit the sick rooms, thus I rely on your discretion to say nothing of it to anyone. Can I trust you, Trooper Wiggins?" She addressed him squarely.

"If'n the surgeon general has authorized you, ma'am, 'tis clearly no concern of mine."

"Thank you, Trooper Wiggins. I will be sure to commend you to my husband, the major."

"Is there aught else you require, ma'am?" he inquired as he escorted Charlotte to the captain's room.

"No thank you." She nodded a dismissal and entered. Closing the door quietly, she froze at the sound of a soft, deep voice. "Charlotte."

Her breath caught. Had she imagined it? She revolved slowly, and their eyes met. After a moment of immobility, she suddenly flew to his side. Falling upon him, she cried, "You have come back! Robert, you've come back to me!"

He was still pale and gaunt and his eyes glassy. "The fever broke late yesterday. 'Twould appear God deems it more fitting for me to die by hanging than by fever."

"Hanging?" Charlotte gasped. "You are yet delirious."

"On the contrary, my dearest love, I have quite recovered my senses and am informed that I am to face charges."

"But how could they? You are still a patient in the sick bed."

"I am deemed well enough. I have committed one of the greatest offenses, Charlotte. 'Tis unlikely I will live to see many more days. You should not have come, my love." He spoke the words devoid of emotion and refused to meet her eyes.

"How can you say this? How can you hurt me so?" Her pain wrenched his heart, but he gazed stolidly through her.

"My life is all but over, Charlotte. I was a fool. There is nothing left for us."

"No! You don't mean it! There is always hope, Robert. Philip has pleaded a lesser charge, a lesser penalty. You could be acquitted."

"The man is a liar, a traitor, a Judas! He is the very reason I am here and is not to be trusted! Promise me, Charlotte, that you will have nothing to do with him. Regardless of how matters progress, you must have *nothing* to do with Philip Drake!"

"B-but, Robert, I—"

"Give me your vow, Charlotte."

Horror gripped her. He would never understand this deal she had made with the devil. Turning away to hide her guilt, she cried, "But there is no one else. As your superior, he is the only one who can help us."

"Swear to me that you will not go to him on my behalf."

Was it fear or guilt in her eyes?

"I must needs explain—"

"Explain what?" His suspicion kindled to rage. "What have you done? What deal have you made with him?"

"Please, not now," she begged. "You could not possibly comprehend in this moment, in your present state of mind. Please let us speak of it later." She prayed for anything to buy her time to think of a plausible explanation for actions she could not creditably defend, any justification he might accept for her actions.

"If you love me, you will tell me the truth and tell me now!" he demanded.

Backed into a corner, she challenged, "If you love *me*, you will heed my request to discuss this later. All will be made right once you are acquitted."

"Made right? Damn it, that's no answer! There will be no acquittal! For the last time, Charlotte…"

She couldn't look him in the eye and lie, but she dared not tell the truth. Their world hung by a solitary thread. Drawing closer, she whispered against his face, "I *defy* you to doubt my love, Robert."

She found his lips with all the love and pain she had harbored, and Robert softened in her embrace, but a flushing Trooper Wiggins interrupted the impassioned embrace.

Clearing his throat, he discreetly announced his presence. "Mrs. Drake," he began tentatively, "Dr. Pringle gave strict orders…"

Robert froze, his stricken gaze fixed on Charlotte. Unable to believe his ears, he repeated, "Mrs. Drake? Mrs. Drake! Charlotte, what the devil have you done?"

Twenty-eight

AN UNLIKELY
CONFIDANTE

Charlotte quit the hospital with only one thought, to find the man responsible for her anguish. She ran blindly out of the doors, crashing straight into Dr. Pringle, nearly knocking him flat as he arrived to make his morning rounds.

"Whoa there, lass! What's amiss?" He lapsed into his native brogue in his excitement. "Has the young Devington ta'en a bad turn, ga'en doun the brae?" He directed his steps briskly toward the hospital door.

"N-n-no, Dr. Pringle. He is much recovered, but I owe him an explanation I am unable to make. It would surely kill him!" she sobbed.

"So you say, lass. I ken no such thing unless 'twould be his love wed another whilst he was in the sick bed."

Charlotte gasped. "Then you knew all the time!"

"Aye. Took no great genius to figure out. 'Twould appear the young captain got the bree o't."

"Everything is such a muddle. It never should have happened this way."

"But if indeed ye married another, it canna be undone, lass. 'Tis aw by nou."

"But you don't understand! No one can understand! And no one can fix it save the man responsible!"

"At whose door do ye lay the blame, lass?"

"Major Philip Drake," she hissed. "If it were not for him, Robert and I would have been happily wed in Scotland."

"The major has his own troubles at the moment, lass. He was placed under arrest this very morning. He and the captain are both to face charges, once I proclaim the lad fit, that is." He eyed her sympathetically.

"What charges, Dr. Pringle? What have you heard of the charges?" she begged.

"There's the question. Several infantrymen witnessed a duel, though the major claims otherwise. Yet another mon has spoken of a kidnapping. 'Tis quite a scandal brewing. The commander in chief will wish the matter resolved expeditiously."

Charlotte blanched. "What can be done? Surely, there must be something. I was also a witness of this so-called duel."

"Were you now? Dare I presume you the one kidnapped?"

"It was an elopement, Dr. Pringle. Robert and I were going to be married."

"As I suspected, but there is naught you can do in any instance. 'Tis a military matter to be handled by due process."

"But what of Robert? Is he to be imprisoned?"

"Nay to that, lass. On my sacred honor, whilst under my care, I shall ensure he sees no walls beyond his hospital room. As for *your husband*, an officer may be placed under arrest for only eight days. The matter will be resolved anon."

"Are you sure there is nothing I can do for Robert?"

"For the captain, nay, but ha'e ye no care for your husband?"

"Philip Drake may rot in prison for all I care."

"'Tis a wee harsh, lass."

"The man is a traitorous, self-serving rogue," she replied, unmoved.

"The mon I knew at Dettingen was as fine and brave an officer as I know and 'twas he who saved your captain's very life. Ye might consider this afore you heap many more curses upon his head."

She lowered her eyes, abashed. "I'm sorry, Dr. Pringle, it's just circumstances…"

"There's nay need to apologize, but I must beg your leave now. Much work to do and little time."

"Dr. Pringle,"—she stopped him—"may I return?"

"Only when ye think to ha'e it all sorted oot," he replied censoriously. "I'll not ha'e ye do more harm to my patient than good." The doctor dismissed her with a nod of good-day.

Charlotte trod despondently back to her lodgings. Perhaps tomorrow would be a better day. Perhaps she would think of some way to convince Robert of her unfailing devotion. Perhaps he would be in a better frame of mind to listen. But would he ever understand?

She had acquiesced to the sham marriage only out of desperation. Her uncle would have surely made good on his threat to throw her out had she refused. But now trapped, she avowed to find a way out of this despicable arrangement the moment Robert was acquitted.

Charlotte arrived at Number Ten Bedford, surprised to find Lady Susannah awaiting her.

"Miss Wallace, you should not go out unchaperoned. London is a very dangerous place for a pretty young woman venturing out alone."

Embarrassed and guilty at having been caught, Charlotte contritely stammered, "I-I was merely taking some air, madam."

"As I have been asked to look after you, my dear, pray notify me when you wish to take air, and I shall endeavor to escort you, or at the least send my maid."

"That's very generous. I am grateful, Lady Susannah."

"Pray join me, Miss Wallace, or may I call you 'Charlotte'?"

"If it pleases you to do so, madam," Charlotte replied coolly.

"Be pleased then to come and take tea with me, Charlotte. You can't have yet broken your fast, and walking invariably raises one's appetite."

Seeing no polite way out, Charlotte sat beside the woman. Lady Susannah poured the tea, asking tritely, "Your rooms are comfortable, I trust?"

"Indeed, madam. Infinitely so."

"I am pleased to hear it. Is this your first visit to London, dear?"

"Actually no, though I remember little. I was very young."

Lady Susannah raised a brow, encouraging Charlotte to continue.

"My father was a barrister of Grey's Inn, and we resided in London whilst my parents were alive. They were both tragically killed when I was a child."

"How sad, my dear. But you are still little more than a child."

"It is unfortunately as you say. Had I yet attained my majority, I would be in a much happier position today."

Mistaking her meaning, the lady's eyes lit with interest. "So, you yearn for a life of independence, do you? Very few women are permitted such, to live their own lives in our society. Most, sadly, have not the slightest notion of freedom. A married woman is the property of her husband, and an unmarried woman lives almost shunned by society, as if fatally flawed in some way.

"'Tis utterly tragic! I was wed once, barely out of the schoolroom, mind you, to a gentleman of eight-and-fifty. He was a wealthy squire, an acquaintance of my father who took a singular fancy to me. He asked no dowry and offered a considerable settlement upon my father, who cheerfully gave me up."

"How unhappy you must have been." Charlotte empathized, warming to the older woman.

"Surprisingly, my dear, not at all. Dear Nigel was as doting as a grandfather, and I was his most prized possession. I had jewels, modish clothing, and a fine carriage, all the best he could provide. He was kind and generous, but also jealously possessive. He paraded me before his peers as his trophy, but on a very short leash.

"In the end, 'twas injustice to us both. He became heavily indebted, and I was irredeemably spoiled. After settling the debts after his death, little remained. I confess, had I practiced economy, I might have lived out a life of modest comfort, but I knew nothing of economy, and I suddenly had freedom." She paused, smiling at her reminiscences.

"Are you never lonely, my lady?" Charlotte asked.

"I have few regrets. I considered remarriage once, but purely for economic reasons." She paused, and her smile vanished. "Suffice to say, my reasoning was flawed. I have since decided that I do not desire a husband at all. I am a spoiled wretch after managing for over half a decade to live as I will.

"How ludicrous it is that society dictates that every woman should have a master, be it a father or a husband. God forbid if any woman dares aspire to the same privileges *every man living* enjoys; she is considered fast and a social pariah. I have spent years walking such a social tightrope, my dear. I tell you this as a warning, sensing a kindred spirit in you."

"But, Lady Susannah, is it not also exercising one's freedom to choose marriage out of love? If two people truly love, marriage binds them together willingly. It is by choice. Have *you* never loved?"

"Heavens, quite the philosopher you are, Charlotte! How delightful to be in such enlightened company." She laughed. "I rarely enjoy the conversation of a woman, empty-headed lot, most of them."

"I am perceptive, as well, my lady, and perceive that you have skillfully evaded my question."

Lady Susannah erupted with renewed mirth. "Indeed, you have me trapped! And such an indelicate topic for maiden ears, but since you persist, I shall disclose all. Although I was content with Nigel, I was never in love with him. Furthermore, my marriage failed to fulfill any physical desires. My husband was unable to… perform in the marriage bed, you see."

The young woman blushed.

"I see that you do understand, but shall I discontinue? Young ladies have such heightened sensibilities."

"I understand what transpires in the marriage bed."

"I am to this day uncertain whether or not it ever transpired in my marriage bed! Only in my widowhood did I discover the hitherto unknown delights."

Charlotte blushed crimson but nonetheless urged, "Is it indeed so, Lady Susannah?"

"You continue to enchant, Charlotte!" She laughed again. "To answer you, in my experience there is much a woman is never taught regarding the physical aspects of marriage. Sadly, they ill-comprehend this God-given expression, which is a sincere articulation of love and devotion by their husbands.

"Instead, they suffer in forbearance their marital obligation to produce a child, believing this distasteful act is performed upon them only to satisfy the primal urges of a husband, which he cannot meet by other means.

"But men are a completely different animal from women, Charlotte, and they desire more than a *dutiful victim to their baser instincts.* A man craves a joyful, playful, loving partner, but sadly many times, he can find it only outside of the marriage. Men have a completely natural need to express their love in a purely physical sense."

Blushing to her ears, Charlotte stared into her teacup. "Do you truly believe this, Lady Susannah?" she asked, "That men require coupling to express their love and devotion?"

"Not just to demonstrate *their* love, but a man will never feel his love is reciprocated in kind without a willing and eager partner in this so-called *coupling.*"

"So a woman who truly desires to prove her love to her beloved would do so willingly with her body?"

"I fear we tread very dangerous ground now, my dear. Countless unfortunate maidens fall to their utter shame and disgrace by giving themselves to young men who plead for proof of their love. 'Tis the oldest ploy in the book, and most of the poor harlots on the street were ruined in such a despicable manner."

Charlotte digested this carefully. "But what if he showed her his love in manifold ways yet never made such demands? Could he not still love her?"

"Indeed! I would then swear he was a victim of Cupid's bow and truly in love. And to think I imagined our first chat was to have been of the weather!" Lady Susannah chuckled merrily and rang for the maid to clear the tea tray.

"I have enjoyed your company immensely, but perhaps our next chat should be in my *private* parlor! Now, if there is nothing you need, I have a social engagement this afternoon and must attend to my toilette." She rose to depart but hesitated at the doorway. "Have you a lady's maid, Charlotte?"

"I did, ma'am, until my uncle dismissed her."

"Are you inclined to locate her?"

"Oh, madam, if it were at all possible. She was with me most of my life and was my dearest friend."

"Then we must find her. I will speak to Philip regarding the matter."

"Philip? What has he to say to anything?"

"He is your guardian, is he not?"

Charlotte nodded dumbly.

"Then as such, he can very well provide you a maid. I shall attend to it, my dear."

"That might present a difficulty at the moment, Lady Susannah."

"Oh? And why is that?"

"He is imprisoned." She spoke matter-of-factly. "I have learned that he faces charges for dueling,"

"What!" Lady Susannah blanched.

Charlotte scrambled for an explanation that would not reveal more than necessary. "I believe it was a matter of honor." That was close enough.

"Was it indeed? 'Tis surely not the first time he has done such a thing, but mayhap it can yet be smoothed over." She tapped her chin thoughtfully. "If Philip is indeed in such a scrape, I must pay a call to an old friend," she said more to herself than to Charlotte and then breezed from the room.

Charlotte later realized that Lady Susannah had once more artfully evaded her question about ever having loved. Although unabashed about her lifestyle, there was at least one secret she kept well guarded.

❦

Over the following days, Charlotte saw little of Lady Susannah, whose life at times appeared a veritable whirlwind compared to Charlotte's own quiet existence. She struggled with her dilemma to no avail. She was still at a loss as to how to face Robert's accusations, but she could wait no longer. She resolved to go back and confront him with the facts. She would make him understand. As Charlotte prepared to go out, she encountered Lady Susannah just coming in.

"Charlotte," the widow asked pointedly, "were you again venturing out with no chaperone?"

"N-no, my lady." Charlotte could not meet her eye.

"My dear, you should never prevaricate unless you can do so quite boldly," she chided and took the shamefaced girl by the arm. "Far be it for me to pry, but I detect that something has you quite distressed. I think it past time for another little chat… in my private parlor."

Warily, Charlotte resigned herself to accompany the determined woman to her sitting room.

"Pray sit down." Lady Susannah indicated a rose velvet settee, where Charlotte nervously perched, awaiting the inquisition. "Shall I ring for tea? I could use some refreshment after my rather full morning," the widow commented airily, moving to a looking glass to rearrange her slightly mussed hair.

"There now," she remarked after pinning a few stray strands back in place and a satisfactory self-inspection. She rang for the maid and then continued. "I have been out this morning on an important errand and bring tidings that should set your heart at ease."

"Indeed? What tidings?" Charlotte asked in befuddlement.

"Why, I've news of your guardian, of course. I feared you must have worried yourself sick, keeping to your rooms as you have. And how could I stand idle, knowing of Philip's troubles when it was within my power to help?"

"But how could you possibly help, madam?"

"After making some inquiries into the matter, I called on one of my dear Nigel's bosom bows. He had served under Marlborough in the Spanish wars, you see, and was well connected with many officers of no small distinction. One can never have too many eminent friends, Charlotte," she advised.

"I imagine so, Lady Susannah," she agreed, wondering where this conversation was leading.

Lady Susannah sensed Charlotte's impatience but evinced no hurry to expiate. "I hold our military in great esteem, Charlotte, and believe all citizens should demonstrate more appreciation for their sacrifice, particularly to those in highest command who carry the heaviest burdens. I expressed precisely these sentiments to dear James just this morning."

"Lady Susannah, not to appear impertinent, but how does your visit to your late husband's friend signify? I fail to see what it has to do with me."

"Dearest girl, you must learn to hear one out with easier grace," she chided gently. "One must cultivate the art of attentive listening if one wishes to earn the favor of others; this is particularly true of such gentlemen as Nigel's friend, James. But perhaps you might better know him as Lord James Dalrymple, the Earl of Stair and commander in chief of His Majesty's forces."

"Oh!" Charlotte gasped. "You are acquainted with the commander in chief? How incredible! Lord Stair was the field marshal at Dettingen where Ro—" She abruptly caught herself.

"You were saying?" Lady Susannah's eyes narrowed in scrutiny. There was a secret here. She felt it.

Charlotte stammered. "I-I was only overcome with your circle of acquaintance, madam. But why have you spoken with Lord Stair?"

Lady Susannah laughed with delight. "Renewing my acquaintance with Lord Stair was the least I could do, in light of dear Philip's present difficulties. After spending quite a lovely interlude, I explained to James the grievous misunderstanding that led to Philip's incarceration. He was all solicitude and inquired instantly how he might assist." Her smile was mischievous. "Lord Stair is a true gentleman, Charlotte, one who would never refuse a lady any service in his power to perform."

"And what service would that be?"

"Why Philip's release, of course. I feared that anxiety over his fate had led you to venture out alone this morning, but you may rest assured the matter is taken care of."

Charlotte's face flushed, but her expression remained guarded, raising further questions in Lady Susannah's mind.

"Are you not pleased, Charlotte? I should have thought you would receive this exceptional news with singular delight."

"You misunderstand, my lady."

"Do I? After our fascinating conversation the other day, I had grown to suspect you have a *tendre* for your guardian, but if I am so shamefully mistaken, I beg you to enlighten me."

"It's not about Philip at all, my lady."

"Is it not? I have begun to deduce as much." Her tone was arid. "What *is* this great secret, Charlotte? Why did Philip bring you here, and what precisely is the nature of your relationship? I believe I have earned the right to know. I do *not* solicit favors of old friends lightly, and having done so for your sake, you had best be forthcoming." Lady Susannah's eyes flashed in growing pique.

"I implore your forgiveness for my mistrust, but for so long I have had no one in whom to confide."

"I am yet far from appeased."

Charlotte sighed. "But where to begin?"

"I suggest at the beginning." She tapped her foot impatiently.

"'Tis such a long and convoluted story, madam."

At this, Sarah interrupted with the tea tray. Once the maid departed, the oh-so-injured Lady Susannah continued. "We have the entire afternoon at our disposal."

Charlotte considered how she could best summarize the high drama of the past months. She took a great breath and began. "'Tis a very tangled web, madam, but suffice to say, I am in love with a certain captain, who until very recently was a close friend of *your* Major Drake. My uncle, who was my *true guardian*, refused our union, which compelled us to elope."

Lady Susannah's annoyed countenance softened. "How foolishly romantic," she murmured.

Charlotte continued. "It proved very foolish indeed after what followed. For reasons known only to himself, Philip aligned himself with my uncle against us. The result was a horrible duel."

"Oh my dear!" she exclaimed. "How very tragic for you!" Filled now with compassion, she surrounded the girl in a maternal embrace. "And your captain?" she asked in trepidation.

"He yet lives, though severely injured."

"Dear, dear girl! What pain you have suffered! But why would Philip have done such a thing? 'Tis not at all in fitting with his character, I assure you."

"Nonetheless, he has caused our suffering. It was Robert whom I had stolen away to see the morning you caught me, and it is want of his fate that torments me." She gazed sadly into the other woman's sympathetic eyes.

"Dearest, have you seen your captain?"

"Yes. I sat by his sick bed, held him, prayed, and wept over him, but when he finally recovered enough to know my presence, he would hear nothing from me!"

Charlotte burst into tears, and Lady Susannah kindly offered her shoulder and lace-trimmed handkerchief. She allowed the girl to weep a respectable period before interrupting.

"I only wish you had confided in me earlier, but as it stands, I have played my best cards. As to Philip's role, I remain unconvinced he is the irrefutable villain. I know him, Charlotte, and absolutely refuse to believe the worst of him. There must be much more to this tale."

"There is indeed much more, Lady Susannah." Charlotte paused. "Philip Drake is my husband."

"Your husband?" She paled.

"In name only, my lady. We were wed under extreme duress. There is no love lost between us, I assure you."

"I don't understand how this should have come about, Charlotte."

"Since you will not believe him the villain, I would rather Philip recount the rest to you. He no doubt has a vastly different perspective from the tale I would tell."

"Then I will press you no further, but I pledge to ferret out the entire history from Philip in good time. Do not dismay on that account. A man discloses much unawares, my dear, if one's methods are subtle." Her smile was one of firm resolution, but she knew Philip Drake was not so easily led as she would have once believed.

"As to your captain, does he know your heart, my dear? Most times, comfort to a man in hopeless circumstances can come only from the woman who loves him. Love has been known to sustain a man when all appears lost. The best succor for him may be your love."

"If he would only listen to me. He is angry, bitter, and hurt. He feels betrayed. He refuses to understand that I acted only out of necessity and that my heart is unchanged."

"You give up the fight too easily. There are other weapons at your disposal."

"I don't understand."

"Mayhap he needs more than just your words to believe your heart. Go back to him, my dear. You will know what he most needs from you."

Twenty-nine

❦

LOVE'S SACRIFICE

When Lady Susannah accompanied Charlotte to the military hospital early that evening, Charlotte was relieved to find Trooper Wiggins at the gate.

"I regret to advise you ladies that no visitors be allowed after dark." Peering closer, he recognized Charlotte. "So, it is you again."

"Yes, and I have brought with me the captain's aunt."

"Mrs. Merring," Lady Susannah interjected.

"The one you said was elderly and infirm in Chelsea?" the trooper asked with skepticism.

"My health is much improved, and I am not so very elderly." Lady Susannah answered, regarding Charlotte ruefully. "Might we have a brief word with Captain Devington?"

"But 'tis after dark, ma'am," he protested.

"Surely there can be no harm, and I am prepared to recompense you for your discretion," Lady Susannah replied.

The Trooper bristled at the intimation of a bribe. "A guard who relinquishes his post or lapses in his duty faces charges, ma'am."

"One could never suggest such a fine and upstanding soldier as you would ever shirk his duty, Captain," Lady Susannah purred. "Your dedication is admirable and shall surely take you far in your career. If we only had more men like you, Captain…"

"I'm no captain, ma'am, leastwise not yet. I suppose since Dr. Pringle has allowed the lady before…"

"Dr. Pringle, you say? Dr. John Pringle?" Her face brightened. "But I am well acquainted with the surgeon. He attended my late husband during an episode of gout suffered one summer in Edinburgh. Is he about?"

"Aye, madam, buried in his books to be sure."

"Then could you inform him of my presence?" she inquired sweetly, giving Charlotte a bold wink.

With matters clearly in the woman's competent hands, Charlotte slipped through the gate. Remarking no additional guards, she cautiously ventured to Robert's room. With only moonlight illuminating the chamber, Charlotte had to adjust her eyes before she took in the shadowy figure sitting by the window.

Creeping silently, she approached from behind, whispering his name. "Robert."

He turned with a start. She registered elation, but it was promptly checked.

"What are you doing here, Charlotte? Or should I say… Mrs. Drake?" He pronounced the name with a snarl.

"Robert, please. I have come to explain. You don't understand the circumstances. Nothing has changed between us."

"Nothing changed? The devil it hasn't!" he cursed and clumsily took to his feet. "You wed another and bloody well claim nothing changed? Do you take pleasure in tormenting me, or are you touched in the head?" He gripped her arm painfully and propelled her three paces to the door. "Leave, Charlotte. Just leave!"

Refusing to give up, she spun around to face him. "But you don't understand how it is!" Tears burned her eyes. How could she make him understand? Make him believe her? She was desperate to break through the barrier he had erected between them.

"It is all just an illusion, Robert. *It is not a real marriage* between

Philip and me. I belong to you and only you. Heart and soul, I have been only yours."

Robert clenched his jaw. "You have been only mine, heart and soul? That's lyrical," he snarled. "I retain your whole heart while poor Philip gets only your body."

Charlotte struck his face with a vicious slap and then gasped at what she had done.

He flinched, but his accusing eyes remained hard as flint.

How could these be the same eyes that once had beheld her in love? "Why can't you believe me? I told you, I belong only to you. I won't let you push me away again." Tremulously, Charlotte reached for his face, tracing the hand print she had left.

"No, I cannot believe you." He moved in closer, pinning her to the door.

This was not the man she knew. What had she done in coming here like this? This was not Robert!

"Somehow I cannot be persuaded that Philip would deny himself," he said with rasping breath that hotly grazed her cheek.

His eyes raked hungrily over her, and he remembered his self-sacrifice the first night they shared in Doncaster, when he had stiffly propped himself in the corner rather than dishonor her. He had watched her that night, guiltily transfixed by the soft, rhythmic rise and fall of her breasts while she slept. He remembered how acutely he had craved her.

Later, when they had again shared sleeping quarters, sometimes so close he could breathe in her scent, her nearness had nearly driven him mad. More than once he had left his bed rather than succumb to the stirrings she evoked.

And in his recent feverish delirium, he had dreamed of her. In his mind he had lived their wedding night, slowly undressing her, stroking her smooth skin with lingering caresses, and lavishing her with warm, open-mouthed kisses while she responded in blissful pleasure to his every touch.

"How was your wedding night, *my love*? Did your heart and soul cry out in agony or in ecstasy when Philip took you?" He laughed caustically then took her lower lip in his teeth and kissed her savagely.

Robert had kissed her many times before, and Charlotte had found exquisite pleasure in the tenderness, but there was nothing tender in *this* embrace. He pressed against her, spearing a hard thigh between hers, holding her captive against the wall. His kiss was fierce, angry, rough in its intensity.

Charlotte froze, trembling violently in her growing doubt and fear. This was not what she had expected, not what she had prepared for! She almost cried aloud. *No. I must not be a coward! He needs to know me in this way, or he will never believe in my love.*

As if reading her panicked thoughts, he abruptly pulled away. His pupils were dilated and face flushed; he panted heavily.

"Leave me, Charlotte. Just go." His voice was hoarse and contemptuous. Turning his back on her, he strode to the window and transfixed a sightless gaze outside as if he waited for the click of the latch to pronounce her departure.

Humiliated, hurt, and her eyes blurred with tears, Charlotte hastened to leave, thankful of escape from this stranger. She opened the door and looked back a final time at the man she had believed she loved. She hesitated, her mind clearing just enough to question what had happened.

If he truly believed in her betrayal, why had he stopped? If he believed she had given herself to Philip, why had he not taken his revenge? Was it all a lie? His behavior only a sham to push her away and make her believe he no longer cared? Perhaps he was not so changed as he would have her believe.

Charlotte closed the door quietly and waited. With the click of the latch, Robert's body racked with unsuppressed emotion.

Her heart wrenched, and she advanced swiftly, catching him

unawares, and wrapped her arms tightly about his waist, binding him to her. Enclosed in her unexpected embrace, Robert finally gave himself up to her.

Charlotte rained kisses on his face and moved to whisper in his ear, "You have failed, Robert. You can never deny my love."

Robert groaned his surrender and took her into an incendiary embrace that ignited them in mutual need. Closing her eyes, Charlotte drank in the sensation of his warm breath and hot tongue exploring her neck, her shoulders, her breasts; the intensity of his ministrations left her gasping. He touched her, and she awakened, her senses bestirred and intuitively responding to every hitherto unknown sensation.

"Are you certain, my love?" His voice was thick and husky, but his uncertainty quashed any remaining doubt she harbored. *This* was truly her Robert, her beloved.

"Body and soul, Robert, I am yours. I am only yours." Her eyes were no longer wide with fear but filled with love. She would hold nothing back to fill the void that had developed between.

"Then we will be as man and wife, as it should have been."

She was, for the present, finally his.

As Charlotte lay curled by her lover's side, physically and emotionally spent, she heard the light scratch at the door. She tried to ignore the call, but the scratch came a second time. She had been promised an hour, and her time had flown. She wished they had the entire night to explore what had unfurled between them. They deserved a lifetime together, but they were cheated yet again.

She rose upon trembling legs, and he pulled her cloak back about her.

"You see what a dangerous thing you have done," he murmured heavily against her hair, his fingers caressing her face. "My hearing is tomorrow. Your coming has only made matters more difficult for both of us, my love."

"But how can you say that now?"

"Because we have no future. My fate hangs by the proverbial thread, and I just pray you suffer no consequences or regrets for your impetuosity this night."

"But how could I?" She bathed his face in kisses. "I could have suffered only by not coming. Above all, you had to know my heart is unchanged."

With the third scratch on the door, he pulled her into a last fervent embrace, their lips meeting for a final tortured kiss. Biting back a sob, she pulled the cloak more tightly about her and left.

Robert spent the remainder of the night in sleepless reflection on all the events leading up to this desperate point of uncertainty. Hours ago he had been lost in hopeless desolation, pensively absorbed by the reflection of an idealistic fool in the windowpane, one who had sealed his fate by a single rash and self-indulgent act. He had regretted wasting his life in pursuit of an empty dream, but Charlotte's coming had changed everything.

In selflessness, she had given her love, proven her devotion, her strength, and her will to persevere. He had taken what she offered, but their joining went beyond the physical. She had somehow given back to him a sense of himself, the sense of purpose he had all but lost.

He prayed that she had not given her precious gift in vain.

Thirty

~~~

MILITARY JUSTICE

As Robert's hands were bound behind his back and the noose dropped over his head, he closed his eyes. His senses awakened to the fetid stench of death emanating from the platform and the sharp prickles of the thick hemp rope, the hangman drawing it snug about his neck and then suddenly pulling it taut. The abrupt, crushing tension on his Adam's apple caused him to gasp and choke. The frenzied crowd roared in a cacophony of bloodlust, sensing the climactic moment imminently approaching.

He shuddered involuntarily. Sweat broke from his brow, slowly dripping down onto his closed lids. His raspy breathing came faster, though he willed it otherwise. Suddenly, as the hangman prepared to release the hatch beneath his feet, there was deathly silence.

His stomach lurched, and he fought for control, willing his body to obedience. If he must die today, by God, he would do it with dignity. He opened his eyes again to scan the crowd, desperately seeking a final glimpse of his love, one last gaze at her lovely face. He sought in vain.

Squaring his shoulders and closing his eyes for the last time, he heard, rather than saw, the hangman release the trap door…

Gasping and choking, Robert awoke abruptly to the sound of the key rattling in his locked door. Sitting bolt upright, he tried to orient himself, slowly recovering from the nightmare-induced panic. This, now, was real. Wiping the sweat from his brow, he rose from his bed, reaching to pull on his breeches when the door opened and the major stepped inside.

Devington masked his surprise at the unexpected arrival of his superior officer… and accuser. He executed a mocking left-handed salute.

"Devington," Philip said earnestly, "I am come to lend what counsel I may in preparation for your trial."

"You are come to help me? I have nothing to say to you, you bloody lying Judas!"

"You don't know how it was," Philip protested.

"I know exactly how it was, you traitorous sod!" Robert retorted. "Sir Garfield gave Beatrix to your brother, so the only way to recoup your losses was to take Charlotte from me. You greedy bastard! Charlotte is everything to me and nothing to you, yet you cast all love and friendship aside and took her for the money! You were a hero to me. I trusted and loved you like a brother. How could you do this?" he cried, tearing at his hair.

"Devington, it was not my intent—"

"Your intent? What exactly was your intent? You maimed and left me for dead. Now you come offering your help?" Robert spoke incredulously.

"Listen to me, Devington," Philip entreated, "I had no intention of settling our differences as we did."

"Did you not, Philip?" he accused. "Then why did you continue pursuit? Why did you draw you sword?"

Philip exploded. "You drew first and gave me no choice, you bloody fool! And had you not acted so rashly, I could have charged you with some minor act of misconduct, easily settled by a flogging, but now my hands are tied. That vindictive sodomite Prescott saw his opportunity and made his report that you assaulted me with intent to kill. He had a half-dozen corroborating witnesses, so you

are to face the general courts-martial as the Mutiny Act requires."
He paused while Devington digested this news.

"I'm sorry, Devington," Philip said grimly. "I wish I could paint
a different picture, but it doesn't bode well."

"Is this what you came for? To tell me I am already condemned?"

"For assaulting a superior, the articles prescribe punishment by
death. I believe your only course is to plead guilty and appeal to the
mercy of the courts."

"Have you ever known of such a thing? Mercy in a martials-
court?" Devington laughed bitterly.

Drake ignored the remark and continued soberly, "The court
convenes at ten o'clock. Field Marshal Viscount Cobham presides.
As judge advocate, he shall act as prosecuting counsel and oversee
the legal proprieties. He is a man with a long and distinguished military career. He will be fair, but you must present your case before
thirteen senior officers, with overwhelming evidence against you.
For what it's worth, I deeply regret the turn of events and would
not, were it within my power to prevent, have you lose your life
over a foolish act of reckless passion."

"Reckless passion? I'd yet kill you even now had I a proper
weapon. If you are finished, *Major*, I respectfully request that you
bugger off." He repeated the mocking salute.

"As you will, Devington," Drake replied with bitter resignation
and departed.

Devington was conducted promptly at ten o'clock to the large
chamber within the inner confines of Whitehall Palace. As Drake
had stated, thirteen officers stood assembled to hear the charges, with
Second Lieutenant George Prescott of the Thirty-second Foot and a
half-dozen of Prescott's subordinates as witnesses. Robert remarked
Prescott's smug countenance, having finally settled his personal score.

The captain confessed to taking up his sword against his superior in defense of his honor, but the articles allowed no legal defense for his actions, regardless of the circumstances.

His trial was remarkably brief; the evidence of two bloodstained swords was overwhelming and the witnesses abundant. The jury of officers adjourned for deliberation, returning the verdict in record time. The entire process had taken less than two hours.

Robert Devington was headed for the gallows as surely as he breathed.

Although unanimous, procedure required that the court's decision and all transcribed documents be taken before either His Majesty or the commander in chief prior to execution of any sentence. Major Thomas Winthrop was appointed for the task.

As the major's carriage departed for the Palace of St James, Philip intercepted him.

"I fear there's nothing to be done now, Drake. Unless His Majesty deems otherwise, Devington's neck will soon be stretched." They both knew the sealed documents included a death sentence.

Philip sighed heavily. "The King's penchant for discipline is as well known as his intractability. The odds scarcely favor clemency."

"I think it would be rather hopeless to appeal to His Majesty, Winthrop said. "The entire episode was embarrassing to the army, and he was exceedingly displeased to hear of it."

"But the Articles of War allow only His Majesty or the commander in chief to mitigate any sentence. Have you any influence with Field Marshal Wade, Winthrop?"

"My acquaintance with him is the briefest, I regret to say. I hardly stand poised to request any boon of the man," Philip replied.

"We fast approach St James; what shall it be? Is there no one with influence who might owe you a favor or a debt of honor?"

Philip's reply was sardonic. "Winthrop, you do understand I do not run in the highest of circles. But a debt of honor?" Philip paused to consider it, then struck by a flash of brilliance, he grinned. "*That* might be arranged. We shall seek out Cumberland!"

⁓

The older of the two gentlemen dealt out twelve cards each. The younger and more rotund of the pair perused his hand and exchanged five. His eyes, revealing the seven-spade straight and four aces in his hand, gleamed in his wine-flushed face.

"Your Grace." The older man nodded, inviting the King's younger son to declare his hand.

"I'm afraid it does not bode well for you, sir. I declare a point of seven."

"Good," his partner replied warily, hoping the suit of seven spades was not also consecutive.

"*Septieme*." His Grace's second declaration confirmed that he indeed possessed seven of the eight possible spades.

"Good."

With no attempt to hide his glee, Cumberland remarked, "That's already twenty-four points, Wade, and I now declare a *quartorze*."

"Good," the elder gentleman replied, holding three kings, all but the spade, and no aces. "I see I am surely buggered with Your Grace holding a seven-card straight and all the bloody aces."

"Buggered indeed, Wade. I've thirty-eight points, and the *repique* makes another sixty. Ninety-eight points thus far before taking a single trick. Do you care to play out the hand, or shall I be merciful?"

"'Twould be purely an exercise in futility for me to continue. I forfeit to your superior hand, Your Grace." Field Marshal Wade threw down his cards in disgust.

"Allowing your two points, I've one hundred four for the final *partie*. Damme, but 'twas a good hand!" Cumberland gloated joyfully as he made the final tabulation. "I win the game by three hundred forty-two points."

"At ten pounds per point, Your Grace, 'tis over five thousand pounds you have won from me this evening. I must concede the field to you." Sitting back and signaling the lackey for more wine, the field marshal scribbled his vowel and handed it to the duke.

Cumberland received it with a smile, remarking, "I fear I might encounter difficulty finding another partner this evening."

"Do you seek another game, Your Grace?" a voice inquired from behind.

"Drake and Winthrop, isn't it?" His Grace of Cumberland eyed the two officers.

"I am flattered you remember." Philip's bow was deferential, and Winthrop responded in kind.

"I endeavor to know my officers, particularly those showing the most promise. Do you play piquet, Drake? I warn you, I've had the devil's own luck this evening." The duke smiled.

"Then it would be a shame not to play it out."

The duke nodded to the vacant seat. "Field Marshal Wade and I have played for ten pounds per point." He waited expectantly.

The major cast a pointed look at Field Marshal Wade's I.O.U. "Might I propose other stakes, Your Grace?"

Thirty-one

❧

A SERENDIPITOUS MEETING

*D*evington." The major entered the chamber and nodded his solemn greeting.

"So it is you, Winthrop. I surmise that you have completed the transactions I requested?"

"Aye. It is done."

"How much… or mayhap I should ask, how little have my meager belongings brought?"

"The returns are far from meager. I have an offer of five hundred pounds."

"The devil, you say! Five hundred for what? My share in the mare was worth only twenty, mayhap thirty pounds, and Mars with my equipage might bring another hundred at most. I asked only for the fair sale of the horses and my accoutrements, Winthrop. As my worth could not possibly exceed one hundred fifty pounds, how could you come by five hundred?"

"You underestimate the stallion. He brings a handsome price," Winthrop dissembled.

"Nigh on five hundred pounds? Unlikely. Though I do not doubt his worth, he is an unknown, and as such would never merit such a price. I care neither for charity nor deceit, my friend."

"What does it matter from whence it comes, when you have dire need of money?"

"What great need should I have of money? Do you expect I wish to carry it to my grave?"

"Devington, are you not aware that your sentence has been amended?"

"What do you say?" he asked incredulously. "How can this be? I had a death sentence upon my head! Do you mean to say I am exonerated?"

"I fear you misapprehend. While you are not exonerated, you are not to pay with your life, but are instead to be transported."

"Transported? How has this come about?"

"You were the fortunate recipient of a debt of honor, but please don't ask me to explain."

"So, I am now to face banishment in the company of thieves, rapists, sodomites, and murderers?"

"Contrary to popular belief, I scarce take to the notion that the American colonies are comprised *solely* of convicts and savages. Transportation is surely more desirable than swinging on the gallows. You will be free to start a new life."

"A new life, you say? Do you expect my eternal gratitude? I am sorry to disappoint you. I find it difficult to generate any enthusiasm when I have bungled the first so remarkably." Robert laughed bitterly. "There is nothing left of my life, Winthrop. I am maimed, dishonored, forced to leave my country and the woman I love. What is left for me?"

"With enough money, you can easily start anew."

"The money again," he remarked caustically. "I wish to know who has offered such an exorbitant sum for the stallion." He asked the question with growing suspicion of the answer.

"What does it matter?" Winthrop replied. "Five hundred pounds is a handsome sum, regardless of whence it came."

"'Twas Drake, wasn't it? Damn you, Winthrop! I told you I want nothing from him. I asked you to sell my belongings so I could assure Charlotte a modicum of comfort. When we spoke yesterday, you gave me your oath that Drake should play no further part. I did not ask for his appeal on my behalf, and I bloody well don't want a farthing of that blackguard's money!"

"I implore you to see reason. You are about to spend your next two months on a crowded ship. Without money, you will be forced to remain below decks with vermin and disease. A full fifth of *those* passengers won't even survive the crossing. Moreover, the rest will be sold into servitude to pay the cost of their passage." The major directed a pointed look to Robert's maimed arm. "The ailing and… injured often die waiting for someone to buy their contracts. With money, you could avoid their fate. Your life is spared, Devington. Is your damnable pride worth taking such a risk?"

"It is if accepting his money allows Drake to buy a clear conscience. Let the bastard live with his guilt! The stallion is no longer for sale."

"What?"

"You heard me, Winthrop. Mars is not to be sold. I take him with me."

"Have you lost your bloody mind? You barely have the cost of your own passage and will be destitute when you arrive. If the sale to Drake so offends you, I shall buy the horse."

"My mind is made up. I take Mars with me."

"You are surely mad!"

"No, I'm condemned, but if I am to begin anew, it shall be on my terms."

"Listen to reason, Devington."

"You know I intended the money for Charlotte."

"With her dowry, Drake has made provision for her. She has no need of your money. If you accept it, a new life is yours, and who knows if in time an annulment might be arranged…"

"Enough! That dream is rent from my heart. For Charlotte's sake, it is best she believe me dead. I have already caused her a lifetime of heartache. I would not have her grieve one more day, let alone waste seven years of her life waiting for something that will never be. Once I depart English shores, Robert Devington is dead."

"Then accept my assurance that the girl shall never be told otherwise."

❧

After receiving the sentence sealed by Commander in Chief Field Marshal Wade, little remained but to relieve the captain of his uniform. Stripped in both the literal and figurative sense, it was as if he had shed his life. Was it only two years ago he had found his identity, his very purpose, as a trooper in the King's Horse? Now it was all swept away. He was lost at sea before having boarded the ship.

"'Tis all arranged as you instructed," Winthrop said. "I still wish you would reconsider the wisdom of your actions."

"You have been a good friend, and I appreciate your concern, but 'tis not a matter of wisdom but of honor. Whatever my fate, I will never again allow another to steer my destiny. I intend to live the remainder of my life, however long it is, on my own terms."

Winthrop sighed with resignation. Devington might have arrived in the colonies with a fat purse, enough to start a new and comfortable life. Instead, his obstinate pride left him with a mere pittance. His net worth after selling his accoutrements and purchasing a new suit of clothes was barely forty pounds. The sum might have given him a cushion had he not insisted on transporting the stallion, whose passage and forage ate up another twenty pounds.

If he purchased a cabin on the ship, he would have almost nothing remaining, but if he took his chances below decks, he would likely not survive the journey at all. Winthrop shuddered at the thought, but with his advice unheeded, he could do naught more but wish his friend Godspeed.

Reunited with Mars, Robert and his escort, Trooper Wiggins, set off for Bristol. Although Robert had overcome the worst of his infection and fever, he was still weak and his arm in the early stages of healing. He was thankful for the small grace that his status as a former officer allowed him to travel without the added hindrance of bonds or shackles. Nevertheless, what he would have once easily endured proved an arduous one hundred twenty miles.

Arriving in Bristol drained of strength, Robert was gratified to hear of the ship's delay, which allowed him a couple of days to rest and recover. Although he had little money to spare, he and his escort took a room at the John Bull Tavern to await the arrival of the merchant ship contracted to carry felons across the Atlantic to the American colonies.

Once settled, Devington and Wiggins entered the taproom crowded with merchants and prospective passengers. They took a table near a soberly dressed middle-aged man and his young companion, presumably his son. Seated in close proximity, they could not help overhear the conversation as the stern-faced gentleman lectured the young man.

"Thy father shall be exceedingly displeased, Master Lee."

"If you could only have seen the horses, Mr. Hanbury! We have none such in Virginia, though the countryside is overrun with the beasts. We have none to compare with this English breed. I have never seen the like!

"The most inferior of the lot was a full hand taller our horses, and I was astounded by their bottom. They raced miles, Mr. Hanbury, four miles and three heats, to be precise. Would that I owned such a horse! With such a prize in the family stables, we would be the envy of the county."

"Vanity, Master Lee, is a sin equal to wagering. Surely, I shalt not settle such a debt, and I must believe thy return home both a judicious and timely event. Elsewise, thy father might grow to regret your half-dozen years spent in England."

"But 'twas only a horse race! Nothing to compare to the vice of playing at dice or cards, and 'tis only ten pounds, a trifling sum that is easily covered tenfold when the ship arrives."

"Surely thou art not suggesting the payment of a gambling debt from thy father's tobacco stores?"

"Why should I not? I must settle the debt before my departure, and I see no reason to trouble my father on this score. Indeed, he need never know of it."

"Now, 'tis not as much the debt at issue as the deception you suggest. I shall have none of it! By my troth to thy father, Thomas, have I pledged to look after thee whence thou arrived to attend Eton. Thy father's purpose was that thou shouldst acquire a gentleman's education, not a gentleman's vice."

Much chagrinned, the lad protested. "I accompanied a few fellows to Newmarket, and what is race without a sporting wager? 'Tis done as well in Virginia, though the usual stakes are made in tobacco rather than coin. 'Tis all the same, is it not? Just a bit of harmless sport. Have you never attended the races, Mr. Hanbury?"

"The Society of Friends forbids gaming, Master Lee, but being well acquainted with Virginia, I understand thy enthusiasm for horse racing. This does not, however, say that I condone gambling. Wagering is an evil pursuit, and no good may ever come of it. Thy present indebtedness renders proof."

The young man flushed. "With the imminent arrival of our ship, I believed you would advance me against the tobacco sale."

"But 'tis thy father's money! Though I am entrusted to care for thy needs whilst thou remain in England, this surely precludes the payment of gambling debts! By my faith, I cannot support it."

"But as a Quaker, you are avowed to honesty in all your dealings. So how could you permit me to renege on a debt of honor?"

"'Tis a small sum, Master Lee, but a larger principle."

"But a gentleman must honor his obligations! I would disgrace the Lee name if I do not pay what I owe to Henry Sharpe."

"Though I offer regrets for thy distress, I am unmoved."

The young man spoke no more, and the pair finished their meal in silence.

Devington and Wiggins ordered two more tankards of ale while the elder man departed to settle his reckoning and inquire further into the anticipated arrival of the ship carrying his tobacco cargo.

"Almost feel sorry fer the young blighter," Wiggins commented.

"Aye." Devington commiserated with the young man, remembering his own similar folly in making his wager with Sir Garfield without the purse to back it up. This one fateful event had brought him to his present predicament. It already seemed a lifetime ago.

"'Tis only tragic, Wiggins, when we fail to learn from our mistakes."

"Mayhap ye should make acquaintance wi' the young gen'leman, Captain. He be headed to Virginia, by the like, and you has no acquaintance in the colonies," Wiggins suggested helpfully.

"I had considered as much. 'Twould appear the young man has connections with a tobacco plantation. Pray excuse me a moment, Wiggins. I think I shall have a word with him."

Feeling that somehow his destiny had revealed itself, Devington staked what little remained in his pocket for an alliance with the Virginia planter's son.

The ship arrived in Bristol a day later and required a full day to divest itself of the vast stores of tobacco. By the end of the second day in port, the new cargo of English goods had been loaded in the ship's hold, and it was ready to take on the awaiting passengers bound for the port of Annapolis, Maryland.

Robert had attempted several times to negotiate transport for Mars on the vessel but was denied each time he brought forth his request. Increasingly anxious, he again approached the first mate.

"Mr. Blakely," he began, "pray might I speak briefly with the captain?"

"If this is about your cargo, I have already told you, Mr…"

"Robert… s, Daniel Roberts," Devington hastily volunteered, resolved to leave his old life and old identify behind.

"Mr. Roberts, this ship is full and unable to accommodate livestock. You might wish to inquire with the port authorities after another vessel. There will surely be a suitable ship within the for'night to carry your cargo."

"But it must be *this* ship," he insisted.

"On the contrary, sir. *It will be another ship.*"

"But 'tis imperative the horse travels with me. I am willing to pay any reasonable fee for his passage. If I might but speak with your captain, sir."

"'Tis no use to petition the captain. This ship *cannot and will not* accommodate your request. Now, if you will excuse me, I have pressing matters to attend." The first mate abruptly directed his attention to the personal cargo of a first-class passenger, the same young man whom Robert had met earlier in the tavern.

"Mister Roberts," the young man began, "I perceive you are having some difficulty."

"'Tis of no consequence, Master Lee," interrupted the first mate.

"I believe I addressed Mr. Roberts," he answered in haughty dismissal. "As you so kindly assisted me out of my own recent predicament, might I perform some service for you in kind?"

"I thank you, Master Lee, but unless you can persuade the captain to take on my cargo, there is naught to be done."

"Indeed? And what cargo might that be, Mr. Roberts?"

"I desire to bring livestock aboard the vessel."

"I am sure Mr. Blakely has made you aware that this ship is not specially equipped to carry livestock, but might I ask why 'tis such an urgent matter that your livestock accompany you when another ship shall soon arrive."

"This animal has a particular value to me."

"Indeed? I am intrigued. Might I inquire after this extraordinarily precious animal?"

"'Tis my horse."

"A horse, sir? You have quite an unusual attachment if you wish to convey him across the Atlantic with another so easily acquired in the colonies. Unlike England, where horses are quite dear, the equine species is right plentiful in Virginia. Indeed, you might acquire a more than serviceable saddle horse for as little as five pounds, far less than it will cost you to transport yours."

"While I appreciate the advice, mine is a vastly superior horse, even by English standards, and I am indeed exceptionally attached to him."

"Is it a racehorse?"

"He is of the type, though he has seen more military service than races."

"But he has raced?"

"In a manner of speaking. He has run several races."

"You've intention of racing him again? Or is your desire to put him to stud?"

"To be honest, Master Lee, I had not yet made that determination."

"I should like very much to see this animal."

"I would be happy to oblige; however, time runs short, and I have yet to negotiate his passage."

"If he is as you say, I shall personally assure his passage. My father is part owner of this shipping enterprise. 'Tis not impossible the captain would make an exception upon my request. Now pray show me the beast," he said excitedly.

True to his word, Philip Ludwell Lee, of Stratford, Virginia, not only negotiated the stallion's passage but also gave up his personal cargo space to make accommodation. Moreover, the young man extended his munificence to sharing his first-class cabin with his new acquaintance.

Having struck the beginnings of friendship, the pair cemented their bond in the following weeks at sea. With a growing burden of guilt at deceiving the young man who had proven so generous, Roberts was led at last to confess.

"What would the high-minded Hanbury say upon the revelation that you have moved from horse wagering to taking up with a transported convict?"

Master Lee reflected for a moment after hearing the entire history and then laughed. "I fear he would be shocked indeed, but the colonies have flourished for having welcomed those cast upon us from our motherland's gaols. You will find no small number of English convicts who have made new lives as honest citizens. I do believe a new life awaits you, Devington."

"Let it be Roberts, if you please. I have left my former life behind."

"Agreed, Roberts, but pray call me by Ludwell, as I should hate to stand a constant reminder of your false friend. I hope to prove more loyal than my namesake."

"You could scarce do worse," he commented ruefully.

"We arrive soon in Annapolis. What are your plans?"

"To be honest, I have yet to make any, not knowing what awaits."

"'Tis only ninety-six miles from Annapolis to my family home of Stratford. If you have no particular destination, why not accompany me? I am confident that among my father's vast circle of acquaintance you could find some manner of gainful employment."

"Even with a maimed arm?"

"You have some education, have you not? Perhaps you could obtain a clerkship. Thomas Lee is very well connected."

"Need I remind you the government would likely frown upon hiring a convict?"

"Indeed. I had not considered that." The young man flushed. "I daresay my father might have qualms, should this become common knowledge. My family suffered misfortune at the hands of vagrants who torched our ancestral home. My mother, heavy with child, was obliged to jump from a second-story window and lost the babe, and a serving girl burned in her bed. Our home, a vast fortune in cash, and priceless books were all lost."

"How tragic."

"It might have been far worse if not for my father's resilience. Thomas Lee is quite an indomitable man and recovered his losses well. As a matter of fact, I have yet to see the new family home. Stratford Hall was completed during my time at Eton."

"Is it a tobacco plantation?"

"We grow tobacco, among other crops. The land is very fertile and conducive to planting, now the more savage Indians are repulsed."

"Savage Indians?"

"Indeed! 'Tis a wild land. The earlier colonists feared for their very lives when they settled. Many were killed in raids on their homesteads. 'Twas a most uncivilized place until a mere decade ago." The young man laughed.

"Then I must give serious thought to my livelihood. A one-armed man might find himself at considerable disadvantage in your Virginia."

"How much use of the arm do you have?"

"Though it pains me less these past weeks, out of the sling, it's rather wont to hang lifeless," he replied ruefully.

"Yet you rode your horse from London to Bristol?"

"I can yet ride, Ludwell. After numerous cavalry charges holding my reins in my teeth while wielding pistol and saber, riding one-handed is no great inconvenience. Just don't ask me to do it while fighting off wild savages."

"If you can still ride, what of training a horse, putting one under saddle?"

"I spent fifteen years of my life tending, driving, and racing horses, Ludwell. Though I confess to limitations, given time, I believe I shall adapt to my disability. After all, horses and soldiering are all that I know."

"I am moved to speak to Mr. Tayloe on your behalf. The man owns the best stables in Virginia, and his horses are nigh unbeatable, though you will find Colonial racing differs greatly from English racing."

"How so?"

"First off, the English regard it as a diversion exclusive to the privileged class, but in Virginia, 'tis prodigiously popular with all men. Secondly, most of our races are run straight out at the quarter mile, though I have heard of a one-mile track at Williamsburg. If your horse is as good as you say, you might consider running him there."

"I shall take it under serious advisement, Ludwell."

Sailing with unusually calm seas and favorable winds, the merchant ship *Venturer* arrived in Annapolis in nine weeks time, and Daniel Roberts disembarked to face a new life.

PART III

Thirty-two

A WOMAN OF INDEPENDENCE

*C*harlotte spent days in her room, alternately praying and crying that somehow God would intervene and spare Robert's life. Was it only three days ago she had gone to him? She had endeavored to give him hope, a reason to go on. She had shown her love in the only tangible way, but now, in mixed hope and fear, she awaited word of his fate. She was at once anxious for word but unready to hear it, as if by deferring the truth she could obviate it.

Emotionally exhausted, she slept, opening her eyes only when Sarah pulled the heavy drapes to admit the noonday sun. She rose stiffly from the bed when the maid returned with a pitcher and washbasin.

"Her ladyship has asked for you, ma'am. She inquires if ye might have taken ill."

"It's nothing a cup of tea won't remedy, Sarah. Please advise Lady Susannah I will be down directly."

"Aye." The maid hesitated at the door. "Ye might wish to know that yer husband waits below stairs."

"My husband?"

"He is yer husband, isn't he? The officer who brought you here? He arrived not a quarter hour hence. 'Tis why her ladyship calls for you."

"Then pray help me with my laces, Sarah!"

It had been nearly a se'nnight since Charlotte had last seen Philip, though never again should have suited her very well. But he might have brought news of Robert. Breathless with apprehension, she hastened to the salon.

"Charlotte." He acknowledged her entrance with a restrained greeting.

She acknowledged him with a nod, wasting no breath on civilities. "Have you news of Robert?"

"I've news." His reply was grim.

Charlotte seized in apprehension. "What has transpired?"

"I shall not beat about the bush. The verdict was guilty. It could have gone no other way." He shook his head in resignation.

Gooseflesh formed on her arms. "What does this mean?" she asked, stiffly lowering herself into a chair. "Wh-what of the s-sentence?" Her voice was now scarce more than a whisper.

He answered in clipped tones. "I know not how to soften the blow. It was a capital offense." He did not elaborate further but directed a helpless look to Lady Susannah, who rushed to the girl's side.

"You are the very one who put the nails in his coffin!" she cried.

"Damme! 'Tis not the way of it, Charlotte, and you know it!" Philip retorted hotly. "Need I remind you? Devington drew first. He induced me at great reluctance to engage him. Had I wished him dead, I should have finished the job myself!"

Charlotte's mind froze with her countenance. She could not think. She could not breathe. She was paralyzed. Lady Susannah knelt beside her, trying frantically to console the inconsolable.

"Philip, is there naught can be done?" Lady Susannah asked.

"There is nothing. His sentence has been carried out."

The reality of his words struck home. Charlotte gasped with horror. As the room swayed, she clutched the arms of the chair. "No! My God, no! It cannot be!"

For three days, Charlotte remained in her room, returning trays of cold tea and untouched food. Lady Susannah let her be until the fourth day, when Charlotte refused to be roused.

"Sarah, what is the meaning of this?" Charlotte protested as the coverlet was torn from her. She attempted to snatch it back, but it wasn't Sarah who answered.

"Three days is enough for such deep mourning, Charlotte. I have granted you this time in peace to wallow fully, completely, and passionately in your grief, but it is finished, my girl. I shall not allow you to put yourself into a decline. Your new life begins today," Lady Susannah proclaimed.

Charlotte met her tyrannical stare in disbelief. "Leave me be, madam! You know nothing of my grief!" Her voice was hoarse from weeping.

"On the contrary, my dear girl, I well know the deep heartache of lost love, but I will not allow this to go on interminably. It is over, love. You must now pick up the pieces."

Charlotte's entire body shook anew. "But how can I conceive of going on?"

"You cannot give up your life, Charlotte. In time, you shall come to accept what has been, and the pain will fade. But now you have the opportunity to make the remainder of your life as *you* choose it to be."

"You mean as you have done."

"Indeed I do. My life is my own. I am free to live as I choose and love as I choose, thought I may not always choose wisely." Her thoughts involuntarily wandered to Philip Drake's reappearance in her life. "No one can ruin my life, save me." She laughed drily.

"But I am not free, madam, and my life is not my own! I'm nothing more than the legal property of the man I most despise!" Charlotte's voice quivered with anger and frustration.

"Indeed you are wed, but you need not view your state as imprisonment. On the contrary, you might yet ascertain the very freedom you gain in becoming a matron."

"I don't follow you."

"Don't fret, child. 'Tis too soon for you to comprehend. For now, let's endeavor to get you dressed and packed. We have a journey to undertake."

"A journey?" Charlotte looked alarmed.

"We are withdrawing to Cambridgeshire."

"Cambridgeshire?"

"Indeed, Cheveley Park, to be precise. Perhaps you have heard of it? I have arranged to lease a cottage owned by the Duke of Somerset, another of dear Nigel's friends. You are in great need of a change of scenery, and I haven't visited the countryside in years. I believe 'tis just the thing for you, dear girl. We shall retire to the country forthwith."

"But I should never cause you so much trouble and expense," Charlotte protested.

"Pshaw! Don't trouble yourself of the expense. It shall be borne by Philip. He is your husband, after all."

"Isn't Cheveley close to Newmarket?"

"Yes, it is scarce four miles. By the by, Charlotte, did you not mention a mare you once owned is stabled at Cheveley?"

"Amoret?" Charlotte spoke the name wistfully. "Philip said she was to be bred and stabled there."

"I thought as much," Lady Susannah remarked thoughtfully.

Philip arrived in the midst of their packing. "Sukey, where the devil are you going?" he demanded.

Ignoring his imperious manner, she answered without looking up from her inventory. "You arrive opportunely, Philip. I had begun to fear you would not respond to my message."

She focused her full attention on him now, but her smile quickly faded at his haggard appearance and the slight whiff of stale brandy.

"But what of Charlotte? Surely you don't intend to leave her alone?"

"Of course not!" she answered in a rebuking tone. "Do you think I would shirk my responsibility, when I gave you my word to look after her? The girl has taken the news very hard, as you might guess, but she must get on with her life."

"So, perceiving my callousness and failure to do so, you have taken matters into your own hands."

"On the contrary, your very presence betrays your concern for the girl. I know you to be many things, Philip, but I don't believe you nearly as jaded as you portray. Moreover, I don't believe her alone in her angst." She raked him in a knowing gaze, and then sitting on the silk-upholstered divan, beckoned him to her side. "Come, Philip." Her voice was both soft and insistent. She clearly detected the pain behind the mask of detachment that he tried to drown in drink. Her heart cried out to comfort him, but he once more spurned her.

"I have no desire to speak of it, Sukey."

"I know, my love," she replied tentatively, reaching out her hand.

He hesitated, a shadow of uncertainty flickering in his eyes, but he turned away. When he faced her again, his mask was firmly back in place.

Hurt more than she wished to reveal, Susannah spoke matter-of-factly. "Very well, we shall only attend to business at hand. I plan to retire to the country for some time, mayhap for several months."

"Do you indeed?"

"Yes, until the girl is standing on her own two legs." Her answer was firm, resolute.

"I gathered you had taken it into your head to play Lady Benevolence, madam, but how to you intend to pay for your bucolic retreat?" Philip spoke with a sardonic glint in his eyes. "I might ask, if perceiving my present weakness, you intend to bleed me dry?"

"You could at least hear me out before passing judgment," she answered sharply. "Had I thought for a moment you would begrudge her such a small request, I should not have appealed to you."

He considered her quizzically, warily. "All right, I call truce. What precisely is your plan, and what do you require?"

"Firstly, I wish to apply to you for the return of Charlotte's maid, if she can be found. The woman would no doubt be of great comfort."

"No doubt," he agreed dryly. "But she could be anywhere in London."

"I shall contrive to locate her, if you agree only to pay her wages. 'Twill be trifling enough, I assure you, scarce more than room and board."

"Trifling," he grunted. "And secondly?"

"I have already arranged to lease a cottage at Cheveley Park. 'Tis a very modest house. The lease is a paltry sum."

"A paltry sum."

"Indeed paltry, Philip."

"'Twould appear you have matters well in hand, my dear," he replied caustically. "And I suppose you have other requests as well?"

"Aside from the maid and the house, we have need only to hire a carriage to convey us."

"A private conveyance, of course."

"And naturally, sufficient money to sustain us," she added.

"Naturally. I should have guessed the fifty pounds I gave you a mere se'nnight ago would have fallen far short of your needs."

She paled at his insinuation. "Have you grown so cynical that you believe everyone is inspired only by greed? I take grave offense coming from one whose own motives have fallen far short of altruistic." The barb struck home. "In addition to what you have already provided, fifty pounds should suffice to cover our needs."

"Fifty, you say? Not one hundred?" he offered mockingly.

"Fifty pounds should more than suffice, Philip."

"And if I am away for an extended period, how then shall you go on?"

"An extended period? But what do you mean?"

He replied brusquely, "I am deployed to Flanders as aide-de-camp to Field Marshal Wade. I depart on the morrow."

"So soon?" Her blurted response was more revealing than she intended. Although wounded by his cynicism and mistrust, she couldn't deny a sharp pang at his imminent departure. "Have you any idea the duration of your absence? I should need to know for Charlotte's sake," she hastily added, mistakenly meeting his gaze while failing to hide the pained look in her own.

Bemused, Philip considered her, wondering if that look, that tone did not belie... something. He dismissed the thought. He would be a fool to believe she possessed a heart.

"One never knows, Sukey. The French continue to amass their forces, and Louis himself takes to the field. I anticipate at least six months, though I don't despair of making winter camp in England. 'Twill all depend on our success." He continued briskly, "I had come thinking you desired to make alternate arrangements for Charlotte, but if you are so willing to involve yourself with her welfare, I shall continue to entrust her to you."

"I am happy to do what I may for one in need of a friend, Philip."

Did she refer to Charlotte or himself? He regarded her quizzically but refused to give any further weight to these thoughts. "Then if there is no more, I shall take my leave of you. I trust a bank draught of two hundred pounds should sustain you?"

"Two hundred? 'Tis more than generous," she answered, hiding her surprise.

He paused, regarding her narrowly. "Might I inquire why you chose Cheveley?"

Her reply was candid. "'Tis by design, as you no doubt suspect, but your question leads to my final request."

"Another? My bounty is not without limits, Sukey," he warned.

"I doubt this last should cause you any undue distress. I merely ask if you yet retain ownership of a mare once belonging to Charlotte. I understood her to be stabled at Cheveley Park."

"If I did, how should that signify?"

"I believe the mare would greatly divert the girl. Would it pain you to give the horse back to her?"

He considered the request. "The mare is bred. I will honor the request with one provision; the coming foal is mine."

❧

With Charlotte pleasantly ensconced at Cheveley, her melancholia slowly diminished. The cottage, though small, was indeed perfect, and although it was a bittersweet reminder of her past, she was delighted with her reunion with Letty and Amoret.

Charlotte began riding again, taking her mare out each day to explore her new surrounds. They rode along the chalk downs and clay-capped hills that ran southeast from Newmarket and comprised Cheveley. She and Amoret, who miraculously had not slipped her foal in their earlier adventure, made their leisurely way along the Newmarket-Ashley Road to the bridge at Broomstick corner and followed the thorn-set ditch that divided the grazing pastures of the heath from the rabbit warrens on the flat summit, aptly named Warren Hill.

At Long Hill, she discovered the hawk ladder and the King's chair used by Charles II, but it was the vista at the site of the Cheveley Castle ruin that inspired Charlotte. Gazing over the sweeping heath and the chalk valley below, her plan was born. After nearly three months in her bucolic idyll, Charlotte was finally resolved to take Lady Susannah's advice and live her life again, and inasmuch as she was able, she would live it on her terms.

Although Robert had been cruelly taken from her, their dreams still lived in her heart, and what better way to honor his memory than to make their dreams a reality. Having already mentally mapped out the landscape, Charlotte began to make inquiries of the available grazing land, lush green pastures that would nurture the foals she would raise.

Charlotte had little money at her disposal, only the quarterly allowance of one hundred pounds that Sukey had negotiated for her, but it was more than enough. What need had she of carriages and ball gowns, when she chose to bury herself in a village populated by farmers?

As her scheme took place, Charlotte leased a modest parcel, comprising ten hectares, in the chalk valley less than a mile south of Newmarket. The proximity of her pasture provided her easy access to the Newmarket Heath and Gallops laid out to train and exercise the Newmarket racehorses. As part of her daily routine, Charlotte would ride along Warren Hill, Long Hill, and Side Hill in unobtrusive observation of the prospective racers that would one day be her adversaries on the turf.

As spring transitioned to summer and Amoret neared the end of her eleven-month gestation, Charlotte contracted laborers to build several large paddocks and shelters that would comfortably house Amoret and the future broodmare band. With Amoret settled for her confinement and only a month to go, Charlotte realized the need for a stud groom. She needed someone knowledgeable about breeding and foaling practices, should anything go wrong. But who? Hopeful of the answer, she dispatched a note and waited.

Knowing that Lady Susannah had experienced her fill of country life, Charlotte reassured her friend that she was ready to stand on her own.

With some hesitation but eager to return to her own life, Lady Susannah returned to London, with a promise of frequent correspondence.

Charlotte continued in newfound tranquility until receiving an unexpected letter from Beatrix. Her cousin had written woefully, pleading for Charlotte to come to Hastings Park and stand as godmother to the unborn child, and had lamented that she awaited the birth in loneliness and isolated confinement.

Charlotte's first impulse was to ignore the letter, but her conscience nagged. Somehow, she felt sorry for her cousin. Had not Beatrix also been a pawn in Sir Garfield's game? Moreover, the infant would be kin. She would be the babe's second cousin through Beatrix, and an aunt through her marriage to Philip. Common civility dictated she at least attend the christening.

Never having previously given thought to the matter, Charlotte also realized she was daughter-in-law to the Earl of Hastings, a man she had never even met. Daughter-in-law to an earl. She pondered the notion, and squaring her shoulders, decided to make the journey to East Sussex.

Was she not now her own woman? She was free to leave at any time she chose. She had learned much from Lady Susannah's example.

Charlotte and Letty packed lightly, travelling by stage, and arrived without incident at Hastings Park. Charlotte shuddered at first sight of the estate, experiencing another pang of sympathy for Beatrix in this desolate place.

Greeted by her aunt, Charlotte and Letty followed her through the empty, cavernous halls to their assigned chambers. Letty unpacked while Charlotte accompanied Lady Felicia to her cousin's rooms, where she found Beatrix reclining in bed and looking pitiful.

Still clad in her dressing gown, her hair tumbling about her pale face in tangled disarray, Beatrix greeted her cousin with a wan smile. "Charlotte! Truly, I did not believe you would come."

Concerned by her appearance, Charlotte inquired, "Beatrix, have you taken ill? Is all right with the babe?"

Heaving a greatly exaggerated sigh, she answered, "'Tis just this intolerable confinement. You have no idea how breeding drains one of life. 'Tis all I can do to dress some days. If it were not for Mama, I don't know how I should go on."

"My poor Trixie," Lady Felicia said, clucking, "'twill all be over soon, dearest. The midwife predicts the pains will commence with the next full moon."

"I should like nothing more than to be done with it, Mama. I have been miserable, exiled to this wretched place! I don't fathom why I could not have remained in London, but Edmund insisted I come here."

"Dearest, you know tradition dictates the heir be born at the ancestral home. All the Earls of Hastings have been born here. Your babe is to be the future earl, after all, and as Viscountess Uxeter, you must abide by all the queer customs of the nobility."

"But how much longer must I remain here?" Beatrix whined.

"I daresay 'tis for your husband to decide. The health and safety of his heir takes precedence over your wishes to reside in London, my dear," her mother answered.

"But couldn't I go to Wortley, Mama? Anywhere but this wretched pile of stone!"

"You are just homesick, Trixie. 'Tis only natural when a girl weds and leaves her home. I daresay Charlotte feels the same. Do you not?" She directed the question to her niece.

"I confess I have been very happily ensconced these past months in Cheveley, Aunt."

"Cheveley, Charlotte? Where on earth is Cheveley?" her aunt asked.

"In East Cambridgeshire, near Newmarket."

"Newmarket, indeed! 'Tis a gentleman's playground and no fit place for a lady."

"Only during the racing season, Aunt. 'Tis quiet enough the rest of the time."

"Horse racing? I am confounded your husband tolerates this infernal obsession with horses! As a married woman, you should conduct yourself with more decorum," Lady Felicia chided.

"I am the wife of an officer, letting a cottage from the Duke and Duchess of Somerset. Who should question the respectability of such an arrangement?"

"Indeed, but I pity you, Charlotte, quite abandoned by your husband and having to make do with so little. Why has Philip not sold his commission and settled you both in a decent house?"

A stab of jealousy caused Beatrix to add, "Poor dear, married to a man who prefers the army to his wife's bed."

"The army is far safer for Philip Drake than my bed, Beatrix," Charlotte snapped. Her remark generated a gasp of horror from the other women.

Her aunt added, "You are duty bound to bed with your husband. If you refuse him, he has every right to put you aside. You provide grounds for annulment!"

"One might only hope, Aunt."

"I cannot countenance such a speech from your lips, Charlotte!" her aunt said in reproach.

Charlotte was moved by her resentment to answer, "I was forced into a union with a vile scoundrel. Did you think I might come to delight in my circumstance? Think again! Philip Drake should live a far healthier life remaining abroad."

Thirty-three

THE TURNING POINT

The Campaign of 1744 began with Louis XV's proud review of his eighty thousand troops at Lisle. By contrast, Field Marshal Wade found his own allied army diminished when the Dutch and Austrians failed again to muster their promised quota. His command, as Lord Stair's before him, was further weakened by the petty jealousies and antagonisms of the Austrian and Dutch generals. As the allied army lay impotent with conflicting counsels and perpetual bickering, the French divided and conquered.

When word of the campaign reached the House of Commons, Mr. Pitt's voice cried in outrage: "Once more we are made to look ridiculous before the world!" He narrated in a mocking voice: "On July the thirtieth, our forces encamped on the road to Ghent within a few miles of the enemy. On the thirty-first, a Scots captain was taken prisoner.

"On August the first, they looked for a field of battle, but no enemy was nigh; on the second, they were put in fear, but danger proved at a distance. The third of August, they slept soundly. On the fourth, the army assembled for review, and on the fifth the Hanoverians foraged, reporting a shot fired at them! But on the sixth, the British forces foraged with no report of fire.

"And on the seventh day they rested."

The chamber echoed with stifled guffaws.

Lord Uxeter leaned over to George Lyttelton. "So proceeds our *third* brilliant campaign. We advance and they retreat, just as two months ago, we retreated and they advanced. Is it any wonder we are ridiculed and our general mocked in farces on the French stage?"

Mr. Pitt's manner grew more inflamed. "Even with the aid of Divine Providence in striking the King of France with fever, our generals proved singularly impotent! I am moved to ask, gentlemen, if this House must petition the Lord Almighty to place his archangel Michael in command, that we might actually be moved to fight!"

࿇

The continued troubles in government and heated debates over the war had given Lord Uxeter valid enough reason to return to Parliament after seeing his bride settled in Sussex, though he would have eagerly invented any excuse to rid himself of the insipid cow.

Overall, however, his marriage had caused little inconvenience, and viewed in proper perspective, he was not completely displeased with how he had managed thus far. At Newmarket, he and Sir Garfield had come to an arrangement. In exchange for the dowry, he had taken Beatrix to wife and agreed to initiate Charles Wallace into his political circles.

Edmund had paid court to Beatrix, sharing his knowledge of her condition and voicing tender compassion for her, followed by righteous condemnation of his vile brother for seducing and defiling such an innocent. He had convinced her that his rogue brother would never have honored his promises to her, and that he would have eventually abandoned her to raise his bastard child alone.

Edmund had vowed to cherish Beatrix and raise the child as his own. He swore that by bearing him a son, she would be assured wealth, comfort, and status as mistress of a great ancestral estate.

With his gentle compassion and earnestly spoken promises, Beatrix had acquiesced to a hasty private wedding.

In dealing with his innate revulsion to couple with her in the marriage bed, Edmund had asserted solicitous concern for her delicate condition. In the most self-sacrificing manner, he had stroked her cheek, lovingly stating his willingness to abstain from conjugal relations to ensure the health and well-being of the bride and child, whom he swore were paramount to his happiness.

Edmund was struck with the irony that his brother's by-blow would truly assure his inheritance and therefore his happiness.

Edmund had then taken Beatrix to Sussex. She had lamented his leaving her at the estate with only the invalid and reclusive earl, but his tender words of solicitude had again prevailed. He persuaded her of the necessity of spending her finals months in the fresh country air. By remaining at his ancestral home, she could forgo the hazards and fatigue of travel when the time came to birth the child. He further placated her by suggesting she send for her mother and cousin to keep her company during her confinement, and promised to return to celebrate the birth.

No, Beatrix had not proven excessively difficult to manipulate, but now word of his heir's imminent birth came amidst a looming political crisis and possible government collapse.

He was acutely aware of the unprecedented opportunity a crisis of this magnitude would provide; nevertheless, Edmund could neither afford to displease his father at this juncture. He consoled himself that he might perform his duty in Sussex expeditiously and resume his normal life within the for'night.

Hoping for diversion along the way, Edmund had sent word to Charles Wallace to accompany him. Directing his coach to the residence at Upper Brook Street, Lord Uxeter collected Charles, and the pair set off.

The coach halted at a small inn in the village of Pembury, about halfway to their destination. The road conditions had been poor, and the hour was late. The gentlemen were excessively tired, hungry, and cramped after nine hours in the closed carriage.

Lord Uxeter sent the coachman to inquire about accommodations. Returning, they spoke briefly. Edmund addressed Charles. "My apologies, dear boy, but there is only one room to be had, and the coachman says 'tis twenty miles to the next lodging. With the lateness of the hour, I fear we have little option but to break our journey here."

Charles responded affably. "By all means, my lord, you take the chamber. I shall sleep in the carriage. 'Tis no trouble at all, I assure you." As he spoke, he stretched his cramped muscles with a slight wince.

Perceiving his companion's discomfort, Lord Uxeter protested. "I should not countenance such a thing! The coachman shall make do with the coach. 'Twill be only minor inconvenience to share the chamber. For now, let us partake of supper, and let the innkeeper attend to the accommodations."

The innkeeper stocked the fire in the taproom and provided two large tankards of strong ale, which he replenished at regular intervals while his wife brought forth a meal of cold chicken, bread, and cheese before departing to prepare the room.

Charles broke the companionable silence as they ate. "Lord Uxeter," he began, "though we've been acquainted for some months, and by marriage you are my brother, it occurs to me that I know very little of your personal history. Were you raised in Sussex?"

"Shall we forgo the formalities, Charles? As I am your brother-in-law, you should call me Edmund."

"Indeed, my lo—"

"Edmund," he corrected. "And to answer your question, I was born at Hastings Park, but one might well argue I was raised there."

"You grew up in London, then? Though I have enjoyed the various diversions of the city, I would not trade my boyhood running wild in the countryside, galloping the heath, fishing, swimming, hunting the wood. Devington and I made all manner of mischief in our youth. 'Tis a pity about Devington. We were boyhood chums, you know... I fear growing maudlin if I dwell on it. My point is," he continued briskly, "there is great freedom for a lad in the country. Don't you agree?"

"As much as I hate to gainsay you, I cannot agree. I never knew the boyhood freedom you describe. My first and most vivid memory of my boyhood was being packed off to Harrow on my fifth birthday. I scarce left its hallowed halls until my eleventh year, when the earl sent for me during my holiday. I arrived to find a stepmother, and the next holiday, a new brother.

"Thenceforth, I developed a decided distaste for my holidays and seldom went home. After Harrow, I attended Cambridge, and moved to London upon taking my degree."

"I daresay, I appreciate my boyhood tenfold after that tale," Charles replied.

"Then I have become a bore! Suffice to say, I prefer the delights of town life. London offers its own kind of freedom. It is a place of many diversions. With proper discretion, one has the liberty to pursue any pleasure, whatever it might be."

His intense regard left the younger man somehow discomfited. Charles yawned and stretched. "The hour grows late; I should like to retire."

"Indeed," Edmund replied. "We've yet fifty miles to travel on the morrow; 'twould be wise to get an early start."

The men quit the taproom for the single chamber, where the apologetic innkeeper's wife lamented that, while she had produced clean linens, there was no truckle to be had.

"At least 'tis a bed of good size," she offered. "Many a night when they patrolled the coast, we had billeted soldiers in this very room. Four at a time didst share the same bed, though they was not of the quality of you fine gents. But there bein' none else, mayhap you might make do?" She gestured apologetically.

"It appears we've little choice," Edmund remarked dryly with a covert glance at Charles, who was already removing his outer clothes.

His fatigue compounded by ale, Charles heedlessly stripped down to his shirt almost before the innkeeper's wife had left the room. The young man forthwith collapsed onto the bed and into deep and easy slumber.

Edmund, however, was far from relaxed in his current situation. He had carefully cultivated an easy familiarity with Charles. He had nurtured camaraderie and trust by taking the young man under his wing in every sense, but he had been leery to reveal too much of himself, choosing rather to maintain a safe distance.

Having grown increasingly cynical, disillusioned, and jaded, Edmund was strongly attracted to the fresh, idealistic youth, but he had tread carefully. Never seeking to press an advantage, he had awaited the right moment to test the waters. Now, gazing longingly at the young man sprawled in careless repose, he was enticed to the point of distraction.

ᑦᔭᓂᕐᑏᐧ

After imbibing too freely of the ale, Charles had fallen fast asleep but awoke to the most profanely disturbing situation. He now closed his eyes in a constrained effort to recall the chain of events but shuddered in revulsion at the images and sensations that evoked.

First he had thought it a dream. What had actually happened? His recollection was vague, as if his brain were suppressing the episode from his consciousness. What little he did remember, he would much sooner forget.

Charles Wallace fled the inn at Pembury on a stolen horse. Preferring to think of it as borrowed without prior notice, he vowed to return the nag as soon as possible, but circumstances had necessitated his actions. Utterly distracted, Charles rode blindly for miles, heedless of his direction, while he struggled to untangle his emotions.

Lord Uxeter! The man whom his father had chosen to wed Beatrix, the man who had been his close companion and mentor for months, the man whom he had trusted and respected, the man his father had chosen to groom him for a position in Parliament. The place his father had arranged for him. His father's choice. His father's desires. His father's ambitions.

Charles's father had achieved much with modest beginnings, but over the years he had become ambitious beyond measure, willing to advance his cause regardless of the price others might pay.

Now he wondered just how much his father had known about the nature and character of Lord Uxeter. Had he known of Uxeter's inclinations? Had he even suspected? Moreover, did he care what befell his son as long as it served his agenda? Charles had a myriad of questions with few answers.

Dutiful and compliant, Charles had never resisted or defied his father's will, had never hesitated to follow his father's set course, even if it ran contrary to his own heart's desire. Even Beatrix, spoiled from birth, had never overtly challenged their father's will.

Ironically, only quiet, demure little cousin Charlotte had ever dared flout him, but she had paid dearly for it. His father's machinations had not only destroyed Charlotte and Robert's lives but had led Beatrix to what he now knew beyond a shadow of a doubt would be a wretched union with Lord Uxeter. He was deeply sorry for both his sister and the child she would soon bear.

Charlotte, however, had demonstrated more backbone and strength of character than any would have previously credited her. Although dealt a serious blow, she had determined to make a life for herself, God help Philip Drake! Charles chuckled briefly before refocusing on his quandary.

To continue to Hastings after what had transpired was completely out of the question. To go back to London and carry on as if nothing had happened was equally beyond his ability to endure. He could head northward, back to his childhood home, but to what possible future?

Or, he reflected, he could for once in his life risk his father's displeasure to follow his own course. He realized there was no longer any debate.

Charles directed his borrowed horse northward to Westminster, the regimental headquarters of the First Foot Guards.

Thirty-four

◈

HEIR TO AN EARLDOM

"Eeeeeeeeeeh!" As Beatrix pushed for the last time, the shriek echoed thru the manor. Her birth pains had commenced with the advent of the full moon, just as the midwife predicted. After twelve hours of exhaustive labor, her final effort brought forth the firstborn of Lord and Lady Uxeter.

"It be done now, my lady!" the midwife exclaimed, attending to the umbilical cord still attaching the babe to its mother. Lady Felicia rose from the bedside where she mopped her daughter's brow.

"Out with it!" she demanded of the midwife. "Is all well?"

The gray-haired woman flipped the babe upside down to clear its airway. Another shriek followed the action, and the babe's cry rang through the manor, mimicking that of its mother.

"Aye, ma'am. All is as it should be," the midwife replied, wiping her bloodstained hands on her apron. She had barely swaddled the babe before the impatient grandmother snatched it from her hands.

"Trixie! You have done it, my girl!" Her mother beamed. "Such blue eyes, he has! Take a look at your son, the future Earl of Hastings." She carried the shrieking infant to its bewildered mother.

"Madam," the midwife began anxiously, interrupted by Lady Felicia before she could speak her piece. "Don't just stand there, woman! We must send immediate word to his lordship, the earl, and dispatch a messenger to Westminster to alert the proud papa!"

"But, madam, you must—"

"Get you hence, Mrs. Lambe! Inform his lordship that the heir is born at last!"

"But, madam, my Lord Uxeter must be informed—" she said with great distress.

"Indeed, Lord Uxeter must be informed without delay! Mrs. Lambe, do you attend me? Why are you standing there wringing your hands? Off with you!"

"Aye, madam. Just as you say, madam." The harried woman left the birthing chamber.

"Beatrix, is there aught you require?" Charlotte inquired of her cousin, leaving Lady Felicia to coo over her wailing grandchild.

"Can't you stop its confounded wailing, Mama?" Beatrix wailed.

"Perhaps the babe is hungry?" Charlotte suggested.

Lady Felicia handed the vociferous infant to its mother, who looked at it askance. "What do you expect me to do with it?" Beatrix asked.

"Why, you must put the babe to nurse at your breast, of course," her mother patiently explained.

"Put it to my breast?" she cried in horror. "If it need nurse, then send for a wet nurse at once, Mama!"

"But my dearest, you are the babe's mother."

"Do you know nothing of better society, Mama? No woman of fashion would think to do such thing. I am a viscountess now and must not subject either my husband or myself to ridicule by putting a babe to my breast as if I were a common shepherd's wife. I must have a wet nurse!"

"'Twas not the way in my day," Lady Felicia protested. "You and

Charles were both upon my teat until your third year, and none the worse for it!"

"Perhaps if you just hold the child?" Charlotte advised. "The babe will surely be comforted in its mother's loving arms."

"Comfort! 'Tis I in need of comfort! Do you know what I have been through in squeezing this *thing* out of my body? I am exhausted, and my nerves are shattered. How shall I ever sleep with that incessant wailing? Take it away from me!"

"Shall I inquire about the wet nurse, Lady Felicia?" Charlotte offered.

"I shall see to it without delay, Charlotte," her aunt replied. "Perhaps you would be so kind as to hold the babe while I attend to the matter?"

"Certainly, Aunt."

With a questioning look to her daughter, she handed the crying infant to Charlotte, who held the babe, rocking it close to her breast. Almost instantly, the protests ceased, and the babe relaxed into slumber. Lady Felicia departed, greatly relieved.

"Thank God for peace at last! You have no idea what I have suffered for that brat, Charlotte!" Beatrix bemoaned.

"I confess I have little understanding."

"It all began with the most excruciating pains. 'Twas unbearable. I thought I should die! I shall *never* bear another child. I swear it!"

"The pain is yet new to you, but in regard to what it ultimately wrought, surely in time, you shall forget. 'Tis a beautiful babe. You should be proud," Charlotte remarked, wistfully gazing at the sleeping child.

"Is it truly? Beautiful, that is," Beatrix asked. "It appeared like a shriveled little prune to me."

"Nay, 'tis a lovely child."

"Mayhap I hadn't a good look at it, then. Bring it to me, Charlotte."

Pleased to have persuaded her cousin, Charlotte rose cautiously from her chair and brought the baby back to its mother.

"It looks like a bundle of rags swaddled so. Pray unwrap it so I can have a proper look."

"Do you think it a good idea? The room is rather chill."

"I want only a quick look at the thing. I am its mother, after all," she remarked churlishly.

Charlotte carefully laid the bundle on its mother's lap, where they proceeded to unswaddle it, slowly freeing the tiny arms, revealing chest, torso, and… Beatrix and Charlotte simultaneously gasped.

"'Tis not a son at all! 'Tis a girl!"

❧

Arriving alone at his family estate, Lord Uxeter stifled his repugnance for the part he must now play—proud papa to his brother's bastard. Proceeding directly to his wife's apartments, he knocked only once and entered without waiting for reply. His mother-in-law met him in the outer chamber.

"Lord Uxeter!" she gushed. "We have awaited your arrival so expectantly. Beatrix shall be delighted to receive you."

"Indeed?" His reply was frosty. "Then I trust my wife is well, madam?"

"Our poor Beatrix is much in need of a husband's comfort after such an ordeal."

"Ordeal?" His expression noted alarm. "Has she lost the child?"

"Indeed not, my lord!" Lady Felicia beamed. "Our little Beatrix has born you a beautiful, healthy child!"

Edmund metaphorically felt the weight of the world, or more accurately, the weight of the earldom, tumble from his shoulders. He had achieved his inheritance at long last. He even found it within himself to smile at his mother-in-law and exhibit a modicum of concern.

"Might I inquire then after the health of the mother?" he prompted.

"They are both quite well," she assured, "but 'twas very trying, you know. Beatrix has always maintained such a delicate constitution."

He had no interest in the details. "Where might I find the child, Lady Felicia?"

"The babe is in the nursery with the wet nurse, my lord. Though we did no such like in my day. Regardless of what the nobility does, I maintain that a babe should suckle at its own mother's bosom. Anything aught is unnatural, if you ask me!" she insisted indignantly.

"Then it was well advised you were not asked. Now, pray direct me to my son."

❧

Edmund came from the nursery ashen-faced. He had made a farce of his life to guarantee his inheritance, and now the worthless cow had failed him! His first impulse had been to throttle the useless life out of her.

Edmund burned with injustice. What right had that damnable tyrant to manipulate his life by forcing him into this marriage in the first place? He was the firstborn. The title and estates were rightfully his!

"You think me unreasonable and my wrath unjustified, you insolent whelp?" the earl had retorted. "The marriage itself was ill-conceived, and now this negligence!"

"I have taken a wife, as you wished, and she has born a healthy child," Edmund protested. "Were not your own parents blessed with daughters, my lord, before the ultimate arrival of a son?"

"You lead me to believe you would breed an entire pack of brats, Edmund?"

"If it is required to produce a male heir, my lord, but I am assured that the next will be a son."

"It shall be required of you to get her again with child. Your time runs out, Edmund. Perhaps it is time I sent for Philip?"

Edmund left the earl's chamber, agonized and unbalanced by his conflagration of emotions, bitterly resentful of his father, filled with jealousy and loathing for his brother, contemptuous and scornful of his wife, and frustrated with unrequited desire for Charles Wallace.

Thirty-five

༄

AN ACT OF VENGEANCE

*T*he firstborn of Lord and Lady Uxeter, Anna Sophie Drake, was christened on a rainy and chill October day in the Hastings's family chapel, with few attending to celebrate the birth. The child's maternal grandfather, Sir Garfield Wallace, had come down from London for the joyous occasion, but notably absent was the Earl of Hastings.

Grimly going through the motions, Lord Uxeter distastefully held the screeching infant, impatiently handing it off the instant the sacraments were completed. Beatrix, determined to play the doting mother, at least whilst in company, received the babe with smiles and coos. As the godmother, Charlotte looked anxiously on, wondering what the poor child's future would hold.

Returning to the great house, the family dispersed, the women taking the babe to the nursery while Lord Uxeter and Sir Garfield retired to the library. Sir Garfield helped himself to a brandy and raised his glass cheerfully. "Congratulations, m'boy, on the first of the brood!" Sir Garfield waited expectantly. He cleared his throat and prompted again, "A toast to little Sophie, Lord Uxeter."

"The devil you say!" Edmund replied contemptuously. "The earl requires a *male* heir." He snatched the bottle and filled his glass.

"'Tis not the end of the world," his father-in-law consoled. "Beatrix was our firstborn, and is to this day the apple of my eye.

Charles came along soon enough, and I must say, I appreciated the boy all the more for his late arrival." He paused with a frown. "Speaking of Charles, I wonder what the blazes has held him up? Indeed, I had thought he travelled down here with you. He left a note to that effect. 'Tis strange indeed for him to miss the christening. Most unlike Charles."

"Perhaps he had intended to depart London with me, Sir Garfield, but I quit the city in such haste that we must have missed one another in passing. Pity. I should have much enjoyed his company." He took a long drink of his brandy.

"Even so, he surely should have arrived long since," Sir Garfield repeated. "I begin to fear he was beset by highwaymen."

"He is a young man, and young men are easily distracted. No doubt some harmless diversion has delayed him, but if it lessens your apprehension, I shall send an express to inquire whether he remains in London."

"Very kind of you, my lord. 'Twould greatly ease my mind," Sir Garfield confessed.

"Consider it done, sir. If you will excuse me, I shall attend to the matter at once." Edmund finished his drink in another swallow, relieved to have some excuse to part company from his insufferable father-in-law. He went to his rooms where he could brood his next move in peace.

Edmund had formed some powerful connections in the Upper House of Parliament, Lords Gower and Cobham among others. The House of Lords frequently presided over civil issues, including acts of divorcement; surely they could also overturn a will.

Surely, he might yet manipulate matters to his advantage. He'd be damned to let the despot rule him from the grave as he had in life. It was time he departed for London.

"What do you mean I am to remain at Hastings?" Beatrix wailed. "You can't keep me here! I have been months in this wretched place with not a soul for company aside from Mama. You said I should stay for my confinement. I have done as you wished. 'Twas no fault of mine it was a girl, but the child is legally yours, and you promised to honor and protect us. You cannot punish me by leaving us here!" She choked on her words.

"You will not leave until you have fulfilled your one duty in this marriage, that of producing an heir."

"Marriage? This is no marriage. What manner of husband have you been? I've scarce laid eyes on you in four months. Tell me the truth, Edmund," she demanded, "did you want me only because Philip did? Was it jealousy because you knew I was his?"

He erupted with a mocking laugh. "You vain, insipid cow! I never *wanted you* to begin with. You were nothing more than a means to an end, but since you have failed, here you shall remain."

"But you can't keep me prisoner. If you won't take me back to London with you, then I shall go to Wortley with Mama. Indeed, I shall. Then you will be sorry." She stilled her weeping as realization dawned. "If I go to Wortley, then what of your precious heir?"

With his barely discernible wince, Edmund betrayed himself. He had revealed the chink in his armor.

She spoke her thoughts aloud. "You need me, Edmund, don't you? You need me in order to become the earl. You need me, or you shall lose everything!" She laughed aloud at her epiphany. "I am not nearly as stupid as you think!"

Edmund's eyes narrowed in an icy and penetrating stare.

Beatrix advanced seductively toward her husband, boldly pressing her abundant breasts to him. She whispered tauntingly, "You need me, Edmund. You must have an heir to become the earl, but you have yet to come to my bed."

Edmund shuddered involuntarily, turning white about the mouth as she breathed these last words into his ear. He tensed when she moved against him, speaking in her breathless whisper, "How can you possibly get an heir and your earldom if you are in London and I am wasting away here?"

Edmund's only betrayal of emotion was a telltale muscle twitching in the left side of his jaw. Did she actually think to manipulate and control him?

"You ignorant, bovine slut!" His blow sent her sprawling onto the bed. He pounced on top of her, muffling her cries with his mouth.

Pinned helplessly, Beatrix utilized the only weapon at her disposal. Biting as hard as she could, she viciously tore at his flesh.

"Stupid bitch." He struck her again and wrestled her onto her stomach, pinning one arm beneath her body while twisting the other agonizingly behind her back. Drowning her efforts to scream, he shoved a thick feather pillow under her face.

It seemed he meant to suffocate her, until he tore at her dressing gown and exposed her from behind. He forced her legs apart with his bony knee. "So, you pine for my attentions, do you? I'll give you what you want." As he fought her exertions, his breath was hot and moist on her neck.

Beatrix bucked and twisted in hysterical expectation of his imminent and degrading invasion. But it never came. He cursed vilely and threw her to the floor.

Beatrix sized him up contemptuously, growing braver with the knowledge that he could not violate her, though he had tried. "I begin to think the getting of an heir might present quite a dilemma for *you*, my lord. Mayhap you should have Philip take care of the matter for you? But you had already thought of that, hadn't you? Philip shall produce the only heir in the end. You shall see, and Philip will inherit all." She laughed in his face, realizing too late that her final taunt had pushed him over the edge.

Edmund ignited. Seizing her white shoulders in a biting grip, he lifted and thrust her against the corner of the bed frame. Twisting her hair around his hand, he snapped her head back. As her skull cracked against the wooden frame, Beatrix gasped with a flash of white. His sinewy frame held her captive. Her spine bore into the post, and he growled in her ear, "You would conspire with Philip against me, you treacherous whore!"

His hand closed like a vise about her windpipe.

She twisted and writhed frantically in a vain attempt to free herself. Struggling for what may have been seconds but seemed eternity, her body, quickly exhausted from its futile exertions, went limp. Blackness closed in.

She had nearly given herself completely up to the darkness when the iron-like grasp gave way. She slumped, clutching at the post, gasping, choking, and sucking in air, precious air, while Edmund regarded her with a speculative gleam, perhaps realizing just how near to death he had actually taken her.

Wild-eyed, confounded, and speechless, Beatrix stared back at him, as with cool composure he buttoned the flap of his breeches, straightened his waistcoat, and smoothed back his hair. Pulling a handkerchief from his pocket, he dabbed at his torn, bloody lower lip and strode abruptly past Charlotte, who stood dumbly in the hall.

Having fulfilled her obligation to stay for the christening, Charlotte was anxious to return to her quiet life at Cheveley. After notifying Letty of their morning departure, Charlotte finished packing and headed to Beatrix's rooms for a parting word.

Approaching the door, she prepared to knock, but her hand was stayed by raised voices. She froze at her cousin's distinct tone of distress, but silence ensued. Charlotte turned to go, but Lord Uxeter

barged out of the room, brushing by her without a word, a bloody
handkerchief pressed to his lip.

Wide-eyed, Charlotte entered her cousin's rooms, finding Beatrix
lying on the floor, shaken and disheveled. Red bands surrounded
her throat, blood trickled from her nose, and a welt covered the
entire right side of her face.

"Good God, Beatrix! What has that beast done to you?" Charlotte
exclaimed in horror. "I heard you arguing. If only I had interrupted…"

"I r-refused to obey, to stay at H-hastings. I d-despise this
wr-wretched place, and he…" She inhaled deeply with a cough.
"He never w-wanted me, Charlotte." Her voice quavered.

"Shhh. Hush now. Don't try to talk anymore."

"He only w-wanted an heir, and I wanted to be a countess,"
Beatrix continued softly, as if to herself. "But I am nothing to him,
less than nothing, now I failed to give him a son. He loathes and
abhors me, but it has taken me a beating to see it. I have been so very
stupid!" She hiccoughed, and her tears began anew.

"You are not stupid! You were deceived, as any woman might
have been. I will get Aunt and Uncle at once! They must take you
away from here and back to Wortley."

"But he is my husband! What can they do?"

"No man, not even your husband, has a right to abuse you. You
must tell your father. He is the only one who might make it right.
You must tell him everything."

"You are right." Beatrix nodded. "I shall tell all I have suffered,
and they will take me back home, where I need never set eyes on
that vile creature again! I am going home, Charlotte." She sniffed
and gently blew her nose.

Charlotte helped her trembling cousin to her bed and set out in
purposeful strides to locate her aunt and uncle.

If only she were a man, she would have surely dealt Edmund
Drake his comeuppance.

For the second time in her life, first with Philip and now with his brother, Charlotte was emotionally charged enough to commit murder.

Thirty-six

A MATTER OF HONOR

$\mathcal{H}$aving spent another six fruitless months in Flanders, stymied at every effort, Field Marshal Wade was all too happy to call an end to the campaign, and with it, an end to overall command of what he had long referred to as the "Pragmatic misalliance."

His reputation tarnished by such an inglorious campaign, Field Marshal Wade promptly tendered his resignation, eager to pass the baton to some other poor sod willing to risk his career on such a futile command.

However thankful the commander in chief may have been at his homecoming, his aide-de-camp, Major Drake, would much rather have stayed abroad than return shamefaced after a third toothless season. Besides, an extended stay on the Continent would have provided him excuse to defer facing his personal troubles, which had in no way alleviated in his absence.

He had had many frustrated months to reflect on his discontent. His career was a disappointment. He was trapped in an unwanted marriage with Charlotte, in which he had seen to all of her needs while receiving precious nothing in return. Although he had promised a union in name only, he vowed that circumstances must change.

He had given her ample time and space to accept her lot. Now it was time she fulfilled her singular obligation in their union. He had bedded and satisfied—he smugly confessed—scores of women, and she would hardly find the experience unpleasant. If she would only come about, they might actually be able to make their inconvenient arrangement somewhat more tolerable.

His deliberations were interrupted by one of his adjutants.

"Major Drake, sir.' He saluted.

"What is it, Lieutenant Barber?"

"I've a message from the commander in chief. He wishes to see you at Headquarters at once."

"Convey to Field Marshal Wade that I will be there directly."

"But 'tis not the field marshal who send the summons, sir. 'Tis His Grace of Cumberland."

"Cumberland, you say?" Philip looked puzzled.

"Indeed, sir. It appears he is now appointed to replace Field Marshal Wade."

The major, annoyed and unsettled by his ignorance of this fact, replied again, "Then pray convey to *His Grace* that I shall come directly."

The lieutenant snapped his heels, saluted again, and departed hastily to carry the message.

How peculiar, Philip thought. Among the inner circle of aides-de-camp, there was precious little news ever withheld from him. As one of the first to learn of Field Marshal Wade's intent to resign his command, why should he not also have been one of the first to learn of his replacement?

Thoroughly perturbed, he checked his appearance and promptly departed for Headquarters.

❧

Upon arrival, Major Drake was conducted directly to an inner sanctum, "the holy of holies," where he was stunned to face a triad of generals seated at a long, gleaming table. Field Marshals Wade, Stair, and Cumberland, looking as if assembled for a counsel of war… or military tribunal… regarded him with reserve.

As Philip saluted the three commanders, his mind raced to recall any incident of misconduct. But he found himself at an utter loss.

"Pray have a seat, Major." General Wade spoke in an attempt to set his former adjutant at ease. He indicated a chair, and Philip acquiesced, regarding the triumvirate in complete befuddlement.

The duke, the new commander in chief, seated at the head of the table, remarked, "You've had a commendable career, thus far, for one so young, Major Drake."

Philip was *almost* amused at the compliment coming from the King's younger son, two year's Philip's junior at four-and-twenty.

"You enlisted even before the commencement of hostilities with France," Cumberland continued. "You were lauded at Dettingen and promoted immediately thereafter. Indeed, your rise in the ranks has been remarkably swift."

"I have endeavored to serve my King and country to the utmost of my ability, Your Grace."

"None would gainsay you regarding your record," commented Lord Stair. "With the exception of one foolish incident involving a captain under your command, your record is without blemish." Philip was reminded with a pointed look that Lord Stair had personally intervened on that particular occasion.

Cumberland spoke again. "Lord Stair and Field Marshal Wade have both spoken highly of your competence and your abilities, and I have personally borne witness to your valor. We have great need of such men. Should you choose to remain in His Majesty's service, I foresee a long and illustrious military career for you."

"Thank you, Your Grace. It is both my ambition and my desire."

"That being the case, I cannot emphasize strongly enough that the loyalty of such men must be absolute, and their conduct beyond reproach."

This struck Philip as distinctly ominous. "Indeed, Your Grace," he agreed, still without a clue as to where this seeming inquisition was heading. His expression must have revealed the questions in his mind.

"You are by this time wondering why you were called?"

"Just so, Your Grace. I truly cannot fathom."

"While having no reason to doubt *your* loyalty to the Crown," Wade interjected, "there are some who begin to doubt that of your brother. *His* allegiance is recently become suspect. Ironic indeed, considering he co-authored the very Act of Parliament that would serve to attaint him of high treason."

The Duke continued. "One would doubt he need be reminded that any correspondence or monetary assistance to the Pretender or his son is considered an act against the Crown. Moreover, if convicted, the penalty is death, dismemberment, and dishonor, with the forfeiture of all your family's holdings."

"But what has this to do with me?" Philip asked incredulously.

"If you've any regard for your family name, let alone your career, Major, it would behoove you to escort your brother to Headquarters. We desire only to question him… for now."

ے

"Here we are at last, home sweet home," the senior of the two officers remarked dryly to his companion and then dismounted.

"You know I have serious misgivings about this, Drake," the lieutenant replied. "I already regret having let you drag me here. I had every hope of avoiding my mother's hysterical weeping at her heartless son, and my father's outraged ranting at what he will perceive only as my outright rebellion. Had I not met you at Westminster, I should never have come." He reluctantly dismounted.

"Trust me, Charles, as one who has seen battle, you would never forgive yourself if you left without word. As the baby's godfather, at the least, you must pay respects to your sister and the child before you bid farewell to all of them. You owe your family that much."

"I know you are right," Charles confessed, "but I still can't like it."

"Where's the bloody groom?" Philip mumbled. "No matter, I know my way about to see to the horses. Don't wait on me, old chum." Philip indicated that Charles should proceed to the house while Phillip, thankful for this brief reprieve, led the horses to the stables.

In encountering Charles at Headquarters, he had learned of Beatrix's imminent delivery and had coerced Charles to travel with him to Hastings to bid farewell to his family. Though unaware of Philip's true errand, Lieutenant Wallace seemed the ideal candidate to accompany him. He might have need of a second officer's aid, if only as intimidation.

Having arrived, Philip now wondered at his errand. Had His Majesty any hard evidence against Edmund, he surely would have arrested him and taken him to the Tower. If Edmund was truly under suspicion, why would Cumberland, Wade, and Stair have revealed as much, let alone sent him on this mission, unless it was to test his own fidelity?

And if being put to the test, to whom did Philip ultimately owe his allegiance? To his family? Or to the Crown? At one time he should never have thought it a contest. He would have scoffed to think he would even hesitate to consider a family who had done nothing but disparage him his entire life. But that was before he found himself in such position. Forced to choose, which would it be?

With disquiet, uncertainty, and an ominous sentiment of foreboding, Philip squared his shoulders to face the inevitable.

Heaving a great sigh, Lieutenant Charles Wallace proudly straightened his crimson regimental uniform and squared his shoulders for his grand entrance. Met by Grayson, he was led to his mother in the first-floor salon.

Lady Felicia's eyes lit with delight and surprise at her son's final arrival... until remarking his uniform. She gasped in dismay. "Charles, what have you done?"

"Dearest Mama, I should think it obvious. I have enlisted in the First Regiment of Foot and am soon off to join Cumberland."

"But what are you thinking! You know your father shall never allow it. He has forbidden even talk of the army."

"For one-and-twenty years I have done all you have expected of me. But now, come fully to manhood, I must please myself, even at the risk of displeasing my father. I have joined the army and will be off for Ghent within the se'nnight. I am not to be dissuaded. I am come only to bid farewell to my family, Mama."

Lady Felicia burst into tears, and into this state, Sir Garfield entered. "What now, Charles!" he exclaimed. "Where the devil have you been, boy? And what are you about, dressed in that preposterous costume?"

"Preposterous, Father?" Charles pulled a face in protest. "'Tis the uniform of the First Foot Guards. I thought it quite dashing."

"How dare you defy me! This is not to be tolerated!"

"Father," Charles interrupted, "the deed is done and not to be undone. I have purchased a lieutenancy in the First Foot and am deployed in a few days time. Pray let us not quarrel about it."

"Quarrel? There is no quarrel. There is only the defiance of an insolent puppy!" Sir Garfield flushed in ire, while Lady Felicia looked on in teary-eyed dismay.

A flushed Charlotte, coming directly from Beatrix's bedchamber, interrupted the emotionally charged exchange. Finding her aunt, uncle, and Cousin Charles assembled, she halted abruptly.

"Uncle, Aunt, Charles. I need a private word. Urgently." Before any of them could reply, Charlotte had dismissed the servants and closed the salon doors behind her.

"What is the meaning of this intrusion?" her uncle demanded.

"'Tis Beatrix. I fear for her life," she said more calmly than she felt.

"Beatrix? Is there trouble with the baby?" Charles queried anxiously.

"No, Charles. Little Sophie is in no imminent danger; however, I predict future peril should she remain in this wicked place," Charlotte replied.

"You have me flummoxed, Charlotte," Charles responded. "Who is Sophie? And what is this peril?"

"Beatrix has already given birth to a daughter, Charles. She was christened Anna Sophie," Lady Felicia offered by way of explanation.

"Charles, Aunt, listen to me," Charlotte interrupted impatiently. "Beatrix is beaten nigh senseless! You must come at once."

Lady Felicia shrieked. "What? Beatrix beaten?"

"Lord Uxeter has nearly throttled her."

"Throttled her?" Lady Felicia repeated blankly. "Sir Garfield!" She turned to her husband.

"Just one moment, madam!" he imperiously commanded. "'Tis no doubt some lover's spat that will blow over soon enough. There is no room for our interference here."

"But she is your daughter! How can you just stand by?" Charlotte looked to her uncle incredulously.

"Hysterical girl!" he admonished his niece. "You should be cuffed yourself for causing such a commotion. Whatever may or may not have occurred between Lord Uxeter and his wife is none of our concern."

"I am not hysterical, nor do I exaggerate," Charlotte exclaimed. "You must remove her from this place at once!"

"Sir Garfield, we must go to her!" Lady Felicia made for the door.

"Beatrix is no longer our daughter. She is Lady Drake and the sole responsibility of her husband. We have no right to intervene in any matter between a husband and his wife. Go to her if it pleases you, but intercede we will not!"

"Your stance is unconscionable, Father," Charles remonstrated. "But if you have no care, as her brother, I shall certainly act! Charlotte," Charles commanded, "take me to her at once!"

EMERY LEE

They departed, nearly crashing into Philip outside the salon. Learning of Charlotte's presence at Hastings, he had resolved to take care of his personal business before attending to his other concerns.

As she made to pass, he restrained her with a firm grasp to her upper arm, pulling her to his side. Charles and his weeping mother swept past.

"Charlotte, dear heart, have you no word of greeting for your long-absent husband?" He smirked.

"Unhand me, you lummox!" She glared, trying unsuccessfully to pull her arm free.

"It quite lacks the warmth I had anticipated. Mayhap we should try again?" His attempt to brush her lips with a kiss was met with a stinging slap. With this answer, he roughly put her away, still not releasing his grip.

"Whoever said absence makes the heart grow fonder was sadly misinformed," he remarked sardonically.

"I have no time to mince words with you, Philip." She again attempted to pull away.

"Wait, Charlotte. What has you so agitated and your family in an uproar?"

"*Your brother*," she hissed, "has sought to amuse himself by brutalizing his wife, the same woman, I might add, who has just birthed *your* daughter. Now release me!"

Stunned, he replied emotionlessly, "I see," and reflexively let go.

Charlotte spun toward the west wing. Philip did not follow, but with single-minded determination, he set out in search of his quarry, the perpetrator of violence on a helpless woman. Although he had long suspected Edmund's deviant nature, he would have credited him with more sense than to expose his vice in such an overt way, under his father's roof, no less. The act reeked of desperation and cowardice. Philip recalled the terms of his father's will.

He stalked from room to room, sending servants scuttling, until he arrived at the earl's private apartments, where Edmund had gone to make his excuses while his valet packed for London.

Remarking the voices within, Philip passed Grayson and unheedingly threw open the doors. Striding fiercely through the private parlor into the bedchamber, he noticeably startled Edmund and his father, who lay pale and wan in his bed.

"What is this intrusion?" the earl croaked. "Where is Grayson to allow it? The man will be sacked!" Not immediately recognizing his younger son, he addressed the elder. "Edmund, throw this scoundrel out!"

"'Twould be my greatest pleasure, my lord," he replied, recognizing the intruder as Philip.

"My dear father," Philip interjected, "I might remark that the only scoundrel is your perfidious eldest son."

Edmund sneered. "Indeed? This is the outside of enough, Philip, *your* attempt to defame *me*. I might even call it laughable."

"Although you have long attributed such crimes to me, Edmund, in the end 'tis *you* who would discredit, dishonor, and vilify the family name."

"Such accusations are insupportable! I insist you explain yourself at once!" Lord Hastings's eyes blazed from his gaunt face.

"I had come here, my lord, on a mission from the Crown, but now I discover my brother's pusillanimous conduct toward his wife by far supersedes his treachery."

"Treachery?" The earl's eyes narrowed.

"I greatly fear the role of conquering hero has gone to Philip's head, my lord," Edmund jeered.

"Only my regard for my family honor forces me to disclose the mounting suspicion of treason from the house of Hastings, my lord. If proven, such would attaint the earldom and forever tarnish our name."

The Earl of Hastings looked to his eldest son. "Edmund, what is this about?" he demanded.

Edmund smirked with a dismissive gesture. "Nothing, my lord. Much ado about nothing. The crime of treason may be ascribed only to those who correspond or provide assistance *after* the first of May 1744. While 'tis true I have lent some manner of support to the Jacobites, this very Act of Parliament with which they would attempt to indict me, *by my very design*, provides my immunity. There is none who can produce any proof of my so-called treason *following* the passage of the Act of Parliament prohibiting aid to the Young Pretender," he replied with total self-possession.

"One must at the least applaud your preservation instincts, Edmund, without which, one cannot survive in Parliament. Mayhap you are ready to assume your place as Earl of Hastings, after all."

Philip was stunned that his father looked upon Edmund's confession with a thin smile of approbation. "You would condone treason, my lord?"

"I fail to see how any such crime can be imputed," Lord Hastings replied matter-of-factly.

"But what of honor? And what say you of a man who brutalizes the woman who is, by law, under his protection?"

The earl scoffed. "Being under his protection, Edmund's wife is no one else's concern."

"On the contrary, my lord, the welfare of any woman, under *his brand of protection*, is very much my concern."

Edmund interjected, "Pray let us forgo the melodrama, Philip. Beatrix had a misapprehension regarding her duty to obey me, and I dealt with her accordingly. She got no more than she deserved, the shameless whore. To my misfortune, however, I made the discovery only after the nuptials that she came to the marriage bed already increasing with child."

"Is this the version you would tell, Edmund? Having a decided preference for the truth, I find I am at odds with it. I submit, rather, that you wed her in full knowledge she was breeding, perceiving it the most expeditious manner to get an heir. You, however, had no contingency when she delivered you a girl, and now, realizing what a bad bargain you've made, she and the child are to suffer for it."

"Until I divorce the slut, she and the child are mine to do with as I will."

Fingering his sword hilt menacingly, Philip instinctively drew it halfway from its sheath.

"Are you bent on playing knight-errant, Philip? My lord's apartments are hardly an appropriate venue for a duel; moreover, I have yet to fathom your preoccupation with the notion. Pray take your sword, brother mine, and go back to playing soldier with Cumberland."

"You really do not comprehend it, do you? To uphold one's name, one's honor as a gentleman. But why should this surprise me? I should be doing the world a favor to rid it of such a perfidious, craven bastard."

"Perfidious, craven bastard?" Lord Uxeter repeated, savoring the bitter words. "Are there no further calumnies, no added denigrations you wish to cast against my character, Philip?"

Another voice spoke from behind. "I might add... misogynistic sodomite."

With these words, Charles Wallace stepped forward and discharged his pistol.

Thirty-seven

AN OLD FLAME REKINDLED

The report of pistol fire reverberated as a thunderclap through the corridors of stone. Chores forgotten and serving trays crashing to the floor, the servants raced breathlessly to the earl's quarters, but only Grayson, after a lifetime in the earl's employ, dared to actually enter his bedchamber.

Charles Wallace's aim had struck true. Shot in the chest, Edmund directed his pain-stricken gaze to his assassin before staggering to the earl and crumpling.

"Edmund, my son! They have murdered my son!" Lord Hastings roared. The earl rose from his bed, pushing Philip away, but without his cane, his weak side failed him. He fell upon his son's body, only to watch Edmund gurgle his last breath.

The vision proved too much for his weakened condition. With his hand clutched to his chest, the earl collapsed with an anguished cry beside Edmund's body. Voiceless and paralyzed, he now lay in his son's spreading puddle of blood.

Grayson miraculously appeared to help Philip carry the fallen earl back to his bed, while Charles stood dumbly over Edmund's body, the smoking pistol still in his hand. With full realization of what he had done, he dropped the pistol, and it fell, thudding to the floor like a lead weight.

Charles stumbled to a chair, where he commenced to shake so violently his teeth chattered. He hid his face in his hands, and his entire body convulsed, giving full vent to its state of shock.

Sir Garfield, the next to arrive, took in the blood, the dead body, and his son's quaking form. He exploded. "What the devil?"

Grayson interjected before Philip could reply. "A tragic accident," the old retainer replied. "I had come to bring his lordship's sleeping tonic, only to overhear shouting. My Lord Hastings was acutely distressed and hardly in his right mind. He must have mistaken Lord Uxeter for an intruder. By the time I entered the chamber, he had been shot!"

He boldly continued his outrageous prevarication. "Master Philip and Lieutenant Wallace appeared almost instantly, but 'twas already too late. Lord Uxeter is dead, and the earl has suffered another apoplectic seizure."

Absolutely confounded, Philip gawked at Grayson.

The housekeeper, Mrs. Baker, chimed in, taking up the blatantly false alibi. "I heard it meself, I did, as I was passing down the hall. Such a profound tragedy!" She fled his lordship's chambers with a muffled sob.

Philip was incredulous at the brazenness of the lies spoken by these lifelong servants. Although he had not pulled the trigger, he had the most to gain from his brother's demise, but with the earl at death's door, Grayson had not hesitated to fabricate a web of deception for Philip's protection.

Though he was not the killer, in truth it was only because Charles had beaten him to it. Philip's conscience tugged faintly, but with no one in the household willing to contradict the tale and the earl unable to do so, he stifled his scruples.

Setting about the task of supervising the aftermath, he mused that should he become the new Earl of Hastings, his first priority would be to raise the wages of his staff.

Two days following the joint funerals of the Earl of Hastings and his firstborn son, Major Drake advised Charles Wallace to play "least in sight." Wisely heeding the advice, Charles promptly departed for Ghent to join his regiment. Sir Garfield and Lady Felicia followed, taking the newly widowed Beatrix and baby Sophie back to Yorkshire.

Charlotte, desiring only peace and tranquility, also could not depart soon enough for her liking. She was shocked by the chain of events following on the heels of Philip's arrival. Was it an omen of what he would bring to her life? She prayed it was not. She had spent the past six months trying to regain her equilibrium and desired none of his presence or influence in her life. Only propriety had made her stay for the funeral and brief inquest.

Now packed, she was anxious to return to Cheveley. She had just sent Letty with word of readiness to the coachman, when she heard a light rap on her chamber door.

"Yes? You may enter," she replied absently. She was startled to see Philip.

"Good morning, Charlotte," he offered in brusque greeting.

"Philip," she said tersely. As she closed and latched her trunk, her eyes flickered briefly over him. "I had thought you the footman, come to collect my things."

"I regret to disappoint you," he said with a smirk. "No doubt it slipped your mind to inform me you were taking your leave today?"

"The need to inform you had not occurred to me."

"Indeed? So my *own wife* would depart without so much as a by-your-leave?"

"Your wife?" Charlotte scoffed. "Since we no longer have an audience for whom to perform, may we not now desist in this preposterous charade?"

Philip grasped her gently by the shoulders. "Charlotte," he began earnestly, "neither you nor I would have chosen this course, had we a choice. You were estranged from your family, with no visible means of support, and I had desperate need to be independent from mine. Nonetheless, I swore to support and protect you. I am yet willing to stand by those vows if you will now show only the slightest inclination to conduct yourself as my wife."

"That was not our agreement." Her voice was pure ice.

"Circumstances have changed. The inquest has absolved me of any wrongdoing, and with this pronouncement, I am to be named Earl of Hastings. With this change of fortune, I have hope of restoring my family estate to a more respectable condition."

"How precisely should this concern me?"

Was she intentionally making this difficult? His patience was strained as he continued. "As my wife, you stand to become the new Countess of Hastings. My requirements in exchange would be minimal, only that you behave with a modicum of decorum appropriate to the station, or at the least with a reasonable amount of discretion, and that you produce the heir necessary to continue my family line."

"A broodmare, Philip? Is that what you propose, that I become your broodmare?" Her mocking reply broke any further pretense of civility between them.

His grip now became like iron, bruising her shoulders, and he fought the urge to shake sense into her.

"You might be more reasonable! I have done all in my power to make your situation tolerable. In the grand scheme of things, I ask a very small sacrifice in return for a title—security and a measure of comfort. I am neither aged, ill-formed, nor unskilled in pleasing a woman. I even dare boast there are many who would welcome my attentions."

"Then I suggest you look amongst *that* herd for your broodmare. Your attentions are not welcome to me. I will allow only a man I love and respect into my bed. You will *never* be that man."

"Do you fully understand what you are saying? Are you aware that your refusal gives me just grounds for annulment?"

"Yes. I do understand. But why should you not set me free? With her husband's recent death, surely Beatrix would be willing to have you." She paused reflectively. "But then would you be uncle or father to little Sophie? I daresay 'twould be much too confusing to the poor child."

The telltale signs of narrowing eyes and slight jaw twitch told her the barb had struck a raw place. Philip struggled to maintain his composure and self-control. His composure prevailed.

"Have no doubt I shall shoulder my responsibilities where Beatrix and Sophie are concerned, but my family faces enough nefarious scandal at present, without my wedding or bedding my brother's widow. You might take more care to reflect upon your own bleak prospects, Charlotte, should you force my hand. I had wished for us to come to some sort of understanding, a truce perchance, but I see you are beyond reason."

"Then do as you see fit, Philip. I will be at Cheveley when you come to your decision. Now, where is that accursed footman?"

༄

The inquiry into Edmund's death had been only cursory. After statements were taken from the "witnesses," the case was simply declared an accidental death, and the earl's demise an unfortunate conclusion due to the shock. No one had even questioned how the earl had come by the murder weapon.

Following the inquiry, Philip had met with the solicitors, only to learn he would accede to the earldom without a bloody farthing to support it! As Lord Hastings had threatened, his last will and testament mandated the entirety of his fortune remain in trust until one of his sons should produce an heir.

Philip had never held any expectation of inheritance, but now it was his, he would have need of every shilling in the trust fund if the estate were ever to be profitable again. His income from the Horse Guard would barely support the bloody inheritance taxes, let alone sustain him. If only Charlotte hadn't proven so damnably bull-headed!

Torn between his past and his future, Philip lingered at Hastings some days in a vain attempt to work out in his mind the hand fate had dealt him. He couldn't even mourn the loss of his father and brother. Their deaths simply represented the cessation of relationships he had done his best to avoid.

For the past ten years, he had fervently wished for freedom from the yoke of his disapproving father. He had spent most of his life in resentment and petty rebellion against his unreasonable expectations, never aspiring to earning anything more than disapprobation, never dreaming he might one day become the earl. His father was dead, yet the yoke remained. Why did he not now feel the weight lifted from his shoulders?

As the new earl, he would be expected to sell his commission and take up his father's seat in Parliament. His father's seat. His brother's desire. Not his.

Philip had chosen the Horse Guard to make a life and a name for himself based solely upon his own merits. Was he truly ready to give it all up? In his mind, none of it seemed real. He was thinking too much. It was this damnable place. He packed for London.

It was either very late at night or very early in the morning when Philip found himself aimlessly wandering the streets between Westminster and the Strand. His perambulations were perhaps not as aimless as he supposed when he found his feet had carried him to Number Ten Bedford Street. Impulsively, he stole around to the servants' entrance and pounded on the door, awakening Sarah from her bed.

Fearful at the pounding, the maid ran to her ladyship's room, where Lady Susannah, rarely discomposed, snatched up her dressing gown and retrieved a small dagger from her bedside nightstand. She accompanied her maid to the side door off the kitchen, but her legendary composure slipped when she recognized the man at her door.

"Philip! What are you about at this hour? Are you inebriated?"

"Foxed quite to the gills, actually, but you needn't fret. I have come by the servants' entrance. None should see me."

"Mayhap not *see you*, Philip, but few have not heard you, with your incessant hammering!"

"I needed you, Sukey. I will desist the so-called hammering if you will only let me in." His tone was glib, but his eyes implored.

Lady Susannah sighed in exasperation. "Very well. You once again prove me weak and foolish on your account. Pray accompany me to the salon. Sarah," she said to her maid, "you may go back to your bed."

"My lady, are you certain?" The maid looked skeptically from the drunken man to her mistress's dishabille.

"Do not concern yourself for my sake, Sarah. He has shown little interest in compromising my virtue." She was at once rueful at the truth of her statement and wistful at the remembrance of the time they had been lovers. But that was six years past.

Sarah shrugged and reluctantly trudged back to her bed.

Entering the salon, Lady Susannah lit several candles. In the increasing light, Philip could now appreciate the full state of her undress. Her thin silk wrapper clung softly to the curves of her still youthful body. Her normally coiffed hair lay in silky chestnut ripples, falling over her shoulders and down her back. Devoid of any artificial enhancement, she appeared, in Philip's estimation, ten years younger, and he thought more dangerously, never more desirable.

He dismissed these thoughts with impatient irritation and silently, broodingly, paced her salon.

Seated delicately on the sofa, Lady Susannah patiently watched his progression, intuitively sensing his struggle with whatever inner demons had led him to her door.

"Well, Philip?" she prompted softly, gently, but with no gesture of invitation.

He turned now to face her. "It would appear that I am now to become the Earl of Hastings," he stated emptily. "The earl and Edmund are both dead, and by default, the title is mine. I should be elated, jubilant even. Yet"—he paused—"I am curiously hollow."

He hesitated, as if collecting his thoughts. "Why have I this void, this emptiness here, Sukey?" He thumped his chest with his fist.

It was not a rhetorical question. He had come seeking her counsel and succor to a pain he couldn't yet acknowledge. Her own heart lurched in sympathy with this angst he had been trying to bury for the past decade. She waited for him to continue, to express what he had been ever loath to put into words.

"I feel as if I cannot find any peace if I don't find the answers I seek. I tried in vain to dismiss the very questions, but without resolution, I cannot seem to carry on with my life."

"What are they, your questions?" she softly prompted.

His back to her, he began pacing anew. "The two questions I have asked myself? The first: why do I suddenly discover this void, when I have achieved an earldom, and presumably with it, the world at my feet?"

"Philip, I speak as both friend and confidante when I say you have yet to truly know yourself. You are empty because you have never attained your heart's desire. Having failed to win your family's love and acceptance, you sought to be free of them. Though that was your conscious decision, your unconscious desire has remained unchanged. You needed the love, acceptance, and affection that should have been your due. Though now free of their bonds, you know that you will never have what you most desired. Any possibility has died with them."

He stopped in front of the window, staring silently into the blackness, digesting her words.

"And your second question?" she asked.

"The second still haunts me after six years." His voice was barely above a whisper.

She closed her eyes, and her heart ceased its drumming that she might better hear every word.

"Why did you refuse me, Sukey?"

She had no breath to respond, glad he could not see her face. It would have given away every secret of her heart. "As to the second question, my love"—the endearment slipped thoughtlessly from her lips now she was committed to bare her soul at last—"I shan't be coy, but my answer, after deeply pondering this question, is exceedingly complex. But perhaps you are now ready to hear it? Perhaps able to understand?"

Philip waited, willing her to continue.

Drawing courage, she spoke again. "I am *not* sorry that I didn't accept you six years ago, but I deeply regret that I *couldn't* accept you."

"What do you mean *couldn't* accept me?" He spun to face her, lashing out at her for his own weakness. "You were widowed and independent. You had means and no one to answer to. You professed love yet dismissed me out of hand. I have tormented over this far too long and now demand that you explain yourself. I *will* be cut loose from this web in which you have once again ensnared me!"

"Ensnared you?" she answered incredulously. "I believed that you would have long since forgotten my very name."

"Never, Sukey. I had believed you completely eradicated from my mind, but I am drawn back again, completely against my will. Like the proverbial moth to the flame, here I stand."

"Against your will, like the moth to the flame? You don't trouble yourself with false flattery nor even any pretension of sensibility for my feelings in dredging up the past." She laughed bitterly.

"No, I have no particular sensitivity for your feelings… if you indeed have any."

"You really want to know why I refused you, Philip?" Susannah rose and came slowly but determinedly toward him. "I said I had regrets that I *could* not accept you. What I mean is, six years ago, I was a woman of nine-and-twenty in love with a rebellious youth. You were scarce past boyhood when you impetuously offered your name, but what was that name worth, my love?

"You were living by your wits and estranged from your family. On top of that, I was your first real lover and knew, even then, I would not be your last. I saw such promise in you, Philip," she said tenderly, "but you had yet to grow into manhood.

"I would have done neither of us a favor by accepting your proposal. Can you not understand me now? I drove you away by feigned indifference, planning to forget you and find my happiness with another, but my happiness has been elusive. I have never remarried because, though I tried valiantly, I have never loved another. The greater jest is that now you are become exactly the man I once envisaged, you are callous and indifferent to me."

"You believe me callous and indifferent?"

"You have rebuffed me at every turn, keeping me at arm's length from the very start. You even brought a young woman to my home, whom I have since come to cherish almost as a daughter, but who is, nonetheless, legally your wife. You do not consider these actions cruel and callous?"

"You have hardly languished for want of me," he answered laconically.

She prickled at the barb. "I never confessed to pining, nor have I been lonely. I have no respect for martyrs, Philip. I have carried on."

She looked away, adding almost inaudibly, "Though I have never loved but you."

"What did you say?"

"You still do not believe me?"

He didn't know if he believed or not, but did it matter anymore? Her words had appeased some of his hurt and anger, but her look of entreaty reached far deeper inside, touching the raw place, answering his need. The force of his emotions overpowered any remaining hesitation. He drew her to him with near-violent intensity, selfishly demanding.

Understanding his need, Susannah gave without reservation.

Philip stirred first, his slumbering lover cradled in his arms, the first rays of daylight filtering through the windows. He shifted carefully, loath to awaken her. What had happened between them was inevitable; he had recognized it the moment he walked back through her door. He had tried to maintain an aloof and detached distance, but his feelings for her ran far deeper than he understood. He was somehow connected with her at a profound level. She *was* his longed-for peace. He wanted her, not just sexually, but in every way. She belonged to him.

He gazed at her face as she stirred in her sleep, a slight frown emphasizing the faint line between her brows. He grazed this place with his lips, an unconscious gesture to erase any sign of worry from his lover's mind. It was a just a light brush, but she opened her eyes into his longing gaze.

"Marry me, Sukey," he murmured softly against her skin as his lips moved to her temple.

"But you are already married," she whispered.

"I can end it, my dearest love." He left a trail of warm, moist kisses along her jaw and down her neck, and his hand moved to cup and caress her breast. She moaned before breathing a reluctant sigh of protest "Please, Philip. I can't think when you do that." Although she could not undo the events of the prior evening, Sukey felt the first stirrings of conscience. Last night she had had no regrets, but as morning dawned, she was painfully and dismally aware that she could have no future with this man.

Her mind reeled as he continued to tease her. "Methinks the lady doth protest too much." He flashed his roguish grin, and she was lost to all reason.

Hours later Susannah reawoke to find Philip contemplating the ceiling. She stretched cat-like and then rolled on top of him, crossing her arms and resting her chin thoughtfully on her hands while she patiently watched him cogitate.

"Do you have it worked out yet, Philip?" she queried, watching his expression.

"To which dilemma do you refer? I find I struggle with several." He splayed one hand on the small of her back, and the other stroked her silky hair. "I want you," he murmured with furrowed brow.

"Yet again? Lesser mortals would have expired by this time." She chuckled, and he pinched her hard on the left buttock. "What was that about?" she cried.

"Your attention was straying, and you were causing mine to follow. We need to *talk* now. We've matters to resolve."

"Such as?"

"I have again asked you to wed me, and you once more failed to answer in the affirmative."

She opened her mouth to speak, but he laid a finger to her lips, arresting her reply.

"Let me finish please. I could press for an annulment. There are unquestionably grounds for one. I could arrange a modest settlement for Charlotte. Although the estate is rather a shambles,

I could provide her enough to ensure reasonable comfort some-where in the country. She could live quietly without fear of scandal touching her.

"If you agree to have me, Sukey, I will sell my commission and make you my lady, my Countess of Hastings in word and deed." He finished by slowly, sensuously tracing her lips with the same finger that had stayed them. He tipped her chin, firmly affixing her gaze in anticipation of her answer.

"Philip,"—she sighed deeply— "please know that I love you beyond comprehension, but what you ask is unconscionable." Had it been any other woman, she would have vanquished her qualms without hesitation, but how could she do such a thing to Charlotte?

"I would with all my soul that Charlotte had in truth been your ward rather than your wife." She regarded him accusingly. "Though I allow you have no tender feelings for one another, you cannot just discard your responsibility for her. Ultimately, it was the choice you made."

He exploded. "Choice? I had no choice! The old sod had me backed into a corner. It was no less than extortion!"

"Philip," she replied calmly, "it was no less a choice. You took the noble path by agreeing to protect a young woman who had no other protection, and for that I love you." She kissed him deeply before he could form another protest. "But there is another matter you have yet to consider." She directed her gaze on the wall beyond his left shoulder. "As a nobleman, you shall require an heir."

"Hell and damnation, Sukey!" he cursed. "Has it always to come back to the infernal heir? My brother, who would gladly have taken his place as Earl of Hastings, a position I never truly coveted, by the by, is in an early grave because of our father's obsession with an heir. What should it matter now? What has it to do with us?"

"You may not care now, but one day that will change. You come from a noble family, and it is your onus."

"Then why should you and I not make a child together? I am willing to make such a supreme sacrifice." He flashed his irresistible grin, but his words ripped her soul to shreds.

"Because I am barren!" she cried. "I was married to Nigel for ten years and never once conceived."

"He was a doddering old man," he protested.

"But you were not. We were lovers and took no precaution. In your inexperience, you may not have known any better, but I did. And at now five-and-thirty, I believe it impossible for me. You need Charlotte because you need an heir." She choked on these final words.

"I don't want her, nor does she want me!" he retorted.

"Give her time. Her emotions are raw, like a cut slow to heal. Treat her with tenderness and patience, and she will come around."

"So this is your answer? You would deny us both for the sake of Charlotte? I thought you had no patience with martyrs, yet you would make martyrs of us both!"

As he threw her words back in her face, she winced.

"I have neither the soul nor the temperament for martyrdom, Sukey."

Philip furiously hauled himself from the tangled bed, renting the sheets in the process. He snatched at his clothes scattered on the floor and began methodically dressing.

"Where are you going?" Her voice quavered.

"As it seems we've nothing further to discuss, I shall go and hire a competent steward for Hastings, then I will go back to my regiment. I find I've no desire to play lord of the manor." He stomped his second heel into his boot and departed half dressed, slamming the door behind him.

Sukey lay dazed in her bed, her wits as tangled as her sheets. She was an intelligent woman, one who knew herself and directed her own path. She had been content with her life *before* his return. But with his departure, *damn him to hell*, from out of nowhere, emptiness flooded her being. In just one night he had made her life a complete and utter muddle!

She longed to be with him and ached with a desire she had never dared confess, even to herself, the desire for motherhood. Sukey yearned with all her heart to bear Philip's children but knew she would never achieve this desire. Charlotte was his wife and had nearly two decades ahead of her to fill his nursery. Could she have said it any other way?

But if she could not be Philip's wife, could she be content as his mistress? she asked herself, not knowing the answer. She had become Charlotte's friend, mentor, and confidante.

How could she possibly countenance such a double life?

Her heart, however, cried louder than her conscience.

Thirty-eight

COUNTESS OF THE TURF

When Charlotte returned to Cheveley, she discovered her request had been unexpectedly answered.

"Jemmy!" she exclaimed. "What are you doing here?"

"Jeffries was asking about in Doncaster, seein' as ye has a need for a stud groom, miss… er missus," he amended. "And being that ye be just starting out, and I don't ask much fer wages…" He blushed.

"So you have volunteered your services?" she finished.

"Somethin' like that. Jeffries hisself weren't inclined to leave Sir Garfield, being he's been wi' the Bart so long. But he says I might could do the job fer ye. I apprenticed last year at Routh's stud up North, and though Jeffries might think me still wet behind the ears, I figures I be as good as any other," he added defensively.

"Far be it for me to scorn your help. I know next to nothing of breeding or foaling. It is hardly deemed an occupation for women," Charlotte remarked ruefully. "I am glad to have you, Jemmy. Although the cottage is small, there is a room off of the kitchen…"

"I be used to living above the stables, missus."

Charlotte blushed now. "As you see, Jemmy, the house is modest. The stables here are barely large enough for two horses. I have leased property and built run-in sheds for the mares, so you will just have to suffer our company—Letty's and mine—that is, at least until foaling time, where you might have to make due in the shed."

"If that be the case, your mare won't drop her foal."

"What on earth do you mean? She's due any day by the look of her."

"Mares be real modest creatures and like to give birth privily. Many a mare that's been ready to pop held off until there was no one around to see it."

"But then how should we know when her time is come?"

"She be already showing the signs. I check on her this very morning."

"Is she?" Charlotte exclaimed. "I must go to her at once!"

With Jemmy in tow, Charlotte walked the mile and a half to Amoret's pasture, where the mare, looking miserable, lumbered heavily toward her mistress. Her nicker of greeting lacked the usual enthusiasm.

Charlotte quickly pulled her skirts aside to climb over the fence. She caressed Amoret's nose. "You poor, poor girl," Charlotte murmured. With soulful eyes, Amoret bumped her, as if to say, "You have no idea of my suffering."

"But dearest, Jemmy says it shall be over soon," Charlotte encouraged as the groom approached the mare's flank.

"Aye, her time be coming soon," he said. As he reached a hand under her belly to her most private place, Amoret kicked out and squealed indignantly.

"No need to be feisty, old girl. Ye've done this many a time," Jemmy said.

"Tell me, Jemmy! What do you see?"

"Yesterday her sack was full, and now she be dripping the premilk."

"Premilk?" Charlotte asked.

"It's watery like and comes in right afore the birth. Ye need to be feedin' her turnips now."

"Turnips?" Charlotte exclaimed.

"There be nothin' better than turnips to make good milk in a mare. Put turnips in her feed, and ye'll be guaranteed good milk and a strong foal." Jemmy retrieved the halter and lead hanging on the fencepost, and slipped it over the mare's head. "Ye best hold her for me now. She already be a bit ill-tempered and won't like me messin' back there."

Charlotte took the lead, and Jemmy approached the mare again. Standing close to her hip and out of kicking range, he lifted her tail. "The passage looks nigh ready, missus. It gets longer and thicker as the time comes. I say she be ready to drop her foal any minute."

Amoret turned her head to look at her abdomen, as if in confirmation.

"What can I do to help? Should we get blankets? Boil water?" Charlotte's voice was shrill and near panic.

Jemmy laughed. "There be no need to fuss. This old broodmare knows what's what. All she need is clean, dry bedding or this nice green pasture. As the time gets closer, she'll pace much, piss much, and mor'n' likely roll on the ground a time or two. There be no worry unless she don't get up. Some mares even drop the foal whilst standing."

"They just drop them to the ground?"

"I'd say they more like slide out. 'Tis not so bad as ye might think."

"Then what should I do?" Charlotte said helplessly.

"Best thing is to leave her be. If naught goes awry, ye're like to have a foal by morning."

"But what if she becomes distressed?"

"I'll be checking on her. If she don't foal within an hour or so, then I needs to help pull the young one out. But 'tis a rare case to intervene."

Amoret turned her head to her belly again and regarded the bipeds with a speaking glare.

"I think she's telling us to leave, Jemmy," Charlotte declared.

"I think ye be right 'bout that. If ye be so inclined to come back in an hour or so, missus, ye might have a pleasant surprise.

Charlotte named the gangly chestnut colt Shakespeare.

Thirty-nine

A COLONIAL CROWN

*T*he late spring day opened warm and sultry, encouraging droves of people to come from all directions for the races of the county fair, the most popular of the Virginia horse races. By noon the throng had strung all along the one-mile course north of York Street in Williamsburg.

Daniel Roberts stood by his aged gray stallion and observed the amassing crowd. Three years ago, he had arrived a near-penniless victim of circumstance, but his sentence had proven a blessing in disguise.

He had found his place in a world that gauged men by their own merits, and he had measured up. Robert Devington, known in Virginia as Daniel Roberts, was outwardly flourishing, but inwardly, no amount of success could counterbalance what he had lost. His drive to succeed was commanded by his burning desire for vengeance, a yearning yet unfulfilled.

Much of his success had sprung from his fortuitous meeting with the young gentleman in the Bristol tavern. The eldest son of the Lee family, wealthy and politically connected planters, had introduced him to those gentlemen of Virginia who shared a passion for horseflesh. In these circles, Daniel Roberts's intimate knowledge of running bloods had stood him in good measure.

The most avid of these, John Tayloe, had offered Roberts a position in his new racing stud. The improvement in the quality, speed, and distance of Tayloe's runners was soon evidence that his confidence in the young Englishman had been well placed. Roberts's talents quickly put him at the head of Tayloe's breeding and training programs, a position that allowed him to bring his own stallion, Mars, into prime racing condition.

In England, with almost no training, Mars had proven himself as a runner. He not only possessed the strength of mind and body to persevere the grueling four-mile distances, he had also demonstrated the incredible breaking speed of a sprinter. The popularity of short-distance racing in the colonies offered a wealth of opportunity to capitalize on this talent.

Roberts began to run his stallion in the "short" races. Entering quarter-mile sprints run on barely better than cow paths, they were abruptly initiated to the rules of Colonial racing; there were none!

The quarter-miler was fast and furious with no holds barred as long as a rider was not actually *caught* unhorsing his opponent. Under these conditions, Robert's cavalry training served him well. Though he was careful to keep his opponent to his left side, where he was less susceptible to foul play, failing this tactic, he was even known to defend his seat by running with his bridle reins between his teeth!

Prevailing against all takers in any distance under two miles, Roberts had garnered nearly two thousand pounds in cumulative winnings. Their names in short racing grew to near legendary proportions, but Roberts and Mars had yet to make their mark where it most counted, in the distance races.

Now at twelve years old, any other horse would have been past his prime and retired to the breeding shed, but Roberts was determined to pit his unlikely stallion one last time. They would run against the very best of Virginia's racing stock in the first three-mile race at Williamsburg. The time was finally ripe to pursue his ambition.

His friend Ludwell hailed him from within the crowd, "Roberts!" and approached. "Just placed a bit of coin on your horse; pray don't let me down, old friend. I shall need the money for my trip back to London."

"You have decided to pursue law, then?"

"I am obligated to follow my father's wishes, though I can't say I should mind the diversions of London now I am older and free to enjoy the pleasures without the particular impediment of Mr. Hanbury's watchful eye." They both chuckled, remembering the Quaker who had done his best to keep his youthful charge out of trouble. "Speaking of obligations and diversions, Roberts, you have yet to respond to mother's invitation."

Since his arrival in Virginia, the Lee family had helped him to navigate his way in his new country. He especially had them to thank for his employment with John Tayloe, but of late, their interest on his behalf had grown a bit too personal.

Mrs. Hannah Lee, the family matriarch, had taken it into her head to find him a wife, and her chosen venue was to be the Lee's annual English-style garden party. Although running contrary to all his inclinations, Roberts feared he was indeed obligated to accept her invitation.

He changed the subject. "'Tis quite a turnout, is it not? I daresay the crowd begins to rival those of my Doncaster days."

"'Tis quite remarkable, indeed. Since my boyhood, I have seen our racing passions burgeon from jovial enthusiasm to fervent obsession. Indeed, I begin to fear the friendly matches of the past, when one pit his best saddle horse against his neighbor's for a bale of tobacco, are nigh gone by. Moreover, the 'English' races are become increasingly popular hereabouts, and one can hardly find a taker for anything less than fifty gold pistoles."

"Do you believe the distance races will replace the quarter mile altogether?"

"While the quarter-milers remain popular to the south and in the Carolinas, I daresay 'tis due only to the shortage of cleared land for proper racetracks, but with these now established in Fredericksburg, Leedstown, Yorktown, and Alexandria, I believe 'tis only a matter of time.

"As evidence, one need look only at the steady stream of imported English blood to Virginia and Maryland in recent years. 'Tis become a constant game of one-upmanship between us, but Virginians do not stomach defeat graciously." Ludwell laughed. "Any losses to Taskers or Byrd of Maryland serve only as impetus to further improve our Virginia stock."

"I am thankful the sentiment is pervasive," Roberts rejoined. "It has provided me a comfortable living."

"Knowing we colonists as both a presuming and fiercely competitive breed, Roberts, 'tis not unimaginable we might one day rival Old England on the turf."

"No, indeed," Roberts murmured, voicing aloud his private ambition for the first time. "Not unimaginable at all."

Once she had secured Daniel Roberts's attendance to her party, Mrs. Hannah Lee made it her mission to invite a number of suitable women, having in mind to end the young Englishman's bachelor days. Mary Griffiths, a quiet young widow with five hundred fertile acres and two rambunctious young boys, was Hannah's primary candidate to become the young gentleman's wife.

It was mainly for her boys' sake that Mary had agreed to look for another husband. Prosaic rather than romantic, she harbored no illusions that she was a beauty and was well aware that the half-dozen smooth-talking fortune-seekers who had paid her court in the past twelvemonth had pretensions only to her property.

Obstinate in her convictions, Mary had not hesitated to refuse them all. She would settle only for a man who would oversee the plantation in the knowledge that it would one day go to her sons; a man who would be a good father, and if not a passionate lover, at least a fond companion. She had begun to despair of ever finding the man she sought, until Hannah Lee had delivered the hapless gentleman firmly anchored to her arm.

Though Mary had put forth her best and brightest smile, Daniel Roberts, unlike those preceding him, had shown no inclination to flirt or flatter. He spoke little and demonstrated no more than polite interest in their conversation, until Mrs. Lee's retelling of the Indian massacre that had left Mary a widow. His sympathy had been genuine, but after a respectable interlude, he had made his escape back to the company of the gentlemen.

"What do you know of this Daniel Roberts?" Mary asked Mrs. Lee with unconcealed curiosity.

"I have gleaned little of his history beyond his meeting Philip Ludwell upon my son's return to Virginia after Eton. You know how retiring these Englishmen are," the matron said.

"I have since learned that he was an English cavalry officer, discharged after an unfortunate injury to his right arm. 'Twas undoubtedly in battle, though he understandably refuses to talk of it," Mrs. Lee added with a note of sympathy.

"Is he quite incapacitated?" Mary asked.

"Indeed not, my dear! One thinks it should have crippled him, but Roberts has proven very resilient. Despite his disability, he has made quite a prosperous living as well as a name for himself among the first families of Virginia. He has a remarkable ability with racing horses, you know. Truly a fine young man, dear Mary." She ended with an encouraging wink and then excused herself to attend her hostess duties.

From that moment on, the previously unassuming Mary Griffith set her cap most resolutely for Daniel Roberts. Allied with the formidable Hannah Lee and her substantial influence, Mary soon found an army of accomplices at her back. Once her campaign commenced, they laid an indefensible siege. The betrothal was announced the autumn of 1748, with plans of a spring wedding. With resignation rather than delight, Daniel Roberts prepared to enter the next phase of his life.

Though it was no love match, Roberts had acquiesced, vowing to be a kind and compassionate husband to Mary and a benevolent stepfather to her sons. Fate, however, intervened in the form of smallpox. Mary Griffiths was taken early that winter, leaving her orphaned sons with no guardian.

Having come from a world where greed and unchecked ambition ruled, Roberts stepped in to protect the young boys and their estate. His public betrothal to Mary had placed him in a strong position to petition the court for guardianship. Suddenly Roberts found himself with a ready-made family and steward of five hundred fertile acres, and under his careful management, the small plantation burgeoned to more than triple its original size.

Daniel Roberts, now having garnered both name and modest fortune, was finally in a position to pursue his lifelong dream. As a Virginia landholder, he had made his mark, yet true happiness remained elusive. Only thoughts of his own racing stud inspired any true passion in him. His time had come.

Breaking amicably with John Tayloe, who desired breeding rights to Mars, Roberts negotiated options on the first of the get from Tayloe's half-dozen prized broodmares. He then scoured the countryside for broodmares of his own choosing.

Although none in Virginia's racing set questioned Roberts's knowledge of horseflesh, he was reckoned to hold some curious notions regarding his breeding shed. Contrary to the designs of his neighbors, who looked solely upon importation to improve their runners, Roberts sought foundation stock amongst the native Chickasaw horses.

Originating from Colonial Spanish horses, this hardy and muscular little breed was highly prized by natives and colonists alike for its practical utility, but these horses were also amazingly swift in short-distance racing. In Roberts's earlier years of short racing, they had proven his strongest competition.

With the growing English trend to run younger horses at shorter distances, Roberts's desire was to produce the ideal middle-distance runner, one with the sprinting ability of the best Chickasaw and the staying power of the English racers. Of all the mares bred to Mars, it was out of his Chickasaw stock that Roberts achieved his greatest success, a blue roan colt with the best qualities of both his sire and dam: speed, strength, stamina, and a powerful will to run. Roberts christened him "Retribution."

❧

WILLIAMSBURG, VIRGINIA, 1751

The subscription race, organized by an elite group of plantation owners, was touted from Maryland to the Carolinas as akin to no other in Colonial history. A test of both raw speed and endurance, the race would pit the top short- and long-distance racers against one another in three heats of varying distance. The victor of the three would be crowned the indisputable king or queen of racing; and with a subscription fee of sixty hogsheads of Orinoco per entry, the winner stood to collect a purse equivalent to seven thousand five hundred pounds sterling!

Roberts's Retribution would be competing in a field of represen-tatives of the premier racing studs from Baltimore to Charleston, the colonies' finest hot-blooded horseflesh, and he was resolved to ride.

For two years, he had not only trained his colt to run but had also prepared his own body for this trial. Light, lithe, and stronger than he had been in a half decade, he willed that this new strength and twenty-plus years in the saddle would compensate for any other limitations he might have.

Aside from the subscription fee, Roberts had wagered the equivalent of an entire year's tobacco crop in a side bet with Maryland's most notorious gambler and horse breeder, William Byrd III. At the current market price of twenty shillings per hundredweight, his combined winnings from this race would amount to a fortune of over twenty thousand pounds should they prevail; but winnings aside, it was something he desperately needed to do.

Though he daily counted his blessings, in seven years he had never lost sight of his objective, to exact long-overdue recompense for all he had lost, and vengeance over those who had deceived and betrayed him in the name of selfish ambition.

Only with this victory could he ever hope to resurrect the man who was buried but far from dead.

❦

The gathered crowd went wild as the baker's dozen, collectively representing the Colonial embodiment of equine perfection, were led out for the first of the three contests, the quarter-mile sprint.

The favored of the lot were Mr. Tayloe's Childers and Jenny Cameron, Benjamin Tasker's imported Selima, Francis Thornton's Chieftain, Governor Ogle's Queen Mab, and William Byrd III's pride, the young stallion Tryal. Mr. Daniels's Retribution, with his peculiar blood cross, was deemed by all to be completely outclassed in the field of thoroughbreds.

Thirteen horses were slated to run, but the track could barely contain ten once gathered abreast. To the jockeys' peril, the horses crowded, milled, and nervously jostled one another as they awaited the starting signal.

The roan jigged in nervous anticipation of the signal, tugging on the bit and pushing his nose out with an irritated snort. He was raring to go. Roberts couldn't be more pleased that the first race was a sprint. There would be no reason to hold back.

His confidence, however, was shattered by the reckless jolt of another horse and rider.

Sizing up the offenders, Roberts recognized the horse as Byrd's Tryal. The bay stallion was known to be a fierce competitor with a vicious temperament. Casting Roberts a malevolent stare, the jockey spurred his horse again and bumped Retribution a second time.

Most times, jostling was unintentional, but there were many jockeys who would use this technique and any other they could command to intimidate the competition. There was no question of this jockey's intent.

Unnerved, Retribution angrily pinned his ears and gave a warning swish of his tail, but the bay struck swiftly with sharp, bared teeth, tearing a chunk of flesh from Retribution's flank. Like lightening, the colt spun to retaliate and poised to strike back. Fearing a disqualification, Roberts hastily spurred his colt forward to disengage from the fracas, but his opponent's goal had been accomplished; Retribution had become distracted and jumpy.

Roberts had taken a huge gamble in believing this colt the answer to his prayers, but perhaps he needed more seasoning. Perhaps the youngster wasn't ready. Roberts was suddenly beleaguered with doubt that gripped and threatened to paralyze him.

Although their position on the inside distanced them from the bay stallion, the roan sensed his rider's lingering tension as the racing stewards gave the call for the contenders to line up. Roberts battled his own nerves, fighting to regain his equilibrium. Only by conquering his doubts and fears could he attend to the needs of his mount.

Blocking out all else, Roberts now focused his attention on soothing his jangled mount. When the moment of truth arrived, he sensed a subtle change. Roberts could feel the stoking tension in the horse, but on the outside, Retribution was deceptively, dangerously quiet, marking his anticipation in subtle signs—in the forward and aft twitch of his ears, in his inflamed nostrils, and in his deeper respirations. He was poised like a tiger readying to pounce and seize its prey.

The trumpet blasted with the reverberation of echoing thunder.

Roberts released the predator, and all apprehension of his colt's readiness evaporated with the blistering speed in which they charged down the track. Roberts hung over his horse's neck, willing him for speed, pushing, driving. Breaking cleanly free of the mill, they blazed past half the pack by the first post and pummeled the turf beneath them. There was no room for error in this brief and frenzied run, and they ran faultlessly.

The crowd went wild. It was later remembered of Retribution's extreme velocity over those four hundred yards that a blink of an eye would have missed it altogether.

While proven quarter-miler Primate, by imported Monkey, came in a distant second, easily defeating Selima and Jenny Cameron, he was believed to lack the bottom to prevail in the longer four-mile run, where the two English thoroughbreds were most favored.

Although Retribution would surely meet with stiff competition against these two mares in the next heat, Roberts had unwavering confidence in his ability to rout them all in the final one-miler.

Following their victory, Roberts proceeded to the rubbing house, where he dismounted to inspect the raw and ugly wound inflicted by Tryal. After applying salve to the injury, he handed the horse off to his groom to rub down, and then he and the other jockeys met with the stewards to determine their positions in the next race.

The second heat found the field narrowed to an even twelve. A fouled sinew had reportedly eliminated Mr. Tayloe's Childers, but Roberts suspected Tayloe's embarrassment of his poor showing, rather a legitimate leg injury, had led to the forfeit.

In the distance race, each rider drew straws. The longest straw would be closest the rail, the shortest, the farthest, and so forth. With four full laps of the one-mile oval required to complete the course, the inside track was held to offer a significant advantage. This position required less distance of the runner, but in Roberts's view, it ofttimes became an inescapable trap. As the competitors bunched up, all vying for the coveted spot, a horse could find it impossible to break out from the pack. As a rider, maneuvering on the inside would put Roberts at the greatest disadvantage. Contrary to the other jockeys, he hoped for the outside.

Fifth to draw his straw, he waited expectantly and breathed a sigh of relief. They would be seventh from the inside rail. In this position, Retribution could ignore those fighting for the inside and run independently until the final furlong, when it would be open for their taking.

His strategy formed, Roberts advanced to the start, discovering to his consternation that Tryal's jockey had drawn the position to his immediate right. Having already shown his colors in the earlier sprint, Roberts tagged him as a jockey with few scruples. Tryal's rider was markedly disinclined to make any attempt to control his mount's rancorous behavior.

Already leery of the pair, Retribution shifted nervously. Roberts circled him before taking his position, but as soon as he turned his back, the bay stallion reared and struck out with his foreleg. His iron-shod hoof missed Roberts's head by mere inches.

Retribution moved to retaliate, but his rider again intervened. Roberts swore through gritted teeth, "If that's how the blighter wishes to play, we'll teach him a trick of our own, my boy."

The incident had again unsettled the entire herd. Horses bumped and jostled one another as they attempted once more to form some reasonable simulation of a line.

Once ready, the trump sounded, and the pack of restless, gleaming beasts exploded off the starting post to charge abreast down the field.

Roberts was acutely aware of the need to set the perfect pace. If too fast, they would lose steam and become vulnerable to a strong closer in the final furlongs. If too slow, they would have to fight their way through the crowd to gain the fore. The distance race, more than any other, required a savvy rider as much as a strong horse. Roberts and Retribution characterized the best of both.

By the time the field of runners approached the first bend, the line had folded inward toward the coveted rail. Roberts maintained his outside position, choosing to make a wider sweeping turn rather than fighting and weaving through the crowd, but as he made the arc, Tryal's jockey, whipping and spurring, came hard upon them. Sweeping across their path, he crowded and bashed into Retribution, simultaneously striking Roberts with a bony elbow to the stomach.

Roberts had been caught completely off guard. The blow paralyzed his lungs and very nearly knocked him from the galloping horse. Unbalanced, winded, and gasping for air, Roberts wrapped his arms about his horse's neck, clinging precariously while fighting to re-expand his lungs.

The race temporarily forgotten, he hung on the horse's left side while Retribution fought to keep his own balance, losing precious ground with every stride. The pack grew farther and farther distant before Roberts, breathing regulated, recovered enough for action. Here he was, dangling alongside his horse while the race was being run without them!

Roberts felt his dreams and carefully laid plans slipping away with every stride, but he could not give up. Not after all he had worked for. He knew to win this heat would be impossible, but if they could only regain the field, third place would be enough to advance them to the final heat.

He had never felt his weakness more than in that moment. With full use of his right arm, he could have easily pulled himself back into the saddle, but it was simply not up to the job.

In a feat worthy of a circus performer, he would have to use his legs to propel himself back into position, at the calculated risk of being trampled beneath his mount.

Grasping a tight fistful of mane, he blocked his mind to all but the rhythm of his galloping horse. Pulling his left foot free of the stirrup iron, he dropped, touching both feet to earth, and sprung. In one fluid motion, he had vaulted back into his seat! Deftly sliding his feet back into the irons, he took up the reins, crouched low over the colt's neck, and urgently called him back into the fray.

He would have to call on every ounce the colt had in him. Did he dare take such a risk? In his training, Roberts had yet to find Retribution's limits. He had demonstrated the heart of a runner, but he had never dared push such a youngster to the edge of his endurance. But now in twelfth place, with the rest of the field barely within their sights, he had no choice.

"Playtime's over, Son; I need all you've got!" Dropping flat to the wind, setting his rhythm with Retribution, he frantically urged the colt with hands, legs, and voice. Roberts rode like never before, incessantly encouraging, pressing, driving.

Responding to his rider's call, Retribution answered. With his ears snapping alertly, he accelerated to a formidable clip and hurled himself down the track. With his nostrils flared and eyes transfixed, he steadily crept up. Gaining little by little, Retribution moved to chase upon the heels of the chestnut filly in eleventh place. Snipping away at the distance, they were now running neck-and-neck and then suddenly hurtling past.

Roberts edged in toward the rail, seeking any advantage to make up what they had lost. Over the ensuing mile, stretching and straining anew, forelegs slicing the air, Retribution relentlessly stalked the field, picking off his prey one by one. By the final lap, he had gained a distant fourth place.

Retribution's body was now darkened, nearly black with the sheen of sweat; his mouth was frothing, his eyes glazed and nostrils flared red with blood, but he showed no sign of quitting. Heart and soul, the roan was giving his all.

With renewed confidence, Roberts studied the three still holding the advantage.

Selima and Jenny Cameron had run a hard race, as predicted, and were holding strong with one another in their contest for the lead. In third place was Tryal, lagging behind by nearly a furlong and noticeably showing strain.

Roberts needed only third, and usurping it from Tryal would be nearly as great a reward as a win. With his foe in sight, Roberts had no need to coax Retribution. With steely determination, the colt gained on the bay, his every stride drawing them closer, first by inches, then by feet, and finally yards, they closed the gap.

Tryal, now furiously blowing, bared his teeth as they came alongside and matched him stride for stride. Retribution tensed, desiring nothing more than to spring, but Roberts kept him back to taunt the stallion. They clung, and the bay fought for all he was worth, screaming to break free. His sides heaved. His jockey frantically spurred and flailed the whip, but Retribution held fast.

The struggle intensified. Tryal and his jockey strained in their exertions to pull free and regain third. Roberts released an inch of rein, and it proved the final blow.

Retribution lunged forward and clipped past Tryal. The stallion's eyes rolled back in his head. Blood issued forth from his inflamed nostrils, and he plunged to his knees, somersaulting onto the track, his rider crumpled beneath. The stallion's heart had ruptured under the severe strain of his efforts.

Roberts was horrified but dared not look back. With less than a quarter mile remaining, Retribution was still running strong, his breathing heavy but still rhythmic and synchronous with his hammering hooves. They had miraculously come from behind to claim third. The finish was in view. Dared he hope?

There was no time for deliberation. He spread his torso flat over the horse's withers and begged Retribution for everything he had. The game little horse answered the call.

With his rider's final cue, Retribution locked his eyes on Selima and Jenny Cameron. Roaring within, he welled and surge forth in a final burst of acceleration. Stealing feet with every stride, he closed the distance in the final furlong, bringing them nose-to-tail with Jenny Cameron, but they had run out of track.

Although finishing a close third, Retribution's rider was no less than elated. The colt had run the last mile and a half at a miraculous clip! Had it not been for Tryal and his rogue jockey, they would have easily won and outdistanced the pack.

Retribution had persevered when all hope appeared lost. He had rallied after a crippling setback. In a grueling test, the colt had proven himself. Roberts had no doubt the one-miler was his.

"The time for our journey draws nigh, my boy. The time of Retribution has finally come."

Forty

A REVELATION

*D*aniel Roberts stood with his young wards, Thomas and Benjamin, on the deck of *Venturer* as it dropped anchor in Bristol. Ironic, he thought, that the same ship that had carried him from Bristol to Annapolis nigh on eight years ago would return him to his former homeland.

Six months ago, he had taken his prized racehorse and tobacco-winnings to Annapolis, where they were loaded aboard the three-masted brigand, *Annabelle*, bound for Liverpool. Roberts had taken great pains to equip the vessel for Retribution's comfort and safety. The horse was the sole occupant of a roomy cargo hold of twelve by fourteen feet and equipped with a sling. In the event of foul weather, the sling would prevent loss of footing in rough seas that would have battered him incessantly against the solid oak walls of his seagoing box. Instead, the sling under his belly would suspend him and gently sway, acting much as a sailor's hammock.

Roberts's most trusted groom accompanied Retribution to his final destination, where the young horse would spend several months training on English turf under John Jeffries's aegis.

It had taken Roberts several inquiries to track down the able horseman who had been his mentor, but he had finally located him in Doncaster, where he had found employment after Sir Garfield's death. Jeffries would know how to bring out the best in the young runner. With the finest running bloods residing in England, Retribution must be trained on their home turf and against their kind. He would be properly prepared, and Doncaster was the place to do so. Quietly.

Although there had been none in the colonies to hold a candle to him, Virginia was not England. The English took their bloodstock in dead earnest, and although many English thoroughbreds had made the transatlantic crossing over the past decade, the very best of English blood would never be exported. It was one of the many ways the English continued to "lord over" the colonists. Roberts would be arrogant and foolhardy to think of accomplishing his ends without due preparation.

And now, Roberts had arrived to set the wheels in motion.

For years, he had awaited this moment, and now he would personally see his plans unfurl. Standing at the ship's rail, he gazed sightlessly at the city sprawled before him, lost in his thoughts, until a crewman's colorful expletive awoke him from his reverie.

"Benjamin! Thomas! Quit the tomfoolery, and stay out of the rigging!" he shouted to the rambunctious boys, who had unwarily provoked the sailor's invective.

The culprits, seven and nine years old respectively, instantly untangled themselves and trudged guiltily over to their guardian as the crew continued docking procedures.

"Is this London?" Thomas asked, eyes wide in wonderment.

"It must be the largest city in the world," Benjamin echoed.

"'Tis only Bristol, lads, a veritable anthill compared to the great city of London!" Roberts answered.

"A city bigger than this? That's impossible," Thomas stated skeptically.

"Impossible? I promise you not, young Thomas. It would only seem so, as your own world has been so very small until now, but we have now crossed an entire ocean to a much older land. You will soon find your universe much expanded."

Bedazzled, Thomas surveyed the city and digested the words.

"Didn't you once live in England, Mr. Roberts?" Benjamin queried.

"I did indeed." He paused, continuing with a touch of melancholy, "I was raised in Yorkshire, a beautiful rolling countryside not unlike our lovely Virginia."

"I should very much like to see London," Thomas insisted.

"Have no doubt I shall take you there. Unquestionably, my business shall require it. Speaking of which, most of my affairs have been conducted by Mr. Lee, you know. He has handled my legal and business affairs, as well as your own for some time, but with his father's recent death, I suspect he will soon return to Virginia."

"Wasn't Mr. Lee also educated in England?" Thomas asked.

"I wish I were going to an English school," Benjamin added wistfully.

"You are yet too young, Benjamin, but at this moment, I should not reflect much upon it. We shall likely spend several months here. There is much to accomplish before I contemplate our return," he remarked soberly.

"Speaking of Mr. Lee, is that not him come to greet us?" Benjamin exclaimed.

"Indeed it is! What sharp eyes you have." He ruffled the boy's hair carelessly and hailed his old friend, who had indeed come all the way from London.

"And now, lads, 'twould appear we should collect our belongings and make ready to disembark."

Mr. Roberts bespoke the very best set of private rooms at the John Bull, ordered supper, and settled his wards before meeting privately with Mr. Lee.

"I offer my heartfelt condolences, Ludwell, on the passing of your father. Thomas Lee was a most remarkable man."

"Indeed he was, and I should never have believed it would have happened so soon. But it appears that now my legal studies are come to an end. As the head of my family, I needs must soon take up the mantle of Stratford." He poured two glasses of port, offering one to his friend.

"But what of your immediate plans, now you have arrived, Roberts? I confess that your intentions in your last letter were shrouded in a cloud of mystery."

"Were they indeed? I am surprised that you, the only one of my acquaintance who knows the truth of my past, would find my journey a mystery."

"You have confided a portion of your story in these years past, but far from its entirety, I would guess. I had assumed, erroneously it would appear, that you had laid it to rest, buried with the unfortunate Mr. Devington. But now I perceive that this unfortunate gentleman is far from resting peacefully in his grave. Are you bent on vengeance, my friend? Is this your motive in returning to England?"

"Lust for revenge is not often attributed to a noble character, is it, Ludwell?"

"Far be it for me to judge! I would call it no more than justice, but I fail to understand what would drive you to the point of risking everything you have worked for these eight years."

"I do not risk everything. The plantation is completely intact. Indeed, it prospers more now than ever. I have not staked my livelihood nor the property, which is not rightfully mine to wager."

"Speaking of which, what possessed you to take on the rearing of two boys? Mary Griffiths was a close friend of my mother, and I knew her well, but why should you involve yourself with her orphans?"

"I confess now that had I any idea of what I was getting into…" He laughed and then sobered. "Mary was a fine woman and a good mother, and the boys had no one. If she had not died, I should have become their stepfather. How could I not step in when it was within my power to protect them?"

"'Tis a good thing you have done to bring them with you."

"They have mourned their mother deeply, and though 'tis nearly two years since they lost her, she has left a void that cannot be filled. I could not countenance the thought of leaving them behind only in the care of servants."

"I know few men who own such scruples, my friend."

"I should not go so far as that, Ludwell. You know why I am come to England."

"We are back to that now, are we? You become a conundrum, Roberts," Mr. Lee said with a puzzled expression. "In our years of acquaintance, you have rubbed along well enough with your fellow man and have duly prospered for your efforts. Why do you now disturb your own peace? Why put yourself to this trouble?"

"One can understand a man's motives only when one stands in his shoes, Ludwell."

"I can only believe that this man, whoever he is, must have been the devil himself, a foul fiend, to have set you so against him."

"On the contrary, he was once my most trusted friend," Roberts replied softly.

"Then if that be so, I can only guess a woman is at the bottom of this."

Mr. Lee's remark drew his friend's countenance into grim, hard lines. He had come far too near the mark. Mr. Lee refilled their glasses and broke the uncomfortable silence that had settled between them.

"I suppose I should waste my breath if I tried to dissuade you? I can't believe any good should come out of this."

"Your breath should be completely wasted. I advise you save it."

"Dare I ask exactly how much you intend to risk?" his concerned friend prodded.

"As much as it takes to answer my purpose." He raised his glass, swilling its contents in one fluid motion.

⟋♥⟍

After only a few days rest from their voyage, Mr. Roberts was anxious to be about his business. He and Lee met to discuss his final arrangements before departing Bristol for Doncaster.

"Item one," Lee said, consulting his list, "I have leased a house for you in one of London's grander districts. Item two: I have deposited the proceeds of your tobacco cargo at the Bank of England and have established your necessary credit, as well as letters of introduction from various respectable gentlemen of my acquaintance. Item three: I have employed a tutor to take charge of the boys while you are otherwise engaged. The last item I had added to the list as something you had overlooked."

"And what might that be?"

"Membership at White's Chocolate House."

"White's, you say? What should I care for such hobnobbing?"

"It would be very much to your purpose."

"How so, Ludwell? How should a stuffy gentleman's club signify in my plans?"

"You overlook the betting book."

"The betting book?"

"White's betting book is an infamous public record of wagers between gentlemen. Much wickedness has been ascribed to it, and since you remain undeterred from your nefarious course"—he paused reflectively—"for purposes of validation, notoriety, and posterity, I suggest you ensure your wager is entered in the book. If one chooses to bring one's enemy to his knees, it is best accomplished most publicly."

"True indeed, Ludwell." Roberts chuckled. "Your insights quite overwhelm me."

"I am but your humble servant," he said with a smirk and took a pinch of snuff. Lee gave a brief shake to his lace cuff then paused to scrutinize his companion. As he critically surveyed Roberts from head to foot, his eyes narrowed.

"What are you staring at?" Roberts asked. Although dressed well enough for a rural Virginia planter, Roberts's unpowdered hair, brown wool suit, and plain white linen would hardly pass muster in the ranks of English gentlemen.

"At the risk of being indelicate," Lee remarked, "might I make a few suggestions to ease your way into the upper ranks?"

Roberts quirked a brow.

"A proper *English* tailor might serve you well, and in the spirit of maintaining your precious incognito, perhaps you would also benefit from a peruquier? I mean no offense, but you hardly impress one as a figure of prosperity dressed as you are. This is England, after all."

"I take no offense. I shall contrive to depart Bristol a proper *English* gentleman," Roberts replied ruefully.

He spent the next day venturing from shop to shop, acquiring the necessary finery. After squandering an entire day and much coin, Roberts exchanged his drab brown wool for suiting of deep blue silk brocade. He replaced his plain white linen for that dripping with French lace, and even his hat brim was now adorned with silver. His final purchase, the *pièce de résistance*, was the white powdered tie wig, a fashionable accoutrement he had always eschewed in favor of his own hair. Adding powder and a silk patch on his face, his transformation was now complete. Roberts regarded himself with amazement in the tailor's looking glass. He hardly recognized himself.

Impatient not to waste another day, Roberts set off from Bristol in a hired coach-and-four, accompanied by the two boys and their tutor. He had commanded a bruising pace, but with scheduled stops at points of interest to allow the boys to stretch their restless legs and the tutor to enrich their young minds with tidbits of English history.

By the fifth day and within thirty miles of their destination, the coachman halted, informing Mr. Roberts of a pronounced lameness in the lead horse, as well as a problem with the rear axle. Although impatient to arrive in Doncaster and assess the readiness of his colt, Roberts was no less concerned for all livestock under his care. He directed the coachman to follow the Sheffield road, instructing him to locate a decent coaching inn where the passengers might rest while seeing to the horse and carriage repairs.

To his great consternation, the coach halted at a place burned vividly into Roberts's memory: the Dark Horse Inn.

"Stokes," he inquired of his coachman with studied indolence, "how have we come by this particular inn?"

"Mr. Roberts, sir, you instructed me to find inn and smithy. As it so happens, here are both."

"Then I suppose we must indeed rest here," he answered skeptically. "Pray tend to the horse, and if he can't be made serviceably sound, you have my permission to hire another team. Have the smith take a look at the axle, but bear in mind I have no wish to delay overlong."

"Aye, Mr. Roberts. As ye say, sir." The coachman directed his equipage to the nearby smithy.

"Thomas, Benjamin, Mr. Thayer, shall we see if this inn offers any manner of fare fit for human consumption? The victuals were dubious at best, upon my recollection." He addressed the boys with a conspiratorial grin, broadening with Thayer's expression of alarm. The tutor's worst expectations, however, vanished when the party opened the doors to the large and crowded taproom with its gleaming wood and tantalizing aroma of roasted meat from its roaring spits.

He was stunned at the profound transformation of the dank and dreary tavern of his memory. A buxom matron with a toddler clinging to her skirts cheerfully greeted the party and led them to a large table.

Eyeing the boys, she remarked, "Now there's a pair of fine lads. Ye look to be right about the age of me own two oldest, Ian and Jack." She gave the boys a friendly wink. "Now, what might I bring ye fine gents? The Dark Horse ale is the finest to be had, if'n I say so m'self, and we be also known for our mutton and our game pie."

"I should say two tankards of ale, two of cider, a game pie, and a platter of whatever you have roasting on the spit should do us very well, madam."

"I am no madam, yer lordship." She laughed. "Just Maggie; Maggie Grey."

"Maggie, you say?" Mr. Roberts said incredulously. His narrowing eyes regarded her sharply in an effort to envision the auburn-haired woman, less the clinging toddler and a good three or four stone. To his amazement, he realized she was indeed the sultry siren with whom Philip Drake had dallied nearly a decade ago.

"Mrs. Grey?" he repeated. "I am no lord, simply Daniel Roberts, if you please. Would you be the proprietress of this establishment?"

"I am, indeed. That is me and me husband John Grey. He be the smith, and most times he leaves the tavern to me."

The inquiry was politely made, but Maggie found herself growing uneasy under his scrutiny. It had been several years and as many children since she had taken the notice of any fine gentlemen passing through her establishment. She felt mildly uncomfortable, and his gaze was strangely familiar. Suddenly compelled, she asked, "Does I know your lordship? I feel as if we've met afore."

"I believe the answer would depend on whether or not you recall an acquaintance with a certain officer of the King's Horse."

"The smile vanished from Maggie's plump face. "And who might that be?" she asked with a slight scowl.

"Do you recall an officer by the name of Philip Drake?"

Still wearing the frown, she said, "I ain't heard that name in years, and don't be repeatin' it around John Grey! He's a jealous husband, John is, and I reckon my poor Ian would only suffer for it. But why would you be askin' after Philip Drake?" she asked warily, and then she suddenly raised her hand to her mouth in a gasp. "God's ghost! If it ain't Cap'n Devington!"

The unlikely reunion proved a serendipitous event. Instead of hastening their journey as he had planned, Daniel Roberts bespoke rooms for the night. To their delight, Thomas and Benjamin, not having shared company with anyone their age for many weeks of travel, found a host of playmates among Maggie's six children. One by one, the Grey brood made their appearance in the tavern.

To Mr. Thayer's dismay, Roberts volunteered the tutor's services to oversee the boisterous brood that he might converse privately with Mrs. Grey, who once recovered from her initial shock, proved a veritable fount of information.

Sir Garfield, she recounted, had two years ago suffered a massive heart seizure while attending Newmarket races. Lady Felicia, beset with grief, divested the estate of all horseflesh, which she believed caused her husband's demise. To her credit, the lady took a good many servants to London with her, elsewise, where could they have found other employment?

Charles Wallace, heir to the entire estate, had joined the infantry years ago and was later involved in that nasty business with the Scots at Culloden, commanded by Billy the Butcher. To Maggie's recollection, Charles had never returned to Yorkshire, even upon his father's death. "But as for that sister of his, I always knew she was no more'n a shameless hussy, though she put on such grand lady airs. There was that scandal whispered about his lordship, her husband, what was shot by his own bleedin' father. Let me say that was some queer business there!"

Placing her hands on her hips, Maggie continued her diatribe. "After that, she, what was so wanting to be a countess, come off her high-and-mighty throne. Though she picked a ripe one in Sir George Tenbury, doddering old squire what he is. But I says, 'tis nobody's business if she makes a cuckold of him with the footmen."

After these telling revelations, awkwardness ensued. Roberts had questions he dared not ask poised on his tongue regarding the fate of another member of the Wallace family. Maggie, however, broached the subject in her circuitous fashion.

"Cap'n... er... Mr. Roberts," she amended, "ye never did say what brings ye back to Yorkshire after all this time."

"My dear Mrs. Grey," he asked, "what do you know of my history these eight years past?"

"Well, Ca... Mr. Roberts, ye was believed dead. That business in Leeds, well that was talked about all over. It was said ye was hauled off in chains and hung by the neck at Newgate, though I never put much stock in that tale, believin' officers is usually killed more dignified like. But Miss Charlotte"—in the midst of her prattle, Maggie missed the shadow that passed over his countenance and the hard lines that formed at the mention of Charlotte's name—"I done heard she mourned you, Cap'n, believing ye dead. Why the fates worked against the two of ye, I'll ne'er understand. *She*, poor thing, ain't known a moment's happiness to any account. Though she be a grand lady now, none thinks she got the better end *o'that* deal!

"As for *him*... though I might once have had feelings for him, that was afore he come back from the wars. After Culloden, he

ain't never been the same as what he was. Black-tempered and jug-
bitten, they say, and carin' for naught but his bleedin' racehorses.
Best thing I ever did was marry John Grey." Her assertion was a bit
too emphatic, as if to convince herself.

"And it appears you have prospered for your decision,"
Roberts commented absently while he struggled to compose his
churning emotions.

"A good man, John Grey," she continued, oblivious. "But
what of yerself? Ye've a pair of strappin' young lads. What of the
Mrs. Roberts?"

"There is no Mrs. Roberts. The mother of the lads passed away
two years ago from smallpox," he replied quietly. "Thomas and
Benjamin are my legal wards, but I care for them as if they were
my own. The elder has come to England for his education, and
not knowing how long I would be away, I could not bear to leave
the younger alone in Virginia. Besides, there is nothing better than
travel to broaden a young mind."

"Aye, 'tis true enough for some, for those restless ones, anyways.
My Ian is one like that, restless he is. Though he works in the smithy,
his mind is always elsewhere. He be far too wont to woolgatherin',
and John has little patience wi' the lad to begin with, ye ken."

"The eldest works in the smithy? You remind me I must see to
the progress of our carriage. I thank you, Mrs. Grey, for your time,
your gracious hospitality, and most of all for your discretion?" He
laid two gold guineas before her.

"Your business ain't no business of mine, Mr. Roberts." She reassured him with a wink. Tucking the guineas deep in the ample
bodice of her gown, she sashayed back to her taproom.

Mr. Roberts then directed his steps to the smithy, where having
already completed the axle repair, the smith was reshoeing the lame
horse. As he held the horse's foreleg between his knees, the lazy
gelding shifted his weight to bear on the man, who barked harshly at

the lad holding the horse. The boy snapped to attention and corrected the horse with a sharp jerk on the lead shank. When the man finished with the final nail, he cuffed the boy roughly on the ear.

"Ye'll pay better attention the next time, Ian! Now lead 'im back to the livery. No dawdling, ye hear!"

"Yes, sir. I won't, sir," the boy answered. His lip quivered, but his dark gaze was direct and his bearing more defiant than submissive. Refusing to be cowed, with his chin raised and stiff shoulders, he led the big gelding out to the livery. Roberts thought the boy resembled a little soldier.

He was about to address a remark to the burly man, but a thought suddenly arrested him. Tall and lanky for his age, which he guessed to be about eight, the contrast in both figure and feature of Maggie's eldest son, Ian, with the five other redheaded, blue-eyed children could not have been more marked. At once he understood Maggie's veiled references to her husband's jealousy and impatience with the boy.

Ian Grey was the spitting image of Philip Drake!

The following day brought a change in Roberts's plans. Rather than traveling by coach to Doncaster, he left the boys at the tavern in the agitated tutor's care and hired a horse to depart Sheffield alone.

In the confines of the coach, he had grown claustrophobic, and his encounter with Maggie had only dredged up painful memories. He needed air and space and time alone to think. He galloped the familiar paths and rolling heath he'd memorized from his boyhood, the same heath where he'd ridden with Charlotte, and was on his way to Doncaster, where his first fateful race had been run.

He shook out of his angst of the past, forcing himself to look forward rather than back. The autumn racing season would soon commence. The time of reckoning was at hand.

Forty-one

AN IRRESISTIBLE CHALLENGE

LONDON, ENGLAND, AUTUMN 1751

*T*he Earl of Hastings sat sullen and brooding, with his customary bottle of brandy within easy reach, as he awaited the arrival of an unknown gentleman who had earlier sent his card. Any who had known the earl a decade ago would be hard-pressed to recognize the handsome and charming cavalry officer he had been.

He had once been one of Cumberland's key men, fighting valiantly against the French at Dettingen, where he had first distinguished himself for bravery, and later in their just-as-heroic defeat at Fontenoy, but it was for the infamous battle of Culloden that he bore his inner and outer scars.

Swiftly and mercilessly, they had routed the supporters of the Young Pretender, the would-be usurper to the British throne. Completely crushing the insurrection, the commander in chief had allowed no quarter. But the price of victory had been high. Too high. Nicknamed the Butcher of Culloden and Billy the Butcher, among his colorful sobriquets, the Duke of Cumberland and all under his command had been condemned in the public eye.

Major Lord Hastings had sold out after the Treaty of Aux Chappelle in '48, resolved to retire to his family seat in East Sussex and put his long-neglected affairs in order, but his vision of bucolic idyll was shattered when he found his properties a shambles.

His estates had suffered decades of neglect under his father, who was more interested in politics and courtly intrigue than in the sowing of fields and mending of roofs. Though Philip had hired a steward to manage his affairs, his own disinterest and elected absence had only compounded the years of decay.

Of all his holdings, the earl discovered only a single profitable enterprise: his racing stud. And to his complete bafflement, the success was singularly credited to his estranged wife, Lady Charlotte Drake, Countess of Hastings.

Having a foundation of only a few mediocre leftovers from the Hastings stud and the broodmare Amoret he had given her as a peace offering, Charlotte had built a stable of superior runners.

The first of these had been Amoret's foal by Lord Godolphin's Hobgoblin, the gangly chestnut colt, Shakespeare, which Philip had claimed for himself. The young horse had more than lived up to expectations. Having been a winner on the track, he was already enjoying success in the breeding shed.

With her first success with Shakespeare, Charlotte was determined with all her being to follow the romantic dream she and Robert had nurtured those many years ago. Maintaining her faith in the superior genetics of the three progenitor sires, she built her stables around the very best mares put to the finest stallions her money could buy.

In addition to Amoret, she sought out descendants of the original royal mares and the daughters of proven runners, adding Mother Western by a son of Snake, Ruby by Blacklegs, Meloria by Portmore's Fox, and Cypron by a son of Flying Childers to her broodmare harem.

Carefully selecting stallions of the Darley, Byerley, and Godolphin blood, she paired them with her choice mares and began to produce winners. A colt, Midas, in '46 and a third colt, Slouch, in '47, followed Shakespeare. Two fillies, Miss Cade and Miss Meredith, by the fine stallion Cade, followed in '48. All had shown the capacity to run. And win.

Charlotte's biggest gamble had been in putting Mother Western to the great Regulus, the still undefeated champion, who had run his first race that fateful day when Robert had wagered against Sir Garfield. The stallion's fee, at twenty guineas, was an exorbitant sum that had drained her available resources, but the resulting filly, Spiletta, was Charlotte's pride and represented her best hopes for the future.

Under Charlotte's guiding hand, the Hastings's stud produced more winners than any other in the region, and although the horses ran under the earl's name and racing colors, Lady Hastings was universally recognized for their successes.

This mortifying revelation came to Philip upon his election to the newly formed Jockey Club, when its members raised their glasses at the Star and Garter to its honorary member, the Countess of Hastings, first lady of the turf.

Shortly thereafter, Lord Hastings took seriously to the bottle. His military career, brilliantly begun, had ended in disgrace. His centuries-old family seat was in such disrepair that it was little better than a pile of rubble. His only success was credited to his wife, and even their marriage, still a celibate arrangement, remained an atrocious farce.

In their eight years together, had Charlotte ever played him for a fool or a cuckold, he would have divorced her. God knew he had just reason. But though she denied him an heir, and with it his full inheritance, she had never crossed the line of adultery. And it was Charlotte's successes, rather than his, that kept them afloat.

Unhappily resigned to his failures, Philip had sought solace in his horses, his brandy… and his mistress. Sukey. His beautiful, witty, laughing Sukey. She was the one and only love of his life, but a life they could never share. Although wanting nothing more than to be his lawful wife, she had settled for mistress rather than allowing him to divorce Charlotte.

He and Charlotte had settled over the years into an uneasy peace. He allowed her full rein over the stud, and she turned a blind eye to his mistress, but even if Philip could have had the woman he loved, she could never give him a son. It always came back to that.

The heir and the inheritance that would never be his.

His trembling hands refilled his glass again to sloshing. He knocked back a third brandy while he waited. Waited and brooded. He had just begun to feel the first dullness of his senses when the gentleman approached, introducing himself with a very correct and deferential bow.

Lord Hastings responded with an arrogant nod and then carelessly waved at the vacant chair opposite him. Mr. Lee seated himself, refusing the proffered drink while his lordship replenished his yet again.

"Lee," Lord Hastings said. "Can't say I know the name, though your face seems somewhat familiar."

"No doubt we've encountered one another at Newmarket, my lord."

"Ah! A racing aficionado, are you?"

"Indeed, Lord Hastings, and as it happens, racing is the purpose of this meeting."

His interest piqued, the earl replied, "You perceive me all ears, Mr. Lee."

"I am come at the behest of a Mr. Roberts of Virginia, a gentleman with a fine appreciation of horseflesh and an even greater conceit."

Lord Hastings quirked a brow at the disparaging remark. "You act as his agent, yet I think you no great admirer of this gentleman."

"Suffice to say, Virginia society is comprised of much closer circles than in England. As we have many mutual acquaintances, Mr. Roberts sought me out, believing I might assist him in his singular endeavor. Believing his purpose is utter folly, it is only for the sake of our mutual friends that I have agreed to act on Mr. Robert's behalf."

"And what is this folly? I am intrigued to know more of your imprudent Colonial friend." He once more offered a glass of brandy to Mr. Lee. Upon his polite refusal, his lordship shrugged, lifting his own to his lips. Slouching in his chair, he beckoned Lee with an indolent nod to continue his narrative.

"It would appear that Mr. Daniel Roberts of Westmoreland County, Virginia, has conceived in his mind the belief that he possesses the finest piece of horseflesh in God's creation. Having been a competitor on the Virginia turf, I was acquainted with his reputation but am no less taken aback by the man's vanity."

"So you say!" His listener barked with laughter and sat forward in rapt interest. "Precisely how did this Roberts come by his peculiar notion?"

"By a fluke, my lord. His four-year-old colt bested the most superior Colonial blood horses for a very substantial purse, the largest prize ever won in Virginia."

"Indeed fortuitous, but what has this to say to me, Lee?"

"Bear with me, my lord, and I shall come to my purpose."

Their discourse was interrupted by the arrival of several gentlemen of obvious consequence. The leader of the trio was a corpulent man of unquestionable nobility coupled with his unmistakable military bearing. The arrival brought about a remarkable change in the earl's seeming state of torpor. He smartly rose from his chair and snapped a salute of greeting to the corpulent man. "Your Grace."

At this address, Mr. Lee, a man of quick faculties, deduced the new arrival to be the Duke of Cumberland. He swept an obsequious bow.

Lord Hastings turned to the duke and his entourage, and said, "I make known to you the honorable Mr. Lee, a gentleman of Virginia, who has entertained me mightily this quarter hour."

"Is that true, Hastings?" His grace appeared amused. "Then I would join you for a spell. God knows how I am in need of diversion *these* days." With a crook of his finger, the duke signaled an army of lackeys to see to his party. Seating himself with a grunt, Cumberland assumed an attentive pose. "Pray continue, Mr. Lee. I would hear this tale that has so amused my jaded friend."

"I have spoken, Your Grace, of a certain gentleman who is come from Virginia to propose a horse race."

"A horse race, you say? This is not so unexceptional. Who is the gentleman?"

"No one of any consequence, Your Grace, but he has an inflated regard of his horseflesh, having defeated our Virginia horses, and has transported his champion with the stated purpose of besting the most superior runners in England."

The entire group burst into uncontrollable laughter.

"Conceited, you say? I would remark that the man is delusional!" His Grace retorted. "What do you make of this, Hastings?" he said to his former aide-de-camp.

"'Twould appear a ridiculous vagary, but I should know what manner of horse he has, this Roberts. By what sire line is he bred?"

"The sire line is unknown, although it is allowed he is of Saracenic origin."

"An unknown Eastern-bred sire in Virginia, eh?" A brief shadow crossed the earl's visage, but he dismissed it with a visible shake of his head, casting off whatever notion had momentarily caught his fancy. "What of the dam, sir? I have heard you Colonials have imported a good many of our English-blood mares. What is the dam's family?"

"The dam is native bred, a mare of the Chickasaws," Mr. Lee replied.

"Chicksaw, you say? What on God's green earth is a Chicksaw?" His Grace barked.

"*Chickasaw*, Your Grace," he corrected. "'Tis a breed of horse domesticated by a tribe of American natives highly respected for their horse sense."

"A racehorse bred by savages? You bloody well do mean *native!*" interjected the duke. "I can't recall the last time I was so entertained."

"Is this meant to be a jest?" Lord Hastings asked Mr. Lee.

"Indeed not. The man is in dead earnest; however, he has of late discovered an impediment to his aspirations."

"An impediment? Aside from the lack of a real horse?" Cumberland asked. "By all means, you must continue this tale."

"The gentleman had in mind to run in the Royal Plates but has learned, to his chagrin, that his colt is ineligible due to his breeding. We have no such rules governing the blood in Virginia, where any horse may race, so I daresay he never considered this complication. He has brought his horse at no inconsiderable expense and is extremely vexed that he should be denied the run."

"If the horse is deemed ineligible, he is ineligible," remarked Lord Hastings. "Although this tale has been delightfully diverting, I fail to see how it involves me."

"One can only sympathize with the deluded creature, eh, Hastings?" His Grace poured a drink and considered his friend.

Mr. Lee replied, "Although the horse is ineligible to run any of the subscription races, the gentleman will not suffer defeat so easily. Thus, I finally come to my errand. Mr. Roberts came desiring to challenge only the most superior horses in England, and since some of the finest are reputedly housed in the Hastings stud, he respectfully proposes that your lordship consider a match race. Any horse of your stable against his Virginia-bred colt."

"What?" Lord Hastings exploded in laughter. "He has in mind to match some half-breed native pony against the likes of Shakespeare? My horses have won three King's Plates this season alone! I would not condescend to such a mockery."

"Mayhap you would be more disposed after considering his wager. He proposes twenty thousand pounds."

The laughter abruptly ceased. "Twenty thousand pounds sterling?"

"Just so. The man has more tobacco than sense and is in dead earnest regarding his horse," Lee asserted.

"Then I shall consider his ludicrous wager *in dead earnest*. What are the terms, should I accept?"

"The race would be run at the distance, time, and place of your choosing, my lord."

"Good God! The man's a complete buffoon!" The Duke of Cumberland slapped his thigh heartily while Lord Hastings battled his sense of disquiet. Something just didn't sit right with him. But twenty thousand pounds? Dismissing his eerie presentiment, he looked to Cumberland. "I find myself compelled to accept him, Your Grace."

"By all means, Hastings! I would that I might also have a horse in this race!"

"Mr. Lee," Lord Hastings said deliberately, "pray convey to your friend that we shall meet at Newmarket on the fourteenth of October, the day before the King's Plate is to be run. He shall no doubt be well pleased to have a wide and sundry audience to witness his most *auspicious* race."

"He shall be pleased to hear of your acceptance, my lord. I suppose all that remains is to enter the wager in the betting book," he remarked casually.

"By all means, Lee." Lord Hastings strolled to the infamous tome and entered the details of the wager, witnessed by Mr. Roberts's legal agent as well as His Grace, the Duke of Cumberland.

When the ink was dry, Lord Hastings reflected, "I am come to mind of an old English proverb, Mr. Lee. 'A fool and his money are soon parted.'"

Mr. Lee smiled politely and softly spoke his reply. "I am in mind of an even older proverb, my lord, 'Do not answer a fool according to his folly, or you will also be like him.'"

Forty-two

RETRIBUTION

NEWMARKET, SUFFOLK, OCTOBER 13, 1751

*T*raveling as inconspicuously as possible, the two Virginians arrived in Newmarket a day prior to the scheduled match race. Anxious to avoid recognition, and particularly any inadvertent encounter with the Earl of Hastings, Roberts eschewed the better accommodations in town to take rooms at a smaller coaching inn, the White Hart, in the nearby village of Bury St Edmunds.

Once settled, he sallied forth to the racing stables to inspect his horse, delivered by Jeffries and Roberts's Virginia groom, Tom, a full se'nnight earlier, to work in earnest on the Newmarket Heath. In his caution, he had instructed Jeffries to take every possible measure to keep his runner under wraps, a near impossible feat with so many congregating en masse for the King's Plate.

The trainer's only recourse had been to stumble about in the dark, conducting their practice runs in the early twilight hours. Though the trainer felt at a distinct disadvantage, the able colt revealed not the slightest weakness. He was in top form, tearing up the Heath with blistering speed.

Mr. Roberts was immensely pleased with the trainer's report. He did not desire a simple victory on the Rowley Mile. No indeed. He would be satisfied with nothing less than the Earl of Hastings's complete and utter humiliation, witnessed by the entire racing world.

Although they made every attempt to do so, the earl and his countess could not completely evade one another's company. Thus, over the years, at least where racing was concerned, they had come to a truce of sorts, agreeing to maintain appearances when encountering one another at public gatherings.

This was no truer than during the twice-annual Newmarket racing season, the only time in which Lord and Lady Hastings actually shared the cottage in Cheveley. This autumn, however, he had sent his baggage coach a day earlier than Charlotte had anticipated.

The event came as little surprise to Charlotte, who imagined he intended to spend the night before the race with Cumberland and his army cronies in a late night of drinking and carousing. She was, therefore, surprised to encounter him at breakfast early the next morning, and even further taken aback to find him clear-eyed, clean-shaven, and dressed to go out.

"Philip, you are certainly up betimes! Have you taken to new habits these days?" she inquired mockingly. "I should not have expected you to bestir yourself before noontime."

"Don't place any great hope on my reform," he remarked dryly.

"Indeed, I should never expect you might suddenly give up the practices of excess and dissipation you have spent eons perfecting," she said with a snort. "'Tis quite a ridiculous notion."

"No reason to get your hackles up so early, darling one. I shall remove myself to town directly, and you may continue in your cherished solitude."

"I do not cherish solitude, Philip; I am simply discriminating in the company I keep."

"*Touché*, dear heart." His answering smirk was provoking. "But pray let us truce, light of my life, for contrary to my fresh appearance and exceeding good temper, I've the devil of a headache." He beckoned the footman for coffee.

"All right, I shan't cross swords with you any further."

"You are forever gracious, dear heart," he said.

She ignored the taunt and filled her plate from the sideboard. She then seated herself to his right.

"Philip," she began, "your sudden change in habits has stimulated my curiosity. What would take you to town precipitately? The races do not commence until the morrow."

"Ah, but there is another to be run *this day*."

"Another race?" she replied with keen interest. "I had not heard of it. Pray, who are the runners?"

"This event should prove nothing but a farce, though it shan't hurt Shakespeare to run a warm-up lap before the King's Plate."

"You are running Shakespeare? Against whom? And why would you not inform me?"

"'Tis hardly an event worth mentioning, sweeting. The challenger is inconsequential, an unknown brought from Virginia by a gentleman of prodigious pomposity, by all account."

"He brought his horse all the way from the colonies to run a match against Shakespeare? I am confounded."

"Apparently, this horse of no distinct breeding has bested the Virginia bloodstock. Thus inflated, the gentleman has the impertinence to challenge the English runners on their own turf."

"How extraordinary! I am incredulous you accepted."

"I should not have, but the wager was such that I could hardly refuse."

"What precisely *do you know* of this horse, Philip?"

"He's a four-year-old sired by an unknown of Eastern descent that was imported to the colonies. The dam, however, is of some indigenous breed created by the savages. Completely ineligible to run the track, of course."

"Indeed? 'Twould appear great folly on his part, unless..." Charlotte furrowed her brow as she sipped her tea. "An obscure gentleman, with a horse of mixed blood, who has come across the ocean, no doubt at great expense." Charlotte frowned at a passing thought. "Have you seen the horse run?"

"What need have I? The Hastings stud owns some of the finest horseflesh in England, all to your credit, I might add." He affected a gesture of tribute. "I should not trouble myself further on the matter, oh dearest one."

"I do, you know," she answered. "I *always* contrive to watch our rivals exercising on the Heath the week before a race. Indeed, just yesterday I witnessed a new one. His small stature and unusual coloration first drew my eye, but as it was barely daybreak, I caught only the end of his session. He was remarkably swift. I am sure I have never seen this one before... I wonder, Philip?" she said in trepidation.

"Daniel Roberts and his Retribution hardly signify." His reply was disdainful.

"Retribution? Is that what he calls the horse? What a curious name."

"One would imagine his owner must carry a great chip on his shoulder."

Charlotte was suddenly overcome with a feeling of foreboding. "Philip," she began, "I wish to attend this race."

"It is hardly an occasion of sufficient consequence to merit the attendance of the *Countess of the Turf.*"

Charlotte scowled at his sarcastic accolade. "Nevertheless," she persisted, "I *am* going with you. Be pleased to order my horse." With this command, she set down her cup and summoned her maid. "Letty, I shall require my riding habit at once."

The match race between Lord Hastings's Shakespeare and Daniel Roberts's Retribution was scheduled for eleven o'clock. The course would be the Rowley Mile track, and the distance two miles, four furlongs, in a single heat, a distance considered most evenhanded, considering the three-year age difference between contenders. Jockeys would ride, and each horse would carry ten stone.

Word of the extraordinary wager, recorded for posterity in White's betting book, spread throughout the countryside. Throngs gathered to witness the spectacle, but the mysterious Mr. Roberts and his peculiar horse were nowhere to be seen.

By a quarter hour before post time, with the challenger still to make his appearance, Shakespeare's owners grew restless and increasingly impatient. At ten minutes before the start, rumors abounded that the challenger from America had pusillanimously turned tail and run.

The crowd, by now thoroughly disenchanted and disgruntled at the forfeiture, had begun to disperse, when finally appeared a grizzled jockey on his slight-statured and oddly colored mount. The flustered gentleman who followed horse and jockey addressed the Earl and Countess of Hastings, making no immediate explanation for the late showing.

"I trust we have not kept you waiting?"

"Arrived in the nick of time, I should say, Lee," Lord Hastings remarked, checking his timepiece, which showed but five minutes to post time. "Might I inquire after the enigmatic Roberts?"

"The gentleman has unfortunately taken ill and is unable to attend. I stand in his stead."

"If the gentleman is unwell, Lee, the race must certainly be postponed." Lord Hastings's voice dripped with exaggerated courtesy.

"By no means, my lord! Should that occur, I fear he would be called craven. 'Tis out of the question! As stated, I stand in his stead."

"As his legal agent?" Lord Hastings asked, growing increasingly suspicious.

"Indeed, as his agent," Lee concurred.

"Lee," Lord Hasting began charily, "as a man of no inconsiderable experience, I confess a degree of skepticism regarding the very existence of Daniel Roberts. It is most curious to me that a man of such reputed vanity, who after proposing such an unprecedented wager, should fail to show his face. I ask you directly, sir, has Roberts fled England in mortification for proposing this race?"

"Indeed not, my lord! Pray disavow such thoughts. He is merely indisposed and resting this very moment at the White Hart."

"Yet I shall not be made a fool, Lee. As a gentleman, I should never ask such a thing, but this mystery has invoked a desire to see the color of his gold before this race is run."

"'Tis indeed a matter of honor, my lord." Mr. Lee blanched at the affront. "I carry the appropriate letters of credit on his behalf. I assure you, Lord Hastings, Mr. Roberts is more than able to settle his bet with you."

"Then I shall take you at *your word* as a gentleman, Lee. 'Twould appear we have a race to run." Lord Hastings signaled the stewards.

The contenders, proceeding to the starting post, stood in stark contrast to one another. Shakespeare, long of leg, sleek of body, and high of wither, stood at fifteen-and-three-quarter hands. His superior breeding could be noted in every line and angle of his body. To any knowledgeable observer, he appeared the consummate English thoroughbred.

Retribution, his challenger, stood at barely fourteen-and-a-half hands. A blue roan, he was truly a horse of a different color among the sea of chestnuts and bays typical of the English horses. The younger stallion was stocky in conformation compared to his elegant contender, with a wider, deeper chest and more powerful hindquarters, and half again as densely muscled as the lean chestnut. His shorter, more compact form appeared nearly squat, lending him more the appearance of a cart pony than a reputed racing champion.

Retribution's strongest attributes, however, were invisible to the naked eye. He had the heart of a runner and the cool-headed temperament of his sire, which his months of training with Jeffries had served only to season and perfect.

Arrived at the starting post, Shakespeare danced in edgy irritation. His rider struggled to hold him back, and the stallion snorted his impatience, touting his eagerness to put down the pretentious usurper.

Jeffries, mounted on Retribution, felt only the tightening of equine sinew as the mounting tension roiled inside the horse. He watched and waited for that certain sign of his mount's readiness. Suddenly, with the prick of his ears, Retribution gave the sign. With a subtle but unquestionable shift in his stance, the colt transferred his weight from front to hindquarters. Thus lightening his forehand, Retribution was ready to explode like a musket ball.

Daniel Roberts had arrived late with the intention of losing himself in the gathered crowd, remarking that everything to this point had played right into his hand. Indeed, the day had proceeded almost as if he had scripted it. To confess the truth, a good portion of it he had!

Ludwell had earned every penny of the cut Roberts promised him; not that he wouldn't have done it just as a lark! His performance had been impeccable. The man should have taken to the stage. Roberts grinned but hastily sobered as the horses proceeded to the starting post.

His attention riveted to Retribution; his hands clenched involuntarily at his sides. He watched with bated breath, anticipating that indication, that subtle shift, telling him all he needed to know. There it was! With this sign from Retribution, Roberts could have walked away, knowing before the start that the race was already his!

At the signal, the pair burst like floodgates. Shakespeare lunged forth, long legs slicing the air, but the elegant thoroughbred hadn't a prayer against the explosive breaking force of Retribution. Launching like a catapult, the roan became a blur of kinetic power. From the raised dais, Lord and Lady Hastings watched with unbridled horror.

"Good God, Philip, I've never seen such a break!" Charlotte exclaimed.

"His jockey's a fool. The horse can't possibly sustain that pace. He'll be used up by the first mile," the earl replied unconvincingly, his heart pounding in his throat and threatening to choke him.

Setting a lightning stride in his own frenetic style, Retribution dropped his head and dug in. And the roan stallion tore up the track. By the first furlong, he had gained three lengths. Stride-by-stride, Retribution ate up yards of turf, leaving Shakespeare scrambling feverishly after him, his jockey pushing, driving, and pleading.

Mr. Roberts positioned himself where he could best observe his vengeance in action. Until this moment, with his concentration focused on the horses, he had not spared a thought of Philip Drake. But now, Retribution had completed the first mile and there was no doubt of his lead. Robert stole a look at the Earl of Hastings, desiring a firsthand witness of his enemy's torment.

Looking to the dais for the first time, he suddenly took in the figure seated beside the grim-faced Earl of Hastings—*Charlotte.* The woman at his side was Charlotte, and time had only ripened her. Roberts's heart seized. He had not expected to see her. He was unprepared. He couldn't tear his gaze away, but hers was locked on the track, her lovely face growing deathly pale. He was overwhelmed as never before with invidious hatred of Philip Drake.

Shakespeare's rider, in sheer desperation, had flattened himself to the withers, urgently cajoling, wildly spurring, and flailing the whip. Accelerating with a groan, the game chestnut answered the call, giving everything he had, but it just wasn't... enough.

Shakespeare was distanced before Jeffries ever plied whip or spur to his plucky runner.

The Earl of Hastings's blood ran cold. He opened and closed his eyes in a vain attempt to blink away the vision before his disbelieving eyes, whilst his mind violently rejected the very notion. Shakespeare had lost the bloody race!

Thus, Daniel Roberts's unknown half-breed native pony from Virginia completely annihilated the Earl of Hastings's champion on his own turf.

Forty-three

❧

RESURRECTION

"Good God, Philip, we have lost!" Lady Hastings cried in dismay. "I have never witnessed such a run! I must go and console our noble Shakespeare at once. What a blow this must be to him. Pray congratulate the victor on my behalf," she declared genially, and oblivious of Philip's stunned anguish, sought out her former champion and his jockey.

He couldn't move. He couldn't hear. He couldn't speak. Frozen, he was unable to process what was beyond its ability to comprehend. Shakespeare had lost the bloody race!

The surrounding voices roared in his ears, yet he was deaf to the words. *Smile, Philip. They are all watching you.* The result was more grimace. Outwardly conceding defeat with grace, he nodded dumbly to those around him, but inside he reeled.

In his supreme confidence—or better said, extreme arrogance— Lord Hastings had recklessly wagered twenty thousand pounds without any consideration of defeat. With the loss of this wager, the fourth Earl of Hastings accomplished a feat no prior generation of supercilious and self-indulgent ancestors had managed to achieve: the total and complete ruination of an earldom.

It took all his strength, all his will, to force his body to obey his incapacitated brain's commands, but once regaining a modicum of control of his impaired faculties, he mechanically weaved through the crowd to his stable block. Entering the first empty stall, he clutched the wall and heaved.

Although Daniel Roberts would like to have congratulated his champion, he could not yet risk detection. Instead, with smug self-satisfaction, he located the carriage to take him back to his lodgings. He had incontrovertibly won the first round but was far too cautious to become cocksure. The game was not over, and the rest would not be so neatly scripted.

Though his earlier investigation had not determined the full extent of Lord Hastings's financial resources, they did confirm that his hold on his family estate was precarious at best. He would have few places to turn for ready coin, and Philip's pride would prevent him from applying to friends for a loan.

The most likely method of meeting his obligation would almost surely be the liquidation of his only viable asset: the Hastings stud, the racing stud that should justly have been his and Charlotte's. Only *this* sacrifice would begin to even the scales.

By the unwritten code, a gentleman had three days to settle a debt of honor, and by the same code, it was best settled in person. Thus, upon Ludwell's return to the White Hart, Mr. Roberts sent his calling card to the Hastings residence and departed for London.

Unable to locate her husband to escort her home after spending a pleasant hour with her horses, Lady Hastings had requested a groom accompany her. To her great surprise, she discovered Philip's horse already stabled, another curious deviation from the Earl of Hastings's normal routine. The stabled horse indicated his direct return follow-ing the race, rather than staying out drinking, gaming, and God only knew what else he did. She dismissed further contemplation of Philip's multifarious vices as unworthy of her energies.

Climbing the stairs to her rooms to change out of her riding habit, she was startled by the resounding crash of shattering glass emanating from the study. She paused then closed her eyes, and her rampant imagination envisaged what she might discover. At first, deciding to ignore it, she then changed her mind. Breathing a great sigh of resignation, she directed her feet to the study.

The scene was much as she had imagined: shards of glass and wasted brandy splattered by the hearth, Lord Hastings himself slumped in his chair in his shirtsleeves, his close-cropped hair completely disheveled, his perruque and coat cast to the floor. Noting the bottle cradled in his arms, she deduced it was merely a glass he had smashed. Far be it for Philip to waste his precious French brandy, she though disparagingly, but when he failed to look up or even acknowledge her presence, Charlotte grew uneasy.

Although Philip was a consummate gambler, she had never known him to accept his losses with anything more than a cavalier shrug. His current state gave her to feel more than a small amount of alarm.

"Philip, what was this wager?"

Ignoring her, he raised the decanter to his lips. Without pausing for thought, she snatched it from his hands, raising it as if to pitch the bottle against the stone hearth. "Now have I your full attention?"

"'Tis none of your affair," he growled.

"Your condition speaks otherwise, and if it is in any way related to the wager, it involves the Hastings stud. If it involves the Hastings stud, it involves me," she finished acidly.

"If you must know, I drink to drown my stupidity in underestimating an adversary. Now give me back the bottle that I might finish the job."

"Philip, you are hardly to blame. Who would have known? I doubt any observers of today's race have ever witnessed such blistering speed, and all from an unknown. From the colonies, no less! Though I chide you for not putting yourself out enough to discover more of the horse before the race, 'tis finished. If one plays, one must eventually pay, so the adage goes."

"Therein lies the problem, Charlotte. I cannot pay."

"What do you mean? You have never wagered beyond your ability to cover a loss."

"The ignoble Roberts proposed such an enormous sum that I had no power to resist. I could never have envisaged defeat."

"'Twas no mere defeat, Philip. Shakespeare was thoroughly trounced today!"

"Your words are less than helpful."

"You said an enormous sum. How much was this bet?" she asked, her trepidation growing by the minute.

"Twenty thousand pounds."

Charlotte gasped. "Philip, how could you! Were you drunk? You were either completely foxed or utterly mad! You don't have that kind of capital. How can you possibly cover it?"

"By any and all means at my disposal. I will not have it about that I single-handedly destroyed my family name and fortune."

"Twenty thousand pounds!" she repeated. "But even I know that we stay afloat by means of the horses."

"I shall do whatever is necessary to salvage my honor and meet my obligation," he replied with grim resolve.

"No, Philip! You cannot sell the stud! I have spent seven years of my wretched life to build something in order to make my life tolerable. You have no right even to think it!"

"I am the Earl of Hastings, and it is *my name* attached to the stud. I have every right to think it! And if you weren't so bloody high-minded and obstinate, I should never have been in this position to begin with!"

"What is that suppose to mean?"

"You know exactly what I mean!" he bellowed. "There is well above fifty thousand pounds sitting in a bloody trust. Money that is rightfully mine, which I cannot touch. If the stud is lost, it is your own doing, madam wife."

Charlotte was speechless with rage.

Philip continued more calmly, "I have already dispatched a message to the Duke of Cumberland. He has long desired his own racing establishment at Windsor Park and expressed great interest in our broodmares a short time ago. I have also sent Jeffries to Richard Tattersall, Master of the Horse to the Duke of Kingston, to assist in dispersal of the racing stock."

"How could you! How could you do such a thing without even telling me!" Tears of helpless frustration and fury burned her eyes.

"If I did not, my dearest heart, we should be obliged to remove ourselves to the Fleet Street debtors' prison." He laughed bitterly. "Now will you return my bottle? Or shall I forcibly remove it from you?"

Charlotte stared blankly at the half-empty brandy decanter in her hands. Meeting his bloodshot eyes with a rebellious glare, she raised it to her own lips and commenced a long, choking swig, and then she flung it against the flagstones at his feet. Whirling from the room, she left Phillip gaping after her in a speechless stupor.

Charlotte lay fitfully awake, her mind racing with all that had transpired in the past twenty-four hours. Although far from content with her life, she had managed to achieve a precarious state of not quite unhappy; but in one fell swoop, her balanced scales had tipped to decidedly miserable. It was Philip's damnable greed and pride that had led to his downfall, and he was about to drag her down with him.

Greed had tempted him to accept a wager he could never cover, but then his stubborn pride had pricked and prodded because an unknown from America had dared challenge his supremacy. He had lost, and she would be forced to pay.

This same arrogance and avarice had led to their accursed marriage to begin with. He cared nothing for her, then or now. She had been only the means of collecting a dowry, and later, the inconvenience he had to bear.

Her entire being railed against the injustice. She was a victim once before and had vowed never again to be anyone's sacrificial lamb. She knew not how, but Lady Hastings resolved with all her being to take matters into her own hands.

Alerting Letty, Charlotte packed enough belongings to maintain her for a few days should her business require it. She had waited anxiously for Philip's departure before calling for her carriage, fretful that he might discover her plans. She had departed shortly after Philip went out, directing her coachman to the London address copied from Mr. Roberts's calling card.

She arrived in the capital six hours later, dusty and travel-weary but beyond caring. Her coach halted at the elegant Mayfair address, and with her maid in tow, the Countess of Hastings descended. Squaring her shoulders, lifting her chin, and adopting her haughtiest demeanor, she rapped sharply upon the door.

The answering footman had little opportunity to question or protest. Lady Hastings stepped boldly into the foyer and presented her card. "Pray inform Mr. Roberts that the Countess of Hastings wishes to speak with him." Her tone evoked no refusal.

"Indeed, my lady. Is the gentleman expecting you? I distinctly recall his mentioning an afternoon appointment with *Lord* Hastings."

"You may inform him that the countess is come in his stead," she snapped imperiously. "It is a matter of personal business. Please conduct me to a place where I may await the gentleman's pleasure, unless you would have it about that said gentleman would leave a countess standing on his door stoop."

The beleaguered servant, knowing not what to make of this, dared not challenge her any further. He replied with due deference, "No indeed, my lady. If you and your maid will follow me, I shall notify Mr. Roberts of your request."

Charlotte seated herself on a sofa near the hearth while Letty took an inconspicuous chair by the window. In a matter of minutes, the door opened to admit Mr. Lee. "Lady Hastings, we meet again. 'Tis a most unexpected surprise. How might I be of service?"

"Mr. Lee," she said with a terse nod, "I fear you are not the gentlemen with whom I wish to speak."

"My sincerest apologies to disappoint, but Mr. Roberts is otherwise engaged."

"As my business with him is of the utmost consequence, I shall be happy to await his pleasure." She regarded him stubbornly.

"I see." Now thoroughly disconcerted, he considered his response. "I shall be happy to show you to my office, where perhaps you might be kind enough to enlighten me. As his agent in London, I have the privilege of conducting the majority of Mr. Roberts's affairs. Whatever your concern, you may be assured of my utmost attention, diligence, and discretion in resolving it on his behalf."

Perceiving she would make little progress otherwise, Charlotte nodded agreement and followed the gentleman up the wide staircase and down the brightly lit hallway to the large doors leading into a darkly paneled office. A massive mahogany desk was positioned near the heavily draped windows, and two of the walls were teeming with Latin and legal texts, with the third opening into an antechamber. Although the connecting door stood slightly ajar, Charlotte could see nothing beyond it.

The gentleman gestured to a large, comfortable-looking chair, but Charlotte perched stiffly on the edge of the seat. He regarded her expectantly, but still composing her muddled thoughts, Charlotte did not immediately speak. Suddenly at sea, she wondered what on earth she was going to say to this perfect stranger now that she had come.

"Perhaps you would care for some tea, Lady Hastings?" he offered in an effort to set her at ease.

"So kind of you, Mr. Lee, but no thank you."

He waited patiently.

Finally, she took a breath to speak. "I suppose there can be little cause for conjecture. I think you must know why I have come."

"Indeed not, my lady." His reply was somewhat disingenuous. "You find me quite confounded."

"My concern relates to Lord Hastings's wager with Mr. Roberts."

"But I fail to see how this should involve *Lady* Hastings."

"Lord Hastings had no right to make such a wager."

Lee's countenance darkened. "I am afraid I do not follow you, my lady."

"The Hastings stud, it is mine. When Philip, Lord Hastings, made the wager with Mr. Roberts, he should have known that a defeat would cost the entire Hastings stud. It was not his to wager."

"You mean to say that *you* are the legal owner of the Hastings stud?"

"N-n-o, not strictly speaking," Charlotte said, stammering her reply. "As a woman, I have no property rights, but in reality, the horses are mine. I have worked seven long years to breed champions. I selected the broodmares and the sires. I raised the foals and personally supervised every aspect of their training. The success of the Hastings stud was due to the sweat of *my* brow and none other.

"Now the threat of losing all I have worked for has brought me to this state of... of... desperation! I have no other word for it. Do you still not comprehend why I have come?"

"Lady Hastings, while entirely sympathetic to your plight, this is no concern of Mr. Roberts's. He and Lord Hastings agreed to a sporting wager, and the earl unfortunately lost. Any concerns you have regarding *how* the wager is to be paid are best discussed with your husband. I am afraid there is nothing I can do for you."

Having been dismissed with such detached indifference, Charlotte boiled over with frustration, indignation, and outrage. "No! You shall not brush me off so easily! You know nothing of my plight! I am not come to beg forgiveness of Lord Hastings's debt. On the contrary, he entered the wager and is obligated to pay. The debt, however, is his and only his. It is not my debt to pay, and I shall never allow the sacrifice of the stud to pay it!

"The racing stud was *my dream*, the dream I inherited from the man I loved, who was cruelly taken from me by the very one to whom I am now legally bound." Charlotte caught herself, suddenly aware of the very personal revelations her outburst had exposed.

"Lady Hastings," Mr. Lee said in tempered tones, "I shall not patronize you further with false displays of pathos. I can again only recommend you take the matter up with your... with Lord Hastings," he quickly amended. "The wager must be paid." He came around the desk and offered his hand. "It shall be my pleasure to guide you back to your maid, my lady."

Recognizing the fruitlessness of her errand, Charlotte had no choice but accept defeat. She rose, ignoring Lee's outstretched hand, determined to comport herself with dignity before melting into a great pile of weeping hysteria. Yet struggling for this composure, she remarked a noise, as of someone restlessly pacing on the other side of the door.

"One moment, Ludwell. I would speak with Lady Hastings."

The voice from the adjoining chamber rang a familiar peal through

Charlotte's near-delirious brain. That voice! It couldn't be! She must be hysterical.

Charlotte spun around to face... a ghost.

Forty-four

REDEMPTION

Charlotte's gaze locked on Daniel Roberts. Her breath seized in a great gasp. Her world whirled about her. Her vision blurred. Her body quivered. Her knees threatened to buckle and give way. She frantically clutched the chair for balance, desperate for support.

"Robert," she whispered, her eyes incredulous.

Instinctively he advanced, as if to lend her support, but abruptly caught himself several feet away.

"Ludwell, pray excuse us," he said to his friend more harshly than intended.

Mr. Lee regarded him questioningly but was more than happy to comply. The tension in the room had become overwhelming.

Charlotte found her voice. "You were dead. I thought you were dead!"

"You were correct, Lady Hastings." His glib answer masked any trace of emotion. "The man to whom you refer ceased to exist eight years ago. Do not be deceived that the one standing before you is the same one you knew."

"They *told me* you were dead!" Her head reeled, and her stomach churned. "They lied to me! Why did they lie?"

Her voice broke into a sob that wrenched his gut, tore at his insides. He longed to go to her, take her into his arms, but his long-cultivated need for self-preservation was stronger than the call of his conscience.

"They told you what I insisted they tell you. There was no point in holding on to something that could never be, so I released you. I set you free to live your life." As her legs gave way, and she collapsed limply into the chair, he moved not a muscle, did not even blink an eye.

"Could never be, you say? Your very existence is proof to the contrary! Why did you not send for me? Why?" she asked in a shrill voice hardly recognizable as her own.

He was paralyzed with uncertainty. It had all been clear to him *before* he saw her, but her words planted seeds of doubt and confusion. Her anguished eyes were a debilitating distraction.

"It was too late for that, Charlotte," he replied softly. "You were already wed to Philip, and then he came into his property and title. What had I to offer you in comparison? What is a Virginia planter to an earl?"

"But don't you understand? I desired none of it! I cared nothing for titles and privilege. I craved only love, genuine respect, and affection. Could you not find it in your heart to fulfill those simple desires?" She lost her struggle with the flood of hot, angry tears.

He turned from her, moving toward the books, running his hand absently over the leather covers while imagining how he might have used these same hands to sooth and comfort her. He abruptly shook away the vision, composing himself anew.

Choosing his words with utmost care, he posed his reply. "Are these simple desires you speak of not fulfilled by your husband, Lady Hastings?" He stole a furtive glance at her, surreptitiously studying yet not daring to hope. Hope had been a great deceiver in his life and the author of his greatest despair.

"Don't call him my husband! There is only one I have loved, one whom I thought long dead, but I now learn abandoned me."

He ached to accept her words as truth, but *her truth* would paint him as the false lover, the betrayer of her trust, and the villain. He was not prepared for any reality other than what he had imagined. *No, it just could not be so. It was all another deception.* He had nearly played right into her hand.

Roberts advanced, his countenance hardening. "My compliments, Countess. You perjure yourself most convincingly."

Her face wet with tears, flushed with simmering ire. "I told you the night we spent together that the marriage was nothing more than a legal bondage. I am wed to a man I despise. Why do you think the Earl of Hastings has never begotten an heir?"

"Do you mean to persuade me that in eight years you never succumbed to Philip's bed; that for eight long years you have languished for a lost love, leading a chaste and lonely existence?" His words dripped with irony. "Why don't you tell me why you have *really* come? Has Philip sent you to beg for clemency? If so, he vastly overestimates your powers of persuasion." His hardened blue gaze swept over her.

Charlotte colored at his insolence.

He drew closer, so close his warm breath grazed her neck. Charlotte closed her eyes, and an unbidden wave of nearly forgotten desire swept over her. Her heart pounded when he murmured in caressing tones, "Mayhap his lordship places more worth on the allure of your charms than on your powers of persuasion. Does he propose to offer his countess in lieu of payment?"

The force of her hand viciously stung his face. He blinked. His breath came harder, but he didn't move.

Charlotte observed, trancelike, the flesh of his cheek slowly effusing in an angry red flush. She had lost control, but in this single act found no release. Her rage had only begun to surface. Mentally replaying his filthy insinuation, his contemptuous words, she erupted like a volcano. Releasing all vestiges of restraint, she assailed him, blindly, frenetically, with all her fury.

"You bastard!" she shrieked. "I loved you! I would have gone to the ends of the earth with you, but you made me believe you dead! You deceitful, lying sod!"

Charlotte attacked with the passion she'd withheld. She raged for years of loneliness and despair; for years of frustrated, self-imposed celibacy that had suppressed the yearnings of her young body; for years of lying alone at night, mourning the loss of her only love. This same love now mocked and cheapened all she held dear, blighted all she had believed.

Robert had stood remote and emotionless as a column of marble while she slapped and pummeled. He had led her to believe a falsehood only that she might get on with her life. He would not cast himself as villain for his self-sacrifice. He caught her fist with one hand and wrenched it behind her back to subdue her. Drained of energy and emotion, Charlotte stood quietly, panting from her vain efforts to beat him into a senseless, bloody pulp.

"Are you quite finished now?" he growled.

Charlotte shook the hair from her face to see more clearly the man who wounded her so carelessly and transformed her love to hate. Fiercely meeting his glower, she asked, "How can you poison it all?"

"How can you convince me otherwise? How can I believe that one of the greatest rakes of my acquaintance would fail to consummate his union with a beautiful woman, and failing consummation, would not have immediately sought annulment?"

"So, you would wish to make a whore of the woman who loved you!"

"Not I, madam. 'Twould be your husband who endeavored to make you a whore."

Charlotte had never anticipated how her intentions might be misconstrued in coming to meet with Mr. Roberts. Heat rose up her neck in mortification at such naïveté, but she replied defiantly,

"I am no man's whore and no man's possession! Now, *Mr. Roberts*, I wish you to the devil!" Flashing sparks of fury, she spun around to leave, but he could not let her go.

"Wait, Charlotte," he cried. Swiftly, before she could resist, he closed the gap between them, blocking her path to the door. Her response should have been outraged resistance, but her flight instincts failed her; the magnetic pull between them was still irresistible.

"I ask you again, why have you come? You did not know it was me, yet you came here. To what purpose?" Deep in his eyes, Charlotte finally perceived it, a brief glimpse into the soul of a drowning man.

"I had wished to negotiate terms to save my stud. I explained as much to Mr. Lee. Surely you heard."

"If what you say is true, then how do you mean to satisfy the debt?"

"There is nothing, aside from my horses, but they are not negotiable."

"But Lord Hastings has few viable assets outside of the stud with which to satisfy me. Without the dispersal of the stud, he faces certain ruin. Yet you find it so preposterous that I suspected his hand in your coming?"

"But you passed this judgment solely upon Philip's character. What of my mine? Have you no faith in my integrity?" She whispered the last.

Their eyes met, searching, questioning, each endeavoring to discern the truth from the lies. He was too exposed to her beseeching gaze, and her allure was too strong. He was weakening by the second but still unwilling to become vulnerable to hurt again. He had been deprived of everything once, nearly his very life, when he had sought to make her his. The price was too high.

He froze; his reply was pained. "After all that has come between us, Charlotte, how can you expect me to trust? How can I ever again believe in love?"

"But I've told you before, Robert, you cannot defy it. Try as you may, you can never defy love," she whispered.

With a groan of defeat, he abandoned his resistance, conceding at last to her will, the will to love and be loved. Evincing no desire to turn back, they came together in a desperate embrace that melted away any remaining reservations.

Finally, mutually, and completely, they released all doubts, abandoned all fears, unwilling and unable to deny this overpowering love.

EPILOGUE

My Dear Philip,

By the time you receive this letter, I shall have boarded a ship for America. Although ours was not a happy union, in our eight years of wedlock, you provided for all my needs and were never truly unkind. For this alone, I am indebted to you and feel you are entitled to some explanation of what will soon become known as my truly scandalous and reckless act.

As you are by no means a man of small intelligence, you may already have deduced the true identity of the enigmatic Daniel Roberts, but should this yet remain a puzzle, you need only reach back eight years in your memory to discern the mystery shrouding the gentleman from Virginia.

I count myself fortunate to have made this discovery before you, lest I may never have found my old love and my new life.

With this letter, Philip, I finally absolve you of any further responsibility for me and set you free to seek annulment of our marriage. Moreover, as to the debt of honor incurred to Mr. Roberts, his spirit being moved by charity and forgiveness, he most generously grants the following dispensation:

Firstly, he shall privately and discretely, to avoid any public knowledge, issue a lien against the Hastings Estate to the amount of twenty thousand pounds, with the provision the debt be repaid in full within ten years time.

Secondly, I leave in your hands the operation of my beloved stud, to include all bloodstock, so that you should maintain a viable living until your obligation to Mr. Roberts is met. Kindly take particular care of my beloved Spiletta. I predict great things from her.

You should imminently be in expectation of several legal documents prepared by Mr. Philip Ludwell Lee in regard to all matters aforementioned.

Furthermore, I would wish you to know that although I obstinately denied you any means of producing a legitimate heir, you have a son, nonetheless, should you choose to seek him out and acknowledge him.

Lastly, I sincerely pray you discover peace and mayhap the measure of happiness of which, while together, we were cruelly denied.

Yours in Earnest,

Charlotte Wallace

BIBLIOGRAPHY

Ainslie, General de. *Historical Record of the First or Royal Regiment of Dragoon*. London: Chapman and Hall, 1887.

Ballantyne, Archibald. *Lord Carteret: A Political Biography 1690–1763*. London: Richard Bentley and Sons, 1887.

Black, Robert. *Horse Racing in England*. London: Richard Bentley and Son, 1893.

Blackmore, David. *British Cavalry in the mid-18th Century*. Nottingham: Partizan, 2008.

British Battles - analysing and documenting British Battles from the previous centuries. 16 May 2009. <http://www.britishbattles.com/index. htm>.

Cassell, John, and William Howitt. *John Cassell's Illustrated History of England*. Vol. IV. London: Cassell, Petter, and Galpin, 1860.

Charteris, Evan. *The Duke of Cumberland: His Early Life and Times (1721–1748)*. London: Edward Arnold, 1913.

Chifney, Samuel. *Genius Genuine*. London: Shury, 1804.

Clee, Nicholas. *Eclipse*. London: Bantam, 2009.

Cook, Theodore A. *A History of the English Turf*. Vol. I. London: Virtue and Company, 1901.

Cross, Arthur Lyon. *A History of England and Greater Britain.* New York: The Macmillan Company, 1911.

Culver, Francis Barnum. *Blood Horses of Colonial Days: Classic Horse Matches in America Before the Revolution.* Baltimore: Francis Barnum Culver, 1922.

Curzon, Louis. *A Mirror of the Turf.* London: Chapman and Hall, 1842.

Day, William. *The Race Horse in Training.* London: Chapman and Hall, 1885.

Earl of Pembroke, Henry. *A Method of Breaking Horses and Teaching Soldiers to Ride.* Lincolns-in-Fields: J. Hughs. 1762.

"European dueling sword/smallsword Information." *Comcast. net: Personal Web Pages.* 16 May 2009. <http://home.comcast. net/~sylvanarrow/dueling-sword.htm>.

Eyck, Erich, and Eric Northcott. *Pitt Versus Fox: Father and Son (1735–1806).* London: George Bell and Sons, 1950.

The Georgian Era: Memoirs of the Most Eminent Persons Who Have Flourished in Great Britain From The Accession of George the First to the Demise of George the Fourth. Vol. II. London: Vizetelly, Branston and Company, Fleet Street, 1832.

"Georgian Index – Horse Races and courses." *Georgian Index – Alphabetical Site map.* 16 May 2009. <http://www.georgianindex. net/Sport/Horse/races.html>.

Goodrich, Chauncey A. *Select British Eloquence Embracing the Best Speeches Entire of the Most Eminent Orators of Great Britain for the Last Two Centuries.* New York: Harper and Brothers, 1852.

Hamilton, Sir F. W. *The Origin and History of the First or Grenadier Guards.* Vol. II. London: John Murray, 1874.

Hammond, Gerald. *The Language of Horse Racing.* London: Fitzroy Dearborn, 1992.

Horse Racing: Its History. London: Sanders, Otley and Co., 1863.

The Jacobite Heritage. 16 May 2009. <http://www.jacobite.ca/index.htm>.

The Letters of Horace Walpole, Earl of Orford–Volume 1 by Horace Walpole–Project Gutenberg. Main Page–Gutenberg. 16 May 2009. <http://www.gutenberg.org/etext/4609>.

Morley, John. *Walpole*. London: Macmillan and Company, 1889.

Picard, Liza. *Dr. Johnson's London: Life in London 1740–1770*. London: Orion House, 2000.

Porter, Roy. *English Society in the 18th Century*. London: Penguin Books, 1991.

Robertson, C. Grant. *A History of England in Seven Volumes: England Under the Hanoverians*. Vol. VI. London: Methuen and Company, Ltd., 1911.

"Royal Plates GB." *The Thoroughbred Racehorse*. 16 May 2009. <http://www.highflyer.supanet.com/royalplatesgb.htm#1743>.

Shirley, Arthur. *Remarks on the Transport of Cavalry and Artillery*. Whitehall: Parker, Furnivall and Parker, 1854.

"The Speeches of William Pitt, Earl of Chatham." *PEITH*. 16 May 2009. <http://www.classicpersuasion.org/cbo/chatham/>.

Stocqueler, J. H. *The British Officer: His Position, Duties, Emoluments and Privileges*. London: Smith, Elder, and Company, 1851.

Stocqueler, J. H. *A Personal History of the Horse Guards 1750–1872*. London: Hurst and Blackett, 1873.

"Stratford Hall | A Virginia Gentleman on the Eve of the Revolution: Philip Ludwell Lee of Stratford." *Stratford Hall Plantation, birthplace of Robert E. Lee*. 16 May 2009. <http://www.stratfordhall.org/learn/lees/philip_ludwell_research.php>.

Taunton, Thomas H. *Portraits of Celebrated Racehorses*. Vol. I. London: Samson, Low, Martson, Searle and Rivington, 1887.

Thormanby. *Kings of the Turf*. London: Hutchinson and Co., 1898.

Waller, T. *Historical Memoirs of His Late Royal Highness William Augustus, Duke of Cumberland*. London: T. Waller, 1767.

Weatherby, J., E. Weatherby, J. P. Weatherby, and C. T. Weatherby, comps. *The General Stud Book Containing Pedigrees of Race Horses From the Earliest Accounts*. V ed. Vol. I. London: 6 Old Burlington Street, 1891.

Welcome to Thoroughbred Bloodlines. 16 May 2009. <http://www.bloodlines.net/TB/>.

Welcome to Thoroughbred Heritage. 16 May 2009. <http://www.tbheritage.com/index.html>.

ACKNOWLEDGMENTS

I would like to extend my heartfelt gratitude to the following individuals, without whose support this book would never have been written:

To my good friend, Diana Maynard, who first encouraged me to pursue such a ridiculous notion as writing a novel;

To my sister, Michelle Nabors, one of the most discerning people I know, who was not only my best critic, but also my biggest fan;

To my husband, John, and sons, Sean and Brandon. No effort of this magnitude can be successfully undertaken without the full support of a loving family;

To my editor, Deb Werksman of Sourcebooks, who perceived a glimmer of promise in this "diamond in the rough";

To my agent, Kelly Mortimer of Mortimer Literary, who helped to cut and polish said diamond;

And special thank you to Thoroughbred trainers, Michelle and Casey Lovell, for providing insight into the fascinating world of Thoroughbred racing.

Lastly, to God above who inspires all good things.

Thank you!

ABOUT THE AUTHOR

Emery Lee is a lifelong equestrienne, a history buff, and a born romantic. Combine the three, and you have the essence of her debut novel, an epic tale of love, war, and horse racing. A member of RWA and GRW, she resides in Upstate South Carolina with her husband, sons, and two horses.

Island of the Swans
CIJI WARE

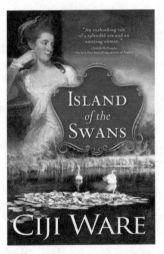

A passionate, flamboyant Duchess and a cruel twist of fate...

Jane Maxwell, the fourth Duchess of Gordon, was one of the most influential women of her time—a patroness of poet Robert Burns, advisor to King George and friend to Queen Charlotte, the mastermind behind her husband's political success, and a rival of Georgiana, Duchess of Devonshire. Spirited and charming, Jane captured the heart of her childhood sweetheart, Thomas Fraser, while her beauty caught the eye of his rival, Alexander, Duke of Gordon. Torn between duty and love, Jane is thrust into a lifelong love triangle that would threaten to destroy all that she holds dear...

"Ware's meticulous research and first class talent for invention reclaims a woman lost to history, a powerful and controversial figure in her day, all but unknown in ours." —*Publishers Weekly*

"An enthralling tale of a splendid era and an amazing woman." —Judith McNaught, *New York Times* bestselling author of *Paradise*

"A deep, complex novel exploring love, betrayal, healing, and renewal in the human heart." —*Affaire de Coeur*

$15.99 US/$18.99 CAN/£8.99 UK ~ 978-1-4022-2268-9

An Infamous Army
GEORGETTE HEYER

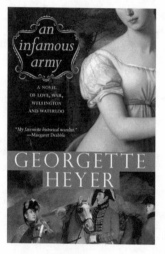

On the eve of battle, passions are running high...

In the summer of 1815 with Napoleon Bonaparte marching down from the north, Brussels is a whirlwind of parties, balls, and soirees. In the swirling social scene surrounding the Duke of Wellington and his noble aides de camp, no one attracts more attention than the beautiful, outrageous young widow Lady Barbara Childe. On their first meeting, dashing Colonel Charles Audley proposes to her, but even their betrothal doesn't calm her wild behavior. Finally, with the Battle of Waterloo raging just miles away, Lady Barbara discovers where her heart really lies, and like a true noblewoman, she rises to the occasion, and to the demands of love, life, and war...

"A brilliant achievement...vivid, accurate, dramatic...the description of Waterloo is magnificent." —*Daily Mail*

"Wonderful characters, elegant, witty writing, perfect period detail, and rapturously romantic. Georgette Heyer achieves what the rest of us only aspire to." —Katie Fforde

$14.95 US/$19.95 CAN ~ 978-1-4022-1007-5

The Spanish Bride
GEORGETTE HEYER

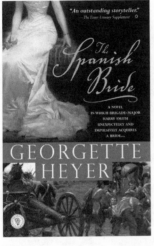

A true story of love at first sight

Known for her exhaustive research and ability to bring past eras to life, beloved author Georgette Heyer follows hot-headed Brigade-Major Harry Smith and the spirited fourteen-year-old Spanish noblewoman he met and instantly married during the Peninsular Wars, when the Duke of Wellington's forces fought Napoleon's army in Spain and Portugal. *The Spanish Bride* illuminates in fascinating detail the wearying marches, deathly battles, and victory in a stirring account of the life of a military wife who "followed the drum" during the Regency period.

"With the aid of considerable research... Heyer has traced Wellington's army in the Peninsula from the bloody storming of Badajos to the final invasion of France, following the fortunes of a British officer who married a Spanish girl and took her with him through the rough campaigns that followed."
—*The Saturday Review*

"Perfect craftsmanship." —*New York Times Book Review*

$14.95 US/$17.95 CAN ~ 978-1-4022-1113-3

Demelza
WINSTON GRAHAM

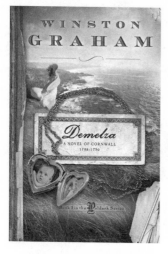

The second novel in the classic Poldark series, Demelza is a heartwarming, gripping, and utterly entertaining saga that brings to life an unforgettable cast of characters and one of the greatest love stories of our age.

Demelza Carne, the impoverished miner's daughter that Ross Poldark rescued from a fairground brawl, is now his wife. Poldark's bitter struggle for the rights of mining communities and the rivalry that ensues, as well as Demelza's efforts to adapt to the ways of the gentry, test their marriage and their love.

"From the incomparable Winston Graham…who has everything that anyone else has, then a whole lot more." —*The Guardian*

$16.99 US ~ 978-1-4022-2697-7

The World from Rough Stones
MALCOLM MACDONALD

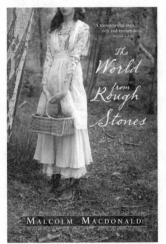

John Stevenson is a just a foreman when a near-fatal accident brings young Nora Telling into his life. Her nimbleness of mind and his power of command enable them to take over the working mill and rescue it from catastrophe. Together with their friends the Thorntons, they are willing to risk any dare, commit themselves to any act of cunning on their climb from rags to riches.

The World from Rough Stones is the epic story of two ambitious but poor young people who, at the very start of the Victorian Era, combine their considerable talents to found a dynasty.

"A monumental saga…rich and tremendous." —*Boston Globe*

$16.99 US ~ 978-1-4022-3608-2

The Rich Are with You Always

MALCOLM MACDONALD

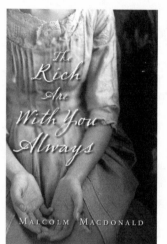

John Stevenson's genius as a builder and his wife Nora's clear-eyed, brilliant cunning promise to make them one of England's richest families. But as their fate becomes more and more entwined with that of their friends the Thorntons—repressed and pious Arabella and secretive, sex-obsessed Walter—whispers of scandal and disgrace threaten to bring them all to ruin.

The second novel in the classic Stevenson Family Saga, *The Rich Are with You Always* is the epic story of two families at the height of the railroad boom, where the lives of the Victorian people rose economically and set in motion forces of passion and struggle that would define a people.

"Engrosssing…a book to revel in!" —*Charleston Evening Post*

$16.99 US ~ 978-1-4022-3609-9